VALENTINE NOOK

EARLY ARC EDITION

LULU MOORE

FOREWORD

Hi Friends,

Welcome to Valentine Nook - the first book in my brand new, small ~~town~~ village series - The Valentine Nook Chronicles.

I'm so happy that you're excited enough you want an early copy, and I want to thank you for trusting me.

Set in the English countryside, it's my first foray into the small town genre, and I've had so much fun that I can't see myself ever leaving. It's been a journey back to my childhood, growing up surrounded by green fields, nosy neighbours and a plethora of farm animals.

This series is my love letter to that time, combined with my obsession for Nancy Meyers movies, and I'm so proud of this funny little world that's been living in my head rent free for what feels like forever.

I don't know if it's because I'm English but everything about it feels incredibly special.

Please do let me know what you think, I really hope you love it as much as I do.

Lulu xo

ps. When you're done, if you want to know more about Alex and Haven, I highly recommend reading the prequel to this series Once Upon a Christmas Tree, which you can find on KU.

VALENTINE NOOK

Valentine Nook

THE VALENTINE NOOK CHRONICLES: BOOK 1

PROLOGUE

LANDO

There's nowhere more beautiful than the English countryside.

Rolling green hills, horses gently grazing in the fields, a brook babbling somewhere in the distance, and the familiar twitter of birds in their nests—it's the perfect antidote to a few days spent in London.

Every time I arrive back home, I only need to take a deep breath of country air and saddle up my horse, Thunder, for the tension in my shoulders to melt away to nothing.

Not today.

It all started an hour ago as I was driving under the old stone arch—the words *amor principum* carved into its center. It marks the threshold to the village of Valentine Nook, one of the oldest villages in Oxfordshire, the heart of the countryside, and has belonged to my family for five hundred years.

Often described as the most beautiful and romantic place in

England, it's believed Valentine Nook is where you will meet your true love. According to legend, it's where Cupid was conceived—hence its name. Cupid's parents—the gods Venus and Mars—popped down for a tryst near an ancient glen on the outskirts of the village, and nine happy months later, Cupid made his entrance.

The concept of love has never been the same.

Just like my family, the people who live in Valentine Nook have been here for generations too.

There's Leon & Daughters, the local butcher who used to be Leon & Sons when his grandfather owned the place, but after he married and had four girls, his eldest daughter made him change the name. Next door is the bakery, where the best sourdough east of San Francisco is made. People come from miles around to grab the early loaves on a Saturday morning, along with a coffee from the shop across the road.

Two pubs, The Cupid's Arrow and The One True Love, stand at opposite ends of Valentine High Street, in constant, *albeit friendly*, competition, usually over who has the biggest blooms on their hanging baskets (Cupid's Arrow), who makes the best pork pie (The One True Love), and who will win the annual Valentine Nook cricket match (currently 34-29 to The Cupid's Arrow).

On the opposite side are the vets, where you'll find my brother Hendricks when he's not out helping to birth the new season's cows or locating Mrs. Winston's runaway goat.

There's a church with the vicar who's always running late because he misplaced his glasses, a fishmonger, a beauty salon, and the village store—The Valentine Cook, which stocks everything you could possibly need, plus anything you didn't realize you needed.

At the other end of the high street, to the stone arch, stands the fountain where year-round visitors come to throw in coins and make a wish that they'll finally meet their soulmate.

All the money collected from the fountain goes toward paying for the upkeep of the village—keeping the rose bushes and flower beds tidy, the cricket pitch in good shape, and the hedgerows trimmed. The lampposts, fences, and buildings all receive a regular lick of fresh paint. It finances the summer fair, taking place in a couple of weeks, the Christmas fair in December, and the Halloween party for all the local children.

It won't come as any surprise to hear the majority of funds go toward Valentine's Day. Because Valentine's Day in Valentine Nook is . . . well, I'm sure you can imagine.

I don't think you'd find a more perfect village.

It's my favorite place in the world.

Unfortunately, Valentine Nook is also home to Agatha Chase, a self-proclaimed high witch specializing in the services of love, and like everyone else here, her family has a longstanding history.

She owns Agatha Chase's Love Emporium, where she brews potions and spells that she believes will summon your soulmate. She gives readings, she hosts full moon parties, and if you're not careful, she'll drag you into her store and try to cleanse you with crystals.

If I didn't think the villagers would riot, I'd have evicted her years ago. But annoyingly, Agatha's good for the local economy.

Love is a powerful motivator for spending.

The people throwing coins in the fountain are mostly here because they're visiting Agatha. Once they're done, they drink at the pub or grab lunch from Mary's Sandwich Shop and buy a tea towel or tote bag from the village store that says they came to Cupid's birthplace. Sometimes if they're lucky enough to get a room, there's Mr. and Mrs. Kilpatrick's delightful bed-and-breakfast, though it's always booked up six months in advance, a year if you want to come in February.

I forgot to mention Valentine Nook is the number one place to propose marriage.

But mostly, people come for Agatha.

When my father was alive, he used to think she added a bit of fun. I *don't* share his opinion. In fact, after Agatha once told me that I was destined to be alone for the rest of my life, I've avoided her at all costs.

It's ironic that the grumpy, cynical man doomed to be single forever owns the most romantic village in England, isn't it?

I used to think it was all nonsense. More recently, I've been wondering if she was right because six months ago, on the night before my wedding, I found my fiancée and my best friend in a position they should never have been in . . . *with each other.*

I've spent the time since trying to erase the view of Jeremy's naked arse and the sound of Caroline's moans from my brain.

Losing a friend and a fiancée in one night was hard enough to deal with, but as England's "most eligible bachelor" is back on the market, two further issues have arisen.

One, Agatha Chase has taken to reminding me of her forewarning every chance she gets. Even if she's correct, I don't want to hear it. Therefore, I cut her off the second she opens her mouth.

And two, a slightly more exasperating matter, is my mother, who has made it her goal in life to set me up with *every single woman* in British high society.

I've declined them all because I have no intention of dating again any time soon.

Anyway, as I was saying . . . my drive through the village this morning—and subsequently my good mood—was totally ruined.

It began as I passed the fountain and spied a larger-than-usual number of visitors crowded around it. Not that I count, but I don't normally have to wait for them to move out of the way and was too deep in thought about what could have caused it to notice the giant moving vans parked outside Bluebell Cottage, where I used to live with Caroline.

I haven't stepped inside since the night I found them.

Slamming the brakes, I make a sharp turn to avoid hitting a pile of boxes in the middle of the road and stop the car.

Not the *best* place to leave a pile of boxes, I feel. And then I realize boxes are everywhere. Boxes from the three giant vans take up almost the entire width of the road.

Peering into the open end of the nearest van, I spy several large house plants, furniture covered in movers' blankets, framed prints . . . nothing that looks like renovation supplies — the only explanation I'd accept. But I already know it's not that. The sixth sense twitching in my gut provides an unnecessary warning. The cottage was redecorated a few months ago, and it's been empty since then.

Purposely empty.

Bluebell Cottage is something I've filed away under the subject of *Things I Don't Want to Deal With Right Now*, which you'll also find next to *Love Life*.

"Watch it, mate," one of the movers yells, shaking me from my darkening mood.

I lower my window, prop an elbow on the doorframe, and lean out. "Could you explain what's going on here?"

Another couple of movers carrying a large, bubble-wrapped, and heavy—from the way their knees are tensed—object stop and stare at me. Because *obviously* they're moving furniture. Moving furniture into *my* house.

"Wassit look like we're doin'?"

I point at Bluebell's front door. "It looks like you're moving furniture into that cottage."

"Proper Einstein right here, fellas." The mover laughs and continues on his way.

In the rearview mirror, I watch the rest of them shaking

their heads in amusement as I shift into reverse, maneuver past the boxes, and hit the accelerator, taking off for Burlington Hall, my home.

I might not have the full picture of what's happening, but *I know* that somehow my mother is involved in it.

* * *

USUALLY, when I approach Burlington, I like to slow the car and take my time driving through the gates. I love the way the road sweeps past the fields—currently slightly parched from the summer sun—and the horses grazing high above the valley where the stables and Foxleigh Park, the polo ground, lie.

If Thunder is out, he gallops over to run alongside me, whinnying for a scratch and any possible carrots or Polo mints I might have with me. I'll stop to oblige him for five minutes.

Farther along, the herd of Aberdeen Angus dots the horizon, and it's here where the turrets of Burlington Hall appear in the distance, growing larger and larger as the car continues its journey. Only when you turn the corner and pass through the long line of oak trees standing proudly like sentinels does it fully come into view.

A vast structure of pale Cotswold stone, set in three sides of a square with neat rows of arched windows across two floors. The asymmetrical turrets breaking up the chimneys staggered across the roof make it look ever-so-slightly French.

It's magnificent.

And my breath catches the first time I see it. Every time. I'm filled with pride and gratitude for this place that's housed my family for centuries.

Now, however, I'm too annoyed to take it in. I don't even get to enjoy the perfect June day, where the sun is high in a cloudless kingfisher-blue sky. Instead, screeching to a halt outside the front doors, I sprint out and go in search of answers.

"Mother?" My holler echoes off the hard surfaces of the entrance hall and the wide pillars on either side of the vestibule. "Mum, where are you?"

I wait, but there's no answer. The only sound I hear is the barking of dogs getting louder, their nails clattering on the stone floor as they rush down the hallway to greet me. My mum may be choosing to ignore me. Her pet peeve with us as kids was when we stood and yelled for someone instead of going to find them. We argued that it was far quicker than spending half an hour searching, while they could move from room to room.

But today, I have no intention of waiting, and one way or another, I'm getting answers.

I'm only slowed down on my mission when three of the Labradors—Hamish, Maud, and Dolly—catch up with me because they all demand I say hello to them before they follow me through the house and back outside.

"Mother!" I try again, marching over the newly mowed grass toward my first stop, the pool, which the dogs immediately launch themselves into.

Giant floats—a unicorn, a fire engine, and a dragon—bob in the center. Max, my four-year-old nephew, has clearly been here, but I only find my sister, Clementine, lying on a navy-and-white-striped sun lounger with her nose deep in a book.

Eleven years younger than me, she's just taken her finals at St. Andrew's, and since she arrived back home a couple of weeks ago, she's been permanently installed by the pool.

"Where's Mum?"

Clementine tilts her head toward me and slowly pulls her sunglasses down her nose until she's peering at me through her Burlington-blue eyes, the ones we all inherited from our late father.

"Oh, hey, Lanny, when did you get here?"

"Thirty seconds ago. D'you know where Mum is?"

She shrugs, ignoring my snapping and lacking interest in whatever has me agitated, and returns to her book.

"Dunno, she might be in the kitchen, or I think she talked about going over to the vegetable gardens. Or it might be the rose garden. Can't remember."

I grunt to myself. Typical. Turning to leave, I then spin back around with narrowed eyes.

Clementine normally has her ear to the ground with anything happening around here, especially when it concerns things that *shouldn't* be happening. If anyone knows what's going on in the village, she will.

"You don't know what's happening at Bluebell Cottage, do you? There are moving vans blocking the lane."

Clementine abruptly sits up and shifts onto her knees, which I should take as my first warning. This time, she whips off her sunglasses, and her expression—only moments ago somewhat blasé and disinterested—is wide with excitement.

Too much excitement for my liking. Especially when she gasps and claps her hands.

"Holy shit. *Today*? You saw them *today*? She's here already. Oh my god!"

"What?" My brows draw together in confusion. "I asked you about moving vans."

"Yes!" Her screech almost bursts my eardrums. "You really saw them? They were definitely outside Bluebell?"

"Saw what? Clementine, why are there moving vans outside the cottage?"

"Mum's put a new tenant in. You'll never guess who it is—"

"What!"

"The new tenant, guess who she is? *Guess*, Lanny!" She balls her hands, pumping them in the air. "Oh my god, let's go down and meet her now. We can take her a housewarming gift."

My fists clench, my blood boils, and my molars are on the verge of breaking from how hard I'm clenching them. This time, my mother has gone too far, and from the look on Clementine's face, she seems to have roped my sister in too.

"She? *She?*" I snap. "Un-fucking-believable."

"Wait for me!" cries Clementine, totally misreading the way I storm off. "I just need to change. Go grab a bottle of champagne from the fridge."

I most certainly am *not* getting champagne.

I march back over the lawns and into the house the way I came. Storming down the corridor, I briefly peer into each room I pass—my study, the library, Max's playroom—but my mother is nowhere in sight. I'm about to take the stairs two at a time when I sense movement next to me. I know instinctively it's James Winters, our family director of operations. The man is stealthier than a ninja.

In hindsight, he should have been my first stop, considering that anything my mother is involved with also involves him.

"Your Grace, if I may—"

My fist tightens around the banister. "Oh, for fuck's sake, James, there's no one else around. You practically raised me. Drop the officiality, will you?"

He tuts loudly. He knows exactly why I'm boiling with rage, and it dawns on me that my mother's absence is purposeful. James is waiting for me as the voice of reason because after our father died, that was the role he took. The five of us children were nothing compared to the thousands of troops he commanded as a former army brigadier.

"I was going to say you can't do anything about it."

"Like hell, I can't." I sprint up the stairs, only for James to follow.

"Lando, I know you're pissed off, but you can't kick her out. The lease has been signed, and she's here until the end of the year."

She. *Her.* It's the only part of James's sentence that has my jaw clenching.

"I didn't okay it. This is *my* land. It's *my* cottage. *I* am the duke. *I* am in charge. *Not* my mother."

James sighs but says nothing more. I know he agrees with me, but I also know he'll do anything my mother asks of him.

"I know exactly what's going on here," I retort. "And don't pretend you don't either. I thought at the very least you'd have my back in this dating agency she seems to be running."

"Of course, I have your back, Lando. But you haven't exactly been *you* the past six months. Ever since . . ."

"Ever since I walked in on Caroline fucking Jeremy?" I snap.

"Yes."

"And how exactly do you want me to be?"

"Well . . ." He waves at my face—more precisely, the beard, which has grown thick and fast.

"Yes?"

"You look like a yeti, for one. When was the last time you shaved?"

I scratch through the thick bush. I haven't been clean-shaven since what was supposed to be my wedding day, and beyond a couple of necessary trims, I haven't touched it. What's more, I like it.

"Six months ago. Caroline hated me with a beard, so I'm bloody well keeping it like this."

James remains silent, only raising an eyebrow.

"What's the second?"

"Your short temper," he replies without hesitation. "It's not like you, Lando. I know what happened was shit—"

"That's not the problem." I carry on up the stairs because I do not want to get into another conversation about Caroline.

When there's no response to my statement, I turn around and find James still where he was.

"What?"

"Then what?"

I sit down with a heavy sigh of defeat, twisting the gold signet ring on my pinkie. "I have a business to run here, a huge multibillion-pound business. We do good, important work. But all anyone seems to care about—and by anyone, I mean Mum—is finding me a wife. I don't know who's worse, her or that dreadful love guru."

James chuckles and joins me on the step. A wet Hamish waddles up the stairs and drops down on the one below us, dripping everywhere.

"So . . . are you going to tell me who I've rented Bluebell Cottage to, or do I have to guess? And why's Clementine acting like it's Christmas morning?"

James reaches out and strokes Hamish's ears. "I don't know much about her. Her representatives managed it."

"Representatives? What does that mean?"

"It was her agent, I believe." He's waving his hands about while he tries to find the correct wording. "Perhaps a manager? I'm not sure which is which. Gerard, from the estate team, brought her credentials over, and the duchess approved it."

"An agent? What sort of agent?"

"I'd need to check her name, but she's an actress. Quite well-known, I believe."

"An *actress*?"

"Yes. American."

"An *American*? Has my mother run out of women in England?" I scoff, although the entire scenario sounds more ridiculous by the second. Hamish groans loudly in agreement.

James shrugs. "Possibly. She's from Hollywood, according to your sister. Won an Oscar this year."

I turn to him, and his face remains as impassive as always. But usually his left eye twitches ever so slightly when he's joking, only not this time.

It has to be, though.

"Are you joking? Is this a joke?"

"No. It's not a joke."

"You're telling me my mother has moved an actress into Bluebell Cottage. She's trying to set me up with an actress?"

"I'm not sure that's—"

"That's *exactly* what's happening here. Stop being so diplomatic. She can't hear you." I laugh, and suddenly, like the sun breaking through dark rain clouds, my mood lifts, and a smile beams from my face.

My mother has truly outdone herself this time.

"An *American Hollywood actress*?" The laugh rumbles up my throat from deep in my belly, followed by another, until I'm laughing so hard I roll back on the stairs. "An actress? Dear god. Really, James, you should have led with that. More fool my mother, I say."

"Lando . . ."

"There's no way I'd ever date an actress. Come on, let's saddle up the horses and ride over to the pub."

HOLIDAY

I've made a terrible mistake.

"Ashley, the house is made of straw. *Straw.* Like I'm one of the three little pigs. And it's *leaking.*"

I pivot my phone so my assistant can see the drops of water slowly seep through a crack in the ceiling and fall into the saucepan I've placed on the floor of my bedroom. A small pool of rainwater collects in the bottom and splashes with every new drip.

Drip, drip, drip.

"Isn't it only the roof that's made of straw?"

"Yes. A roof that's supposed to keep me dry."

I *knew* this would happen. Roofs are not supposed to be made of straw. They should be brick or tile or, if you're the Chrysler Building, hubcaps, but not *straw.*

"Okay. Do you want me to find you somewhere else?" she asks, pulling the face she does sometimes when she's really trying to look concerned for me.

It's a look that could also be misinterpreted as judgment because I'm behaving like a brat and being a pain in her ass. It's almost like I don't pay her a generous salary.

I fall back onto my bed with a loud groan and try to ignore how I sink into the incredibly comfortable mattress. I'm loath to admit it might be the best mattress I've ever slept on.

It's one of the many surprising things about this quaint English cottage and its leaky straw roof that looks all kinds of ramshackle and whimsical from the outside, with wisteria creeping across the walls and a rose-lined path leading to the powder-blue front door.

Seriously, the Jane Austen vibes are on point.

I, of all people, should know you can't judge a ramshackle-looking house by its cover because the front door is where ramshackle stops.

Once you've crossed the threshold to this deceptive little place, you'll find a beautifully laid out, super cozy yet spacious, and incredibly well-put-together home. A kitchen with professional-level appliances, three perfect bedrooms including a primary suite overlooking a backyard I'd die for in LA, along with furnishings my interior decorator would call "country cottage chic" before sending me a mid-six-figure bill.

But all that money, and the goddamn roof leaks.

It's what's taking this place I've rented for the next six months from utterly perfect and charming to I-need-to-move-back-to-Los-Angeles-where-it-doesn't-rain, stat.

It's been raining *all morning*.

"No," I say eventually, sitting up and re-plumping the pillows. "No. I'll call the maintenance guy. There's a maintenance guy here, right?"

I'm ashamed to say I don't know.

In my defense, I've had an insanely busy eighteen months, after an insanely busy two years, after an insanely busy three years before it. You get the picture. This is the first time since I started my career that I haven't worked. It's a much-needed respite in a quiet and private setting.

And hopefully relaxing.

Ashley did what she does best and organized my chaotic life so I could escape from it.

She gave me a list of options, and I chose the prettiest, jumped on a plane, and now here I am, sitting next to a saucepan.

"I'll do it."

"Oh *thank god*." I sigh with relief.

"I think this place will be good for you, boss. I printed off everything you need about the village, and it's in your travel wallet. You've only been there a few days. If you still hate it in a week, I'll see if your second option is still available. Or book you a flight home, whichever you prefer."

"Thanks, Ash. What would I do without you?" I peer into the phone to catch her mumbling a response I don't hear, which is when I notice her background and the sun rising over the Pacific. "Where are you, anyway? And come to think of it, why are you up so early? I said call me when you wake up, but I didn't expect it to be before the sun."

"On my way to surf camp. I decided I'm going to learn while you're out of town this summer."

A pang of homesickness flickers in my chest. I could have learned to surf this summer too, but maybe I'll learn something else—how to fix a roof, for example.

Or bake. I've always wanted to learn how to do that.

"What time is it?"

"Five o'clock."

I groan again. That's why I'm being so grumpy. Jet lag. I'm still on LA time, and I've been traveling so much recently that my body has no idea whether I'm coming or going.

"Hope the water isn't too cold."

"I need cold. It's been over one hundred degrees every day this week."

I peer out of the rain-splattered window.

In fairness, even on this miserable day, the views from my bedroom are stunning.

Fields upon fields upon fields stretch as far as I can see, broken up by tall, thick hedgerows. Patches of brown tell me they probably haven't had rain in a while. In the distance, I can make out horses grazing, and when I crack it open, all I can hear are birds and the occasional moo of a cow.

It's not one hundred degrees, but it's warm, and the air is fresh with that just-rained scent, which is something you could never say about Los Angeles, where smog rules the sky. The blast of the English countryside has sufficiently reinvigorated me, and I'm taking control of the rest of my day—today's the day I'll be brave and venture out.

"You go enjoy the water. I'm going to get my shit together while I wait for the maintenance guy."

"Okay, boss. I'll call him now. Message me if you need anything."

"Thanks," I add before ending the call.

Tossing my phone on the bed, I peer around and drum my fingers against my cheek while I decide what to do.

What I *really* want to do is speak to my twin brother, Tanner. My favorite person in the whole world, and the one I always miss the most when I'm traveling. He's the best person at talking sense into me.

But it's still early in New York, and he's recently become a dad, so if he's not asleep, he's probably attempting to soothe my gorgeous nephew back to sleep.

I pad through to the bathroom and stare at myself in the wide mirror above the sink. The dark circles under my eyes seem a little less prominent than they did when I arrived but still mauve enough to tempt me back to bed.

I should probably unpack.

The couple of days I've been here have been mostly spent sleeping, and my unpacking so far leaves a lot to be desired.

Two of my four suitcases are open on the bedroom floor and, considering I've existed solely in pajamas or sweats, are virtually intact with everything I brought still neatly folded. The closets are waiting to be filled.

I also have to unpack a couple of boxes Ashley shipped from home—trinkets, prints, my favorite cozy blanket—that I like to take with me when I travel to make everything seem more familiar. It was a trick I learned a few years ago when I was on location in Vancouver for three months. And even though Vancouver is only a couple hours' flight from LA, having my own things made it feel a little bit closer, so now I do it wherever I go.

Scraping my hair back, I secure it with the tie that's almost permanently on my wrist and pick up the coffee I made before Ashley called. It's time to roll up my sleeves and get my shit together.

I'm about to start on the first suitcase when a loud knocking stops me, and I forget I'm not at home for a second. This cottage doesn't have an intercom—just a good old-fashioned door knocker.

I'm singing Ashley's praises with every step I tread down the super-narrow and very steep, uneven stairs, trying not to add to the bruises on my shin from where I've already fallen twice.

But when I open the door, it's not a maintenance man standing there. Well, as far as I know, this isn't what maintenance men look like in the English countryside.

A tall woman about my age, maybe a little younger, stands there in muddy dark green rain boots, a pair of denim cutoffs, a navy sweater, and a wax rain jacket that looks a hundred years old. Dark blond hair falls over her shoulders in thick waves that look so natural I'm tempted to ask her where she gets them done and how she manages them.

She's incredibly pretty, wearing a broad smile, and her blue eyes are so wide with excitement that it immediately makes me a little anxious.

Back in the US, I never open the door to strangers.

I have gates on my property in Los Angeles that Ashley always answers. Where I lived in New York while filming my last project, there was a buzzer and a concealed entryway so no one was allowed in without being seen first. While this charming English cottage has a large-ish hedge and a tall gate, clearly neither deters people from walking up the path. This *girl* definitely isn't a maintenance *man*.

But her expression doesn't say I look different in person from how she expected me to. That I'm shorter, taller, fatter, or less pretty.

Which also happens.

It's not that I'm not used to people staring at me like she is, because I am. Just not on my doorstep, and I figured it would take the public a lot longer to find me here.

"Hello?" I ask, trying not to sound nervous or too standoffish, but she doesn't seem to notice.

"Hiii," she draws out, pulling down the hood of her rain jacket. "Oh my god. Hel-*lo*." She wrestles an enormous bunch of pale pink roses from one hand into the other and tucks a bottle of champagne under her arm. The basket of eggs she's also holding rattles precariously as she stretches out her free hand. The eggs are all different—some large and brown, some small and white, and a couple are the exact shade of pale blue as the front door. "I'm Clementine Burlington . . . call me Clemmie. I've come to welcome you to Valentine Nook."

My shoulders drop a little. Despite her smile making her look somewhat crazed, Clementine has the face of a person I intuitively know I'll like.

I have two options.

I can either invite her in to get out of the rain or politely excuse myself and go back to unpacking. However, I've rented this place for six months—assuming it stops raining—and it occurs to me I'll need to make friends.

In two days, she's the first person I've spoken to in real life.

Therefore, I take her hand and shake it. "Thank you, that's very kind."

"These are for you. They're from the Burlington rose garden," she says in a confident tone like I'm supposed to know what that means as she thrusts them at me. "And these are freshly hatched this morning." She holds out the eggs.

The roses are incredible. Huge silky petals give off the most intoxicating scent, mingling with the warm, rainy air. It's the first time I've been outside today because opening the window earlier doesn't count, and despite the damp, it's glorious.

"Wow, these are awesome. Very thoughtful of you. Thank you . . . um . . . would you like to come in?" I ask, trying to mirror her smile. "I'm Holiday, by the way."

"I know. I'm a *huge* fan." She grins wider. "Your latest movie, the one about New York? Saw it twice. Loved it. Can't wait for part two. Your Oscars speech was perfect. So was your BAFTA."

My hand freezes on the doorframe. Shit. Maybe I'm wrong, and she isn't a local, and my face must give every internal thought away.

"Don't worry, I'm not a stalker. You're renting this cottage from my family."

"What?" I ask with a frown, still wondering if I should retract my offer to let her in.

"The cottage . . . it belongs to my family . . . my brother really. I'm not sure anyone knows you're here, and we won't say anything if that's what you're worried about. I assumed you realized who I was when I introduced myself."

I shake my head. "No, my assistant and business manager dealt with it all. I wanted to get away for a few months, and they gave me some different places to choose from. This looked the cutest, even if the ceiling drips," I add.

"The roof's leaking?" Clementine asks with a frown.

"Yes, I thought you were the maintenance man." I nod and realize we're still standing in the doorway, holding champagne, eggs, and flowers between us. Clemmie's probably safe, so I say, "Sorry, come in. I'll put these in water if I can find a vase."

"There's probably one in the pantry. I'll show you," she replies, toeing off her rain boots, which she leaves slumped next to the front door. "How're you settling in?"

"Good," I reply out of habit, hurrying after her through the small hallway to the kitchen, which leads out to the back of the house, "but I've mostly been catching up on sleep. I haven't been out yet. It was something I planned to do today."

Placing everything on the counter, I lean against it and peer outside to a backyard as pretty as the front.

Large apple trees, ripe with fruit, take center stage by a seating area I had my morning coffee at yesterday before going back to bed. Today, the rain has knocked some of the last vestiges of blossoms off the trees and scattered the petals among the wildflowers growing along the borders.

There's a beauty to it that brings back a sense of calm I've not felt in a while.

"I'll take you around and introduce you," Clemmie offers, appearing from the small pantry off the kitchen with a huge mason jar in her hands. "Here, this is the best I can find, but I'll have some proper vases delivered in case you need them."

"I'm good. The jar is fine." I huff out a small chuckle. "It kind of goes with the vibe of this place. It's really cute."

"My mother will be happy to hear it. She got a bit carried away with her interior designer," she replies as she places the roses one by one into the jar before filling it up with water and positioning it on the counter. "There."

From the sunlight creeping through the clouds, the roses

take on all different shades of pink and immediately add an extra brightness to the kitchen.

"Thank you, they're stunning. Where did you say you got them from?" I ask because I fully intend to go and buy weekly bunches of these to fill the house.

"My mum's rose garden."

I blink. Wow. That has to be some rose garden. My mom takes care of the garden at my parents' house in Maine, but there's no way she's ever grown anything of this caliber, and if she had, there's even less chance she'd be cutting it down to put in a vase. I'll have to find a different supplier.

Maybe there'll be one in this little place I plan to call home, and I'm suddenly excited to explore.

Clemmie turns away from the window. "Come on, it's stopped raining. I'll show you around Valentine Nook."

I glance down at the sweats I pulled on this morning and realize I haven't even brushed my teeth. "Can you give me ten minutes to change?"

"Of course, take your time," she replies.

I run back up the stairs, adding one more bruise to my growing collection.

I'm definitely going to break something on these if I'm not careful.

HOLIDAY

"Have you spent much time in England before?" Clemmie asks as we make our way out of the house and down the road.

Except I soon learn it's not really a road. It's a lane with no sidewalk and only wide enough to fit one car down at a time.

We've already had to move out of the way of a tractor carrying bales of hay and a couple of large, frisky-looking horses being led by a teenage boy. I almost fell into the hedge while trying to avoid them.

I shake my head. "Not out here. I've only been to London, and usually, it's a quick visit with press junkets or award ceremonies. Never longer than a week."

Clemmie's blue eyes widen. "Wow, really?"

"Yup."

"And you're here for six months?"

I nod again, because technically, that's the idea as long as the roof stops leaking.

"What's your plan?"

"I don't have one," I reply truthfully. I didn't get that far. I *usually* have a plan. Perhaps I should come up with something. "I've never had time off before."

I wait for Clementine to be shocked or pick up on my nerves at the prospect of doing nothing, but instead, she loops her arm through mine as though we're lifelong friends. It creates a comforting familiarity.

"Then you've come to the perfect place. You'll absolutely love it here."

Her grin is so wide and enthusiastic, the reticence I felt earlier vanishes. Large hedges we've been walking alongside give way to a fence lined with the same blossom trees I have in the backyard of my cottage. A little way up is a pale green gate too high for me to see over, but it doesn't stop Clemmie from pushing it open.

Perhaps privacy isn't a thing in the countryside.

"This is my brother Miles's house."

I peer around the wide open gate to find a cottage as equally cute as mine but with a collection of rain boots and mud-covered sneakers stacked up by the front door. A saddle is resting on a beam in the porch along with a pile of blankets.

"As you can see, he's not the tidiest. He's not the quietest either. His parties keep the whole village awake. But he gets away with it because he's *Miles,* and because he invites everyone. I'd decline if I were you, though you'll likely be the guest of honor."

"Sounds exhausting." I chuckle. "Is he younger or older?"

"Older. I'm the youngest, and I have four older brothers."

"Four?" I gasp. "I have three siblings. An older brother and a sister, and a twin brother. I always think that's enough. I can't imagine four brothers."

"It definitely has its disadvantages," she groans ominously and shrugs out of her raincoat, only to hang it on the gate as she closes it. "I'll get that later . . ."

It hasn't been long since the rain stopped, but the heat is already drying the puddles dotted around the ground, and the birds have commenced chirping. It's warm enough that I'm hoping I won't regret wearing jeans because while I'm used to the dry Californian heat, this humidity will stick to me.

"Anyway, where was I? Oh yes, Miles and my brother Hendricks are identical twins. They used to live in that cottage, but Hendricks became a dad, and their place wasn't exactly child friendly. He and Max, who's four, now live in Burlington, our family home across the fields"—Clemmie points in a general direction although there are too many hedges in the way for me to see anything—"along with my mum, and my eldest brother, Lando. My other brother Alex lives across the village."

There's something about Clemmie I can't quite put my finger on. It makes me think her upbringing was different from mine, with her rose gardens and perfect chickens, and the way the tractor driver and the kid with the horses were almost deferential in their greetings to her. And now she's telling me she still lives at home with almost her entire family.

My parents' house isn't small, but with the four of us kids plus six grandchildren, the most I can manage under one roof is a week during the holidays.

As much as I love my parents, the thought of moving back home makes me break out in hives.

"Sounds like a houseful."

"It is. Especially with the mood Lando's been in lately. I do what I can to stay out of his way."

"Why's he in a mood?"

"He went through a breakup." Clemmie tuts.

Her deep eye roll tells me exactly what her opinion is and makes me laugh because it sounds like her brother is as dramatic as mine. And considering I act for a living, that says a lot.

I'm about to say as much, but then we turn a bend in the road. Suddenly, I'm walking over a stone bridge under which flows a stream coming from a large fountain at the end of the prettiest main street I've ever seen.

I must have been more tired than I thought on arrival here, because there's no way I noticed this.

It's seriously stunning and so quintessentially English that it doesn't look real. It could be a film set, but even the movies couldn't make anything this cute.

While it's not *busy* busy, it's not quiet. Everywhere I look are people, and out of habit, I pull my sunglasses off my head and slip them on to cover my eyes.

The main street is easily the length of a football field, with a lilac explosion of wisteria climbing up two-thirds of the stone storefronts, which pops against the pale green window frames on each building. Store signs swing ever so slightly in the breeze as customers enter and exit, their bags overloaded with goods.

I spot a couple of black Labradors sitting obediently by a flower stall laden with a rainbow selection of buds and blooms, and a long line snakes halfway down the street from what looks like a coffee shop, but it could be a bakery.

Someone's tied their horse up outside a store called The Valentine Cook, which sells groceries based on boxes of fruit and vegetables stacked outside, reminding me of a rustic version of Erewhon. And I now understand why New England is called New England if this is what they were trying to replicate.

But the best bit, I realize, is that no cars are driving down it, and none are parked. All the cars passing by have come around the road and headed over the bridge past my cottage.

"Welcome to Valentine Nook."

I turn to find Clemmie beaming proudly, eager for me to love it like she does.

"You grew up here?"

"Yes." She nods. "Gorgeous, isn't it? I can be having the worst day, and I'll come and sit by the fountain, and suddenly, everything seems okay again."

I join her as she perches on the edge of the fountain's stone wall, and I turn to study it. A large cherub takes center stage, aiming his arrow down the middle of the road. He's surrounded by dozens of woodland creatures and animals all carved into what must have once been an enormous rock.

Around the opposite side, people throw coins into the water, making the bottom glitter in the sunlight, reminding me of the Trevi Fountain in Rome, except smaller.

I can understand why Clemmie loves it so much. I've been here two minutes, and I've already forgotten my bad mood from this morning and the water dripping from the ceiling.

"Yes, gorgeous."

"I'm so happy you like it." Her arm loops into mine and squeezes gently. "It's one of the oldest villages in England. Been in my family for five hundred years."

My neck snaps around. "Whoa, what?"

I've never heard of someone owning a whole town before, and the concept of something being five hundred years old is a little hard to grasp, but Clemmie just nods enthusiastically, like it's totally normal.

"My great-great-*great* . . . whatever . . . grandfather owned the land and built the village. If you can believe it, it hasn't changed much, although my father modernized it a lot, bringing in more money for the village and its businesses. And now my brother is in charge."

"Which brother?"

"Lando, the moody one."

Shit. I really should have read the information Ashley printed off for me.

"Now . . ." Clemmie pushes up from the fountain wall and points down the road away from the main street. "Down that lane is the village cricket pitch, and a little farther on is Foxleigh Park, the polo club where my brother Miles plays. There's a game every week, but next month is the big summer tournament, so you must come. It's lots of fun. Ooh . . ." she gasps. "The Valentine summer fair is in a couple of weeks too."

"Summer fair. Cool. Polo. Got it. Cricket? I don't know what that is."

"It's kind of like baseball. But also nothing like it. You'll have to see for yourself," she replies and catches sight of my confused expression. "Sorry, I know this is a lot to take in. We can do cricket and polo another day."

I chuckle. "Thanks. Information combined with jet lag is making it hard to compute."

"How about I show you the shops? And there's a spa one road over that does the best mani pedi outside of London."

"Lead the way."

I soon figure out Clemmie is that person who knows everything and everyone.

It takes us twenty minutes to get about fifty yards because she stops to speak to each person we pass, or rather, they stop her. Three times she gets invited to afternoon tea.

People are so focused on getting her attention that no one has noticed me, and honestly, it's refreshing, especially when she introduces me as her friend Holly.

"And that's the vet"—Clemmie pulls me out of my daydream and points at a building across the street—"where my brother Hendricks works, although he's never there. Usually, he can be found in the middle of some crisis he has to deal with. Goat on the loose, that kind of thing."

A laugh escapes so quickly it's almost a snort. Goat on the loose. I'm definitely not in Los Angeles anymore.

Walking a little farther, we pass by a clothing store, followed by a homeware store that sells locally made pottery, which I know my mom would love. There are skincare and beauty stores, a hair salon, and I spy a bookstore across the street.

I'll need to buy more suitcases before I go home.

We're passing one of the older-looking buildings when Clemmie grabs me and pulls me into the entrance.

"Shit, quick," she hisses as a tall woman wearing a long, billowy patchwork dress marches by determinedly. The sunlight catches on the large crystal around her neck, and the dozens of bracelets around her wrists jangle as her arms power her forward. "Sorry, that's Agatha. We *definitely* don't have time for a chat with her today. It's impossible to escape, and she'll only want to talk about Lando."

The woman seems far too focused on wherever she's going to pay attention to us, but I peer around the doorway and watch as she disappears past the fountain. Turning back to Clemmie, I find she's walked inside, so I quickly follow her. It's like I've been transported back in time.

It's a bar called The One True Love, the inside of which is all old beams and walls made of thick stone slabs, and I can totally believe this was here five hundred years ago.

The first thing I see is an unlit fireplace, as tall as me, with carvings around the outside depicting nature and the same cherubs and hearts I've seen everywhere. Heavy-looking wooden tables are crammed together, lining the walls.

The dark wood adds a coolness to the air, and I breathe it in. It's the sort of place where poets and playwrights from centuries past came with their quill pens and pots of ink to work, but today, they're full of people eating a late lunch and sipping their glasses of wine.

Colored sunlight beams through stained windows and hits the floor I'm hurrying over to catch up with Clemmie. The bar itself is marked with drink rings and etched with scuffs and scratches. It doesn't look like it's been polished in forever even though the beer taps along the top gleam so brightly that I can see my reflection.

Like everything I've experienced so far, this bar is both surprising and beautiful. There's so much character in here that it would probably take my entire six months and more to hear all the stories. I've never been anywhere so old.

Behind the bar, however, with his arms crossed over a sturdy chest, is the grumpiest-looking man I've ever seen. A thick gray mustache droops down from his heavily lined face, making his scowl seem even deeper.

"Well, look who the cat's dragged in."

"Hey, Eddie," replies Clemmie, rushing forward. To my surprise, she wraps her arms around him in a hug, which melts the scowl off his face.

I think it does. It's hard to tell behind the facial hair.

As she pulls away, Clemmie's expression is more guilt than anything else. "Sorry. *Sorry.* It's been a busy few weeks since I got home. I haven't seen anyone."

He grumbles under his breath. Without being asked, he turns and pulls two large glasses from the shelf behind him, fills them with ice, followed by Diet Coke from the fountain, and slides them toward us. My mouth salivates immediately. There's nothing like a crisp Diet Coke, and I've been dying for one since the plane touched down at Heathrow.

"And who's this you've brought with you?"

Clemmie throws an arm over my shoulders. "This is my friend Holly."

Eddie pushes his bifocals onto his head and narrows his eyes. "You the American actress who moved into Bluebell Cottage?"

Well, that lasted all of twenty minutes. Guess I'm no longer incognito, but I try not to let the disappointment show.

"Yes, sir," I reply, giving him my best smile. "That'll be me."

"Hmm. *Sir.* I like that. You've got good manners, young lady. I like you. Clementine, however—"

"How do you know about Bluebell?" Clemmie demands.

Eddie's gaze shifts from Clemmie to me and back. "Your brother was in here grumbling about it."

Next to me, Clemmie groans, and I blink hard. Grumbling about *it*? What exactly does *it* mean? Is he talking about *me*?

"God. Lando's such a dick sometimes."

Lando. The moody one.

The pair of them are looking at each other in the way I know I'm missing ninety percent of the conversation.

"Sorry . . . what's happening?"

"Nothing . . . *nothing*. Don't worry about it." Clemmie turns to me, her expression full of frustration. "Lando just didn't know we'd put Bluebell Cottage up for rental, and he's kind of annoyed. But, like I said, he's been in a mood for months. He'll get over it eventually."

"Oh."

I pick up one of the glasses and take a large mouthful because I don't really know what to say. I feel bad that he's annoyed, but on the other hand, I had nothing to do with the rental, and I'm paying ten thousand dollars a month, so he probably needs to lighten up.

"And Eddie won't say anything about you being here, will you, Eddie?"

Eddie looks like he couldn't care about anything except making sure his beer taps are polished.

"Secret's safe with me," he replies, and I'm pinned once more by his steely gray eyes. "As long as you remember this is the best pub in the village, not The Cupid's Arrow."

"Got it. I can remember that for sure."

"And you're joining our cricket team for the summer fair."

"Um . . ."

"Eddie, leave her alone. She's only just arrived," Clemmie chides playfully and picks up her Diet Coke. "And please can we grab a couple of bags of salt and vinegar? I'm showing Holiday around the village."

Turning around again, Eddie removes two of the smallest bags of chips I've ever seen from a basket and passes them to Clemmie, who shoves them in her pockets.

"Don't leave it too long next time," he grumbles.

"We'll be back tomorrow. Now I have a new buddy," Clemmie replies.

"Nice to meet you, Eddie," I add, reaching for my purse. "What do I owe you?"

"Don't worry about it. He's put it on my tab." Clemmie nudges me gently. "Come on, I want to show you something I think you'll like."

I figure Clemmie's taking me to another store or another part of the main street, but five minutes later, we're walking through a field toward a cluster of huge oak trees. My sneakers have soaked through from the rain clinging to the long grass, but I forget all about it when we reach the center.

A tiny waterfall about twenty feet high drops into a perfectly round rock pool.

My gasp echoes around us. It looks like something you'd find in the rainforests on a remote island off South America, not in the English countryside.

I make out a small ledge behind the waterfall, which, over time, has carved a couple of steps leading to the pool. The water is crystal clear—no moss, no leaves or dirt. Nothing. I can't tell how deep it is, but at the bottom, I can see a large pink rock, the exact shade of the blossom trees.

There's a magical quality to it. Although that could be because Clemmie's whispering and the buzz of Diet Coke has gone straight to my head.

I'm genuinely speechless, and it's totally worth the fences we climbed over to get here.

As if reading my mind, Clemmie says, "There's a much easier path leading from the gate at the back of Bluebell Cottage. If you ever want some privacy outside of the cottage, you can come here."

Having seen how busy the village is, I'm surprised at how quiet it is.

"Do people swim in it?"

"No, it's on our private land. If anyone's here, they're trespassing, but you're welcome to," she replies, sitting down on the grass verge and patting the spot next to her. "No one ever comes here, though."

"What is this place?"

Removing the packets of chips from her pocket, she rips them both open with her teeth until they're flattened out and places them between us.

"It's Cupid's Waterfall. He's the symbol of our village, and legend has it his parents came here for a quickie." She giggles through a sip.

"Oh, that's the cherub I've seen everywhere."

"Mm-hmm," she mumbles, laying back. "It's kind of cute but totally cheesy."

Leaning back, I prop myself on my elbows and close my eyes. "Nice story, though."

It's probably the warmth of the sun, the birds chirping, and the crunch of chips as we slowly eat them, all combined with the tranquility of this place, but for the first time since I arrived in England, I feel truly relaxed. Content, almost.

"Anyway, you're welcome to swim here or read books, whatever you want, but if you'd rather a proper swimming pool, come over to Burlington. I plan to spend the entire summer on the sun lounger while contemplating my life choices. I promise it doesn't rain every day."

Clemmie closes her eyes, and her breathing evens out as she drifts into a nap. I lie next to her, thinking about what she said because contemplating life choices sounds exactly like what I need too.

And perhaps doing them in the English countryside makes staying here not such a terrible mistake after all.

LANDO

A snail is crawling across my desk.

"Max!" I yell loud enough that I know he'll hear me.

A silvery trail crosses the document I need to read, along with tiny nibble marks around the edges. And while many documents are probably only fit for eating, this one I do actually have to sign and send back to my solicitors. Picking up the snail, I open the window and carefully place him on the ivy outside.

"There. Now go and find something else to eat." I turn back to my study and yell again. "Max?"

"Yeah?" he replies from the doorway, leaning against the frame just like his father does, wearing the same expression of pure insolence. Except I rarely see his father dressed as Spider-Man.

"Not yeah, *yes*. And what have I told you about snails in the house?"

Spider-Man shrugs. "Sometimes they come in without me. I've told them they're not allowed, but that must have been a particularly naughty one."

"Hmm." I narrow my eyes, but he holds my stare without blinking. I swear this child will grow up to be either a barrister or a dictator. A leader of something at the very least, which suits me fine. "Well, perhaps you need to have another word with them."

"I will."

"Where's Birgitta?" I ask, just as I remember Wednesday is her day off, though Max's nanny is rarely around when she should be. "Never mind, where's your father?"

"Churchill got out of the field again."

I tut loudly. That bloody goat is a better escapologist than Houdini.

"Where's Granny?"

"Don't know."

"What about Auntie Clemmie?"

"Did I hear my name?" asks Clementine, appearing at the door as stealthily as Max had and peers down at him. "Ooh, I didn't know superheroes were coming for breakfast. How exciting. What's going on?"

"Uncle Lando's still in a bad mood," Max replies, his eyes rolling just like Hendricks, or rather, *Miles.*

Given Hendricks and Miles are identical twins, Max has annoyingly inherited all of Miles's equally annoying habits, including his ability to shit-stir.

"I'm not *still* in a bad mood. I'm not *in* a bad mood," I say, holding back the irritation I know will make an appearance if I let it. "I'm fine."

Max and Clementine stare at me until they're joined by Dolly, one of the Labradors, who also stares at me.

"What? I'm not in a bad mood," I repeat. "I just don't want snails in the house, and no one seems to be concerned that Max is going to be late to school."

One look at Max and it's clear I'm the only one concerned about his tardiness.

"I'm taking Max to school," Clementine answers in a level of calm that directly correlates to my mood and only serves to irritate me further. She turns to Max. "Come on, Spider-Man, go and get changed. We need to leave in five minutes. We can have a second breakfast in the car."

Max groans but decides against protesting and trots off, followed by Dolly.

I slump down in my chair with a sigh only to find Clementine still staring at me. I don't bother to ask her why she's staring at me because I know. Just like I know I can't escape the conversation about to happen because it's been a daily occurrence for the past week.

"Come on, Lanny, you can't seriously keep this bad mood up. Go and meet her. You'll like her."

"I don't need to like her. She's my tenant. It's a business transaction and nothing more. As long as she pays the rent every month, I never have to see her."

"She doesn't know anyone."

"Then she shouldn't have moved here, should she?"

"Lando—"

"Clementine, I'm *not* having this discussion again. Bluebell Cottage belongs to me, just like this house belongs to me. I did not give you permission to rent it out, but you and Mum did it anyway. And if you think I'm going to endure the pair of you ganging up on me for the next six months, then you can both move out tomorrow. Bluebell still has two spare rooms."

Okay, maybe I am in a bad mood.

The cause of it is standing opposite my desk, blue eyes squinting, arms crossed over her chest while she taps her foot on the floor. She's one of the causes, anyway. The other is my mother because I seem to be related to the two most infuriating women in England.

Once more, I curse the day I ever met Caroline Montague.

Along with the day I was stupid enough to ask her to marry me.

It didn't take me long after we broke up to realize how badly suited we were. Or that my entire family despised her.

I was too blinded by a woman who perfectly fit the role of the future Duchess of Oxfordshire. I ignored every one of the tiny niggles that constantly followed me and all the giant red flags waving in my face.

I'm still boiling with rage that it got to the night before our wedding for me to see what should have been obvious. My best friend—*ex*-best friend—and my fiancée—*ex*-fiancée—were having an affair.

I'd spent the evening with my groomsmen, including Jeremy and my three brothers, Alex, Hendricks, and Miles. We'd played poker, had a delicious dinner, and overall, it had been a relatively sedate and early night.

For reasons I can't explain, when Miles left to go home, I decided to walk back across the fields with him. He lives next to Bluebell Cottage, where Caroline was sleeping the night before our wedding while I was staying at Burlington.

I hadn't planned to go in and see her because, after all, it's bad luck. But as I passed, the gate had been open and so was the front door. Being naturally curious and wanting to make sure the cottage was shut for the night, I walked up the path.

I was only halfway down when I heard them.

Groaning, deep moans, and breathless panting. They'd been so desperate to get to each other they hadn't even had time to close the door behind them. At first, I wasn't sure exactly what I was seeing, except as the light adjusted, all I could make out was my fiancée's legs wrapped around someone who wasn't me.

When Jeremy and I were eighteen, we went to Thailand on a boys' trip with a group of our friends. It was to be the final vestiges of freedom for me before I officially took over the dukedom I inherited when my father died.

I doubt there was a sober moment for any of us, and one afternoon, Jeremy lost a bet. His forfeit was a tattoo on his arse. He chose the Superman logo.

Now, everyone knows the rules of tattooing is you have to wait before getting your skin wet. But Jeremy was eighteen, drunk, and the temperature was a scorching forty degrees Celsius. The minute he arrived back at our villa, he forgot about the still drying ink and jumped straight into the pool.

From that day forward, he was the not-so-proud owner of a permanent red and yellow smudge on his left arse cheek.

As I stood there in the doorway of my cottage, that smudge burned into my retina.

Before I knew what I was doing, I punched Jeremy square in the face before calmly walking away without another word.

Our wedding had been hours away. The entire country was primed to watch the spectacle that had been tabloid gossip for months—how much the flowers had cost, where the honeymoon was, who would be attending—and canceling everything didn't seem like an option. Instead, I got blind drunk.

If Alex hadn't found me and taken charge of the situation while my mother and James dealt with the fallout, I would now be in a very unhappy marriage.

I have no intention of making that mistake again.

"I saw Agatha yesterday, you know . . ."

My molars grind as my jaw clenches. I open my desk drawer and rummage around for no other reason than to show Clementine I'm ignoring her.

"I was with Holiday . . ."

I stop what I'm doing and take a deep breath. *Holiday.* What a stupid name.

Really, I should feel sorry for the woman who's become an unwitting pawn in my mother's attempt to get me into a relationship, but all it's done is solidify an idea I've been toying with for a while.

Renting out *my* cottage was the final straw.

I've asked my mother a thousand times to stop setting me up on dates, yet each request has fallen on deaf ears. The time for politeness is over.

Hence, the paperwork. Pulling out a tissue from the box on my desk, I wipe as much of the snail goop up as I can, but it's already dried. No matter, everything will still be legal.

Picking up my fountain pen, which had once belonged to my father, I'm ready to scrawl my name along the dotted line at the bottom of the page, except I remember I need a witness.

I'm not going to waste my breath by asking my sister.

She wouldn't do it anyway.

Clementine hasn't moved when I glance up.

"We're not ganging up on you, Lando. We just want you to be happy."

"I'll be happy if you stop trying to push me into a new relationship."

"We're not—"

"Clem—"

"*I'm* not, at least. Holiday Simpson moving into Bluebell has nothing to do with you. Mum didn't want it sitting empty with bad memories for you, and as you weren't going to do anything about it, she did. Holiday was the perfect candidate."

My eye roll is thick and heavy, just like my scoff. The manure in the cow pasture smells less like bullshit.

"Fine. As long as we're all clear I am not interested in anyone. Including the American you're such a huge fan of."

"We're clear," she snaps. "Can I go now?"

"I was never stopping you."

Her hair flicks behind her as she turns and marches away without another word. I hear her yelling for Max to hurry up and slump back in my chair. It's not even nine o'clock, and I've already had a day of it.

Sometimes I wonder how my father managed.

I pick up the phone and hit the button that takes me straight through to James Winters's desk—the only person I do want to speak to this morning.

After my father died when I was fourteen and I inherited the dukedom, James and my father's other advisers took me under their wings and taught me everything I needed to know about running a multibillion-pound company. That was twenty years ago, and I could never have done it without him.

The Burlington Estate Group was established in 1511 by the first Duke of Oxfordshire, and over five hundred years later, it owns approximately six hundred thousand acres of land across the United Kingdom, Europe, Asia Pacific, and North America, as well as business holdings in property, technology, and sustainability.

As the current—and eleventh—Duke of Oxfordshire, I am the head.

At thirty-four years old, I'm responsible for the salaries of close to twenty thousand people globally. While there's a CEO for the Burlington Estate Group, along with CEOs for each of the subsidiaries within the business, I prefer to stay closer to home.

I have the legacy of Burlington to keep intact, which includes fifteen thousand acres of Oxfordshire countryside and Valentine Nook.

It keeps me immensely busy, and I want to be able to concentrate on that instead of who I'm going to marry. Or not marry.

Legacy is exactly the reason I'm calling James, along with why I'm a little more tense than usual this morning.

"Good morning, Your Grace."

"Have you got five minutes?"

"Yes, now?"

"Yes."

"Certainly. I'll be right over."

One of the best things about James is his appreciation for a sense of urgency.

I imagine him jumping into the Land Rover outside the staff offices on the other side of Burlington Estate, zipping around the track, and passing the polo fields and the dairy before reaching the lane, which takes him straight to Burlington Hall's side door.

By my estimation, he'll be here in less than fifteen minutes, which gives me enough time to get a coffee.

Walking into the kitchen, I find Alex sitting on one of the stools at the breakfast counter, a piece of toast dangling from his mouth as he turns the page on the *Financial Times*. It's the first time I've seen him this morning. He usually comes over much earlier for breakfast before heading to the estate offices to check on the staff, but he's leaving for Hong Kong this afternoon.

While all of my brothers work for the family in some capacity, I work with Alex most closely. He manages our overseas portfolio across Europe, the Americas, and Asia Pacific, making investments globally and primarily acquiring land for sustainable agriculture. His trip today will be to check on the progress of our work in the Far East, as well as the quarterly earnings reports.

"Anything interesting in there?"

He shakes his head, removing the piece of toast from his mouth as he does. "Not really."

I pick up a cup set out for breakfast and pour out a coffee. I'm toying with whether to tell him what I'm planning, but I don't want to be talked out of it.

"Where's Mum?"

"Not sure. In the garden probably."

I peer out of the window, thinking I might catch a glimpse of her, but I don't see anything.

"Morning, James," Alex booms, and I spin around and see James striding in.

"Good morning, my lord," he replies and turns to me. "Your Grace."

"James."

He stands there staring at me, but he knows better than to ask what I need him for, especially with Alex present.

"By the way, I passed Lord Hendricks on the way over. He said to tell you he's gone to check on the new calves."

We're coming to the end of birthing season. Over the past two months, one hundred of our heifers gave birth, and only a couple are due over the next week or so. Hendricks, along with half the farm staff, have been working through the nights as the calves have arrived. Thankfully, they've all been healthy and sound. Once I'm done here, I'll pop in to check on them too.

"Did he find Churchill?"

James nods. "Yes, he was in the orchard again. I'll get the fencing around there checked today."

"You'd be better having Mrs. Winston's fencing checked. That's where he escapes from."

"Don't curb his freedom," Alex mumbles, stuffing the last piece of toast into his mouth. "He's having fun. Mrs. Winston's so boring, and he's all on his own there. Goats need company."

"Then it'll be up to you to deal with Mum when she discovers all her trees have been stripped," I grumble.

"Hmm." Alex ponders. "On second thought—"

"Exactly."

I gesture to James that we leave before Alex asks what we're doing, but he's gone back to his breakfast and whatever he was reading in the paper.

James follows me into my study and silently takes the document I pick up from my desk to hand him.

"I need you to witness me signing this."

If he notices the silvery snail trail, he doesn't say anything, although perhaps that's why he's frowning. It could also be a frown of concern because I know what's written on the document in his hand will come as a surprise to him.

"Lando—"

"I just need you to witness me signing it. I don't need a lecture or your approval," I snap. James raises one of his thick brows. "And I don't need you to try to talk me out of it."

"Of course."

It's the way he elongates the vowels that has me answering the question he didn't ask.

"It's none of my mother's business. I'm the duke. I get to say who inherits my title."

James drops his head with a shake, and his eyes scan over the words again. "You know there are rules in place to prohibit this from happening."

"Which is why I want to change them." I flick the paper he's still holding that says exactly that and let out a loud sigh, scratching through my beard.

As much as I love my "fuck you, Caroline" beard, I have to admit it's become itchy. It needs a trim at the very least.

"Lando—"

"If something happens to me, Alex is next in line to inherit, but he's only two years younger than I am. We need the next generation to be cemented in before we're too old and decrepit to do anything about it. Max should be the rightful heir after me. He's the first grandchild."

There. I've said it out loud. This plan kills two birds with one stone.

Confirms the heir to Burlington and, by doing so, gets my mother off my back.

If an heir is in place, I don't need to find a wife like we're still living in the sixteenth century.

Does it seem drastic? Probably. But desperate times call for desperate measures.

"Have you spoken to Hendricks?"

"Not yet."

This particular part has my usual nerves of steel jittering slightly. Out of all my brothers, Hendricks is the most laid-back, the least unruffled—you'd have to be with Miles as your twin—but I'm certain this will likely get his blood boiling.

Still, needs must.

"Don't you think you ought to? Legally, you have to, seeing as Max is his son."

"Yes, and I will. But I wanted everything in place first."

He stares unblinking. I can tell he's concerned, and truthfully, as the closest thing I've had to a father in the past twenty years, I'm amazed he's not already yelling at me that I'm making a mistake.

"You're writing off your future."

Close enough.

"I'm not. I'm taking the pressure off all eventualities and buying myself some peace and quiet. If I ensure the future of Burlington and hand it to Max, then everything else is irrelevant."

James drops the document on my desk. "This is imprudent."

"I disagree."

"Look, consider sleeping on it a little longer. Please, Lando—"

"No. If you won't sign it, then I'll find someone who will."

He remains silent but pulls a pen out of his blazer pocket. I'm aware of his disapproval with every letter I scrawl at the bottom of the page, and the moment I'm done, he snatches it away and signs on the dotted line next to my signature.

"Thank you," I say, and I mean it. "Would you please courier it to Arthur?"

Arthur is our family solicitor. Just like everything else at

Burlington, we've inherited him from his father and his father before him. His firm has served our family for one hundred and fifty years. I see him once a month when I head to London for monthly meetings, but I was there last week to collect this document, and I have no plans to leave Valentine Nook again quite so soon.

"Certainly." He turns and walks out without another word.

That went about as well as could be expected, though I really hope he doesn't mention it to my mother before I do because that wouldn't be ideal.

My cheeks puff as I exhale loudly and turn back to the windows. Following the much-needed rain yesterday, the sky is cloudless and a glorious shade of blue. The stacks of papers on my desk are crying for my attention, as are the dozen unreturned calls—most likely about the summer fair—but after the last hour, I need to reset my day.

I'm tussling what to do when my phone beeps from an incoming message.

JEREMY: Can we talk?

I stare at the screen, fighting the urge to punch something. It's been six months since I last spoke to him, and even then, it was only a cursory *fuck off*.

Instead of reiterating my stance, I take a deep breath, delete it, and change into a pair of running shorts.

I'm definitely not doing any work now.

Five minutes later, I'm sprinting down the drive. Cutting through the first field on my left where Thunder has been turned out, I stop to give him a quick scratch and a Polo, then continue on my way. Aside from working Thunder around the land, running is the best way to check on my property.

I can go where the Land Rovers and tractors can't. I can see where hedgerows need repairing or fences are down. Where the cows can sneak out or goats can sneak in. It helps me feel more than a CEO when I'm actively contributing to Burlington's mammoth upkeep.

I run until I arrive in the one place I come when I need to be alone.

Just as I've always done since I was a child, I strip off completely and dive into the water until I touch the pale pink rock that's in the middle of the pool. It's a little ritual I've had whenever I swim here and the first thing I do.

If anything could convince me magic exists, it's this place. The water should be freezing cold, yet it's not, even in the winter. It's crystal clear, and as it's quite warm, I stand under the waterfall, allowing its power to pummel my shoulders, releasing the persistent tension I've been carrying. It also helps me think.

I have *a lot* of thinking to do—about my life, my future, about whether I'm doing the right thing. About what my father would have done and whether I'm living up to his expectations. Whether he would be proud.

It's where I came to grieve after he died.

It's where I came to lick my wounds after my marriage ended before it began.

Unfortunately for me, I don't get to think today.

Suddenly, my peace is shattered by a loud gasp followed by a deafening screech.

A blond woman is on the other side of the pool frozen in place, hand clasped to her chest with blue eyes as wide as dinner plates as they scan over me in horror.

Her hair is scraped back from her face and wrapped in a messy knot on top of her head. Loose wisps of gold catch the light and pull my attention to her immaculate bone structure, peachy smooth skin, and full, plump mouth that's currently dropped open.

She's wearing the tiniest white bathing suit I've ever seen; the material is cut so high on her thighs that it makes her legs go on forever. Toned bronzed skin that, even from this distance, I can see how soft it is, how lithe she is.

She's fucking beautiful.

I've never seen another person here in my life. For a split second, I wonder if she's real or if my brain is short-circuiting through the haze of spray.

As I wipe the water from my eyes, I remember I'm stark naked. Before I can say anything or cover myself, she darts away back down the path leading toward Bluebell Cottage.

So that's my tenant.

Fan-fucking-tastic.

HOLIDAY

"And he was naked?"

"Yeah. Naked."

"Totally naked?"

"Totally naked."

"You saw his—"

"Yup, everything."

"And?"

I shift on the unicorn float and lift my glasses up so I can properly see Clemmie's face. She's lying in the middle of a fire-engine float, and as I thought, her expression is as eager as her tone. She wants *all* the gossip.

"And what?"

"Well, before we try to figure out who he is, I want to know if he's worth figuring out. Was he hot?"

Swinging my legs around while trying to maintain my balance, I paddle my hand through the water until I reach the side, and the tanning lotions neatly stacked in a little wicker tray. The scent of coconut and sunshine permeates the air as I spray it over my legs and rub it in.

My preconceived ideas about England always being cold

and rainy have been proven incorrect because the past few days have seen heat similar to California but with added humidity.

It's also without the AC, but that's a totally separate issue that I'll have to deal with another day.

For now, I'm content lying on this unicorn float, sipping cocktails, and soaking in the rays. It's glorious.

I hadn't planned to come and hang out with Clemmie again so soon, but after two days of unpacking almost everything and sweating my ass off, I caved the second she invited me over.

Anything to stop myself from going back to the waterfall.

I haven't dared, yet I can't stop thinking about it.

My legs are still scratched from the brambles catching me as I ran away. By the time I reached my cottage, chest heaving from exertion, I didn't know whether to collapse or laugh.

"It was hard to tell. He was standing under the waterfall. Dark hair, beard—"

"Any tattoos?"

I shake my head. "No, but there was a lot of chest hair, so maybe underneath."

"He was hairy? Gross. I hate hairy men." Clemmie shudders dramatically. She picks up her plastic cup with the curly watermelon straw sticking out of it. The sun bounces off her pinkie ring as she attempts to swing the straw into her mouth. "What else?"

"Nothing. I ran off."

"Hmm."

I leave out the bit about his powerful thighs and rock-hard chest, stacked abs. I don't tell her this guy looked like he swung tires over his head and threw hay bales for fun. Just because he could. Even in the few seconds I stood there while the water poured over him, I could tell his wasn't a body carved from spending hours in the gym, not like the guys I knew anyway. Movie guys.

It wouldn't occur to this guy to watch what he ate. He'd burn it off by wrangling a few cows. Or by spending a hard day in a saddle. Whatever guys did around here to keep fit, anyway.

"What was his dick like?"

The mouthful of margarita I've just swallowed is inhaled with my laugh, and it takes all my strength not to topple off the unicorn. As it is, I have to grab the horn and lower myself back to lying down.

Even though this is only the second time we've hung out, I've decided the best thing about Clemmie is she says exactly what pops into her head.

My mind flashes back to the waterfall guy and his little trail of dark hair leading down from his belly button, and it takes effort to push it away.

"I mean . . . I don't think a girl would be disappointed, let's say."

"He doesn't sound familiar." She giggles before her tone takes on a more serious note. "I don't know everyone who works here, but I'll find out who it was. He could have been dangerous. Definitely a pervert. He could be a streaker or a sex pest."

"He didn't seem like a pervert. I was the one who walked in on him. I don't think he knew I was there. He seemed shocked to see me."

"Can't be too careful these days," she mutters, and this time, I stay silent because I know exactly what she means.

In my early days as an actress, I had experiences I don't want to relive, which makes me all the more certain this guy was doing nothing except enjoying nature as it was intended.

But thankfully, she changes the subject. "How's the cottage? Are you all unpacked?"

"Nearly. You should come over for dinner. I'll warn you now that I'm a terrible cook, but I can dial a mean takeout." I grin wide. "And I can get early screeners of movies if there are any you want to see. We can have a girls' night."

Clemmie lifts her head. "I would love that. I haven't had a girls' night in yonks. Growing up in a house of boys, I missed out on a lot of that. And having been away at boarding school, my friends are scattered all over the country."

I don't fail to notice the sadness in her tone. I feel it too. I wasn't at boarding school, but I know what it's like to have your friends scattered around. The closest girlfriends I have are my twin brother's wife and her best friend, but they live in New York.

The more well-known my face has become, the harder it's been to make friends. Harder still is coming to terms with people only wanting to be friends with you for the association, for your connections, your time, and your money.

But with Clemmie, I don't get any of those vibes, which is rare in itself. I love that she's never once tried to impress me, and beyond her first declaration of being a huge fan, she hasn't brought it up again.

"I'd love it too. Maybe make it a regular thing before I go back to work," I reply. There's heaviness in my tone.

"You mean on another movie?"

I nod. "Yeah."

"Have you got anything scheduled?"

"I start on the press for part two of my last movie. I had another movie scheduled to begin at the end of next year, but I pulled out. I told my agent I wanted a real break before she brought me anything else."

What I don't tell Clemmie is that my agent said it would damage my career if I took time off, but I did it anyway.

It makes me too nervous to think about.

Turning her float next to mine, she pulls up beside me and shifts so we're facing each other. Her legs swing on either side of the fire engine, and it looks like she's riding on the top of it. "Do you know what you want to do next?"

"No," I reply without a beat. "The last couple of movies I did were intense."

"You won all your awards, though."

"I did." I omit that I found them in one of the boxes Ashley packed and left them in there.

"That must have been incredible."

Clemmie's smiling at me with genuine happiness because she thinks that's what I must be feeling—*happy*. Because who wouldn't? An Oscar is the ultimate goal. Instead, I'm chewing on my lip, pondering whether I admit out loud what I've only told my therapist.

The water slips through my fingers as I paddle, a metaphor for my life.

"It wasn't as awesome as I thought it would be."

"What d'you mean?"

I sit up, dangling my feet instead. "I worked my ass off for eighteen months, and before that, I worked eight years almost nonstop because I thought that's what I needed to do to be recognized as a serious actress. By the time the nominations came around and the ceremony arrived, I was so burned out that I couldn't enjoy it, but I kept smiling all night because that's what people expected. I can't honestly say I deserved it more than any of the other actresses nominated. All I could think about while I was being congratulated was how tired I was."

Out of nowhere, the urge to cry burns my eyes.

I should be happy. I should be grateful.

"I haven't told anyone that before."

"Your secret is safe with me," Clemmie replies and flops back onto her float. "I know what it's like to feel you have to live up to other people's expectations, but it's nothing like the weight of expectation you put on yourself."

She sounds as lost as I feel.

I glance over at the house. House is a little misleading. Downton Abbey would be more accurate. I can imagine living here comes with more weight and expectations than most people could cope with.

We lie there in silence, floating and contemplating life choices.

"You don't know anyone who can teach me to bake, do you?" I ask, thinking about my apple trees. I'd like to learn how to make a pie. "The kitchen in the cottage really deserves to live up to its potential."

"No. But I can ask our chef—"

"Do you think he'll know someone?"

"No, I'll ask him to teach you."

"Oh." My head turns toward the house again, and I wonder how many staff work here. Beyond the one who brought out the margaritas, I haven't seen any.

"I'm sure he has way too much to do. I was thinking something smaller scale."

"He'll love to do it. He's probably bored of his days always being the same. He taught me one summer." She pauses, and a smile pulls on her mouth. "The basics anyway. I wasn't a good student, but I do remember how to roast a chicken."

"I like roast chicken."

"Then I shall cook you one," she replies, lifting the jug to fill our glasses, but it's empty. "First, I'll fetch more drinks."

"That's a better idea." I laugh.

Getting off the floats gracefully is much harder than getting on them, especially with the generous levels of tequila in our drinks. She manages to step off hers onto the pool edge, but I'm not so successful. The cold water immediately refreshes and reinvigorates me. The wooziness I felt a second ago vanishes, so I decide to swim a few lengths as Clemmie ambles off toward the house.

I'm finishing my fourth lap when the gate in the middle of the rose bushes surrounding the pool area opens, and in walks the last guy I saw naked. Except this time, he's clothed, and truthfully, he looks just as good.

His eyes flare as they lock onto mine, and he pauses mid-stride while my momentary panic stops me in the middle of the pool. At least I don't swallow any pool water when I inhale sharply.

"What are *you* doing here?" he spits.

His long legs eat up the distance from the gate to the pool edge until he's towering over me. If he wasn't scowling quite so furiously, I might consider him good-looking. The ferocious thumping in my chest says he's good-looking regardless.

I don't reply immediately. I'm still trying to decide what to do when two Labradors come hurtling down the path he's entered from and leap into the water. I figure this is my cue to get out in case he decides to dive in after them. Who knows what this handsome lunatic is capable of, and I have no idea how long Clemmie will be.

"Dolly. Hamish. Out," he bellows at the dogs, only to be ignored.

I realize the steps are on the opposite side of the pool to where I've swum, and I'd need to pass two frolicking Labradors to get to them. It must be the margaritas that make me braver than I am. I'd have never attempted to pull myself out otherwise. But thanks to the grueling training regimen I've been on for the past eighteen months, I'm strong enough to do it in one smooth movement.

Up close, this guy's much taller than he seemed under the waterfall. Even taking into account the inch or so from his thick boots, he towers over me.

He's wearing a pair of slightly muddy jeans that stretch around those powerful thighs I can't stop thinking about, and I've spent enough time in clothes fittings to know that the button-down shirt he's wearing with the sleeves rolled up his forearms is custom.

If we were in America, he'd be wearing a Stetson.

He may have been naked the last time I saw him, but it had crossed my mind he could very well have been homeless and in need of a shower. Now I'm not so sure.

For someone who looked so rugged, he's remarkably well-kempt, with curls of thick chocolate-brown hair brushing along his collar. Even his beard looks tidy and soft enough that my fists clench to stop from finding out for myself, and I bet it's hiding a dangerous set of cheekbones.

But it's his eyes that I can't tear myself away from.

I always thought mine were blue. But his eyes are *blue* like the Caribbean seas are blue or a cloudless sky in the dead of summer blue.

As I watch, those blue eyes drop to my feet and travel up slowly, causing my body to heat from more than the early afternoon sun. Then I remember not only am I wearing one of my flimsier bikinis but I'm also dripping wet, so I snatch up the nearest pool towel and wrap it around myself so tightly and aggressively that I almost cut off my air supply.

"Are you following me?"

"Following you?" He has the audacity to scoff. "No. Now answer my question."

It takes me a second to remember what his question was. I can't even blame it on jet lag or being slightly intoxicated. To quote Nick Miller, this guy smells like strong coffee and going to see a man about a horse. It's entirely distracting.

"What are you doing here?" he repeats, and each word he enunciates stiffens my spine a little bit more.

"I'm swimming. What does it look like?"

"I don't know how it is in America, but you can't just break into people's gardens and use their pool. This is private property."

First off, how dare he? Who does this guy think he is?

Crossing my arms over my chest, I glare at him. "I haven't broken in."

"Then how did you get here?"

I have no intention of divulging any information to him, a perfect stranger. An unhinged one at that. It doesn't matter how good-looking he is, even with the snarl.

Come to think of it, *why* is he snarling at me?

Then it dawns on me. This guy doesn't like me.

Huh.

This is *new*.

I don't think I've ever met anyone who doesn't like me. And while I understand not everyone likes everyone, this guy doesn't like me on sight, the waterfall incident not included. Surely, it's not that big of a deal that I saw him naked. Not sufficient reason for him to be looking at me the way he's looking at me, anyway.

Nope. This guy doesn't like me. He doesn't even know me.

He hasn't even *tried* to get to know me.

His eyebrows lower so much with his scowl they become a dark slash across his face. But if he thinks I'll cower, he's scowling at the wrong girl. While I might *look* sweet, I'm well practiced in holding my own against hard-nosed men who think they can tell me what to do. Thanks, Hollywood.

We're still locked in this glaring competition when Clemmie arrives back carrying another jug of her lethal margaritas. I expect her to tell him to get lost or call the police, but she doesn't. It hasn't occurred to me there are still two dogs happily swimming about in the pool like they own the place.

"Oh goodie, I'm so glad you've finally met."

My eyes snap to hers, and she's wearing that same grin she wore when she came to my cottage. The borderline-crazy one.

Finally *met?*

"Holiday, this is my brother Lando." She turns, totally oblivious to the way he's standing rigid and glowering in my direction. Even under his beard, I can tell his jaw is set hard. "Lando, this is Holiday. She's renting Bluebell Cottage. I invited her over for a swim. Do you want to stay for a drink?"

My brain is firing a half second slower than Clemmie, but as soon as it catches up, my eyes bulge. Oh *shit.*

Her brother. The naked waterfall guy is my new friend's *brother.*

Lando, the moody one.

She certainly hit the nail on the head with that description. I've never met anyone so irritable, and I say this after spending less than five minutes in his presence. Then I remember what Eddie the barman said, that Lando was grumbling about me renting his cottage.

That's why he doesn't like me? Because I *rented* his *cottage*?

"No, I don't," he snaps and turns to his sister. "Are you planning to drink your entire summer away?"

"Maybe." Clemmie shrugs, placing the jug on the table.

I swear once her back is turned that Lando's scowl intensifies.

"Oh hey, Lanny, Holiday was telling me she saw a trespasser in the glen the other day. You don't know if any of the farm staff have been down there, do you? Particularly any hairy ones? Holiday said he was gross and hairy, and completely naked standing in the waterfall."

It's almost in slow motion how Lando's head tilts and one of his brows slowly rises. "Gross and hairy, was he?"

I dare not look at Clemmie.

Not for one second do I want her to know that this is the guy whose dick she asked about. If someone described my brother's dick to me, I'd want to puke. Figuratively *and* literally.

"I never said gross," I mumble.

"It sounds like you did. Unless Clemmie's lying. Are you calling my sister a liar?"

I look at Clemmie, hoping she'll rescue me, but she's too busy filling our glasses, one of which she passes to me.

"Oh, and Pierre said he'd be happy to teach you."

"Who's Pierre?"

"Our chef. He said he'd happily teach you what he can."

"What?"

The pair of us turns to Lando, whose face hasn't changed, though it's slowly becoming redder.

"Holiday wants to learn how to cook. Pierre said he'd teach her," Clemmie explains.

"Pierre has enough to do here without running a culinary school."

Clemmie's giggle does nothing to lighten the tension. I don't think she's even noticed it.

"Lando, what are you on about? It's not a culinary school. It's a couple of lessons for Holiday while she's having some time off. She wants to learn how to cook."

I can't decide what's worse—Clemmie's obvious happiness at helping me or her brother's annoyance that she has.

Lando realizes he won't have any luck persuading Clemmie to give up her idea of their chef teaching me to cook. So he tries me instead.

"It's not included in your rental, if that's what you're thinking."

"Lando!"

Oh. Perhaps that's what his problem is. He's short on cash and needs money. My eyes flick to the mullioned windows of the mansion / castle. It can't be cheap running this place. I bet they're one of those rich-on-paper families, but all their wealth is tied up in property or gold mines or something. Old money problems . . . something I know nothing about.

My money is so new it's still shiny.

I smile my sparkliest smile, the one I save for billboards,

chat shows, and magazine covers. Maybe that will win him over. "Of course, I'll happily pay him."

"No. Absolutely not." Clemmie gasps. "Lando, what is wrong with you? Holiday, I apologize, he's not normally so rude. Although he has been much more of a dick than usual lately."

Lando stares at his sister, and I swear I hear his teeth grind together. I can tell he's on the verge of retorting, but instead, he silently turns on his heel.

I watch him storm off. My eyes linger on his ass for way too long.

So he's my landlord.

Fan-fucking-tastic.

LANDO

"So then . . . listen to this . . . Clementine announces that Pierre's offered to give her cooking lessons. *Cooking lessons.*" I throw my hands in the air. "Have you ever heard anything more ridiculous?"

There's a snort of laughter to my left.

"Amazing. I'm so glad I woke up early for this."

I glare at Miles, who's wearing one of his more annoying smirks. Not an ounce of him is bothering to hide how amused he is by my plight. There's no feign of support. Nothing.

I turn to Hendricks, hoping for a shred more empathy. "Henners, don't you think it's ridiculous?"

He removes the earbuds of his stethoscope and loops it around his neck.

"I'm a little busy right now. If you're going to be in here, at least make yourself useful and give me a hand," he snaps, one of his palms soothing over the heifer's neck. The other one is nowhere to be seen. "Easy, mama, they'll be here soon."

"Sorry. What d'you need?"

I jump down off the stable gate and step closer to Elsa.

We don't normally name our cows, but Max took it upon

himself to name all the cows last year, and this one stuck, along with Minnie two corrals down. She's also in active labor, with one of Hendricks's veterinary assistants monitoring her.

Elsa lets out a loud moo followed by a series of grunts, just to reiterate how uncomfortable she is. Usually, we leave the cows to deliver their calves by themselves like nature intended, with Hendricks keeping a close eye from a safe distance, but Elsa is having twins, so we're being more hands-on.

At least I am. I'm not sure why Miles is here.

These calves are the last to be born this season. It's been a busy two and a half months adding to our small herd of Aberdeen Angus cattle. It usually finishes in early May, but Elsa and Minnie needed to be inseminated twice, having failed the first go-around.

"Just keep her calm. I need her to lie down," Hendricks replies, peeling off a pair of long gloves. "Her amniotic sack is still intact, but we need to get this one out without the other one bursting. I think he's a big boy."

A couple of the chickens have come to see what's happening, unlike Hamish, who's snoring loudly under the gate. Every few minutes, one of the farm staff pops their head into the corral to check, and we get an update that Minnie's calf arrived safe and sound.

I stay with Elsa as Hendricks runs the portable ultrasound across her stomach, nodding in approval, and there's nothing else we can do except wait. Twins are not something we've had often. In fact, in the sixteen years I've run the Burlington Estate, we've only had twins half a dozen times.

I'm about to ask Hendricks how long he thinks we should leave it before we step in and help when Elsa drops onto her front legs and rolls onto her side.

Her huge belly convulses as her first calf finally decides to make an appearance.

"There we go," Hendricks murmurs as the pink birth sack appears. "Excellent, I can see a hoof . . . and a nose."

While Hendricks and I have moved to the side to give Elsa some room, Miles, being Miles, kneels in the hay and strokes through her mane. "Well done, darling, you can do it. Babies will be here soon."

Amazingly, Miles's presence seems to calm her, proving it's not just women he has this hypnotizing effect on. It's females of all species.

God, he's annoying.

"Come on, girl. Push."

Another round of intense contractions, loud mooing, and heavy breathing, and the calf's legs, head, and shoulders make an appearance. From where I'm standing, this all looks good. The sack still hasn't burst, but it's a nice, healthy color, and one more big push should have it sliding right out.

Which is exactly what happens, followed by a flood of amniotic fluid, blood, and the placenta, which splatters everywhere.

The little black calf twitches on the hay. Miles is still kneeling next to Elsa's head, stroking her neck and whispering in her ear, but she's in no condition to move. Dropping down, I rip the sack open, clear out his nostrils, and clean all the goop off the calf's face with a handful of hay, trying my best not to touch him before Elsa does.

He takes one big sneeze, spraying me with cow snot, and his first breath comes out in a little squeaking noise. Elsa turns her head toward him but makes no attempt to get closer.

"It's okay, Elsa. We got him," I tell her. "You get his brother out."

Her breathing is labored, and it's clear she's becoming distressed. Another set of contractions rolls through her, but nothing happens. I can just make out the tips of one hoof appearing, but that's it, and there should be more. Sensing the same, Hendricks kneels and feels Elsa for the next calf.

"Shit. Just what I didn't want. The sack burst with the first calf. If he doesn't progress, we'll have to pull him out."

We wait a couple of minutes to see if Elsa manages to push any more, but after another round of contractions where her mooing is almost deafening, Hendricks steps in to help.

He might be twenty-six and only fully qualified for two years, but Hendricks has spent his entire life caring for animals. Watching him work still fills me with awe. Over the years, I must have been present at the delivery of hundreds and hundreds of cows, a dozen or so horses, and many, *many* puppies, but it was the first time we ever delivered a calf together that set him on the path to becoming a vet.

It wasn't long after I took over Burlington. I was eighteen, and Hendricks was ten. We'd taken a four-wheeler out into the fields to check on the pregnant heifers and came across one in early labor. Along with Burt Easton, the previous Valentine Nook vet, we stayed with her for ten hours.

Unfortunately, the calf didn't survive, but after that, Hendricks made it his mission to learn everything he could, eventually specializing in large animals. He took over Burt's practice after he retired, and now Hendricks services the farms around Valentine Nook and the Burlington Estate, as well as the ponies of the Polo Club. Plus, Mrs. Winston's constantly escaping goat.

Taking hold of the legs, Hendricks shifts his weight back and tugs hard on the calf. His face puffs through his exertions while I stay out of the way, keeping my eye on the first calf as he attempts to lift his head.

"You're okay. You're okay," Miles coos to Elsa. "Nearly there."

"Fuck, this calf is massive." Hendricks heaves.

"Bigger than the first?"

"Yeah, his shoulder is twisted around, I think. It's what's sticking." Hendricks stops pulling and eases his hand inside Elsa to see if he can move the calf before starting up again. After thirty seconds of doing whatever he's doing inside Elsa, Hendricks steps back and takes hold of the legs again. "That's better. C'mon, buddy, let's get you out."

It takes another minute of grunting all around before the calf arrives with an unceremonious plop onto the hay, followed by another round of blood and goop.

Miles jumps up, joining Hendricks and me by the gate as Elsa eases to standing. She gives both her calves a long lick, beginning the process of cleaning them and bonding, and next to me, Hendricks takes a long, hard sigh of relief. By now, we have an audience of twenty or so chickens, a couple of the stable cats who are busily sniffing the newest arrivals, and even Hamish has woken up.

"Excellent work, bud." Miles holds his hand up to Hendricks for a high five as we all watch on. "Looks like one little happy family now."

Hendricks lets out a tired chuckle. "It sure does."

"Congratulations on another successful birthing season," I add with a laugh.

It has been successful too. We haven't lost any calves this year. Which is not something I can always say, but those are the realities of farming.

We don't have a huge herd. It has always been kept small, allowing us to personally manage it. These calves will have an incredible life and will eventually be either kept for stud purposes or used for meat. The income received from the Burlington Estate farm is directly allocated toward the upkeep of Valentine Nook and supporting the long-term residents through supplemental income.

It's a process that has been ongoing for the last couple of

centuries, and it's what allows us to ensure Valentine Nook stays pristine, attracting tourists who spend more money.

We watch in silence as the second calf makes a wobbly attempt to push to his feet and join his brother, already drinking hungrily—a good sign after such a stressful birth.

"I think we can leave them to it," Hendricks says eventually.

"Always enjoy being present at a birthing," says Miles, throwing his arm around my shoulders as we walk out into the main yard. "Feel like we should be passing around cigars."

"I'd rather have a coffee," I reply, stopping by one of the yard's large outdoor sinks to wash our hands and clean up as best we can.

Even using a scrubbing brush and a bar of soap doesn't get me fully clean, but it'll have to do until I take a long soak in the bath later tonight. If I didn't have to go to London once a month, I'd quite likely be permanently covered in mud.

Running seven days a week, the yard is the busiest place on the Burlington Estate. A staff of fifty is responsible for everything from maintaining the machinery to rolling the hay and plowing the fields and taking care of the various animals, including—cows, of course—horses, sheep, chickens, geese, pigs, goats, and the farm cats who keep the mice away.

Every day is an all-hands-on-deck situation, and I come down here each morning to make sure everything's running smoothly and check in with the yard manager.

Normally, however, the staff is too busy to hang around. Not today, it seems. It's like everyone suddenly decided to pick up a sweeping brush or fill the buckets with water, although on closer inspection, three-quarters of the staff I can spot are female. Which has everything to do with Miles being here.

I don't know why I haven't banned him from the yard because I'm convinced productivity drops by fifty percent when he's around. On the flip side, I don't need to ask anyone to bring us coffees because they're already being brought over by someone who's going to trip on something if she doesn't stop staring at Miles instead of paying attention to where she's going.

"Coffee, Your Grace, my lords."

"Thanks." I nod to her with a smile, though she's obviously not looking at me.

"This is perfect. Thank you." Miles flashes a smile that is way less professional than I care for, and I swear she swoons. She's walking away, backward, mind you, because god forbid she wastes an opportunity to stare at Miles when he calls her again. "Also, could you call over to the yard and let them know I'm running a little late? Ask them to get Chester ready. I want to stick and ball with him."

"Oh yes, absolutely, sir. No problem. I'll do it now, sir."

Foxleigh Park, the polo yard that Miles runs with his own team of stable hands, is a couple of miles across the fields and where you can find him when he's not causing havoc elsewhere.

Amazingly, even though Miles is chaos personified, the polo yard is run with an unarguable attention to detail. There isn't a speck of hay out of place. The ponies are treated like Olympic athletes. Their diets are closely monitored, and their exercise schedules are strictly regimented.

"Thank you," he replies, watching her as she hurries off as quickly as possible without breaking into a run.

The number one rule of any yard is no running. You never know what will be coming around the corner.

Bringing the cup to my lips, I sip while my to-do list floods my brain. Calving season might be over, but that just means something else moves to the top.

"Hey, I ran into Eddie this morning," Miles says, and I groan because I know where it's heading. "He wants to know if you're playing in the cricket match at the summer fair. Henners and I are on The One True Love team this year, and Al is playing for The Cupid's Arrow."

The Valentine Nook Summer Fair is held in the field next to the cricket pitch. It's an eventful weekend with a hive of activity from music and food to games and competitions. When the weather's good, we can get ten thousand visitors across the weekend.

However, the summer fair, like the Christmas fair, is run by a committee, overseen every year by one member of my family. It's my least favorite thing about Valentine Nook, and no matter how often I've tried to change it, I get voted down every time.

But this year, I really *really* don't want to head it up. Because this year was supposed to be Caroline's year. Her first time as my wife and an official member of the Burlington family.

Six months on and the looks of pity still haven't stopped. Nor have the sympathetic head nods and understanding smiles.

I see them every time I'm walking down the high street, and people stop me to ask how I'm doing. I hear them whisper as I pass. Even though I try my best to block it out, late at night, I wonder how many of them knew about her and Jeremy.

And the summer fair will bring it all back a thousand times over.

I shake my head in disappointment. "I can't—"

"Lando—"

"I'm head of the committee this year," I interrupt before Miles starts up his usual argument about how I'm too weighed down in duty to have fun. Easy to say when you're the youngest son with zero responsibility. I peer between my brothers with pleading eyes. "But I'll give you ten thousand pounds if you swap with me."

"Nope. I did it last year."

"C'mon, Milo. You're way better at judging all the competitions than I am."

"I know, but I'm still not doing it." He grins. "I want to win the cricket match. Ask Alex. When's he back, by the way?"

"Day after tomorrow."

"Max is entering Sherbet in 'Best Turned Out Pony,'" Hendricks says, leaning against the wall. "We had to order red wraps because he wants him to match his Spider-Man costume."

It's amazing how quickly my bad mood can appear these days. "Well, if I'm judging, you'll need to warn Max he can't expect favorable treatment."

Even Hendricks, who's usually too laid-back to react to anything, is momentarily taken aback by my snapping. "What's wrong with you?"

"Lando's still sulking because of the starlet in Bluebell, remember?" Miles answers for me, unhelpfully *and* untruthfully, but I don't bother correcting him. "Have you seen her yet?"

Hendricks shakes his head. "Nope."

"Me either. Although I watched one of her movies with Clemmie the other night. It was good," he says and turns to me. "What's she like, Lan?"

You'd think I'd have gotten used to the really annoying face Miles pulls when he's shit-stirring, but I haven't. Especially when I'm the target.

"How would I know?"

"You've met her."

"So—"

"So what's she like?"

"She's . . . I dunno. Blond. What do you want me to say?"

I *know* what he wants me to say.

He wants me to say that she's the most insanely beautiful woman I've ever seen, with curves that Renaissance artists would have killed each other to paint. That while it should be her dripping wet body I can't stop thinking about, what's really seared into my brain is the way she glared at me, arms rigid over her chest while enough anger blazed in her eyes she could have melted me if she'd glared any longer.

I was with Caroline for four years, and I never saw that level of emotion.

But I'm not telling Miles that. I'm not telling anyone. It will stay my secret until I'm dead and buried.

"Is she hot? Marriage material?"

"Marriage material? Jesus Christ, you sound like Mum."

Miles throws his head back and barks out a laugh. "I just wanted to see if I could get that vein in your temple to pop."

I narrow my eyes at him. "Why are you such a dick?"

He doesn't answer, just takes a sip of his coffee and leans back against the wall next to Hendricks. The pair of them stare at me with their arms crossed, and it's almost impossible to tell them apart. In fact, very few can outside of situations where Hendricks is elbow-deep in a cow or Miles is galloping down a polo field swinging a mallet.

"C'mon, Lan, go back to what you were telling us before we got rudely interrupted by Elsa giving birth."

To be honest, I can't remember where I'd got to. The annoyance I've been feeling since she moved in is bubbling too near the surface of my skin to allow me to think clearly.

"Did I tell you about the waterfall?"

Hendricks's eyes slice to Miles, and he's doing his best to keep a smile in check.

"Waterfall?"

I nod. "Yeah, you know, the waterfall over on the edge of the village? You can cut through from the back pasture, but the path is pretty overgrown. There's a track leading from Bluebell, which I used to use." I stop talking because the twins are staring at me like I've grown two heads, and Hendricks is no longer holding down his smile. "What?"

"Nothing. We just know the waterfall, is all."

I frown. "Why are you saying it like that? I'm talking about my waterfall."

"It's not *your* waterfall."

Technically it is because it's my land, but whatever. "I'm the only one who goes there."

Hendricks shakes his head and laughs. "No, you aren't. We used to go there all the time. It was our favorite party spot when we came home from school."

"What? When? I wasn't invited."

"That's because you'd have told us to stop."

My gaze flicks between the pair of them. Sometimes it's impossible to tell when they're joking, and it would be so typical of them to wind me up for no reason. It's times like these when the eight-year age gap feels so much bigger, and it takes so much more effort on my part not to resent their freedoms when my teenage years were spent preparing for leadership.

"Are you serious?"

"Deadly." Miles clasps a hand to his chest, as dramatic as always. "The waterfall has a special place in my heart. It's where I lost my virginity to Isobel Carruthers. It's where I ended up with Mabel last Friday night."

"What? Last *Friday*?" I was there last Friday too. I squeeze my eyes tight shut and scrub a hand down my face. That is not a visual I want in my head. "Stop ruining my thinking spot for me."

"You're ruining my fucking spot. What about the next time I want to go? I'm going to get performance anxiety, thinking my big brother will walk in on me—"

I spin around, checking no one's listening. Even though everyone knows what Miles is like, he's talking far too loudly for my liking. I try to keep some level of professionalism around here. "Milo—"

"Kidding. I'd never get performance anxiety—"

"*Miles*."

"Sorry." He sweeps an arm out in front of him. "Continue."

I sigh so deeply I'm certain my bones rattle. I can't even remember what I was going to tell them. They'd only laugh anyway.

"Why is she so under your skin?" Hendricks asks when I still haven't said anything.

"Who?"

"Holiday Simpson."

"She's not."

"Sounds like she is." His mouth curves down in one of those I-don't-give-a-shit pouts, and his shoulders jerk.

"Well, she isn't."

"Then why do you care whether Pierre teaches her how to cook?"

Fucking Hendricks. He *was* bloody listening earlier. He's the dark horse to Miles's bull in a china shop. Quieter, pays attention, but you don't realize until it's too late.

"Because he's got enough to do, and I don't want her hanging around the house."

"In case Clemmie and Mum get the wrong idea?"

"Or because maybe you like her, but you don't want to admit you like her because then Mum and Clemmie would be right?" Miles adds.

"I've met her twice." I hold up two fingers. "Twice. For a total of about ten minutes. It's not long enough to form an opinion."

"What a load of bollocks." Miles scoffs. "And we both know you're going to apologize to her because you're not really the colossal dick you're so good at pretending you are. So maybe get it over with today and tell her she's welcome to the Burlington kitchen whenever she likes."

"I wasn't a dick."

Hendricks and Miles raise identical eyebrows.

"Okay, fine."

Miles slaps an arm across my shoulders. "Proud of you, big brother, and on that note, I have a date with my favorite girl. Legs up to heaven, beautiful chestnut red hair, so soft it feels like silk. And she fits just right between my thighs." He winks, and I can't help the grin pulling at my lips because I know the idiot's talking about Chester, his polo pony.

And just like that, my anger dissipates.

Miles might be the most annoying individual I know, but he also makes me laugh more than anyone else.

* * *

DESPITE HAVING ABSOLUTELY no intention of apologizing, I've parked outside Bluebell Cottage, opened the gate, and am currently knocking on the door.

I try not to think about the fact the last time I was here was the night before my wedding.

Today, there's a brand-new pair of wellies lined up neatly by the step. So new I wonder if she's even worn them yet. I mean, there's not a speck of dirt on them.

The kind thing would be to chuck a bucket of mud over them, but she probably wouldn't appreciate it.

After a second attempt at knocking, it becomes clear she's not home, so I decide to leave. It was stupid to come here anyway. Unfortunately, that's the moment she returns.

She doesn't see me standing on the doorstep as she closes the gate behind her. She's too busy humming loudly to whatever she's listening to while trying to open a bottle of water with her teeth. Based on the light sheen coating her skin and the very tight workout pants and sports bra sculpting her body, I'd say she's come back from a run.

I've only ever seen this woman in the skimpiest clothing, and I'm starting to wonder if I'm being tested in some perverse way. Maybe Miles has put her up to this. That would make sense because fuck me if I can't take my eyes off her.

I rarely have time to watch movies, and I've never seen anything starring Holiday Simpson, but I have the sudden urge to go home and binge everything she's ever made.

I also have about three seconds before she spots me, and it becomes very awkward, so I decide to preempt it.

I wave in her face. "Hello?"

"Bag of dicks," she screeches, and the bottle flies out of her hand.

I manage to snatch it mid-air before it hits the ground, twist the cap off, and pass it back to her.

"What an extraordinary greeting."

She's still staring at me, blue eyes wide with shock, and I feel bad that I startled her, but I've also never had this reaction from a woman before.

It's both confounding and mildly amusing. I could live without the screeching, though, because so far, we're three for three.

Eventually, she pulls out her earbuds and takes back the water. "Thanks."

"You're welcome," I reply with a smile, hoping I don't startle her further. But I'm not sure she's blinked yet. "Are you okay?"

"Is that blood?"

I glance down at my jeans to see that I am indeed covered in the remains of the morning. I hadn't realized quite how gross they were, and I take a step back.

"Yes, yes, it is. Um . . . we had some calves born this morning."

"Oh. Cool," she says, her lips rolling into a straight line, and her head bobs as she takes a long sip of water. My eyes are transfixed on the delicate curve of her neck as she swallows. "So did you come to yell at me some more?"

"No—"

"You're fixing my roof?"

"Your roof?"

She sidesteps around me and walks to the front door, where she toes off her trainers and lines them up next to the wellies.

"Yeah, the roof. It's leaking. You know it's made of straw, right?"

No idea why I glance up to check. "Yes, it's thatched. But I didn't know it was leaking."

"I told Clemmie. She said she'd get it fixed."

"Ah." I chuckle, hoping to defuse any impending annoyance. "That's where you went wrong. Clementine is notoriously forgetful. But I can promise you that I will have it fixed. Where is it leaking?"

Holiday pushes the door open and gestures me inside. "Come in, I'll show you."

I try to take a step forward, but it's like my feet are glued to the ground. It seems the end of the path is the farthest I'm prepared to go. If this house wasn't part of the village, I'd happily burn it to the ground.

Peering in, however, the dread I was expecting doesn't materialize.

I know my mother refurbished, but I never paid attention to anything she was doing. Even from my narrowed view of the hallway, it looks completely different.

Where the walls used to be cream, they're now wallpapered in thick blue stripes. The wooden floor is stained dark instead of its previous pale oak, and I can see the edges of a curved table with a huge bunch of roses sitting in a vase that wasn't previously there.

It's not the house I found Caroline and Jeremy in, but I still can't bring myself to investigate what other changes have been made.

"That's okay, I won't disturb you. I'll have someone around this afternoon, and you can show them. They'll be here in an hour." I pull out my phone and shoot off a message asking James to get it handled. "Will that be okay?"

"Sure. Thanks."

"You're welcome," I say, taking a step back followed by another.

She's still standing there as I turn and walk to the car.

It takes all my self-discipline not to check and see if she's still watching when I close the gate. Will I be disappointed if she isn't?

As I get behind the wheel, I realize I never apologized, and I never mentioned the cooking lessons.

This means I'll have to see her again, and for some inexplicable reason, I don't seem to mind.

HOLIDAY

TANNER: How's the straw roof?

HOLIDAY: Stopped leaking, thank god.

TANNER: Can you seriously believe they make their houses out of straw?

HOLIDAY: No, yet here we are.

TANNER: And you're definitely staying?

HOLIDAY: I'm staying. I like it.

TANNER: Then we'll be over to visit as soon as the season is over.

HOLIDAY: You better. And can you send me some more pictures of my nephew in the meantime please? I haven't had any this week.

TANNER: In the morning, once I've had more sleep. Love you.

HOLIDAY: Love you too.

I'M ABOUT to toss my phone onto the bed when it rings, and my agent's name flashes on the screen. It's eleven o'clock here, which means it's six o'clock in New York, and while my brother was awake for his son's morning feed, it's been rare I've heard from anyone before lunchtime the past couple of weeks.

I hit the button right before it cuts out, and Marcy's face fills the screen.

Marcy was my first agent when I entered the industry fresh out of high school. Straight black bob, hitting just below her jawline, and a face pumped so full of Botox that I have no idea how old she is because she looks exactly the same as the day I met her.

She taught me everything I needed to know about standing on my own two feet, and I owe my career to her. On the flip side, she likes me working, and I know she'll have been slowly driving herself crazy from declining any offers coming in for me.

From the looks of it, she's already in her office, and I'm ashamed to say I'm still in bed. I woke up, made a coffee, and decided to get back under the comforter. I've had a delightful morning trying to read a book while listening to the birds and the occasional *clip-clop* of horses' hooves.

"Hey Marce, how's it goin'?"

"Holiday, honey, boy, are you a sight for sore eyes," she crows, though her face doesn't move.

"Oh yeah?" I laugh.

"Yeah. Tell me everything. I want to hear it all."

I pause for a second. I haven't done much more than sleep late and read. I've jogged. Clemmie and I have been to the pub (*pub*, not bar as Eddie corrected me). And after a trip to the local grocery store, I've eaten whatever I've wanted.

I've been here almost two weeks, and I'm starting to feel like myself again.

Ashley has been an excellent gatekeeper, so in the absence of dozens of emails and calls she's fielding every day, it's also been incredibly relaxing. And freeing.

But bizarrely all that pops into my brain is Lando, the moody one.

In the end, I go with, "Oh, you know, I'm still getting used to the time difference and that everything is the wrong way around."

True story. I almost got hit by a car yesterday because I was on the wrong side of the road and not looking in the right direction. I mean I was looking right, but I should have been looking *left*. Even in the English countryside, where everyone seems to be super chill, that *really* pisses people off.

"Not ready to come back?"

I shake my head and settle back into the pillows. I'm not even ready to get out of bed.

"Nope, not ready."

Marcy takes a breath, sucks her cheeks in, and her lips purse. "I thought as much, but I wouldn't be doing my job if I didn't check. However, you are a very popular woman right now . . . I told you this would happen . . . I told you after the award season, everyone would want you. And they do, but it's fine. I got you."

If this is going to be a call about how dramatic Marcy thinks I'm being, then I'll hang up right now.

If I'm not careful, I'm going to get to thirty / forty / fifty, and my entire life will have gone by in a flash with nothing to show for it but a bunch of movies no one can remember.

"Now, the reason I'm calling you is because I had an enticing offer come through—"

My finger hovers over the end call button. "Marcy—"

She holds her hand up. "Just listen."

"Okay."

She pauses again and sits back in her chair. It's the same as the chair she has in her LA office, with high wing backs that almost make it seem like she's sitting on a throne. Because in case you didn't realize when you enter her space, Marcy is important, and she makes shit happen.

"L'Oreal wants you to join their global brand ambassadors lineup. Five-year contract, eight million for the first year, and the potential to renegotiate higher for years two through five. But it won't lower. Minimum forty mil. Half up front."

I watch Marcy's mouth moving, but I can't hear anything else. My jaw drops. Holy crap.

Forty million dollars.

The only time I've stepped outside of acting was to front a fragrance campaign for Gucci, but it was nothing of this caliber.

I might have twenty-five films under my belt and won a couple of awards in the process, but I still feel like that struggling young actress auditioning for her first role. It's there every time I step onto set, and they decide I'm too young to know what I'm talking about, or when I walk into a meeting with an executive, studio head, or film director and know I'll have to prove myself all over again.

But this? This is more money than I've ever been offered in one go before. Even after all the percentage cuts for my lawyers, manager, Marcy, and tax, forty million dollars is enough to make it work for me.

I wouldn't need to start another movie next year.

I could set up my own production company. I could direct.

I've always wanted to do theater, even though the thought terrifies me more than anything else in the world, and this contract would allow me to be more choosy with the roles I take on and free up the time to do so.

Marcy takes the silence as hesitation.

"You can have a couple of weeks to decide where you want to negotiate, but this is a good offer, Holiday. You need to meet with them in Paris in a couple of months' time for some initial shots, which they'd pay extra for. I'm gonna fly over so we can discuss it in person."

I balk. Marcy and the countryside would not mix. For one, I don't think I've ever seen her out of five-inch heels. For another, the air is way too fresh.

"You're coming here?"

"Yeah, you said you're not ready to leave."

"To the English countryside?"

"Sure, why not? Send me a list of all the clothes I need to buy," she says, and she's dead serious and more enthusiastic than I've ever seen her outside of a conversation about making money. Though this is still about making money. "It's all tweed and shit, right? I look great in tweed."

I stifle a laugh. Now that I think about it, I've not seen any tweed. Maybe it's one of those ideas perpetuated by movies. I'm almost tempted to share the rain boots I ordered only to see what she'd do, but then I change my mind.

"Why don't I meet you in London?"

I can almost feel her sigh of relief. "Thank *god*. We'll do Claridge's. I'm sending the proposal now. Read over it."

My email pings, and I nod silently. "Thanks, Marcy. Thanks for looking out for me. You're the best."

"I know. I know." She grins. "Anyway, gotta go, I have another meeting. I'll leave you to your English peace. Call me if you have questions."

"I will."

The second she hangs up, I open the email.

It's fairly top line but laid out in black and white is what I need to do for forty million. Photo shoots, filmed campaigns, press. A total of ten full days per year, which would work around all other commitments.

Easy. And huge. Hell, this isn't just good. It's a dream deal.

Since the first movie contract I signed, I typically get a

surge of excitement coupled with acute anxiety whenever a new job offer comes in, but this is different.

Adrenaline rushes through me until I'm shaking. Tears prick my eyes.

Someone *somewhere* has deemed me worthy to join the lineup of incredible women who currently serve as ambassadors to the world's largest cosmetics company. Women I've looked up to for years. Idolized. Wanted to be.

Me. Holiday Simpson from Augusta, Maine.

The years and years of auditions followed by rejections are too ingrained in me to believe this is real, that I've earned it through my hard work and nothing else. For a split second, I forget I'm not still that little girl putting on plays in my parents' backyard and forcing the whole neighborhood to come watch.

I glance back at the screen.

I'm tempted to message Clemmie and ask her to meet me for lunch. But I also want to sit with this news for a little bit before anyone weighs in with their opinions.

Therefore, I'm going to do what I always do whenever I get an offer. Buy myself a coffee and a donut and go for a manicure.

* * *

I'M DECIDING what donut I'm going to buy when I round the corner, and right there next to the fountain is Lando, deep in discussion with Eddie from The One True Love.

The first thing I notice is he's not scowling, and his smile is kind of nice. Full mouth, straight white teeth, and his beard has been trimmed such that I can make out the hard line of his jaw. The shadow from the peak of his baseball cap only enhances it.

Yeah, this guy is all kinds of hot.

On second glance, he's also cleaner than I've seen him before, aside from the nakedness. But I don't think about that.

I'm so engrossed in watching him that I don't notice the enormous black horse standing calmly next to him. I mean, *enormous*.

This one might look chill, but I'm not about to chance it isn't.

Unfortunately, the wide berth I take means I walk right into the eyeline of Eddie.

"A'right 'Oliday," he greets. "How's it goin'?"

Lando spins around. His eyes widen a split second before he catches himself, and the surprise is replaced with amusement.

Now what's his problem? I have no idea what to do with this guy.

I've met him three times, and he's either naked or yelling. And don't get me started when he turned up at the cottage covered in blood with a story about baby cows. At least he seems to have washed since then.

I'm usually good at reading people but this guy's impossible, because right now he almost looks happy to see me.

I tear my eyes away from Lando's, trying not to frown, and focus back on Eddie. "Hey, Eddie. I'm all good. How 'bout you?"

"Can't complain. Can't complain. But while you're passing, maybe you can help us out. I'm telling His Grace here about the bunting—"

"Bunting?"

Eddie thumbs behind him, and the pair of them turn around so we're all facing Valentine High Street.

It's as busy as it usually is, but since I was here yesterday, the entire length of the street has been festooned in multicolored flags strung up from lamppost to lamppost traversing the road. Down on the far end, I spot a couple of guys up on ladders, adding the final touches.

It reminds me of the Fourth of July and brings a huge smile to my face.

"It looks so cute."

"You think?" asks Lando. "It's not—"

"Your Grace, we always have the bunting," Eddie says with more than a little exasperation. "It's the summer fair."

"I know, but this is my second year in charge." Lando shrugs. "I wanted something better than bunting."

"What's better than bunting?"

I'm wondering that myself when I glance between them and realize they're waiting on me to provide it.

"Oh . . . um . . ." I hate being put on the spot. "I dunno. Balloon arch?"

Eddie sighs because obviously a balloon arch is *not* better and turns back to Lando. "You want to come and check out the rest of the decorations?"

"Sure, lead the way," he replies, his gaze flicking to mine. "Um . . . d'you mind? Can you hold Thunder for a second?"

Before I have the chance to say absolutely fucking not, he tosses me the reins and takes off after Eddie followed by a chocolate Labrador I hadn't noticed.

Now what?

I'm not great with horses.

A few years ago, I was riding a horse during filming when it got spooked and took off down a path, but only after deciding he didn't want me tagging along. I could have been competing in the rodeo for his attempts to buck me off, and I was catapulted through the air onto the road.

Luckily, I didn't break anything, but the concussion and overnight hospital stay put me off ever getting back in the saddle.

I'm frozen in place, figuring out what to do when I realize a couple of girls are standing near the fountain staring at me, but because of this monstrous beast, I can't do what I usually do when people stare at me, which is drop my head and walk away.

I push my sunglasses firmly up my nose instead.

"Your horse is gorgeous."

"Oh . . . thanks. Yeah, he's not mine." I smile back, wishing I hadn't replied because it only encourages the girls to step forward and stroke him.

Even though Thunder—*Thunder,* I mean, that's not the name for a super chill horse—has barely moved an inch, I don't know how he's going to react to two strangers touching him, but he doesn't seem to care in the slightest. Of the two of us, I'm the one fending off a panic attack.

The first girl holds her hand out, allowing him to nibble at her palm, and I catch a glimpse of his giant horse teeth chomping on nothing but air. What a tease.

Even *I* feel disappointed for him.

"How old is he?"

"I'm not sure."

I'm trying not to be rude, but I'm also staring at the door Lando disappeared through because where the fuck is he?

From the corner of my eye, I notice the second girl tilting her head as she stares at me, but I'm too focused on the pub entrance to feel the weight of it.

"You seem so familiar," she says eventually. "Did I see you at the polo last weekend?"

I shake my head. "Nope, not me."

She's about to ask something else when the pair of them turn around, and a little way down the street is a small group of girls calling and gesturing them over. I breathe a sigh of relief.

"Thanks for letting us say hi to your horse." Girl one smiles. "Bye."

"He's not mine," I mutter and follow it up with a "see you

around" out of habit just in case she remembers where she knows me from.

Because having the gossip sites say I was super nice is always more preferable than being called a miserable bitch.

I figure Thunder would go back to standing still, but the tiny attention he just received seems to have piqued his need for more. He nudges me hard in the ribs, running his soft velvety lips all over my shirt pocket.

"Dude, this is clean. Don't eat it." I step back before his teeth make contact with my skin, but I'm talking to half a ton of horse, and of course, he follows me, nibbling at the soft cotton. "What are you after?"

Pushing his face away, which is harder than it sounds, I reach into my pocket to find a tin of breath mints from the plane ride over. Huh, maybe this shirt wasn't clean.

"Is this what you want?"

Given he tries to eat them before I open it, I'd say so.

Maybe he's expecting something different because when I tip the tiny white pellets into my hand, he stops what he's doing and stares at them, disappointed.

"Sorry, pal, it's all I got." I hold my hand out.

His hot breath blows over my palm, and he leaves a trail of saliva as he licks the mints up and crunches down.

"What are you doing to my horse?"

Spinning around, I find Lando sauntering across the street, all thick thighs and broad shoulders, with the same amusement as before sparkling in his eyes. There's an insolence to it, giving me the feeling he's laughing *at* me, not *with* me.

I snap the tin shut. "Nothing."

As he steps between us, the scent of wood and amber dances through the air. Holy *shit*, it's all I can do not to run my nose along his collar. Because Lando smells *good*. Better than he has any right to.

Cupping his hand around Thunder's nose, he pushes his

fingers up into his long, thick black mane. Thunder is more interested in the mints or my shirt, it seems.

"He likes you."

"He likes the mints."

"True, but he wouldn't be rubbing his nose over you if he was only after mints."

My cheeks warm under his gaze, and I step away, only for Thunder to crane forward for further investigation of my shirt, causing Lando to raise a thick brow at me. His point is proven, and it's followed by a twitch in his cheeks suppressing a smile.

"Buddy, I don't have anything else for you," I tell Thunder as he moves on to sniffing my hair.

I take another step back. My shirt might now be covered in horse slobber, but I draw the line at my freshly washed hair. Then I realize there's no reason for me to still be standing here, holding the reins and staring at Lando while he laughs loudly.

I should be on my way to get a coffee and a donut. Yet I'm not because I'm watching Lando's hands stroke Thunder's silky neck and wondering what else he can do with them.

My moment of insanity is broken when Eddie reappears carrying a large box, followed by the Labrador ambling behind him who promptly lies down between Thunder's legs.

"Right, Your Grace, we're settled on the bunting, and we've got the ribbons for the lampposts. Anything else you want?"

That's the third time Eddie's called Lando something other than his name. Or the name Clemmie introduced him as, and I'm a little confused. What I should do is hold my tongue or walk off in search of my coffee and donut. But I don't, obviously.

"What did you call him?"

"Who?"

My eyes slide toward Lando. "Um—"

Eddie's brows crease together, and his thick mustache

droops even lower because I'm obviously making no sense. "His Grace?"

"Yes, *that*. I thought your name was Lando."

Lando's—or whatever his name is—cheeks redden. "It is."

"Then—" I look at Eddie for some explanation. I shouldn't have asked. This is one of those complicated English things where everything is called something different.

Eddie nods at Lando. "His Grace 'ere, is the Duke of Oxfordshire. You address him as Your Grace. Same way you and me are like mister or missus. Or whatever they say in America."

Duke.

I'm normally much smarter than the last week or so would suggest. Maybe if I'd read Ashley's notes, I'd already know this, but I should have figured it out the day I spent at the pool with Clemmie. I've watched *Downton Abbey*. No regular person lives in a palace-sized house.

Address him? "Am I supposed to call you that? *Grace*?"

Next to me, Eddie snorts, and the ends of his mustache twitch while Lando looks like he'd rather be anywhere else. It's odd because even the few times I met him, he doesn't strike me as the sort of person to be uncomfortable in any situation. His self-assuredness is both incredibly alluring and infuriating.

"No, you may call me Lando," he replies eventually.

"Lando," I repeat.

"It's short for Orlando."

I remember enough of my schooling that I know *Orlando* has to come from Shakespeare rather than just being a name or a destination. He totally fits that broody, handsome sulky hero thing he has going on.

Lando is the guy I've met. The moody one.

So this uncomfortable, almost bashful expression he's wearing right now looks all wrong, and I hate it.

Therefore, I'm going to put things right.

"Orlando? Like Disney World?"

Lando's thick brows drop, giving me the exact reaction I was hoping for.

Eddie barks out a laugh and slaps his round belly. "She got you there, Your Grace."

"Hey, your name is *Holiday*," Lando shoots back, ignoring him. "Or how you Americans like to say—*vacation*?"

His eyes narrow, and I'm guessing he expects me to get all offended and storm off. But Eddie's chuckling next to me, and it's all I can do to stop my own laughter from escaping, especially as *Orlando's* gone back to glaring at me.

"That's a terrible American accent."

Lando opens his mouth, only to close it again and drop his head in defeat, but not before I catch the curve of a smile. "You're right, it is. I'm sorry. I'll leave the acting to you."

"My English accent isn't much better," I concede. "I try my hardest, but my dialect coach would tell me I *overpronounce my consonants*."

"Sounds okay to me."

I'm trying not to stare, but standing this close, I can see how clear the blue of his eye is. Not a fleck or swirl of green present, just pure blue. It's hypnotizing.

"If you two don't mind, I need to find someone to deal with all these ribbons," Eddie says, clearing his throat. "Your Grace, you want anything else added?"

Lando shakes his head, breaking our connection. "No thanks, Eddie, this'll all be superb. I'll pop back later, and we can discuss the cricket."

"No problem. See you later. Bye, 'Oliday."

I lift my hand to wave goodbye, only to find I'm still holding Thunder's reins, and I pass them back to Lando.

Thumbing over my shoulder, I say, "I should go—"

"Where are you heading?"

"To find a coffee."

"Then you need to go to The Beanery. We'll come with you."

I glance down at the Labrador and up at Thunder, then back at Lando. Surely, he doesn't mean all of them? But he does, and the four of us start walking down the street in silence, except for the *clip-clop* of Thunder's hooves.

I'm silent because I'm figuring this must be a super weird sight for anyone passing us, though no one seems to notice. They're too busy darting between stores or admiring the hanging baskets overloaded with blooms. But I don't know why Lando's silent, and it's got me curious, especially as I'm sure he keeps opening his mouth to speak only to close it again.

I figure I'll just wait. I'm waiting until we almost reach the coffee shop.

"Actually," he begins. "I'm glad I ran into you, I wanted to apologize for you know . . . my behavior. I should have done so yesterday. I was exceptionally rude to you the other day, and I'm sorry. And you're welcome to have lessons with Pierre whenever you want. I'm sure he'll welcome the change."

Air hisses through his teeth as he puffs out his cheeks like he's been holding his breath through his entire apology.

I'm so taken aback by his sincerity that I stop walking. I don't think anyone's ever apologized to me so earnestly. And yes, he was kind of rude, but I work in an industry where you need a thick skin to survive, and it was nothing compared to some of the vitriol I've been on the receiving end of, so I'd almost forgotten about it.

But I don't tell him that. Instead, I accept it on behalf of all the apologies I should have gotten over the years and didn't.

"Thank you. I appreciate that."

"You're welcome." He smiles and nods toward The Beanery. "What would you like?"

There's no way I'm standing out here while he goes inside and leaves me with Thunder. Plus, I want to choose the donut. And I also want to pay.

"I'll go, but you tell me what you're drinking."

He doesn't do a very good job of hiding his surprise at my offer, he looks like no one's ever bought him a coffee before. "I'll take one black, please."

"You got it."

It takes me no time to order and even less time to choose my donut because there's only one option. A round ball filled with raspberry "jam" and covered in sugar. It's not what I wanted, but a ritual is a ritual, and I'm superstitious enough that if I don't celebrate with coffee and a donut, things will go wrong.

I expect Lando to leave once I've handed his coffee over, but he doesn't. And the four of us continue making our way along Valentine High Street, where the final yards of bunting are being fastened.

I haven't ventured this far down before. I don't even know where we're going, but it's not like I have anything else to do. I'm still getting used to all this free time I have, and that I can spend it exactly how I choose to.

Eventually, we walk past The Cupid's Arrow, the other pub in the village. I have yet to go in. I'm too scared Eddie will catch me, and considering he was one of the first people I met here, I have a sense of loyalty.

"Has Eddie got you playing cricket, or are you part of the opposing team?" I ask because I'm not walking in silence any longer. If he wants to keep me company, then we're talking.

"Neither. Sadly," Lando replies. "I should be playing for Eddie, but I'm chairing the summer fair committee again. So I can't."

The way he says *again* makes it sound like the task should have fallen to someone else.

"Do you not normally head it up?"

"No, our family takes it in turns every year."

"Who dropped out?" I ask with a chuckle, expecting him to

say Clemmie because I can see Clemmie being a person with expert powers of persuasion to get her out of things she doesn't want to do.

He rubs along the back of his neck. "Um . . . actually, that would be Caroline."

"Oh, I don't recall Clemmie mentioning her. Is she another sister?"

"No, she would be my fiancée."

I don't know if I gasp or if Lando isn't used to not having a fiancée yet, because he immediately follows it up with, "Ex-fiancée."

I remember Clemmie telling me her brother had broken up with someone, but she'd made it seem like a casual girlfriend, not someone major. Someone he was going to marry. Someone he planned to spend his life with.

"I'm so sorry," I say eventually, which is more of a reflex than anything because I have a weird reaction to hearing him say ex-fiancée.

It's followed by curling in my belly, wondering if that means he's single.

Lando shrugs.

It might be a small movement, a casual brush-off, but it thickens my throat anyway.

As if sensing Lando's mood, Thunder maneuvers himself between us and nudges my arm hard enough that my coffee spills.

"Hey, what was that for?" I grumble, shaking my hand dry.

He does it again, only gentler this time, and I realize he's trying to get the paper bag containing my donut.

"Do you not feed your horse or something?"

Lando grins, the last thirty seconds forgotten about, and tugs on Thunder's bridle. "I do. But obviously not enough."

"This is my celebration donut," I say, opening the bag and

taking a deep inhale. It smells divine. "You can't have it all, but I'll share it."

Jelly oozes out as I break it in half and pass it to Thunder before realizing I probably should have asked Lando if it was okay to give a horse a donut.

"Celebration? What are you celebrating?"

I lick the rest of the jelly off my fingers, wondering if I should tell him.

"Oh . . . um, I got an offer this morning for a contract."

"Well, that does sound like something to celebrate. Congratulations."

"Thanks. It's a big deal actually. For me, anyway." I pause and take stock. Think about what my therapist would say to me. "No, it's a big deal for anyone. Not just me. It's huge."

"I'm sure it is."

"Forty million over five years," I blurt from nowhere.

What am I doing? Why am I telling him this? It's so obnoxious. It's braggy.

His full mouth rolls into a line. "I don't know anything about movies or your business, but if you're happy, then it sounds like a good deal. And I'm certain you're worth every single penny. Or *cent*, in your case. Very Hollywood, either way."

I nod. It's not a platitude. He's not trying to be nice. He believes what he's telling me. This almost stranger, who only shouted at me before today, thinks I'm worth it.

And his validation does something to me. *For* me.

"Thank you."

We stop at the wide stone arch, which marks the end of Valentine High Street. Unlike the fountain with its elaborate carvings, the arch is plain except for words running along the top.

Amor Principum.

"What does that mean?" I ask, pointing at the inscription.

"Love is the beginning," he replies quietly, his eyes locking onto mine so intensely I feel like I'm swaying. "Anyway, I need to be going. Thanks for the coffee, Hollywood. And the donut."

Hollywood. A smile pulls at the corners of my mouth. Two can play at this game.

"Anytime, Gracie."

The laugh he belts out almost has him toppling out of the stirrups as he mounts Thunder. And dear god, this guy on a horse . . . it shorts my brain.

"See you at the fair."

I stay there, under the arch, watching him ride off as I finish the remainder of my donut. Which is way more delicious than it looks.

Not the only thing deceiving today.

Lando, not quite as moody as I originally thought.

Quite the opposite.

LANDO

"Uncle Lando . . . Uncle Lando . . ."

I stop my search through the crowds of people and turn to my nephew.

"Yes, Max?"

"Did you *see*?"

"Um . . . see what?"

"Uncle *Lando* . . . did you see Sherbet?"

Max's little face is so filled with excitement as he stares at me through big blue eyes, I immediately feel guilty for not listening to a word he's said. In my defense, he does talk *a lot*, and I have to filter it.

Plus, it would be a full-time job replying to everything, and he already has a dad for that.

It's his dad I turn to now.

"Want to help me out here? What am I supposed to have seen?"

"Sherbet and Max are twins today. Max is dressed like Spider-Man, and Sherbet's wraps are red and blue. His mane and tail have been plaited with red and blue ribbons,"

Hendricks replies, his tone slow and deliberate like I'm hard of hearing or something.

I'm not hard of hearing. I just have other things on my mind today.

Max is staring at me from his elevated position on Hendricks's shoulders. This time, I give him a genuine smile and tug on his Spider-Man boots. "Well done, Maxy, I bet he looks splendid."

"He does. I helped with the ribbons." He beams with pride.

"And I can't wait to see. What time's the competition?"

"Two thirty," he cries, pointing aggressively at the crowds in front of us.

The pointing quickly turns into wriggling, and before Hendricks manages to stop him or drops him, Max has slid halfway down his father's body on the way to the ground. "Daddy, Daddy, there's Granny. Can I take her to see Sherbet?"

Hendricks isn't given the opportunity to reply.

Max sprints off as fast as his legs can carry him, running straight for our mother who's walking toward us with James Winters by her side. She barely moves as a miniature action hero crashes into her and grabs her hand.

We watch as she bends down to listen to Max's pleading, nods, glances up at Hendricks and me, then allows Max to drag her off in the opposite direction. I make a mental note to buy Max and Sherbet a bumper bag of carrots for saving me from a conversation I'm sure I don't want to have because I'm equally sure that's what was about to happen.

"Close call." I lean into Hendricks as we watch them disappear into the crowds. "And can I ask, wouldn't it have been better to dress Sherbet as a spider?"

My brother rolls his eyes, though I catch the twitch of a smile. "Have you already buckled under the pressure of the summer fair committee?"

Hmm. That's debatable.

The Valentine Nook Summer Fair officially opened an hour ago, and the crowds have been steadily building.

However, my day started much earlier than that with a call from Dave, the Burlington yard manager, who'd had a call from Mrs. Williams to say someone had left the gate open between the cow fields and the one we were using for the fair. The cows had wandered through and were now eating the hay bales that had been left out for sitting on.

While it didn't take long to get them rounded up and back into the correct field, we then spent the next two hours cleaning up the mess they'd left and bringing down extra "non-edible" seating.

The rest of the morning had been spent calming the committee, reassuring them that everything would be fine, and doing my best to avoid any further issues. While vowing not to run the committee for at least another five years.

I don't want to speak too soon, but the past hour has been problem-free and appears to be running smoothly.

The band is set up on a stage in the middle of the field, providing a soundtrack of the chosen jazz classics for the day.

Dogs are running around, swiftly followed by children.

The makeshift stables on the far side—where Max has taken our mother—are full of ponies being groomed and readied for the Best Turned Out Pony competition. It's the most popular event of the fair, so popular that we have to do one for each age group between four and twelve.

We also host show jumping competitions, dog agility, and a best pet category—which was won by a rabbit named Nail Varnish last year.

The hay bales that weren't used for a midnight snack are scattered around, while more seating is provided through striped deck chairs laid out in rows. Visitors already occupy half, while more patrons sit on picnic blankets, emptying their baskets and preparing to visit the multitude of stalls offering local produce.

If food's not what you want, there are tractor rides, a petting zoo, welly-throwing, cornhole, the coconut shy, and everyone's favorite, "guess the weight of the calf," where the closest to the number gets to pick the name of our newest herd member.

On the other side of the field is the cricket pitch, where the annual Valentine Nook cricket match between The One True Love and The Cupid's Arrow will begin shortly. The hardest part of today will be to show I'm not still smarting over not getting to play this year.

I shake my head. "As long as nothing else escapes, I don't have to discuss the bunting at any point during the day, and someone brings me a cider, then I shall be happy. Which reminds me, where's Churchill?"

Trust that bloody goat to get loose and terrorize everyone's picnics.

"Locked in the stable with a bucket of water and half a dozen apples."

"Excellent work. Thank you."

My eyes sweep over the crowds again. I make a convincing argument that I'm searching for Miles and Alex, who should have been here twenty minutes ago. But I'm also wondering where Clementine has gotten to because I overheard her talking on the phone to someone she was agreeing to meet before the fair began.

And not that I know all of my sister's friends. I've only recently become aware of one.

But whatever. If she's here, she's here. If she's not, then who cares?

Not me. It's not like I've been thinking about her since she bought me a coffee. Or shared her celebration donut with Thunder. Or that a celebration donut was even a thing.

I didn't think it was cute or anything.

"Where are the others?"

Hendricks flips his wrist over, checking his watch. "They'll be here soon."

As his sentence ends, Miles and Alex appear through a gap in the hedgerow and make their way over.

"Fine turnout today, Lan. Very impressive." Alex slaps a hand on my shoulder. "Love the bunting."

I roll my eyes. Bloody bunting. "Sure you don't want to trade places with me? I'll give you ten grand."

"Sorry. Even if I wanted to, which I don't, Clive would put a bounty out on me if I missed this match," Alex replies.

Clive, The Cupid's Arrow landlord, is even more competitive than Eddie, if that was believable. Alex is easily their best player, easily the best player on both teams having played England under 21s, and Eddie's still rues the day Alex went to work for Clive instead of him during one Christmas holiday.

"Anyone seen Clementine?" I ask, totally casual. Nonchalant, even.

"She went to collect her friend . . ." Miles's eyes widen, and his head tilts at me. "Oh . . . why are you asking, Lando?"

"She's helping out with the stalls, and I haven't seen her yet."

A perfectly reasonable and truthful response, which Miles sees right through.

"Clementine or her friend?"

"Is this Holiday Simpson?" Alex asks. "Did you see her last film? I watched it on the flight back. It was very good. You'd like it."

"Is this the one she got an Oscar for?" Hendricks asks.

"Yeah, Scorsese directed it. The second part is out at the end of the year." Alex turns to me. "What's she like?"

It's Hendricks who responds, his chin jerking at something behind me. "See for yourself."

The three of us turn to where Hendricks is staring and find

Clementine and Holiday walking toward us, though I barely notice my sister.

Holiday's pale blond hair is tied neatly back into a ponytail, dropping just below her shoulders. Big sunglasses take up most of her face and draw attention to her lips. Plump lips that form perfectly into the shape of a heart. She's wearing a white dress, one of those billowing ones that are soft and delicate, unlike the wellies she also has on.

I have to bend my head, so no one catches me smiling.

She looks like summer.

I'm immediately aware of myself. How I'm standing, how I'm looking at her, what I do with my hands . . . and in the end, I shove them deep in my pockets.

It's a level of self-consciousness I've never experienced.

But I'm not about to be overly friendly in front of my siblings. They're sharks circling for the tiniest drop of blood before going in for the kill. I'd never hear the end of it.

Ever.

"Hey, guys, meet my friend Holiday. She's renting Bluebell Cottage."

"My new neighbor." Miles throws her a wink that immediately has me scowling. "You'll have to come over for a cup of tea. Better yet, after-party at mine tonight."

It would probably be inappropriate to punch him. Right?

"Shut up, Milo." Clementine rolls her eyes at him. "Holiday, these are my brothers Hendricks, Miles, and Alex. And you remember Lando?"

The way Clementine makes the introduction has me wondering if Holiday mentioned to my sister that we'd actually seen each other since the day at the pool or that we walked down Valentine High Street and drank coffees together. And if she hasn't, why hasn't she?

But typically, I'm jolted from my thoughts by my youngest brother.

"From what I gather, she'll definitely remember Lando." Miles laughs.

"What does that mean?" Clementine asks.

Miles is too far away from me to punch him, and I can't do anything other than glare when he turns to me. I've learned the deeper Miles's dimples become, the bigger the shit he's about to stir.

I totally forgot I told them about the waterfall incident. My gut suddenly feels very heavy.

"Our new American friend spotted Lando in his birthday suit, having a merry old time in the waterfall."

Alex stares at me, as confused as Clementine, who's turned to Holiday, no doubt extremely grateful for her giant sunglasses. I can't see her eyes, but I'm certain they're shooting daggers at me.

It's so silent I can almost hear the whirring of my sister's brain, and Holiday counting down until the penny drops.

Clementine's brows shoot up. "*You're* the gross, hairy naked guy?"

"I never said gross," Holiday protests loudly, but no one hears her.

Miles is laughing so hard, I only need to bump him, and he'd fall over. So I do just that. Hendricks also has his head back snorting with laughter, just like Alex, although his amusement is coupled with confusion because he was in Hong Kong and has no idea what's happening.

I try to catch Holiday's eye to apologize, but she's not looking at me.

I wait for the explosion, the mood, the black cloud that will follow me for the rest of the day for embarrassing her. For telling my brothers, for Miles's joking around.

Based on experience, that's what usually happens.

Instead, she's shaking her head, wearing a wry smile while she watches Miles pick himself up off the ground.

"Oh, *Lan*. Gross and hairy. What a perfect description." He giggles.

"Lando, why were you naked?"

"I didn't think anyone was going to walk through the bushes, did I? It's private land," I grumble, which only sets Miles off again. "Milo, shut the fuck up, will you?" My eyes fall on Holiday. "I apologize about my idiot brother, and you know . . . the waterfall."

I should probably add another apology for everything else that's happened up to this point, but Holiday brushes it all off with a laugh and a flick of her hand.

"Don't worry. I have brothers. I know how it is."

That's it. That's her entire reaction. Laughing it off. I don't know what's more overwhelming, my relief or my surprise.

Over the tannoy an announcement is made for all members of the cricket teams to make their way to the pavilion for the coin toss and the start of the match. It's not a moment too soon.

"Right, boys, once more unto the breech . . . Loser buys the drinks later, right, Al?" Hendricks slings his arm over Alex's shoulder.

It's enough to start an argument about which team will win today, with Miles and Hendricks teasing Alex for being a sore loser. It's also enough to provide a distraction that I can step closer to Holiday.

"Hollywood—" I begin quietly.

One of her brows raises above the rim of her sunglasses, and I earn myself a smile. "Gracie."

Just like the first time I heard it, the nickname has me biting down on a grin because hell, if I don't find the lack of deference amusing. Kiss-arses surround me daily, and meeting someone who couldn't give a shit about me, my title, or my money isn't just novel, it's energizing.

Clementine swings an arm around Holiday's shoulders. "I

need to go too. I'm helping Eddie behind the bar. You're welcome to come and help, but if you want to stay and look around, Lando will show you. Won't you, Lanny?"

With that, my sister becomes my favorite sibling, and it takes all my effort not to break out into an enormous smile.

"I'd be happy to."

"Great, see you in a couple of hours."

"Keep your clothes on this time." Miles snorts. He leans in closer and nudges his elbow into my ribs. "Still want to offer me ten thousand to switch places?"

"Fuck *off*," I hiss after him as he sprints off with the others, leaving Holiday and me alone, though my tone is only filled with amusement.

It's hard to be annoyed when your heart is beating so hard it might burst.

HOLIDAY

"Welcome to the Valentine Nook Summer Fair."

I manage to tear my eyes away from watching his brothers and Clemmie hurry toward the cricket field. Holy hell, that is one good-looking family.

Miles and Hendricks could walk straight onto a Times Square billboard and fit right in. Alex too. All the same dark hair and bright blue eyes, long legs and broad shoulders. But that's where it stops.

If Miles is the smooth talker of the group, Hendricks is quieter and more analytical. And not just because Miles likes the sound of his own voice. Being a twin, I can easily spot the balance between the two because it's what I have with Tanner.

Then there's Alex, the cool one, who seems most similar to Lando.

But where the other three are good-looking, Lando is *handsome*. There's an edge to him that's missing from his brothers. Hardened and serious, intimidating.

Older.

If I hadn't bumped into him yesterday and walked the length of High Street, shared a donut with his horse and heard him laugh, I'd have never believed he was capable of anything other than extreme grumpiness.

I suspect it's a side of him that few get to see.

Nor do they see the smile he's currently directing my way.

"Thank you."

"Have you been to a summer fair before?"

I can't tell if he's teasing me or if he's genuinely wondering.

Popping a hip, I cross my arms over my chest. "I'm American. I'm not from another planet."

"Oh really?" Deep creases frame his eyes, and a genuine grin spreads across his face. "So you *have* been to a summer fair, then?"

"Yeah. In fact . . ." I tap a freshly manicured finger against my cheek, and my new baby-blue polish catches the light. "I think we invented the summer fair. Our one in Maine has a quarter million visitors every year—" I turn and make a big show of peering around, taking everything in, including how much tweed is being worn. "This is small fry in comparison."

Lando's laugh booms out, and warmth radiates through me. "Then I expect you to give me a full assessment and provide any pointers for where we can do better next year."

"Don't worry. I will."

He sweeps his hand in front of us. "Shall we?"

"Lead the way."

I've never loved crowded spaces, the jostle of people, the feel of being too close to someone. It's gotten worse as my career has grown. It's one of the reasons I keep my personal life so low-key. I don't court publicity. I stay off social media and usually avoid all the classic haunts where celebrities hang out.

Today, I don't seem to mind how crowded it is because it gives me an excuse to stick close to Lando. Close enough that his hand brushes against mine more than once.

"How's Thunder today?"

"He asked me to bring him back some donuts," he quips, making me chuckle.

I'm still smiling to myself as we pass by several booths selling local produce, cute tote bags, and souvenirs. I spy Valentine Cook's display of fruit and vegetables, and The Beanery selling coffee and donuts, which I nearly stop and buy for Thunder.

There's one with a line easily three times the size of anyone else's. It's the final booth along the row, with double the space of the others, and covered in a pink glittery cloth.

As we get closer, I see the table is heaving with products—bags of herbs, candles and incense burners. Crystals of all sizes are on sale next to bottles neatly lined up and filled with colored liquid.

The sign hanging above says this booth is the number one purveyor of love potions and spells in England, and next to it sits an A-frame listing out times for card readings.

It's cute and eye-catching, and I want to stop to see what it's all about.

I could certainly do with a little extra help in the romance department, but I'm hurrying to keep up with Lando's long strides, which appear to have lengthened.

"Orlando—" the lady from behind the table calls, and I recognize her as the woman Clemmie pulled me away from on my first tour around the village.

Lando appears to share the same opinion as his sister. "Not now, Agatha. Must dash."

I'm still jogging to keep up with him as we enter a second field.

"Yoo-*hoo,* Your Grace. Your *Grace . . . hellooo—*"

Lando turns at the sound of his name being called to find a small older lady rushing toward him, carrying a large wicker basket. She's moving with surprising speed for how heavy the basket must be, given it's full to the brim. She must have bought up half the stalls already.

She's also wearing rain boots with her skirt. I *knew* I'd blend in.

I want to laugh, but next to me, Lando stiffens. It's so slight, virtually imperceptible unless it was a movement you were also familiar with. It's that protective need to slip into another version of yourself and don your armor. One I know well.

I get the impression that if he could rush away from this lady too, he would. But it's too late.

"Good afternoon, Mrs. Fraser."

"Wonderful fair this year, Your Grace." She beams up at him adoringly. "We're so happy to see you out and about again."

She makes it sound like he's been locked away with a contagious disease.

One glance at Lando and I can tell he's not sure he wants to be out and about. It's also painfully obvious that his being out and about is not a subject he wishes to discuss, but Mrs. Fraser isn't one to pick up on social cues.

"I was just saying to Judy Dennett that you're much better off . . . with the right woman—" Her gaze moves slowly in my direction.

Lando clears his throat loudly enough to stop her talking. "Okay, thank you, Mrs. Fraser . . . I appreciate it . . . Don't want to keep you, that basket's looking heavy, and we must dash . . . Best pony to judge . . ."

Lando's long fingers grip my arm, and he tugs me away before Mrs. Fraser can continue, and I get enough information to piece together what she's talking about.

"Sorry about that," he mutters, releasing me but only once we've disappeared through another wave of people who've arrived in the last ten minutes. "I didn't mean to grab you."

"That's okay. She seemed . . . *enthusiastic*." I grin.

Immediately, his shoulders relax, and he nods. "You could

say that. Mrs. Fraser is—how should we put it? She loves getting in people's business."

"A nosy old hag?"

"Something like that." He sighs, though the beginnings of a smile reappear on his face as he stares at me.

I can see that he's expecting me to ask what she was referring to. I can tell he's bracing for it, but if it's a subject that makes him *that* uncomfortable, I don't need to know unless he wants to tell me.

Instead, I go with, "So we're judging a pony competition, are we?"

The expression that flickers across his face is both gratitude and relief. "Yes. Yes, we are. If you'd like to join me, that is. I have to warn you, though, we don't usually have celebrities of your caliber here."

"Oh?"

"No, it's usually the local newsreader, perhaps a B-lister visiting the area. No one as Hollywood as you." He grins. "It might cause quite the stir."

My hand clasps my chest. "Will I need security?"

In the split second, before I blink, I catch his pupils flare, and he slowly shakes his head. "No, I've got you."

And my throat goes dry.

Sadly, a small child running between us breaks the moment, followed by several other slightly larger children.

"Where were we?" Lando clears his throat and asks. "Oh yes, the pony judging. It's not for another hour, so what do you say we visit the coconut shy? How are you at throwing?"

I have no idea what a coconut shy is, but thanks to my brother, my throwing arm is pretty darn good.

"Better than I am at shooting," I reply.

"And have you tried our cider yet?"

I shake my head. "No, but I have a feeling I'm about to."

"You catch on quick, Hollywood. Let's go."

I follow Lando through the field to where the games are set up on the opposite end to the cricket, beyond a wide boundary. Thanks to my brother's lengthy explanation this morning, I've almost grasped the concept of cricket. At least enough to know that it's called a pitch, not a field, and a match, not a game.

"So, as a summer fair aficionado, what's your favorite part?" Lando asks.

"Hmm. Good question." I tuck away a loose strand of hair that stuck in my sunglasses. "The food, obviously."

"Obviously."

"But also I really love the old-fashioned games, you know where you shoot at a bullseye and win a stuffed bear, that kind of thing."

"Then the coconut shy will be ideal."

I'm wondering if I should pull my phone out for a quick search on Google when we reach the bar Clemmie's serving at, which turns out to be an Air Stream version of The One True Love.

"Hey, guys, how's it going? Having fun, Hol? Hope Lando's behaving himself," Clemmie calls out when she spots us walking over.

I push my sunglasses up and watch him roll his eyes at his sister. "He's been the perfect gentleman."

There have to be ten people serving, but they still can't pour the drinks quick enough. Every time someone's departure creates a gap, it's quickly filled by a surge of new customers.

It's not the first bar I've seen in the fields, but it's the busiest by far. Patrons carry away trays holding half a dozen glasses at a time. One guy walks off with four cups clamped between his giant hands while he holds another between his teeth, and the small gaps they leave behind are quickly filled.

Luckily because Clemmie is serving, or because I'm with the guy running the place, we step around the side where it's quiet.

"Quit yapping, Clem. Walking around is thirsty work. Hollywo . . ." Lando pauses, and there's amusement in his tone when he finishes the sentence. "Holi*day* wants to try our cider."

"All right, keep your knickers on," Clementine shoots back, passing over two dark green cups that have been pre-poured. Similar to Solo cups, these have Valentine Nook Summer Fair printed on them.

Clemmie and Lando watch me as I take my first sip. The crisp, bubbly apple taste hits my throat. It's incredibly refreshing and immediately goes to my head.

"Well?"

I take another sip under their watchful eyes. "Hey, best cider I've ever tasted."

Clemmie whoops. "Correct answer."

"It's made from Burlington apples. The ones Churchill doesn't eat, anyway," Lando adds, taking a huge gulp of his own.

Clemmie's already moved on to serving more customers. As there's not enough space at the bar for us to stand here and drink, I pick up my cup and once again follow Lando.

"See you two later. Don't have too much fun without me," Clemmie calls after us as we make our way over to the field of games.

The coconut shy is essentially nine coconuts balanced on the top of ten evenly spaced poles set into an overlapping diamond formation, ready to be knocked off.

What's shy about it, I don't know.

It also looks easy enough, though from the way Lando's looking at me, I suspect he thinks otherwise.

"Afternoon, Your Grace," the man behind the counter greets. "Come to give it a go?"

"We have, Mike," Lando replies, peeling notes off a stack he pulls from his pocket. "And we'll take a couple of buckets. It's my friend's first time at the coconut shy."

I thrust my hand out to Mike. "I'm Holiday. I'm new here."

Mike gets that look people do where he can't quite place me, but he shakes my hand anyway and heaves the buckets of balls on the shelf in front of us. They're roughly the same size as a baseball, though a little heavier, but I'll make it work.

I *knew* all those hours spent pitching to Tanner would come in handy one of these days.

I curl my fist around the first ball. "So what? I have to knock the coconuts off?"

"Sure do. Just aim and throw," says Mike.

"Let's see what you've got, Hollywood."

I grin wide at the two men staring expectantly at me, and as I pitch my fist back, I realize the back of the booth is empty.

"Hang on, what do I win if I get them all?"

"Anyone who knocks them all off wins dinner for two at a restaurant of their choice in the village," Mike replies.

"No stuffed bear?"

Lando shakes his head. "No."

I put the ball down. "I'm used to winning a stuffed bear."

"You need to knock them all off before we can negotiate prizes."

I was going to go easy, but the smile he's wearing is so placating that I'm going hard.

"I'd like to negotiate now if it's all the same to you."

Lando scratches through his beard, and one thick eyebrow rises. "All right, if you knock them all off without missing a throw, I'll add a stuffed bear to the prize."

"An extra-large, life-sized one."

"Life-sized?"

"It's what they have at the fairs in America."

"Okay, a life-sized bear." He holds his hand out, and I shake it.

"You have yourself a deal, Gracie." I toss the ball into the air and catch it. "Let's see what I can do."

Pitching my arm back, the first ball flies out of my hand with enough speed and accuracy not to only knock the coconut in the middle but crack it open.

"What the . . .?" Mike's reaction is exactly the same as Lando even though I can tell he's trying to hide it.

"Beginner's luck." I lift a shoulder and throw him a wink.

The second coconut doesn't crack, but it falls off just the same.

The third, fourth, and fifth follow.

By the time the sixth flies off its perch, a small crowd has begun to form behind me. But as I'm sure Lando's guessed by now, this isn't my first rodeo. In fact, he's standing with his arms crossed over his chest, a wide grin stretched over his face.

I don't hate it.

I channel Tanner and all those times I've watched him play or practiced with him over and over in the backyard until the ninth ball hits the coconut square in the middle, and it topples to the ground.

A couple of people behind me clap. A group of boys step forward to give it a go of their own, while muttering it can't be that hard.

I push the remaining bucket of unused balls over to Mike and hold my hand out.

Silently, he pulls an envelope from his pocket, places it in my palm, and grins wide. "I guarantee no one else is going to do that today."

"Thank you," I reply, turning to Lando whose eyes are open wide. "Why are you looking at me like that?"

I can see he's battling with himself while he tries to figure out a way to tell me he's impressed without coming across as sexist or offensive. It's kind of cute, so I decide to go easy on him.

"My twin brother, Tanner, plays baseball in the major

leagues. I was the one who practiced ball with him for hours and hours on end growing up. You learn some things."

Lando nods slowly. "And what did you get out of it?"

"He practiced my lines with me." I laugh. "Don't worry, you're not the first guy who's underestimated me."

Two deep creases appear between his brow, and his smile drops. "I don't doubt that. And I'm certain it's never a mistake made by the same person twice."

The last part of his sentence is spoken with such sincerity that I can only shake my head in response.

As we say goodbye to Mike and turn to leave, a couple of boys have blocked our path. Though they're not boys. They're men, young men but still men.

One of them steps forward, phone in hand. "'Scuse me, are you Holiday Simpson? Can we get a picture?"

It was going to happen sooner or later. I'm not exactly hiding myself in the village, but for the past couple of weeks, there's been peace in walking around undisturbed.

Any disappointment I feel, however, vanishes when I realize Lando's stepped Rottweiler-like between me and the guys because his natural instinct is to protect. Even before he figures out what's happening.

I place a hand on his arm to let him know I'm okay, then nod to the guys.

"Sure. No problem."

I put on my best smile, the one I practice for moments like this. The one that's shared and viewed millions of times over. It's the one that everyone knows, that makes me look happy all the time. Friendly.

Hollywood's Golden Girl.

But as my eyes flick to Lando and his scowl, my smile morphs into a wide grin. Right now, he looks like he wants to rip the guy's arm off for slinging it around my shoulders.

"Thanks. Big fan. We loved your last film."

"That's kind, thank you. Thank you for your support," I reply, easing away from them for their own safety, given the murderous expression on Lando's face.

As soon as there's a gap, Lando steps close to me again.

He stares until the guys have walked away out of sight, then turns us in the opposite direction, like he's worried they'll come back.

"Does that happen a lot?"

"Yes," I reply, folding up the dinner envelope and slipping it into my purse. "Not as much as some actors because I keep a lower profile, but yes. First time here, though."

"Must be annoying."

I take a breath. I'm always careful to respond to comments like this in case it comes back to bite me in the ass. But with Lando, it sounds like he's speaking from a place of experience. If that older lady from earlier is anything to go by.

"Sometimes. When people don't respect boundaries. With social media, everyone feels like they're entitled to a piece of you. But this is a career I chose, and meeting fans comes with the territory. And I do love it most of the time. It's just a bit more intense right after a film releases."

"And you just had one come out?"

It's a question, not a statement.

I stop walking and glance up at him, pushing my sunglasses on my head.

It's been a long time since I met someone who's never seen my work, even from my early days.

It's been even longer since I spent time with anyone who had no interest in films or fame or Hollywood. It's a strange experience meeting someone who already knows a ton about you, thanks to Wikipedia or whatever tabloid outlet they'd got their hands on that day.

It's even stranger to meet someone who doesn't.

But Lando's asking because he genuinely wants to know. Because this is all new to him.

"Are you telling me you haven't watched my films?"

He takes in my shocked expression and his mouth drops. "Um . . . um . . . I—"

"I'm messing with you." I laugh and shove him playfully in the ribs.

"That may be . . ." He clears his throat. "I'm still embarrassed to say I haven't, but that's nothing on you. I just never have the time to sit and watch a movie. Alex said it was very good, though," he adds quickly.

"Well, then, please thank him for me. If you ever do find yourself having time, I can recommend a few good ones. Not mine, just really good movies."

"But I'd like to see yours," he replies, "as long as you bring the popcorn."

"I can do popcorn."

A huge roar of cheers erupts from the cricket pitch, and everyone around us spins to see what caused it. But there's too much in the way to see. I want to ask Lando what he thinks happened, and if we can go watch a little when I notice an impossibly glamorous older woman walking toward us.

The type of woman I aspire to be when I reach her age.

Perfect hair, perfect skin, perfect makeup.

She has to be mid-sixties, wearing navy blue slacks and a white button-down that doesn't look like it's ever had a speck of dirt on it. She's dressed in that impossibly expensive and put-together way, but only if you know what you're looking for—custom fits and the highest quality fabrics.

She's so *English* and proper. I imagine she has afternoon tea with sandwiches every day.

I notice people watching her as she passes them, though her eyes are on no one but Lando, and as this woman looks exactly how Clemmie will look in forty years, it's not a stretch to figure she's his mom.

"Oh *god*." I barely catch what he's mumbling from the side of his mouth. "Holiday, I apologize in advance for anything about to happen."

"There you are, darling. I've been searching everywhere for you. I haven't seen you all day."

Lando bends down, placing a brief kiss on her cheek. "Hello, Mother."

But she isn't looking at Lando. Her entire focus is on me, and she thrusts her hand out. Lando's watching me, and I can't tell if it's through nerves or curiosity.

"You must be Holiday. Welcome to Valentine Nook, my dear. My daughter has been singing your praises. It's so wonderful to finally meet you. I'm Victoria Burlington, Lando's mother."

I have met so many people in my life, which instilled in me the ability to be both incredibly charming and not easily intimidated, but right now, I have to dig deep. I also fight the urge to curtsey.

Removing my sunglasses, I give her my very best smile. A genuine one. "It's lovely to meet you."

"How are you enjoying the cottage?" she coos. "Lando used to live in it, you know. If you have any problems at all, he'll be able to help."

I turn to Lando. I'm certain he's not mentioned that before, and I'm also certain Clemmie hadn't either. No, it's brand-new information.

That uncomfortable expression is back on Lando's face, and this time, it's coupled with a hint of embarrassment, and I wonder why. But then again, this lady is his mother, so it comes with the territory.

"He's been awesome help. He and Clemmie have been welcoming me to the village."

"I'm so happy to hear that." Her eyes bounce between Lando and me. "And you must come for supper. How about next Friday?"

Lando tuts loudly, "No, Mum. Holiday doesn't want to come for supper."

"Lando—"

"Mother—"

I don't know what's going on between Lando and his mom, but I have a sneaky suspicion it's something to do with me. You learn to pick up on cues when people have conversations about you *in front of you.*

But next Friday is the Fourth of July, something I'd normally celebrate with my family. I was going to plan something at my cottage, but I hadn't yet gotten around to it. This invitation not only saves me from hosting, but it also means I get to see Lando's family all together.

I'm not sure who's more surprised—him or his mom—when I answer.

"Actually, I'd love to."

LANDO

JEREMY: Mate, I need to talk to you.

JEREMY: I know I fucked up but pick up your phone. It's important.

THE VISION of Jeremy's Superman logo'd white arse burns in my brain, and until the day comes when it's not the first thing I think about when either of their names are mentioned, I have no intention of speaking to them ever again.

Wherever Caroline is, I'm sure she's happily wearing the four million pounds' worth of jewelry I bought her over the course of our relationship and was allowed to keep.

And Jeremy? I have zero fucks to give about what Jeremy's doing or why he needs to speak to me.

On the plus side, the messages do make me realize I haven't thought about either of them in a few weeks. Unless you count Mrs. Fraser at the summer fair or when I went to Bluebell to see Holiday, my thoughts have been adultery-free.

And I plan on keeping it that way.

Just like all the others before it, I delete the messages and go to slip the phone back into my pocket. On second thought . . . I bring up Jeremy's contact details and hit Block.

There.

No point in ruining a perfectly lovely day with a stream of unwanted messages.

A lovely day that I intend to continue by taking Thunder through the fields, one of his favorite things to do. First, however, he's got a new set of shoes being fitted.

Arriving at the stable yard, I'm only greeted by silence. Silent enough for me to notice Thunder isn't where he should be. Usually, when I arrive, he's whinnying his head in excitement, hopping about while a groom is trying his best to tack him up.

All I find is Max's pony Sherbet, a fat little Shetland, face first in a bucket of feed, snorting up his breakfast like he's never eaten before, and Sunday, Thunder's best friend, kicking his door in annoyance because Thunder isn't there.

The rest of the stables contain their usual residents. It's only my horse who's not where he's supposed to be.

"Good morning, Your Grace." One of the stable boys walking past with two very full buckets of water nods.

"Morning, Will. Where's Thunder?"

"Jack's out in the field trying to get him in. He wasn't waiting at the gate this morning, so I brought the rest of them in, and Jack went to fetch him."

I frown because my horse is too astute for his own good.

There's a reason we're doing the farrier's visit at breakfast time—Thunder doesn't like to miss his breakfast. He's usually fighting Sherbet to be first in line and into his stable for a bucket of feed, followed by a long nap. But as much as he loves breakfast, he *hates* the farrier.

"You should have called me earlier."

"Sorry, Your Grace, he's just gone over to the far field, is all. Jack's gone out with a headcollar."

We try to keep the horses contained within designated spaces, but Thunder does what he wants and will jump a fence without a second thought, which makes it all the more inconvenient when he has an appointment.

I run into the stable office, grab the keys for one of the four-wheelers, and take off for the far field at the top of the valley. I'm going so fast, it only takes me ten minutes to reach the place where Will said he'd be. In the distance, I spot Jack, hurrying up the bank to the top of the hill, and hit the throttle.

Jack spins around as he hears the engine, his red cheeks puffing from his unexpected morning jog. Or perhaps his annoyance at a misbehaving horse.

I've had Thunder since he was a foal. His father, Zeus, was my father's favorite horse, and every time I ride him, I feel like I'm closer to my dad. But just like his father, Thunder has a tendency to misbehave, which I find more amusing than Jack does.

"Mornin', Your Grace."

"Where is he?"

He taps the binoculars around his neck. "Walking the fence line."

"But he's okay?"

"He's fine. Just bloody stubborn," he grumbles. "Won't come in if he doesn't want to."

Jack's ahead of me, so he doesn't see me smile. Because if *I'm* grumpy, there's one person who could legitimately be called grumpier than I am, and it's Jack. Now in his late sixties, I remember him when I was a boy running the stable yard for my father, and even then, his temperament was less than sunny.

But regardless of his mood, everyone loves him. Humans and animals alike. And while he's less keen on the humans, no one cares for horses more than Jack, even when they're misbehaving.

As we pass through the final gate and reach the top of the hill, I spot Thunder for the first time. Sure enough, he's prancing back and forth along the fence line.

"What is he doing?"

When I take the binoculars from Jack for a closer look, it appears that Thunder is absolutely fine—no limp, no sullen posture, no signs of trauma or anxiety—just doing everything he can not to visit the farrier.

It's as he jumps around that I notice something on the other side of the fence. Or should I say some*one.* A blond someone.

I don't know what she's doing or how she's found herself there, but if I'm not mistaken, Holiday's talking to Thunder.

My lips twist, and before I can stop it, a laugh barrels up my throat and belts out. Jack turns to me with a quizzical expression.

"It's okay. I got this. You take the four-wheeler back, and I'll bring him down," I say, holding my hand out for the headcollar.

I approach slowly, taking my time to watch Holiday make her way along the drive with Thunder walking beside her, his glossy black coat shining in the early morning sun. At seventeen and a half hands, he's a big boy, and as docile as he can be, it's unusual for him to be quite so enthusiastic about a stranger. But there he is, matching her short strides with his long legs.

I'm wondering how she got here because it's not an easy road to walk along from the village, when Thunder turns and spots me. His nostrils flare, and he lets out a long whinny, galloping over to me and grinding to a halt just in time to nudge my pockets.

I stroke down the thin white stripe on the bridge of his nose. It's the only marking he has, like whoever painted him missed a spot.

"You get nothing until after the farrier."

In response, he puffs out an annoyed snort, then turns and trots back to Holiday, who's leaning against the fence. A pair of aviators hang off the neck of her T-shirt, which means I can see her whole face. The edges of her clear blue eyes crease from her smile, but aside from those, her face is devoid of lines.

As I get closer, I notice a constellation of freckles along her hairline and down the rim of her nose, which spills out onto her cheeks.

Once again, I realize how incredibly pretty she is.

I can see exactly why she's Hollywood's darling or whatever Miles called her.

"What are you doing here?"

She's trying to pull her smile in, her mouth rolling in on one side.

"Well," she begins, and I'm all ears. "I have my first cooking lesson with Pierre, but this morning, I realized I'd never been to your . . . um"—she's waving her hand around—"*place* before. Except when Clemmie drove." Her smile breaks out again. "I guess I hadn't been paying attention to how far it is or how dangerous the road is. You know there's no sidewalk, right? On the plus side, *this* road is quieter."

I cross my arms over my chest and tilt my head. "It should be. This is the drive. It's private."

She peers left, then right. "This is the *driveway*? It's got to be two miles long."

"Something like that." I chuckle. "Didn't you go through a set of gates?"

She nods. "Yeah, but I thought they were just gates, like the arch in the village."

"Nope. They're entrance gates." Which should have been shut, but I don't tell her that because I don't want to discourage her from coming again.

"Okay, then. Well, I should ask what you're doing all this way up here without a car. And maybe I need to add 'get a car' to my list."

"I came to fetch my horse. He's late for an appointment. But it seems he's being distracted."

Truthfully, I can't blame him. Holiday would make anyone lose track of time, and right now, he's back to being by her side like he's hoping she'll protect him.

"What's the appointment?"

"The farrier. He needs fitting for some new shoes."

Turning to Thunder, she lets out a loud gasp, her eyes wide. "You're going shoe shopping? Oh, Thunder, what a fun morning for you. What are you going to pick?"

I move to stand alongside them, though I'm thwarted by my horse. He's decided he's the only one to get Holiday's attention today and blocks me from getting near the fence.

"He's going to have a very attractive steel horseshoe-shaped pair."

"Steel. Hmm. Well, I'm sure you'll pull them off nicely."

I know he doesn't understand her or have any clue what shoe shopping is. But something about the way she's combing her fingers through his forelock has him standing statue still, his head bent so she can reach between his ears.

I'm not convinced he hasn't fallen asleep.

"You seem to know a lot about how to manage a horse, Hollywood."

She peers around his huge head. "I can make anything seem believable. I'm an award-winning actress, aren't I?"

"So everyone keeps telling me."

This time, she sticks her tongue out, and I decide this is my favorite version of her. The one with her chin jutted in defiance, with fire behind the blond hair and blue eyes, especially when it's followed with a laugh that finishes in a snort.

"I've spent some time around horses. But I had a bad accident once, so now I keep my feet firmly on the ground. I'd also prefer to keep my distance, but Thunder here doesn't respect personal space."

"It's because you fed him donuts. He's never going to leave you alone now."

She chuckles and drops a kiss on his nose. I watch the movement—Thunder's eyes closing as her lips touch him—and have a sudden and alarming desire to know what it feels like.

To be kissed by her. To *kiss* her.

I realize she's talking, but my heart is thudding so hard I can barely hear her.

". . . my bear."

"Your bear?"

One perfect eyebrow arches at me. "The stuffed bear I won. I believe we shook on it."

Ah yes, how could I forget? Even though I did forget. "I can't just magic up a stuffed bear, you know. These things take time."

She sets off walking again, Thunder following. "Not too long, I hope. Can't a duke hurry things up?"

"It'll take as long as it takes."

Speaking of which, I really need to take Thunder back to the stable yard so he can have his breakfast and get fitted. I don't have the time to walk back to the house because I have meetings for the rest of the morning. As it is, I won't be able to take him out until later this afternoon.

Yet we continue along the fence line because it seems that both Thunder and I wish to enjoy Holiday's company for as long as possible.

"What are you making in your first class?"

"I don't know. Something easy, I hope."

"Rice Krispies cakes?"

From the other side of Thunder, I hear her snort another laugh. "Not quite *that* easy. I'm not looking to become a Michelin chef, I'd just like to know my way around a kitchen better than I do right now. I want to know how to bake a pie. The Fourth of July is coming up, and I've never made one."

"You could bake your own celebration donuts," I suggest. "Start a new tradition."

"I *could.* But the real magic of the celebration donut is having someone else make it."

"Ah. I see."

"What about you?" She peers around Thunder and shoots me a wry smile. "How does the duke celebrate?"

I'm silent for a second because *for that second,* I'm confused about who she's talking about. Then I realize it's me, *the duke.*

My birthright, my title, my *life*—all of it momentarily forgotten about.

Worse still, I can't answer her question because I can't remember the last time I had something to celebrate.

Between running things around here, ensuring all aspects of Burlington Estate are staying efficient, meeting with my financiers, lawyers and advisers, seeing the year's young are all born healthy and their mothers are taken care of, and attending the various Valentine Nook monthly meetings, I don't have enough hours in my day.

"Gracie? C'mon, tell me," she presses. "What do you do to celebrate?"

"Um . . . I don't recall. Probably open a bottle of champagne. Something like that."

"Okaaay," she drags out, making it clear she's less than impressed with my response. "Then tell me what you do for fun."

That question is better but also *worse.*

It's better in that I have an answer ready, like "I take Thunder through the fields, watch Miles play polo—"

But worse, because it reminds me of every time Miles accuses me of having a stick up my arse, that duty comes before fun.

Because again, I realize I can't remember the last time I truly had any fun.

Like uninhibited, falling-into-bed-after-having-the-best-day-ever fun. The most recent example of this would be last Christmas when my brothers dragged me off to Aspen on the day I was supposed to get married.

It was the week away I needed, even if I was hungover for half of it and mute for the rest, dreading my return to England.

"That's cute."

"What about you? What do you do for fun?"

"Hmm." She pauses. "Well, I try to catch as many baseball games as possible. But I also like to start the day without a plan and see where it takes me. I'll meet my girlfriends for brunch, and we'll go from there." The knowing laugh she lets out makes me want to beg to hear more. "Sometimes we end up dancing until the morning. But I also like learning new things . . . cooking, for example."

"And we all know how you celebrate."

"We sure do. But I'm only twenty-five. Maybe that'll change in time."

Twenty-five.

It's a sobering thought. It reminds me she's a year younger than the twins, and two years older than Clementine. That she's Clementine's friend.

Then I'm wondering why I care. Many people fall within the age range of twenty-four to twenty-six. What difference does it make to me?

She's my tenant and nothing more.

"How old are you?"

"Thirty-four," I reply.

The silence that drags on makes me feel even worse than I did for not remembering the last time I had fun.

Thunder brings me out of my morose spiral and into the present when we've reached the edge of the fence line. He could jump it with little encouragement, but instead, I use it as an opportunity to let Holiday continue without us.

"You only need to follow the drive for another ten minutes, and you'll get to a row of oak trees that leads to the house."

Holiday nods. "Thanks, Gracie. Clemmie's going to come meet me so I don't get too lost."

"That's good," I tell her. "Enjoy your class, Hollywood. Try not to burn the house down before you come for supper next week."

"I shall. Tell your mom I'm looking forward to it."

A light laugh rings out as she walks off. It's a laugh I want to hear more of, the laugh I listened to all day at the summer fair.

And then it hits me.

The last time I had fun was with her.

* * *

HOURS LATER, after I've seen Thunder safely through his shoeing ordeal and taken him on a long ride through the estate as a reward, I head into my study to take the first meeting of the day I'd pushed.

There, in the middle of a pile of papers, I find a small wicker basket filled with fresh jam donuts and a note attached.

DEAR THUNDER,

I made you some celebratory jelly donuts to enjoy while you're prancing about in your new shoes.

With love, Holiday.

P.S. Gracie, I made extra for you just in case you found something to celebrate today.

I PICK one up and bite into it, because I did. I *did* find something to celebrate.

I have a new friend, and her name is Holiday Simpson.

HOLIDAY

I sprint the final forty yards the same way I always do—like Tom Brady heading for the end zone.

I kick up my pace as I round the corner of the lane, pass the field where the calves have been grazing for the past week, and take the home straight right up to the gate of my cottage.

In the absence of a home gym, I've started running again, and I truly can't remember why I stopped. There's something so freeing about sticking in your earbuds and pounding your feet against the gravel.

I also seem to have acclimated too well to the English summer because it's baking hot today, and I'm gasping. I should have left much earlier—like when I woke up—but I'm having the hardest time getting out of bed these past weeks because I'm so damn comfortable. I can't remember the last time I had such a long stretch of perfect nights of sleep.

I'm wiping sweat from my face when I see it.

A giant stuffed bear.

A giant stuffed bear is in the front seat of an SUV. It's one of the farm Land Rovers I've seen around here, with the logo of Burlington Estates printed on the side, and it's freshly washed.

Therefore I'm looking around for the driver—preferably one around six feet three, thick stubble, piercing blue eyes—but all I see is a woman about my age exiting through the gate next door to mine.

Miles's place.

She's dressed in a pair of jeans with a shirt thrown over the top. All perfectly innocent and casual, cute even, especially with the slides she's wearing, but something about her messy hair makes me think she's not just been over for a coffee.

Or maybe she has, if the coffee was served last night, followed by *a lot* of tequila.

No, this girl is freshly fucked.

A pang of envy stabs me in the belly because I can't remember the last time I looked like that. Or if I ever have.

Maybe this car, along with the bear, is hers, or Miles was driving it. All the endorphins I earned seem to melt away into disappointment. I'm waiting for her, but instead she peers inside, then back at me, with her head tilted.

"Cool bear." Bracelets jangle as she pushes her sunglasses up. "Are you Holiday Simpson?"

"I am." I offer her a smile, but it's not returned, not really.

Half a smile, perhaps. Enough for me to know she's not looking to make friends.

"Cool," she says again. "I heard you'd moved here. I'm a friend of Miles's." She points behind her in case I didn't notice her exiting his place before her eyes drop to the ground and slowly drift back up. "We're kind of seeing each other."

It's an odd thing to say. I don't know how to respond, especially as she's staring at me. Then it clicks.

This girl's warning me off.

I might have been slightly jealous about the way she appears to have spent her last twelve hours, but that's where it stops. It certainly has nothing to do with *who* she spent it with.

I try not to laugh as I refrain from telling her I'd need an offer that dwarfed my L'Oreal contract before I hooked up with a guy like Miles.

I met him for all of ten minutes. In that time, he not only checked me out but also another four girls who walked past me. No, Miles is not the type of guy to ever be labeled as "seeing" someone.

I know guys like Miles. I've *met* guys like Miles.

They ooze charm and charisma, and you're their entire world for a whole twenty minutes before they get bored and move on.

But she doesn't look like she'd care for me to tell her that. She also probably wouldn't appreciate knowing she's not the first person I've seen leaving his cottage in the mornings.

Instead, I hold my smile and say, "That's good to know."

"There's a note on your car, by the way," she calls behind her as she walks off.

I peer across the hood, and sure enough, there's an envelope with my name scrawled across the front. Inside, I find a note and a set of keys.

Dear Holiday,

Thank you for the donuts. You can use this next time you visit me, so you don't get run over on the country lane.

Love, Thunder.

P.S. Sorry about the bear. He refused to get out of the car.

By the time I reach the bottom of the note, my cheeks ache from the size of my smile. I might have left Lando and Thunder a basket of donuts, but I never expected them to be reciprocated.

I don't even know *why* I left the donuts. But the look I

caught on Lando's face when I asked him what he did for fun punched me in the gut.

I never want to see that look again.

Tugging open the door, I grab the bear and pull him out.

He's much bigger than he looked sitting behind the front seat, bigger than me even. Heavy. I've never seen a bear in real life, but it's possible he's life-sized if a little squishier than a real bear would be. Softer too.

I need two hands to wrangle this bear. I manage to kick the car door closed with my foot and drag him over to the gate, where I have to set him on the ground so I can flick the latch. Then it's a tussle to fit us both through the narrow opening and up the path to the front door, where he gets dropped again.

All in all, it takes five minutes from opening the car door to setting him in my kitchen.

I had plans to follow my run with a small workout on the yoga mat in the backyard, but carrying a fifty-pound stuffed animal twenty yards has me pooped. While I'm deciding on a permanent place to keep him—because there's no way in hell I'm carrying him around with me—I flick on the coffee machine and open the fridge.

Another five minutes later, I'm on the back patio, coffee in hand, with a plate of eggs in front of me while the bear sits on the opposite bench. He's staring at me as I lean into the squashy outdoor cushions and take a sip of my coffee.

It doesn't take long before my eyelids feel heavy again. I'm convinced the birds chirping in the trees have me drifting off. It's like a white noise machine, only more effective, and I'm tempted to take a nap.

It's almost noon, and I've done nothing except go for a run.

When I'm working, Ashley manages my schedule, which usually begins with a pre-dawn visit to the gym. Currently, she's handling everything in my absence, overseeing my affairs in LA, looking after my place, and keeping me informed only on matters I *need* to know, so I receive a brief, non-urgent email summary to review.

Aside from that, I have a handful of other things to do, but for someone who's used to her day being planned to the minute, it's amazing how little I can fit in if I really put my mind to it.

I could make them stretch out the whole week.

It's hard to decide which one to do first, especially with the time difference.

My parents won't appreciate a super early wake-up and neither will Tanner.

There's a book I keep starting and putting down. I also need to review the contract terms with my lawyer so I fully understand them when Marcy flies over.

The fruit trees in the backyard are ripe enough to pick, and Pierre said he'd teach me how to make an apple pie if I brought them. I also need to practice the donuts.

But what I really want to do is something I probably shouldn't.

I'm trying to figure out how I can see Lando when a goat hops over the hedge at the end of the backyard.

From the way he trots up the path toward the apple trees, I can tell this isn't his first time here. However, after he stops and stares, opens his little mouth and lets out a bloodcurdling scream, I assume he's never seen a stuffed bear before.

Then he falls over, stiff as a board.

"Oh fuck." I scramble out of the chair so fast it falls over and so does the coffee. "Please don't be dead. Please don't be dead. Please don't be dead."

Dealing with a dead goat was not on my list of things to do today. Or ever, if I think about it.

But then, as quick as he fell down, the goat's eyes blink open, and he jumps up, at which point I wonder if maybe *I'm* having a heart attack. Especially when he trots over to the apple tree, rises on his hind legs, and munches away at the first one he finds.

Some days, I think I could easily move to England and live an idyllic life in the countryside, and then other days, when I may or may not have killed a trespassing goat, I want to board the first plane back to LA.

What the fuck is happening?

And not that I care so much, because who am I to get between a goat and his five-a-day, but he's eating all the fruit I was supposed to be making pies with, and I can't stop him on my own.

I dial Clemmie, the first thing I can think of doing.

"Hey, what are you up to? Want to come for a swim?" she says before I can get a hello in.

"Sure. But first, I should tell you there's a goat in my backyard, and it may or may not have had a heart attack. Or a stroke. Is that something goats do? Now it's eating the apples."

I'm glad I have her on speaker because the next thing from Clementine is her yelling, "Lando, Churchill's got into Holiday's garden."

There's a muffled response before Clementine adds, "We'll be right there." And the phone goes dead.

I freeze.

Shit.

This wasn't even remotely close to any idea I had about how I could legitimately see Lando today. But I'm going with it.

And if he's coming too, then I have approximately ten minutes to wash this running sweat off and make myself vaguely presentable.

I sprint up the stairs, and for the first time since I arrived here, I manage to get to the top without adding more bruises.

* * *

If Clemmie's grinning widely when I open the front door, then Lando's doing the exact opposite.

He looks like he'd rather be anywhere else, which confuses me because no one's forced him to come. I called his sister, not him.

The smile I greeted them with falters a little.

"Hey, thanks for coming. I wasn't sure what to do."

"Oh, no problem," Clemmie replies, breezing through the door into the hallway.

My eyes are still on Lando, his jaw tight as he steps over the threshold. He's looking around like it's the first time he's seen the place even though I could have sworn his mom said he used to live here.

Not to mention, he owns it.

"Lanny, you okay?"

Lando glances up at his sister and blinks. The trance he's in breaks.

"Yes, fine," he replies, and a pair of stormy gray eyes meet mine and turn away. "Fine. Hi, Holiday, where's Churchill?"

He's curt. Gruffer than he's been since the first—*second*—time I met him.

He's never called me Hollywood in front of other people, but he still managed a smile, yet I don't even get that.

I point out into the backyard where the culprit has moved on to the pear tree.

"Great, Lando will deal with him. I must pee," Clemmie says, running into the downstairs bathroom.

I glance over at Lando, who's back in his trance. There's a weariness to him as he stares at the wall, an unguarded sadness in the way his shoulders stoop. I want to ask him what's wrong, what's causing his brow to drop so deeply it could give *me* a headache.

But in the end, I lightly touch his arm and go with, "Hey—"

When his eyes flick up, they don't quite meet mine. "Right.

Goat." He marches through to the backyard and loudly claps his hands. "Churchill. Out."

Churchill stops chewing and spits out the pear, then turns and jumps back over the hedge the way he came.

Seriously?

"Well, I could have done that," I grumble.

The ghost of a smile hits Lando's mouth, and for the first time since he arrived here, he looks like the Lando I've become acquainted with in the past month.

"Now you know for next time."

"Hopefully, there won't be one."

"Don't count on it. There isn't a garden in Valentine Nook un-raided by that bloody goat."

"I appreciate it." I stare up at him, smiling. Clemmie's still in the bathroom, so I take the opportunity. "Thank you for the loan of the car and the bear. It was very kind of you."

His head dips, and a smile forms. "The bear you won, remember? And the car . . . that was Thunder's thank-you for his donuts."

"Then please thank him for me."

"I shall."

We stand there, staring at each other. I'm fighting the urge to run my thumb over his brow and smooth out his tension, but Clemmie walks into the backyard, so instead, I take a step back.

"Hol, what are your plans this afternoon?"

My lips make a little clicking noise as I purse them and scroll through my very short list of things I *could* do today but could also put off until tomorrow.

I glance at the pear Churchill spat out and grin wide. "Now that I don't have any fruit for my pies, I guess nothing."

"Do you want to come back with me for a swim and some lunch?"

I hesitate, and my eyes slide to Lando.

"You should come and keep Clementine company. She's getting bored being on her own by the pool all summer long."

I nod slowly. Message received. Lando won't be joining us.

I hide my disappointment with an extra cheery, "Sure, that sounds great. Let me run and grab my bathing suit."

Snatching up the first one I find, I then spot one I've not worn yet. The tags are still attached, and I decide to go with that one instead. The fact it's the smallest, skimpiest suit I own is irrelevant. It's not like I've been thinking about the way Lando's gaze skated the length of my body the day he spotted me at the pool.

He made it clear he won't be joining us.

Clemmie's waiting for me in the hallway when I walk back downstairs, with Lando already outside by the car.

"Ready?" she asks.

"Sure am. Let's go."

As we're leaving, she spies the bear, who I moved to the couch in the living room just in case the goat had another heart attack.

"Bloody hell, where'd he come from?" Clementine peers at the tag still attached to the bear's foot. "Hamley's. *Christ.* He's enormous."

"I won it at the fair."

"Did you? *Wow.*"

I don't know why I don't tell her it's from Lando because it's no big deal that he gave it to me. So I don't understand why it *feels* like a big deal.

And every time he catches my eye in the rearview mirror on the way back, it has me wondering all over again.

LANDO

It feels like I'm waiting for a date.

I stop pacing, ram my sweaty palms into my pockets, and take a deep breath.

It doesn't stop my heart from thumping erratically, but it does make me realize how ridiculous I'm being.

I'm a grown man, and this is *supper*.

A supper my mother planned, nothing more, nothing less. The same family supper we've had every Friday night since I can remember. The one where all manner of friends are invited, because as long as the six of us plus Max are in attendance, it doesn't matter who joins.

Once, there were twenty-seven of us.

Tonight, there will be only one extra person. It just so happens to be the one sending me into a spiral.

"Your Grace—"

I turn to find James walking across the floor of the great hall to where I'm staring out the window and trying not to have a panic attack.

"The barbecue's fired up, and the chefs are outside. I've let the duchess know the table is set for when you're ready."

James's volume drops. "And the fireworks are being prepared on the upper lawn."

"*Fireworks*? Who's having fireworks?"

Bollocks. Why did I think fireworks would be a good idea?

I'm putting it down to a momentary and highly irregular bout of self-pity. It's all Holiday's fault for asking me what I do for fun.

And what's more fun than fireworks?

The one—rather pressing—issue I didn't foresee was that they would open me up to a slew of questions I'm not prepared to answer. And while family supper night is normally a loud affair, it's not loud enough that no one will notice a bunch of fireworks going off.

I glance at James, silently pleading with him not to say anything to Alex. Because we both know why I requested tonight to include after-dinner entertainment in the form of colorful explosives.

We never have after-dinner entertainment unless Miles drinks too much.

"We are."

Alex's confusion deepens. "Why?"

A perfect example of a question I don't want to answer.

"Why not?"

"Um . . . okay . . . because—" Alex's pause gives me the exact argument I need.

"See, you can't come up with a reason not to either."

He looks at me like I've lost my mind, and perhaps I have, but it's too late now. On the plus side, the conversation's distracting me enough that my palms have stopped sweating.

Alex is still trying to come up with a response when a fire-engine siren blares out from the corridor to the left. It's a sound that usually grates to my core and has me threatening to remove the batteries, but right now, I'm wondering how I can use it as a distraction tonight.

"What's going on?" Hendricks asks, followed by Fireman Max driving along on a toy fire engine.

Alex takes one look at James's and my blank faces and shakes his head. "I have absolutely no idea, but it involves fireworks."

"Fireworks?"

"Fireworks?" Max screeches, jumping off the fire engine with enough force that he slips on the floor, banging his head on the stone slabs. Luckily, his fire helmet saves him, and he barely seems to notice as he scrambles to his feet. "Fireworks? I want fireworks. I love fireworks."

Truthfully, I thought Max would already be in bed before the fireworks began, which is why we have silent ones, but I'll take any support I can get.

"See. Max thinks they're a good idea."

"He's four. This morning, I discovered him painting himself green so Birgitta wouldn't find him during hide-and-seek in the garden."

Definitely can't blame him for that. I try to hide from Birgitta too, something I'd say Alex agrees with, given he's smirking.

"Sounds like a good camouflage technique, wouldn't you say, James?" I elbow him in the ribs. "Isn't it how the army does it?"

"Not exactly, Your Grace, but close enough," he replies in his usual diplomatic tone.

"Uncle Lando, can I have a firework?"

Scooping up Max, I prop him on my hip and straighten his helmet. "Of course you may. We have special ones just for you."

"If you're talking about sparklers, Miles used them all up at his party after the fair. So you'll need to find some more. Otherwise, you can deal with the tears and fallout."

Bloody Miles. At this rate, I'll be the one in tears.

Taking another deep breath, I turn to James. I don't even need to ask.

"I'll see what I can find," he replies wearily.

"Thanks, James. You're the best."

Max decides he's bored being propped in my arms, and in his bid to get back on solid ground, he kicks me in the stomach.

"Thanks for that," I call after him as he pushes open the doors leading to the garden and sprints out, the three of us close behind.

It's a beautiful, balmy summer evening, not too hot but warm enough to spend it outside in relative comfort. The fragrance of the roses from our mother's garden drifts through the air, a strange contrast mingling with the scent of the coals heating up on the barbecue, while the birds are performing their twilight serenade.

For half a minute, everything's perfect until Alex ruins it with more questions.

"Are you planning to explain the fireworks at any point, or are we just going to pretend it's a normal Friday night occurrence?"

"What's there to explain?" I reply, taking a beer from the drinks table, which has been laid out.

Alex shrugs, and hopefully, he's done with his Spanish Inquisition. Hendricks picks up a beer and takes a long draw. Once again, we stand in blissful silence until the next interruption.

This one is far more welcome.

Alex's and Hendricks's backs are turned so they don't see Clementine walking around the corner on the far side of the lawn next to Holiday. It's going to take at least thirty seconds for them to reach us, and for that thirty seconds, I get to enjoy the sight of her before anyone else notices.

Enjoy watching her laugh at whatever my sister is saying.

I'm thankful the beer is cold in my hand, stopping my palms from sweating again because that erratic thump of my heart returns.

Her pale blond hair is loose and bouncing around her shoulders. The last few times I've seen her, she's had it tied back, but today, the soft waves make her face even more heart-shaped than usual. Her pink cheeks stretch with a smile, and when she looks up to find me staring, it freezes for a split second before widening even further.

A tugging sensation stirs in me, a long-forgotten feeling of attraction, and for the first time in a long time, I feel single.

Not tied to someone. Not someone's ex-fiancé. Not the guy whose wedding was called off the night before.

Just Lando.

"We're here. We're here. No need to send the search party. Happy Fourth of July, everyone," Clementine announces loudly when she's ten meters out.

"Fourth of Ju . . ." Hendricks's eyes meet mine. "*Ohh.* Oh. And it all becomes clear. Nice, Lando. Very smooth."

"I agree. *Very* smooth." Alex slings an arm around my shoulders and leans in. "I like you like this."

"Like what?"

"Just . . . like *this*. It feels like the old Lando is coming back to us."

I want him to explain what he means, but Clementine barges in with Holiday next to her.

"What are we drinking?"

"We have beer."

Clementine pulls a face. "Hard pass. Hol, how about a glass of champagne, as it's Friday?"

Holiday puts down the large basket she's carrying, and as she bends, I notice a small sparkly American flag fastening some of her hair back. "That sounds good to me."

I'm too busy trying not to stare at her to be quick enough to open the bottle. Hendricks gets there first, pours out two glasses, and hands them over.

"What a perfect way to start a weekend," Clementine says, lifting her glass. "Cheers. And so lovely Holiday could join us, especially on America's birthday."

A warm glow spreads over Holiday's cheeks. "Why, thank you. I accept on behalf of all Americans."

"What would you normally do to celebrate today?"

She brings the glass to her lips. "Usually watch my brother play baseball, barbecue, hang out with family. When we were growing up, we watched a big fireworks display. It's not the Fourth without fireworks."

I don't look at Alex or Hendricks. I don't need to. I can feel their eyes on me, identical smirks curving their lips.

Okay so? It's not a big deal that I realized this week's family supper would fall on July fourth and that Holiday would be coming, and subsequently asked James to put together a display that would make her feel like she wasn't missing out on celebrations.

Anyone would have done it if they'd thought of it first.

"It certainly isn't the Fourth without fireworks," Alex repeats.

I ignore the mocking expression on his face. I have a feeling I'll be ignoring it a lot this evening.

Clementine slowly spins a full three sixty, waving to Max on his fire engine. "Where are Mum and Miles?"

"Mum's just returned from Wimbledon, so she's changing. Miles . . . who knows?" I reply.

On cue, our mother walks through the open patio doorway at the top of the steps. She sees Max first and waves, then she spots us.

"Oh, why didn't you tell me our guest had arrived?" Her eyes skate over Alex, Hendricks, and me with a frown before they land on Holiday, for whom her expression transforms into a broad smile. "Holiday, my dear, welcome to Burlington."

"That's really very kind." Holiday puts down her glass and takes my mum's hand, only to be pulled into a hug.

Hendricks's brows shoot up as Alex and I watch on in astonishment.

Easing out of her grip, Holiday picks up the basket, peeling back the gingham covering.

"I brought you homemade apple pie. Apples from the cottage, and I promise they were made under supervision." She laughs, and my mother laughs along with her. "Thank you for the lessons Pierre is giving. And also, a little thank-you gift for tonight." Holiday hands her a familiar orange store bag with its horse and carriage logo. "I noticed you wearing one the other day."

There's a look of genuine shock on my mother's face. An expression rarely seen on a woman who's usually ten steps ahead of everyone else. It makes her so impossible to argue with because she already has answers for every question you've thought of.

"*Hermes*," Alex mutters next to me, as my mother's profuse levels of thanks increase as she opens the box and ties the scarf around her neck. "I'd say that's already earned her a hundred points more than Caroline ever had. She was at least negative five million by the time the wedding got canceled."

I don't argue. Of all the people who didn't like Caroline, my mother didn't like her the most.

The final nail in Caroline's coffin was when she rejected my grandmother's engagement ring, a seven-carat antique-cut diamond that once belonged to Anne Boleyn and had been in our family for generations. I'd proposed with it, only for her to ask if she could have one from Graff's instead.

"Now, where's Miles?" asks my mother.

"Running late as usual."

"Then we shall start without him *again*." She tuts, turning around to where Max is still playing with his fire engine, having been joined by Hamish, Dolly, and Maud. "Max, come and eat."

The long table set out on the patio has candles burning down its length. It's where we'll always be when the weather allows.

As much as we might all complain about this compulsory mealtime and the curtails it placed on our sacred Friday nights growing up, we all love it. It's one tradition I hope we keep forever.

And we usually take the same seats, but tonight, Holiday is sitting in my spot, so as Miles is yet to grace us with his presence, I take his. Because it's opposite her.

Food is being placed down, though not fast enough for Max, who's grabbing pieces of chicken, half of which Hendricks promptly removes to put on his own plate, along with sliced steak and shelled prawns. Summer salads made with leaves and vegetables from the Burlington gardens and freshly baked bread come next.

While everyone's preoccupied with piling their plates, I pick up a bottle of wine and gesture to Holiday.

In response, she pushes her glass across to me. "Why, thank you, Gracie."

I'm so focused on smiling back at her that I fill her glass almost to the brim.

It's only been two days since I've seen her, but it feels like longer.

In those two days, I've found my mind drifting to her more often than it should have. Where she could be, what she might be doing, how her baking is going. Once I found myself on the way to the kitchen, hoping to see her, only to turn around again.

It's noisy enough that the two of us can have our own conversation without being overheard.

There's a strand of hair that's come loose from the clip, and I want to reach over and fix it. But instead, I ask, "How's your week been?"

"Goat aside, it's been good. I've been reading through the terms for this contract—"

"The one you were most clearly worthy of receiving? And celebrated with coffee and a donut?"

Her lashes flutter down, giving me the impression she's embarrassed or uncomfortable like she can't take the compliment. Or perhaps she doesn't know how to take the compliment from *me*.

"Yeah, that one. My agent's coming over next week to discuss terms."

"Ah. Always important to discuss terms. Are you happy with it?"

She nods. "I think so. It's a good offer. I've never had one quite so large before. I usually take a smaller fee and larger profit share, but it hasn't always paid off."

"Who manages your money?"

She tilts her head. "My dad. He worked in finance, and now he just manages Tanner and me."

"Your brother?"

"Yes, he earns ten times what I do. It keeps my dad busy."

I'm about to tell her I'd be happy to look over it for her when my youngest brother's arrival shatters the peace.

"I see you all started without me. How was the tennis?" Miles leans down to kiss our mother's cheek and as he does so spies the Hermes bag to the side. "Managed to fit in a spot of shopping too."

"A gift from Holiday, actually." She beams with a smile usually reserved for Miles, only now it's directed at Holiday.

Pulling out the chair next to mine, Miles bends close enough to whisper, "*Hermes.* Oh, *Your Grace,* Holiday is *good.*"

"Nice of you to join us," I drawl, the only response I'll give him even though he has a point.

Gifts aside, Holiday's so charming and effusive that it's easy to see why she's so popular.

Winning over the Duchess of Oxfordshire is not for the fainthearted, but she seems to have managed it with little effort.

The calm of the table prior to Miles's arrival vanishes.

"How's my new neighbor doing?" He winks at Holiday as he piles his plate up with more than he can fit on it, earning himself a frown from our mother. "Fitting into the village nicely? When are you coming over for a cup of tea?"

Opposite him, Alex rolls his eyes.

"I don't drink tea." Holiday pushes a fork through her salad and turns to Miles. "But I sure am fitting in well. Everyone's super friendly, and I met your girlfriend the other day."

Next to her, my mother splutters into her wine before recovering herself immaculately, but I can see she's now on tenterhooks like the rest of us.

"I don't have a girlfriend," Miles replies with a coolness to his tone. "Right, Maxy? Girlfriends are bleugh."

"Yeah, girlfriends are *bleugh,*" Max mimics and sticks out his tongue.

"But she was coming out of your place and introduced herself to me as your girlfriend. Though tell her I prefer her hair blond to the dark she had last week. We blondes have to stick together."

Holiday couldn't look any more innocent if she was wearing a nun's outfit and had a halo around her head.

For a moment, I genuinely wonder if she realizes Miles would never ever commit himself to a girl. But when she lifts her fork to chew down and throws me a wink, I realize exactly what she's done.

Holiday one, Miles nil.

His eyes flare, and Hendricks snorts with laughter.

"Oh, I like you, Holiday," Alex barks loudly, leaning back in his chair until it almost topples. "You can come again."

"Maybe I will," she replies before excusing herself to use the bathroom.

Which is the exact moment my mother has been waiting for.

Her elbow hits the table, and her chin is propped on her fist.

"You know, darling . . ." She leans forward. "You seem very happy tonight."

"Do I?"

My mother hums softly. "Yes, and it's not just tonight. It's the past month or so, you've been much more . . ." She waves her hand around. "Relaxed, I suppose."

A month is the exact amount of time Holiday's been in Valentine Nook. Sometimes I wonder if my mother thinks I'm stupid.

"It's probably the weather," I reply.

It's not the weather.

"Perhaps," she muses, sitting back and folding her napkin. I know this move. I've fallen victim to it many, *many* times because the real subject of the conversation is about to reveal itself in three, two, one . . . "And isn't it wonderful that Holiday's settling in so well? And she's delightful. We must host a party for her."

I roll my eyes. "She doesn't want a party, Mother. She's come here to get away from everything."

"Maybe a family movie night, then?"

I shift my chair closer, so it's just the two of us. I want to beg her to stop, but I can't bring myself to because right now, at this moment with my family and Holiday here, I wonder if my mum's onto something.

I am relaxed.

And for the first time in a long time, I'm enjoying myself. Perhaps movie night isn't a bad idea.

I'm ruminating on it, along with Alex's comment from earlier, when Holiday plops back down into her chair.

"You okay there, Gracie?"

I nod. "You know, Hollywood, I think I am."

"Good," she replies and turns to Alex while I sip my wine.

As I stretch out, my feet hit something I assume is the leg of the table, but when it shifts, I realize I'm actually resting against Holiday's feet. The polite thing would be to move. But I don't.

Her eyes flick to mine, looking at me from under thick black lashes.

In the dimming light, her irises seem even more piercing than usual. I expect her to shift away, but she resumes her conversation with Alex instead. I swear the pressure of her leg deepens.

I can't be sure, but I think I might be playing my first game of footsie.

And so the evening continues as most family mealtimes do. Miles makes everyone laugh by being as outrageous as usual. Max regales us with tales from his week at school, and Hendricks updates us on the progress of all the calves.

Clementine and Alex bicker over which pieces of Valentine gossip are true, and my mum watches on. It's hard to believe she's as disapproving as she comes across when her expression holds nothing but amusement as she laughs out loud at the next outrageous things Miles says or weighs in on the argument between Clem and Alex.

It's moments like these that I miss my father so profoundly, because I know how much he cherished family time and ensured we had quality moments together despite his busy schedule.

We carry on laughing, drinking, and joking around until the sun is close to setting and Birgitta comes to collect Max for his bath.

Usually, this is followed by a lot of pleading and crying on a Friday, but not tonight.

"Don't start the fireworks without me," he orders, shouting louder than any four-year-old should be able to shout as he marches off, holding her hand.

Holiday immediately sits up. "Fireworks? Do you always have fireworks?"

"No, never." Miles frowns. "Why are we having fireworks?"

I wait to see which one of my brothers outs me. It's Alex, but instead of announcing it to the entire table, he leans into her.

"Fireworks are usually reserved for bonfire night. Lando organized these for you."

"It's not the Fourth without fireworks," Hendricks adds.

Her eyes find mine. "You did?"

The flame of the candle flickers in her irises when I lean forward. "I can be fun when I want."

"I knew it." Happiness flashes across her face, and all the worries I had about whether fireworks were a stupid idea become insignificant.

After what has to be a record bath time, Max returns in his pajamas and a dressing gown, which makes him look like a sheep.

The sun has dipped below the horizon, leaving an inky sky behind with stars making their debut for the evening.

"Fireworks time," Max screeches.

We stand on the patio and watch as they burst above us, a rainbow of colors lighting up the sky. There's something about fireworks that has even the most stoic personalities become awestruck for that moment.

Catherine wheels, rockets, and spirals explode, but I miss most of them because I'm transfixed by the joy on Holiday's face.

It's something I didn't know I needed to see. I never realized how much happiness I could derive from someone else's, yet here I am, heart pounding at what feels like a thousand times a minute.

Max squeals with excitement until the very last one, and Hendricks takes him up to bed.

"Thanks, Gracie, this has been a really awesome evening. I can't believe you organized fireworks just for me."

"Anytime, Hollywood." I grin down and fight an urge to kiss her. "Some would even say *fun*."

"I would say *super* fun. And while we don't have celebration donuts, I think apple pie would work just as well."

"Apple pie is perfect."

My eyes follow as she rushes off to fetch them, and immediately her spot is taken.

"What did she just call you?"

Damn Miles and his exceptional hearing. "Nothing—"

"And what did you call her?"

"Nothing—"

"But you did call her *something*." Miles's finger points right in my face, and his mouth drops open. "Oh my god, have you guys got *nicknames* for each other?"

"What's going on?" Alex asks, his head appearing in the gap between the two of us.

"*Nothing*," I repeat for the third time.

Except third time's not the charm in this case, and Miles turns us all to where Holiday and Clementine are slicing up her apple pie and placing it on plates. This time his finger is less accusatory, but no less pointy.

"Our big brother has a thumping great crush on our Hollywood starlet, *and* they have nicknames for each other."

Alex lets out a low whistle. "*Nicknames*? Does this mean—"

"It does, Alexander. It means Lando might be happy again," he says, before adding, "and that stick up his arse is finally loosening."

Ignoring the identical guffaws from both my brothers, I take a long sip of my wine.

I don't know what's worse—having a crush on my tenant . . .

Or that Miles is right.

HOLIDAY

"And I'm confirming Paris for next month." Marcy scribbles more notes onto my contract.

I nod, which turns into a yawn. "Do they know I don't speak French?"

"Yes, everyone speaks English."

"Which I'm sure they *love*."

Maybe I should learn.

I've always wanted to speak another language, and if I sign a five-year contract with a French company, now's the perfect time. Plus, I've always heard that the French hate Americans. Or hate people who don't even try to speak French.

And I don't want to be one of those.

I mindlessly reach for the afternoon tea tray between us and take a macaron, breaking it in half, only to put it down again.

I've already eaten three, plus all the sandwiches. Not the self-discipline L'Oreal would expect before the start of a beauty contract. It's right there in the fine print that Marcy's finalizing —I'm required to look after myself.

Instead of the sugar from a macaron, I signal the server for a strong cup of coffee. Less carbs and more effective at keeping me awake.

Why am I tired, you ask?

Because the goddamn English countryside has ruined me.

A month in Valentine Nook and it seems it's impossible to sleep without my windows open, listening to the sound of the stream running through the village.

Last night, I opened the patio door of my suite at Claridge's, and all I could hear were sirens. Even with the doors shut, and after I'd called down to the concierge for a set of earplugs, I didn't get to sleep until after two a.m.

I planned to stay two nights in London, returning to the city I've always loved visiting.

Last night was spent at dinner catching up with friends who are in town filming. This morning, I was pampered from head to toe in the spa before my meeting with Marcy, and this evening, I'm supposed to be catching a show in the West End, but as soon as we wrap up, I'm calling time on London and heading straight back to Bluebell Cottage.

"Okay, honey. I gotta go. I need to get this finalized and sent over to the lawyers before a call with the West Coast. Expect me to confirm the schedule by the end of the week —"

I stand as Marcy gathers everything up—papers, pen, phone, laptop, you name it—and shoves it in her bag, which must now weigh ten pounds.

"Thanks, Marce. I appreciate you," I tell her, giving her a hug.

"Yeah, yeah. And once I'm done with this, we can discuss what you're working on next. You've only got a couple of months until we have to ramp things up before the junkets in November and then . . ."

God, even listening to her makes my brain ache.

It sets off a swirl of unease that sits right in my chest. All that relaxation from my morning massage lasted about thirty minutes.

"But I'll see you in Paris." She squeezes me hard, waves goodbye, and powers toward the elevators.

A million miles an hour is the speed at which she runs. There's nothing else.

It's what's made her one of the most successful agents in the business. But it's what's going to kill me if I'm not careful.

Slumping back in my chair, I drain the rest of the champagne in my glass, knock back the espresso the server brought over, and ask for the check.

My eyes are closing when my nose catches a scent that has my heart beating fast. I'm too tired to compute why my body is on high alert until he's standing in front of me.

It's not the server.

My tiredness is forgotten.

It takes me far longer than it should to realize it's him. And it's not because we're in the Claridge's tearoom instead of a field, it's because he looks *completely different.*

Over the past month, there may have been an occasion or two when I wondered what Lando would look like in a suit accompanying me on the red carpet. Sophisticated, I assumed, because what guy doesn't look good in a custom suit?

I was way off.

Some guys look good in a suit, and some guys make the suit look better.

Lando is the latter.

Dark navy slacks, a cream button-down cut exactly to his body, wide shoulders, narrow waist. The jacket's hanging off his finger, and I notice the cufflinks have the same emblem as his pinkie ring, the one Clemmie also has.

His beard, which was thick only a few days ago, has been trimmed down to long stubble, enough that I can see the dimples pulling at his cheeks.

But as mouthwatering as he looks, it feels all wrong. I can't see this guy galloping over the fields on Thunder or birthing a calf.

Yet I can't look away.

"I thought that was you."

His deep baritone reverberates over my skin. If I hadn't already woken up, that would have done it.

"What are you doing here?"

"I come in for a couple of days every month or so. Investment meetings and so forth."

Yeah. Investment. That's exactly how he looks. Like a city guy.

"What are you doing here?"

"I came up yesterday. My agent's here."

Lando glances at the chair Marcy vacated. "Ah, the contract."

I nod. I'm still positively speechless. I want to ask him to sit down and join me for a drink, but I'm staring at him too hard to remember the words I need to form.

"Okay, well, I'll see you in Valentine Nook," he says when it becomes clear I'm mute.

"You're leaving?"

He pauses, his hand on the back of Marcy's chair. "Yes. You?"

"I'm leaving too . . . for Valentine Nook."

"How are you getting there?"

"I have a car service."

Lando's face splits with a smile that almost has me melting. "Well, now I'm even happier that I bumped into you. If you cancel the car, I'll drive us both."

I snatch the check from the server as he hands it over, and I can't sign it quickly enough. "I have to collect my things. Can you give me twenty minutes?"

I glance up to find a pair of radiant blue eyes staring at me, edges crinkled in happiness. "Now that I know we're going home together, I'll give you as long as you need."

* * *

Twenty minutes later, I've checked out. Lando's waiting for me at the hotel lobby while a valet brings his car around.

I expect his muddy Land Rover to pull up, but instead, a sleek Aston Martin arrives. It's black everywhere—black rims, black chassis, black leather interior.

I've never been into cars. I have a Range Rover back in LA, and that's only because I told Tanner to find me a car that wasn't too flashy or complicated to drive.

But now I'm wondering if maybe I *should* get into cars, because just like his suit, Lando makes this car look good. No, Lando makes this car look *sexy*.

The valet hands the keys to Lando, switching them for a wad of notes. "See you next month, Your Grace. Hope you enjoyed your stay, Miss Simpson."

"Thanks, Henry. See you soon," he replies, holding the passenger door open and gesturing me inside. "Hollywood."

"Whose car is this?"

His head quirks. "Mine. Why?"

I shrug because I don't even know why I asked, but as I slip into the cool interior, I realize I'm seeing an entirely different side to Lando I never imagined existed. Lando, with his bespoke suit and sexy car, who visits Claridge's often enough that he's on a first-name basis with the valet.

The engine roars as we pull away, and my eyes are drawn to his hands around the steering wheel. I've seen his forearms dozens of times and watched his fingers thread through the leather of Thunder's bridle, but now that he's removed his cufflinks and rolled his sleeves up, there's a decadence to them.

I can't stop watching the way they flex.

I'm so engrossed in the movement I don't realize he's talking to me.

"How did your meeting go?"

"Good, we went through the contract, and Marcy—she's my agent—will now redirect all my queries to my lawyer before it goes back to L'Oreal. It takes a while."

"Yes, because how else would lawyers earn their keep?" he drawls, making me laugh.

"Exactly."

"But you're happy with it?" he asks, turning left onto a busy road behind one of London's red double-decker buses.

Except this one has an ad on the side of it, a Gucci ad featuring *my* face from the campaign I shot earlier in the year.

I'm stretched along the length of a dark green velvet couch, wearing nothing more than a bra and panties.

My breath judders in my throat, and I'm wondering if Lando's noticed, when he turns to me. The heat in his eyes zips over my skin, and my core clenches until the hairs on the back of my neck stand on end.

I worked out for three hours every day for an entire month before that shoot and always wondered if it was worth it. For the first time, I can wholeheartedly say yes.

It's a good thirty seconds before either of us speaks again, but the bus stays there in front of us, mocking me.

Eventually, Lando clears his throat. "So you're happy with the offer?"

"Yes, it's good."

"What did your dad think?"

"My dad?"

"Didn't you say he manages your money?"

"Oh," I reply, trying my best to focus on the conversation instead of that bus and Lando's forearms. My body continues to throb from the way he mentally undressed me, and all I can wonder is whether it will ever become a reality. "Yes, he does.

He's happy with it. Largely, I stay out of it because he invests everything for me through a couple of different businesses I have set up, and I pay myself a salary."

"Sounds sensible. Always good to diversify, and if you ever want a second opinion, I'd be happy to look over it or introduce you to my investment team."

Diversify. Investment team.

His response—along with this car, the suit, and everything I've experienced of Lando in the past hour—has me rethinking my assessment of Lando's financial situation. His money can't be all tied up in gold mines or whatever.

"Can I ask you a personal question?"

There's a beat of silence before the corner of his mouth tips up. "Yes, but only if I can ask you one."

"Do you have a lot of cash?"

"What?" His response is part guffaw, part bark. "That was not what I thought you were going to ask."

"What did you think I was going to ask?"

He shakes his head as he chuckles away. "Doesn't matter."

"Well, do you?" I press because I already feel like a dumbass, and now I need to see it through to the end.

"Okay . . . yes. You could say that. Why on earth do you want to know?"

"Um . . . because I keep thinking about that day a few weeks ago when I told you about my contract. I didn't want you to think I was bragging—"

His eyes flick to mine before going back to the road. "Hollywood, you don't have to justify what you earn to anyone. You work incredibly hard, and you should be proud of it."

"I am. But forty million dollars is a lot of money . . ." I don't know what I'm asking or what I'm implying. I should have just kept my mouth shut because it's none of my business.

I'm beginning to think the rest of the journey will continue in awkward silence when he says, "My personal wealth is approximately nine—"

"Million?"

"*Billion.* Though that's in pounds, so with today's exchange rate, it would be more around twelve billion dollars. Plus stock and investments. Then there's the value of Burlington Estates."

My entire body turns toward Lando. I can't tell if he's joking because he still has that wry smile tugging his mouth.

"Twelve *billion?*"

"Give or take."

"Cash?"

He nods, and boy, was I way off base. I *am* a dumbass.

"So you really didn't think I was bragging when I told you how much my contract was worth?"

"No, and I don't know why you think I would have."

He sounds so offended that I honestly want to crawl inside myself and redo the last twenty minutes.

"Because it was kind of gross for me to tell you that I earned so much, even though you could look it up, but the day at the pool when you said Pierre wasn't part of the rental, I figured you were one of those English old money families where your net worth is in antique oil paintings or gold mines . . ." I stop babbling.

"*Gold mines?*" Lando groans in despair. "God, Milo's right. I'm such a dick. I'm sorry. I'm so sorry for the terrible impression I left on you. Please believe me when I say it really had nothing to do with you, but I'm sorry nevertheless."

"I'm sorry I started this conversation in the first place." I pick at an invisible thread on my pants and ignore the heat in my cheeks. "But now I know you know what you're talking about, so maybe I will take a second opinion."

"And I'd be happy to help. We don't own any gold mines, but that's not a bad idea."

I force a chuckle. "Thank you."

"You're welcome. Now it's my turn for a question."

"Shoot. But if it's about money, I'm all out."

He laughs. "In the time you're here in Valentine Nook, should we be expecting a boyfriend of any kind to turn up for a visit? Or, you know, be waiting for you when you get home?"

I'm not buying the innocence in his tone because if I'm not mistaken, he's trying to figure out if I'm single.

I can't answer quick enough, and I don't even care because my heart's fluttering.

"No. No boyfriend. Here or there."

"That's good to know. And Hollywood, if you did have one and he's not coming to visit, then he damn sure isn't good enough to be waiting for you when you get back."

I'm wondering where this conversation is going, but Lando remains silent, and the second we hit the interstate, he shifts gears, and the car rockets forward.

It doesn't take long for the urban surroundings to give way to leafy fields filled with yellow rapeseed, and soon, we pass a sign welcoming us to Oxfordshire right as a huge clap of thunder echoes through the sky.

The nearer we get to Valentine Nook, the lower my heart sinks in my chest, and as Lando pulls up outside Bluebell Cottage, I know I'm not ready for this day to end.

Out of nowhere, I remember the restaurant voucher I won at the coconut shy.

So, for the first time in my life, I ask a guy on a date.

And he says yes.

LANDO

The first time I went on a first date to The One True Love, I was seventeen, and she was Madeline Baxter.

I'd been a bundle of nerves leading up to it because I *really* liked this girl.

I spent the afternoon riding with Jeremy, galloping through the fields, checking the calves and the fence line. Anything I could do to distract myself.

Madeline lived in Lower Slaughter, a village about twenty miles from Valentine Nook, and at exactly seven o'clock, I pulled up outside her parents' house to collect her.

I genuinely thought I was having a heart attack as I knocked on the door. I hoped she'd be just as nervous, but she was completely unfazed instead, which made it worse.

Madeline's dark hair was fastened back with a band, and she wore the skinniest pair of jeans, making her legs seem longer than usual. To my seventeen-year-old self, she was hot. I was still growing into my size and gangly enough that it made me self-conscious.

The drive to dinner was conducted in silence because I didn't trust myself to open my mouth and not be sick.

The rest of the evening didn't fare much better.

Eventually, Eddie, stealthily watching from a corner of the bar, felt so sorry for me he poured out a triple whiskey, then ordered me to knock it back and get a grip.

It worked. Sort of. It gave me enough confidence to get through dinner but not enough to ask for a second date.

All first dates since then have been a marked improvement.

But when Holiday and I walk through the doors of The One True Love, Eddie takes one look at my face and silently places a triple whiskey on the bar.

Perhaps I can swap it for a towel.

One of the perks of owning a village is that I can park anywhere I want, but even sprinting in from the spot outside, we get drenched. The rain is coming down so hard that it's almost drowning out the sound of thunder.

A fork of lightning illuminates the bar for a second before plunging us back into a dimly lit atmosphere. The weather must have kept people home because it's much quieter than it usually is.

"Evenin', Your Grace, 'Oliday. Rainin' is it?" Eddie smirks, holding out a large towel, which Holiday immediately takes to pat her face dry.

"You could say that," she replies, scraping her wet hair away from her forehead.

"The fire's lit in the back. Take whatever table you like, no one will disturb you. I'll come over and serve you myself."

I don't know whether he's offering the privacy for Holiday or for me, but I clap an appreciative hand on his shoulder anyway and guide us through.

"This place is so stinkin' cute," she whispers. "I keep meaning to come in here and bribe Eddie to tell me all the stories."

I pull out the chair for Holiday to sit, then retrieve a second towel from behind the bar and run it over my head. "I don't think you'll need to bribe him. He'll give it up for free, but you'll be here for days. Maybe months."

"Oh yeah, and what stories do you have of this place?"

I take the space opposite. She's cupped her face in her hands as she eagerly awaits story time. The low lighting and the flames flickering in the hearth make her appear starry-eyed as she looks at me, and I'm here for it.

"See that corner over there?" I nod to the opposite side of the room, where the wood paneling is carved with an intricate scene of Venus and Mars behind an old square table. "Rumor has it that was Shakespeare's favorite spot to write."

Holiday's eyes widen. "No way. That's seriously cool. Is that where you got your name from?"

I shake my head, trying to keep my expression as impassive as possible. "No. Walt Disney named me, remember?"

Confusion flickers on her face before she picks up a beer mat and whips it at me. "Idiot."

"Actually, Orlando is an old family name," I tell her. "What about yours?"

"My mom listened to a lot of Billie Holiday when she was pregnant with me, and Tanner got the family name."

"It suits you."

"You think?"

"I do." I nod. For the first time since I spotted her in Claridge's, I get to really look at her again. Wet hair scraped back, flushed cheeks, rain-smudged mascara. She looks exquisite. "A holiday, by definition, is happy, relaxing, and energizing. And that's what you are."

Her bottom lip rolls in, and I catch the flash of her teeth biting into it as she looks away. I have no idea where *that* came from, but it's out there now, and I can't take it back.

Plus, it's the truth. Holiday Simpson has energized me more in the past month than I've felt in years.

"You're very sweet. You know that, right?"

Now it's my turn to be bashful. The way she's looking at me has my cheeks heating, and if it wasn't for my beard, my face would be bright pink.

I'm blushing. Fucking blushing because a girl called me sweet.

"Not sure how many people would agree with you on that."

"It doesn't matter. I don't care what other people think."

Her magnetic eyes hold mine, and the sincerity behind them is almost frightening.

I look up at the bar to find Eddie watching us, waiting for the right moment to come over. I imagine he's also waiting to see if I'm going to down the glass of whiskey still taunting me, but I have no need for it right now.

Nerves don't exist tonight.

In fact, I realize, they rarely do around Holiday anymore. Spending time with her is easy. Talking to Holiday is *easy*.

Because to her, I'm just Lando, her landlord. She doesn't want my title or my money. She wants nothing more from me than my time, and for her, I have all of it and more.

"A'right, you two, the specials are on the board. 'Oliday, what are you drinking?"

She glances at me. "Wine?"

"Sounds good. Eddie has an excellent cellar. He'll pick one out for you once you order."

Eddie leaves us to read the board on the wall by the bar. Holiday's mouth silently forms the words as her eyes scan down the menu, but every couple of seconds, she turns and smiles.

I simply wait for it to happen, so by the time Holiday's decided what she wants to eat, I still have no clue and just go with the steak pie.

She grabs Eddie before he leaves. "Wait, that's what I want instead."

"Good choice."

Eddie returns shortly with a bottle of red, showing it to me before he opens it.

Out of nowhere, my throat tightens.

We both know this bottle was my father's favorite, the one he liked to drink on special occasions. I didn't even know there were any left here.

It's not particularly fancy, and there are much more valuable wines in the cellar, but he loved it.

I swallow away the lump in my throat. "Not seen one of those in a while."

"There are still a few left. Thought you might like it tonight. You know, 'cause it's raining and such."

He's much more subtle than my mother, I'll give him that, and not that I need it, but I quite like that I have Eddie's approval of this dinner with Holiday.

Date with Holiday.

She lifts her glass once he's poured the wine. "To a few days of successful meetings."

"To successful meetings," I respond, taking a sip and savoring the burst of berries on my tongue. I try not to feel guilty about drinking it without my brothers and Clementine. "When do you start work for L'Oreal?"

Her fingers run up and down the stem of her wineglass. "I haven't got a formal date, but the first campaign will launch in January. I have to go to Paris next month for initial meetings."

"You don't sound that excited."

Her shoulders jerk up. "I am. It's new, is all."

"But I saw you on the bus today . . . you don't seem that much of a novice." That fucking bus. I nearly swerved into the next lane because I was too busy looking at her.

Once or twice, it crossed my mind to buy every single bus with that advert on it, just to have it removed. I don't want anyone seeing her like that except me.

"No, I'm not a novice." She laughs, but there's weariness in her tone I don't like. "Anyway, how were your meetings? Investments go well? What exactly do you do apart from making more money?"

I ponder her for a moment, the speed at which she changed the subject. Or shut down. It's a move I know well, which makes me all the more curious why she did that.

I also know enough that pushing her for an answer won't work, so I answer her question.

"It's not me who makes the money, but yes, the investment reports for the month were better than expected. Alex has been in Hong Kong finalizing a deal on some land, which will be lucrative in the long run."

Her eyes widen. "I like Hong Kong. What was he doing there?"

"We—Burlington Estates—bought a plot to redevelop, which will become a mall. The biggest mall in Hong Kong, actually."

The glass stops halfway to her lips. "Wow, that can't have been cheap."

"Two billion dollars for the plot, another seven for the build."

She sips her wine and puts it down. "Then it's good we have the dinner voucher tonight."

A laugh belts out, and it's oddly freeing.

I never used to discuss business with Caroline because she wasn't interested, and my mother inputs every so often when she has her quarterly reports, but for the most part, she keeps her distance.

But this, this feels . . . like we're sharing something. A commonality. Our fields of business might be completely different, but the basics are similar enough to understand.

"Yes, it is. It clearly pays to know you."

One perfectly shaped eyebrow lifts. "Do you travel?"

"Not much. I like being here."

"Hanging out doing duke things?"

"Exactly, duke things." I grin again.

There's a pause as Eddie brings over our steak pies. Holiday's eyes widen at the size of it, and she picks up one of the green beans on the side and bites down.

The gravy inside still bubbles away when I stick my knife and fork into the thick puff pastry lid. "There's nothing better than Eddie's steak pies."

After her first mouthful, she seems to agree because the next few minutes are conducted in silence. I must have been much hungrier than I thought, and the rain definitely added a chill to the air that's made me crave warmth from more than simply the fire.

"How long have you been doing this?" Holiday asks, spearing a piece of steak.

"Doing what?"

"Running everything, being a duke. How do you become a duke anyway?"

Putting down my cutlery, I pick up my wine and sip. "My dad was the tenth Duke of Oxfordshire. He died in a car accident when I was fourteen. I became the eleventh that day and officially took over Burlington Estates on my eighteenth birthday."

"Your dad died?" Her voice becomes a whisper. "I'm so sorry, I didn't know. I figured your parents were divorced or something, and that's why he wasn't around."

"It was a long time ago but thank you."

"You've been in charge of this since you were eighteen?" Her hands sweep around the pub. "Of the village, and your house . . . and everything?"

"Yes." I nod. "I have a lot of help. I don't do it by myself. But the final decision falls to me."

She's quiet again, pondering as she takes another mouthful.

"I guess that's kind of the same as me." She sighs. "I started auditioning when I was fourteen. I had my first proper movie role at seventeen, and it's been my life ever since. I have a team helping, but all final decisions are mine. It's hard sometimes, huh?"

No one's ever asked me this before. Not one person has asked if I enjoy what I do. Or even if I wanted to do it in the first place.

I am the eldest child. Therefore, it's my birthright.

There's a burning sensation behind my eyes that I need to blink away. "It is hard, yes."

Holiday sits back and pushes her plate aside. "It's why I'm here."

"Because your industry is hard?"

"It's *exhausting*. Before I arrived, I honestly thought I could leave acting for good."

I pick up the bottle and fill our glasses. "And now?"

"I earn a lot of money." She peers at me over her wineglass, and her eyebrow rises again. "Not as much as you, obviously, but it's hard to walk away from it. This new contract will enable me to pursue other projects, such as theater. But on the flip side, I still need to work to stay relevant."

I nod. I know exactly how she feels, which is surprising because a month ago, I would never have thought I'd have anything in common with a Hollywood actress. However, Holiday is the first person I've talked to in a long time who has made my life seem less lonely.

That someone else understands the pressure.

"How do you deal with it?"

My mind drifts to the waterfall, which reminds me of the last time I was there, and a chuckle escapes.

"What's so funny?"

"Remember the day we first saw each other?"

Her expression flickers, and then her cheeks tint. I wonder if she turns that shade *everywhere*. "Yes. The waterfall."

"I go there to think. Something about that place clears my head. I also take Thunder out for a ride, and I remember the many reasons I love Burlington so much."

"Maybe I need to borrow Thunder."

"I'm sure he'd love that." I laugh. "And if that fails, I tag along on one of Alex's overseas trips."

We both glance up at Eddie as he collects our plates.

"Thanks, Eddie. That was the best steak pie I've ever tasted." Holiday beams up at him, and one more victim succumbs to her charms.

"Shout if you want anything else," he gruffs out as he walks off.

"Does he have a girlfriend?"

"Eddie?"

"No, Alex."

I shake my head. "Nope. He's hung up on a girl he met last winter in Aspen on a family ski trip."

"They're dating?"

I shake my head. "No, again. He's tried to get in contact with her, but she's ghosted him."

"I love Aspen. It's so pretty."

"Then we shall go." The words are out of my mouth before I even think about what I'm saying.

That I'm planning any trip with Holiday is preposterous, especially since I have no idea where she'll be in December, because it won't be Valentine Nook.

And the idea of that makes me unbelievably sad.

Her finger is back to running up and down her wineglass. "What did you think I was going to ask you earlier?"

"When?" I reply, trying to shake the thoughts of Holiday leaving.

"In the car, when I asked if you had a lot of cash. You thought I was going to ask something else."

The journey back home feels like eons ago, and I wrack my

brain. When I remember, I wish I hadn't.

I could say I'd forgotten, but she'll find out sooner or later, and I'd rather it was from me.

"I thought you were going to ask about Caroline."

Holiday's jaw flexes. "Your ex? Do you miss her a lot?"

I shake my head. "No, not really. Not at all, actually. In hindsight, we weren't well suited."

"You were getting married?"

"That was the plan."

"And you got cold feet?"

I shake my head again. Holiday's looking down at her wine, trying to come across as casual in her questioning, but I can see how badly she wants to know.

Except I get the impression it's not for the same reasons as everyone else—for idle gossip. And when I open my mouth to tell her, I realize the humiliation I usually feel is missing.

"I visited her the night before our wedding and found her screwing my best friend."

Blue eyes flare impossibly wide, and I brace myself for the same reaction everyone else likes to give—the pity, the head bob. What I don't expect is Holiday smothering a laugh.

But that's exactly what she does.

She tips her head back and laughs. It's one of those laughs that begins deep in your belly until it rumbles up your throat and bursts out.

"Oh, *man.* That's spectacular. I'm so sorry, I shouldn't be laughing. It's not funny. But also, wow. That sucks." She wipes a tear away, trying and failing to contain her amusement as she waves a hand in front of her face. "Please ignore me. I laugh at the most inappropriate things. Sorry, are you okay?"

"Yes," I reply truthfully.

The anger I've been holding on to since December is absent. I don't even feel annoyed. Holiday's laughter is so infectious that I start to chuckle, which sets her off into another round of loud, uninhibited, raucous laughing.

Fuck me if I don't enjoy watching her.

And that's how Eddie finds us.

"Are you going to let me in on the joke?"

Holiday shakes her head, wiping away tears, and squeaks out, "It's really not that funny."

"Hmm. Well, the bar's closing soon if you want anything else."

"No, thank you, just the check. I have a voucher."

"Do you now?" he replies, trundling back to the bar.

"Come on, I'll leave the car and walk you back to Bluebell. It looks like it's stopped raining," I tell her, and after we've settled up and said goodbye, we make our way outside.

I don't even look at the whiskey still waiting on the bar.

The rain has left a chill in the air, but after the warmth of the last few weeks, it's a welcome change. The scent of the wet ground settles around us.

There's something else too.

Expectation. Anticipation. The buzz of electricity.

We're walking so close to one another I can feel the heat coming off her body. It's followed by the slip of her soft hand in mine, and I glance down to find her smiling at me.

It's so small yet monumental at the same time, and the surge of happiness is almost overwhelming. I want it to last forever.

We pass the fountain, and out of habit, I stick my free hand into my pocket. My fingers brush against the cool edges of a coin, which makes a soft plop as I toss it.

Holiday's gaze follows the movement, and she turns to me. "What did you wish for?"

I don't tell her. I just stop us walking. My hand's still curled around hers, and I lift it, placing it on my chest. I want her to feel my heart thudding as clearly as I can.

Her soft mouth parts, her tongue darts out, and she slowly wets her bottom lip.

I step farther into her space.

I don't ask permission because I don't need to. Her eyes, expressive to a fault, give everything away. She wants this as much as I do.

I think about how fucking beautiful she looked through the spray of the waterfall the first time I met her. I think about the day she was talking to Thunder and the kiss she pressed on his nose and I wondered what it would feel like if that were me.

And when it finally happens, and her tongue slips alongside mine with a soft moan, I realize that I must have been doing it wrong my entire life.

This is how kissing should feel.

HOLIDAY

Lando kissed me.

Kissed me *good*.

So good I'm wondering how I'm waking up alone.

Twelve hours later and my knees are still weak.

I'll be amazed if I can stand, and I know without looking, there's still a smile on my face. It's been there since he walked me to my front door and kissed me goodnight.

If it's possible, that kiss was even better than the first. Soft yet firm. Totally delicious. Big, strong hands cupped my cheeks, the calluses on them scratching my skin.

I could relive it all day.

I stretch out of my sleep with a long *mmm*.

I've woken up far earlier than usual. It's not the crack of dawn, but it's close. Early enough to hear the rooster crowing from the other side of the fields.

The city might have sirens, but the countryside could easily compete for noise levels with its loud farmyard animals, clip-clopping horses, and tractors.

And that's not counting the church bells going off right

now. Whoever thought nine o'clock on a Friday morning was a good time for bell-ringing practice needs to get laid.

I never thought church bells would be louder than a rock concert, but man, do they give it a go.

Throwing back the covers, I pad into the bathroom and stare myself down.

I stare until I see things I haven't seen in a very long time.

The whites of my eyes are whiter, the freckles across my forehead—the ones they always cover in makeup—seem to have quadrupled in quantity, and right now, my lips are totally bee-stung, and I freaking love it.

There's one thing missing. And that's any sign of mauve.

I'm so busy staring at myself that I don't immediately notice my phone going off, so I snatch it right as it falls off the edge of the sink.

Ashley's face fills the screen.

"Hey, boss, sorry it's early."

I'm immediately confused. "Early? Where are you?"

"Home. I meant early for you."

"Why are you awake? Is everything okay? What time is it there?" I fire out because there's no way Ashley would be calling me at this time, which means something's wrong.

The confusion gives way to a stab of panic.

"It's all good, nothing to worry about . . . I've had some queries come through—"

"What kind of queries?"

"After your meeting with Marcy, you were snapped getting into a car with a guy. They just want to know who he is."

"Oh. *Oh.*" Immediately, my heart rate returns to its normal pace, and I pick up my toothbrush to squeeze paste onto it and puff out the breath I'd been holding. "I thought it was something serious. Did you respond?"

"Of course not. And I've forwarded everything over to Patty to deal with," she replies, mentioning my publicist.

"Thank you," I mumble as I begin to brush.

It's been a while since I got spotted with *anyone.*

There was a time when it didn't matter who I was with, they were automatically tagged as someone I could be dating—from Tanner to a random guy who just happened to be standing next to me at the valet.

The only people I saw in London were my friends and . . .

I stop brushing and spit the paste. "Wait. Did you say *after* my meeting with Marcy?"

"Yeah, yesterday afternoon, London time."

"Shit."

"What?"

Cupping my hand under the faucet, I scoop water into my mouth and rinse. "Is there a picture?"

She nods. "Yes, but it's literally you getting into a car with a guy. It's cute, actually. Who is he?"

I rub against my temples at the telltale signs of an impending headache. Goddamn it. And I woke up in such a good mood.

"My landlord."

"*That's* your landlord?"

I nod. "Yeah, I ran into him in Claridge's, and he gave me a ride home. It's nothing."

It *was* nothing. Now, it's *not* nothing.

"*Sure.*" She chuckles, adding *Liar, Liar, Pants On Fire* with her tone. "You never said your landlord was hot."

I shake my head. I'm not getting into this conversation now. "Okay, time for you to sleep. Can you email me the picture?"

"No problemo, doing it now."

"Thanks. Night, Ash. Let me know if you get any more queries."

I sit on the edge of the tub and wait for my email to ding with the picture Ashley sent, opening it the second it does.

There it is plain as day. Evidence that *it* is definitely *not* nothing.

There's no denying it. There I am, staring up at Lando like he's the jelly in my donut.

I've been caught unawares plenty of times, but those pictures have rarely told any more of a story than:

"Holiday Simpson Walks Down The Street Next To Someone."

This is more in the region of:

"Irrefutable Proof That Holiday Simpson Absolutely Has The Hots For Her Landlord And Wants To Climb Him Like A Tree."

Lando's hand is resting on my back, and the other is on the doorframe as he guides me into the car, and we're both laughing.

I know the exact moment this was taken. It was when I was trying to figure out who this suited and booted version of Lando was. While I want to be mad, I can't because all I see is how he's looking at me and how happy I seem.

Would it be inappropriate to use it as my screensaver?

Shooting off an email to Patty telling her exactly what I told Ashley—that it's nothing and not to be commented on—I finish brushing my teeth.

Then it dawns on me that I'm going to have to tell Lando, and my panic reappears because I have no idea how he'll react.

Is he going to be mad?

Will he regret kissing me?

Have I blown my chance with him?

I'm working through all possible scenarios when a loud knocking sounds on the front door. Another equally loud and insistent knock follows it.

Why is everyone up so freaking early today? I haven't even had my coffee.

The third time has me hurrying down the stairs, and

because my morning decided to go to shit, I slip on the wonky step. I should have stayed in bed.

If I hadn't grabbed the banister, I'd have bumped my ass all the way to the bottom.

"Fucking bag of dicks," I screech, shaking out my elbow, which has lost all feeling. "Ouch, *fuck*."

Flinging the door open, Lando has one hand raised, and the other's holding a huge bouquet of roses.

Black riding pants are hugging his thighs so tightly they should be illegal—the thighs and the pants. The loose black tee isn't much better because it falls exactly right to emphasize the tightness of his chest and the thick vein running the length of his bicep.

The black baseball cap is a step too far because under the shadow of the peak, his eyes are even more piercing than usual. His scent is like a hit of dopamine straight into my brain.

I still don't know what time it is, but it's far too early for *this*.

My good mood is officially gone.

"Are you okay?" Lando asks, concern all over his face.

"Oh, yeah." I rub at the pain throbbing through my arm. "The stairs are wonky. I always trip on the step."

"Wonky?"

"Yeah, there's a wonky one near the top." I nod, forcing out a laugh. I'm still rubbing my arm, only now it feels wet and a little sticky.

Lando's not laughing. "Shit, you're bleeding."

Before I can take stock, he's dropped the flowers and tugged me by my good arm through to the kitchen, where I'm ordered to sit on one of the stools.

I watch in silence as Lando gets to work, pulling a first aid box from the kitchen cabinet I didn't realize was there. I'm not going to lie, as gross as it is, having a guy clean your own blood off a cut and fix it with a Band-Aid is hella sexy. I kind of hope he might kiss it better too.

"It's minor, but you'll have an impressive bruise," he says, only to walk off.

Without a mirror, it's impossible to look at your elbow, so I get up and use the reflection of the coffee machine instead, where I remember I still haven't had one.

I hear the front door close, and Lando returns carrying the roses. I think he's talking to me, then realize his phone is crooked into his neck.

"Yes . . . Bluebell." He looks at me. "Holiday, what stair is it?"

I blink. "Um . . . third from the top."

"Third from the top . . . yes . . . today. Great. Thanks, James." Lando cuts the call and places his phone down on the counter. "A couple of the guys are coming this morning to fix it, so you need to be out of the place for a little while, but that's fine since I have plans for us."

Holy shit, this guy. I don't know what's sexier right now, the way he fixed my cut or the way he gets shit done. I know it's his place, and technically, he should fix it, but I've experienced my fair share of crappy landlords to know this service isn't the norm.

"You do?"

"I do."

"What are they?"

"A surprise," he answers as he rounds the counter, steps toward me, and tosses his hat to the side.

Any initial next-morning post-kiss awkwardness was taken care of when I fell down the stairs, so there's no hesitation when his hands snake around my waist.

Like last night, I place my hands on his chest, enjoying the softness of the tee contrasted with solid muscle.

"Shall we try this again?" he asks, and he's so close I can

smell mint on his breath. "Good morning, Hollywood. Did you sleep well?"

Biting down a giggle—I mean, *c'mon*—I reply, "Yes, I slept very well, thank you. Did you?"

"Best night's sleep I've had in years. And I woke up thinking of you." His eyes drop to my mouth as he speaks. Heat flushes over my body, and the urge to kiss him again is overwhelming.

Thank *god* I brushed my teeth already.

I lift to the tip of my toes and stop a hair's breadth before our mouths touch. His stubble tickles over my top lip, and he inhales deeply, like he's breathing me in until that minuscule gap closes.

When I open, his tongue slips inside with a quiet moan.

I didn't imagine it. This guy can *kiss*. Soft, firm licks against my tongue, around my mouth, rediscovering everything he left behind twelve hours ago.

This is the reward for waking up early. My hands push up Lando's neck while his kiss deepens.

In one swift movement, I'm scooped up onto the kitchen counter, and he steps in closer. That's all it takes. That shift to position himself between my thighs, protected only by my flimsy pajama pants, sets off a tugging sensation deep in my core that soon radiates across my body.

Hands fist my hair, pulling me back. His lips stray from mine, traveling along my jaw, my neck.

"Lando," I hiss, and a big hand grips my ass, yanking me half off the counter, enough that I have to wrap my legs around his hips.

And then I feel it, his dick pressing between my legs in the exact spot I need it, and I become a panting, wanton hussy, grinding on him.

My breath labors, my chest heaves, and I'm about to have the first non-battery-powered orgasm in forever when there's pounding on the door. Lando immediately jumps back.

"If they work for me, they're getting fired," he snarls.

Even though the tight pants are holding it down, the bulge of his dick is impressive. And I'm still staring at it when there's another knock.

"Holiday," Lando croaks and clears his throat. When I look up, there's an infuriatingly wide grin on his face. "Are you going to get that?"

Easing off the counter, I glance down at my crumpled pajama shorts and the T-shirt from my brother's baseball team, then make a poor attempt to straighten it and re-tie my hair. By the time I reach the front door, I've also thrown on my raincoat, which was hanging up.

I find a FedEx guy who shoves a box at me, followed by a form to sign, then takes off without a second glance, for which I'm grateful.

Lando's standing at the patio doors, like he needs to keep a safe distance, though I take great pride in how mussed up his hair is.

Tossing the package down, I pick up the roses and take a deep inhale. "They're stunning."

"From my mother actually."

I blink in surprise. "Your mom is so sweet."

"Oh yes. A real treat." He laughs.

"You don't get along?" I call back as I fetch the last vase I used for roses and fill it with water.

"We do . . . of course, she's my mother, and I love her. But also, *she's my mother*."

I laugh because I know exactly what he means.

"However, I didn't come empty-handed. You'll have to come outside to see it, though."

"Outside?"

"Yes. Your surprise." It only takes four large strides, and he's in front of me again. This time, when he bends to kiss me, his lips brush against my cheek, keeping it chaste. "Go and get changed, and I'll show you."

I turn to head back upstairs, only to hesitate. My mind rewinds the last twenty minutes to the reason I was so flustered in the first place.

"What's wrong?"

Spinning around, Lando's looking at me curiously.

"Um . . . I need to tell you something. My assistant called this morning. There's a photo of us getting into your car yesterday. I've seen it, and it's no big deal. I thought you should know. My photo gets taken sometimes. There were questions—"

When he steps up and takes hold of my shoulders, I realize I've been babbling.

"I already know."

"You do?"

"Yes, I was going to tell you, but you fell down the stairs. We have a media team, which is mostly kept busy with whatever Miles has done, but sometimes my photo gets taken too. I rarely pay attention and I never comment. We're getting into a car. It's not that interesting."

I blink. The relief's immediate, and so is the surprise. I'd expected him to be pissed at the bare minimum, but it's refreshing, to say the least, that he barely cares.

"Now go and get dressed."

* * *

When I see what's waiting for me fifteen minutes later, it's mission accomplished. I am surprised.

Thunder and a smaller brown-colored horse are tied to the fence in the field opposite the gate.

"What's this?"

"We're going for a ride. I need to check a couple of fields, and I thought you might like to come. You said you wanted to borrow Thunder."

Maybe I need to work on my delivery because I was *joking*. Wasn't it clear I was joking? I'm sure Lando must have known I was joking.

Because there's no fucking way I'm getting on Thunder.

"Um, yeah, I don't know about this. I didn't mean—"

Lando brushes his thumb across my cheek. "You're not riding Thunder. Don't worry. Only I ride Thunder."

That doesn't make me feel better. "I haven't ridden since my accident."

"I know, that's why I'm going with you." He vaults over the fence, jumps down on the other side, and pats the brown horse.

Next to Thunder, from across the road, the brown one looked smaller, but up close, he's fucking humungous.

"This is Sunday. You couldn't find a more passive, dopey horse if you tried. I promise he'll look after you."

"Sunday?"

"Yes." Lando grins. "Because he's lazy like one."

I stare at Sunday. I can't get a good read of him because he's too busy eating grass, which I guess is better than prancing about.

Thunder nudges his head forward as if to say "you can do it"—*or it could easily be "hey, donut lady, move your ass"*—so I step on the fence and climb over. Sunday doesn't even bother looking at me, but Lando sees me hesitate, nonetheless.

"You need to think of it like riding a bike. If you've done it once, you can do it again. But anytime you want to stop, we'll stop."

I wish I shared his enthusiasm or even half his confidence. Lando's gathered up Sunday's reins and is holding them out to me.

I take a deep breath. I'm literally getting back on the horse.

After slipping my foot into the stirrup, I grip the saddle and heave myself up.

"Okay?" I'm so high up that Lando's head is tipped back.

I manage a nod and try not to focus on how hard my heart is pounding while I take another big inhale through my nose.

Leaving me with Sunday's reins, Lando mounts Thunder, who immediately leaps about whinnying with excitement.

Lando doesn't shift, just sits there laughing while telling Thunder to stop being such a dick.

I hold my breath, expecting Sunday to do the same thing.

But he stays munching on his grass.

Lando wasn't kidding when he said Sunday was passive. I think he might be stoned.

At this rate, it will take us forever to get anywhere.

But it turns out Sunday was just waiting for Thunder to get his shit together because the moment it happens, Sunday stops eating, lifts his head, and trots after his friend.

"Sorry, Thunder gets a bit excited sometimes. Taking a long hack through the fields is his favorite thing to do."

Sunday and I level up beside them. "What's Sunday's favorite thing?"

Lando chuckles. "Thunder. He has a massive crush and follows him everywhere he can."

Poor dopey horse of mine, I know exactly how he feels.

Leaning closer to his ears, I stroke along his silky neck. "Don't worry, Sunday, we can stick together."

"Ready to go?"

"Sure."

Both Thunder and Sunday have long, smooth strides, and we spend the next couple of minutes peacefully walking side by side. The heavy rain from last night has cleared the dryness and added a sweetness to the air.

We pass through fields where the grass is almost waist

height. Bunnies sprint away into their warrens, while above us, birds of prey circle and dive.

It doesn't take long until we reach the stream crisscrossing our path. It's the one that runs through the village and is just as crystal clear. I figure we're going to walk alongside it, but Thunder walks straight up to it and steps right in.

And so does Sunday.

I hadn't realized how fast it was flowing until I felt it pushing against Sunday's legs. It's high enough to brush along the bottom of the stirrups, but he gets us safely through, and I relax back into his undulating stride.

Lando's meticulous as he checks over the land we pass. His eagle eye misses nothing. Twice, he dismounts to examine a fence post loosened from the dry earth and calls back to the yard to have it fixed.

Just like he did with the staircase.

After riding through fields for thirty minutes, we haven't seen a single building. It's all horses, cows, and sheep.

"Is all this yours?"

Lando nods, and there's gravity to him when he speaks. "Yes. Fifteen thousand acres, including the village. It's all mine."

I can barely manage a small backyard. I can't imagine what it must be like to have this much space.

"A lot of work."

"Yes, but I love it," he replies, leaning forward to rub Thunder's ears. And I see the love all over his face. I can hear the emotion in his voice. It's how I used to feel when I walked onto a film set. Lando sweeps his hand around. "This is what my father left me. It's where I grew up, and it's why I work so hard. Alex leads the international subsidiaries because I want to stay here. I want to make my father proud."

"I'm sure he's very proud," I tell him because how could he not be? "What's your favorite place?"

"You've been there, remember?"

He turns to me. There's definitely insolence to the smile curving his mouth, and I can't stop staring at it.

It's a beautiful mouth.

"The waterfall?"

He nods, and a heavy throb begins between my thighs. I haven't been to the waterfall since I saw him there.

After what happened in the kitchen this morning—or what didn't happen—the coiled spring inside me is quick to tighten.

There's no mistaking my meaning when I reply, "How 'bout you show me why you love it so much?"

Lando's eyes blaze. "Okay, Hollywood. You ready for a gallop?"

* * *

If it's possible, the glen is even more beautiful and magical via the entrance Lando leads us through. Dark vines coupled with trailing wisteria create a curtained appearance, like we're walking into an exclusive club for two, while Thunder and Sunday stand guard, tied up to an exposed root of the tree.

The echo of water hitting the pool is quieter than I remember, and the dappled sunlight breaks through the spray, creating an eerie glow around us.

The impulse to dive right in has me easing off my boots while Lando looks on in amusement.

"How deep is it?"

"Deep enough."

Pants and tee follow my boots until I'm standing in front of Lando wearing nothing but my bra and panties. Throwing him a wink, I march to the edge and plunge.

I was expecting the water to be freezing, but it's almost warm.

Warm and clear like bathwater.

I swim down to the bottom, to the pink rock I spotted the

day I came with Clemmie, which turns out to be more quartz than stone.

When I come back to the surface, Lando's watching me from the rock under the waterfall, wearing nothing but black briefs. The water hits his shoulders, runs down his chest, and disappears into the dark curls.

It's six weeks, give or take, since I walked through the bramble path and discovered him here, and I'd be lying if I said I hadn't thought about it every day since.

He crooks a finger at me. "Come here."

I swim over to the rungs worn into the rock and step up slowly.

Taking my hand, Lando pulls me into him, using his massive body to protect me from the water cascading down on us and the jagged wall behind me.

Both hands sweep through my hair, slicking it back. The movement forces me to look up, and when I do, a pair of bright blue eyes peer down at me.

"You are so beautiful."

I've heard those words a thousand times and read them in a million press cuttings. But they've never been more than page fillers, lip service to a celebrity they want to flatter.

Until now, I haven't ever really *heard* them, felt the weight of them. Or truly believed them.

But Lando's gaze is so earnest as it holds mine, it has every inch of me glowing.

I run my fingers through the silky black curls covering his chest. "So are you."

The corner of his lip quivers with the beginnings of a smile and breaks the seriousness threatening the moment. Pressed against him, I feel the thickness of him swell against my pelvis, then his mouth falls on mine.

It's not like last night's kiss or the kiss in the kitchen. This kiss has the power to disintegrate me.

He kisses me on and on.

And on.

Without breaking contact, Lando hauls me up in one swift movement, sets me on the ledge, and spreads my thighs. His gaze narrows until all I see is the onyx moon of his pupils.

"I've been wondering what you would look like spread out like this for my eyes only, Hollywood."

I squirm under the intensity of his stare, the stillness of him —save for the rise and fall of his chest—and a shiver whispers down my spine. I'm so exposed. With my underwear on, it feels indecent almost, yet the goose bumps wracking my body aren't because I'm cold.

"And?" It comes out more croak than word.

"Fucking fantastic," he hisses.

The calluses on his palms are rough against my skin when he slides them up my thighs, and it's a reminder that Lando is no Hollywood pretty boy. He doesn't spend his days reciting a bunch of lines. He *works* for a living. There's power in his hands, and right now, they're on me, spreading me wider.

"You've been so desperate for this all morning, haven't you?" Lando's voice is steady and deep. "For me to touch you. Your pussy is aching for it."

My nipples are so hard they poke through the lace of my bra. When his palm ghosts up my stomach, and he grazes the pad of his thumb over one, my head falls back with a groan that echoes off the rock.

"God, *yes*. Lando."

Another groan from me is followed by a deep chuckle from him.

Bunching my panties, he rubs the thin cotton between my slit until the friction is almost too much to bear.

His fingers ease beneath the elastic, between my legs, and the slipperiness of my pussy is all he needs for a green light to push them inside me.

It's everything I've been waiting for, and I whimper his name.

"My name sounds good on your lips, Hollywood."

Behind me, the water pounds down, inches from my skin, the vibration ripples across my body until it aches for release.

Thick fingers stab inside me, fucking me with reckless abandon.

Mine dig into the rock so hard I can feel it under my nails.

The pressure builds in my spine, and black dots fill my vision. All it takes is a swipe of his thumb on my clit.

And there, in broad daylight, under the force of a waterfall, the orgasm that I almost had in the kitchen explodes.

LANDO

"Lando, I forgot to ask about your document last week," my solicitor barks down the phone. "If you've had a change of heart, that's fine. We'll keep it on file until you're ready. If you still want to go down that route."

Holiday is paused on the TV screen. Somehow, I've managed to stop it at the exact moment when her face beams with a huge smile.

It's the smile I've come to know, though everything else about her is different—dark hair, brown contact lenses, not one freckle appearing on her nose.

But underneath all the makeup, she's still Holiday. And she's mesmerizing.

I can't tear my eyes away. She steals every scene she's in, and even though I'm only two-thirds through, this might be the best film I've ever seen.

I was supposed to be working, but after the first two calls of the day almost put me to sleep, I lay back on the sofa in my study and somehow began watching the movie Alex had been raving about.

"Lando, you there?"

Typically, Arthur never introduces himself, just launches straight into whatever it is he wants, but no one could mistake his crusty baritone for anyone else. And being a lawyer, he likes to get to the point.

Time is money and all that.

"Sorry, yes, I'm here. What did you say?"

I get up to stretch my legs and open the window for a blast of fresh air. Outside, Max is playing with Dolly and Hamish on the lawn. He's set up a series of mini agility courses, and he's trying to bribe them over each jump with a biscuit.

"The document you were signing. Did you change your mind?"

I chuckle. "Which particular document? I must have signed a dozen for you since Monday."

He tuts, and I know he's rolling his eyes. "The primogeniture."

I freeze.

I'd completely forgotten all about the papers Arthur had drawn up to start the process of changing the line of succession for the Burlington Dukedom.

I signed it and asked James to courier it back to Arthur. I never gave it another thought because that was the day I met Holiday.

Six weeks and I haven't thought about much else.

I scratch through my beard, my eyes drifting back to the screen on the wall, so I switch it off. Holiday Simpson is far too distracting for her own good.

"You never received it?"

"No, sir. I checked the files this morning."

"It should have been couriered. What happens if it's lost?"

"If you still want to sign it, I'll send you another one."

Hearing a cheer from outside, I find Max has managed to get Dolly over the first jump, but Hamish has decided it's far too energetic for him, and he's taking a quick nap. When Dolly gives up jumping to do the same, Max picks up a bucket, takes it over to the edge of the lawn, and crouches.

I just *know* it's going to be filled with snails. It's rained every evening since the thunderstorm last week, and snails are everywhere.

"Lando—"

"Sorry. Leave it with me, and I'll get back to you."

"Fine. Speak soon." He ends the call in the same brusque manner he started it.

I drop down into my desk chair and think.

There's a framed photo of my dad and me when I was eleven years old. I'm sitting on a stable door, and my father's old horse Zeus is poking his head out while my father looks on laughing. It's one of my favorite photos of us, which is why the photo belongs on the corner of my desk.

I stare at it now.

"Come on, Dad. What would you do?" I mumble. "Mum has been such a pain since Caroline. She won't leave me alone."

As I speak the words aloud, I realize that's not entirely accurate. My mother *has* left me alone recently. Aside from a couple of less-than-subtle allusions to Holiday, she hasn't brought up my dating life in over a month.

It has to be some kind of record. Who am I kidding? Going one day without bringing it up would be a record.

Picking up the phone to call James, I put it back down. I could do with a stretch of the legs, so I'll go and see him instead.

I take the shortcut past the swimming pool, which I'm shocked to find is empty. I assumed Clementine decamped here at the first hint of a sunny day, and truth be told, I'm a little disappointed because when Clementine is here, Holiday's usually around too.

My groin tightens at the thought of Holiday out here in her bikini.

Even after the last two hours watching her on screen, I have a sudden craving to see her in the flesh, all blond hair, blue eyes, and freckles. I think about the way they disappear into her hairline every time she smiles, and how her nose wrinkles up right before she belts out a laugh.

When my mind drifts back to the waterfall, my need to see her becomes an incessant tugging in my chest. It's been a long time since I wanted someone so badly that the sight of them literally made my body ache.

But that's nothing on how I feel about that deep rumble from her throat when she came on my fingers. Raw, husky, and genuine, as my name fell off her lips like a plea.

And fuck me if that sound didn't do something to me.

She might be one of the most famous actresses in the world, watched by millions of people, but under that waterfall, she was for my eyes only. *Mine.*

I don't know how long I can go before we finish what we started in the glen because as desperate as I was to fuck her right there on the rock, I didn't want to rush her. Or *me*.

But a couple of days have passed, and all it's done is solidify how quickly Holiday has gotten under my skin and how needy I am to see her again. I'm ruminating on it when I walk across the yard and into James's office.

Thoughts of Holiday dry up, and my face immediately drops into a deep frown.

James, my mother, Alex, Miles, and Hendricks all stop talking. It's a scenario so bizarre I don't even know where to begin, only that there's no question they were talking about me seconds before I entered.

"What's going on?"

"Nothing," Miles replies, shifting closer to the window.

The fact he hasn't cracked a joke but also won't look at me means it's absolutely not *nothing*.

"What is going on?" I repeat.

"Nothing, darling," my mother coos. "We were all here separately. It's a coincidence, that's all."

James sits down behind his desk. I've known the man twenty years, and as stoic as he might seem, he has a terrible poker face.

Alex and Hendricks are staring at the floor, and my irritation begins to take hold.

"If one of you doesn't tell me right now why the fuck you're all in here, then I'm really going to lose my shit."

"Tell him," Miles presses, staring at Alex, who's pinching the bridge of his nose. "Oh, for fuck's sake. Caroline's getting married."

"Who the fuck's Caroline?" I snap a second before it hits. "*Caroline*? *My* Caroline, Caroline Montague?"

Hendricks gives one deep nod.

Well, fuck me. That didn't take long.

"Who to?" Though I don't need any guesses to figure it out.

This time, Alex speaks. "Jeremy."

Wow. Okay.

I guess that's why he's been messaging me.

I lean back against the wall and let out a long breath. One of the louder thoughts I've had spinning around my brain since last December is how long had Jeremy and Caroline been screwing behind my back.

Whether it was worth throwing away our decades of friendship and a future.

It clearly was, and I don't know how I should feel.

For so long, my presiding emotion was humiliation, and guilt that somehow it was all my fault. But now, all I can find in me is relief.

Five sets of eyes watch me process the news.

"When did you find out?"

"This morning," Miles replies.

I don't want to know how. I don't want to find out it's the

latest idle gossip on the London to Oxfordshire network. I don't want to think where the gossip will lead.

Because I know it'll be to me. My reaction.

I dig deep. I try to find something, *anything* that tells me how I feel.

But there's nothing.

And maybe that's my answer. I don't give a shit.

"Fine. Well, good for them. I couldn't care less. Caroline and I should never have been together in the first place."

My mother purses her lips. I'd imagine she doesn't hold the same opinion, just like I know I'm going to hear why.

"It's so tacky. How dare they announce this so soon after everything they put you through?" she fumes, her nostrils flaring. "You should have been the one to announce any marriage first. And you've seemed so happy recently, darling."

Over by the window, Miles bites down a smile.

"I'm still happy, Mum."

"Well . . . I don't know. I think perhaps you need to start dating again."

Oh fuck no. I'm not going through this for a second time. Miles snorts, but his smile dies when he takes one look at my face.

"Enough," I shout, loud enough for all five of them to raise their eyebrows. I try again, softer this time but no less firm as I pin them all with a glare. "Enough. This goes for all of you."

"What've I done?" Miles grumbles.

"I do not want to hear one more word about Caroline." I hold my finger up as my mother opens her mouth. "Nope. I'm still speaking. Today, we draw a line under the whole situation. And I need you all—*Mother*—to back the fuck off. Caroline getting married does not give you the green light to start banging on about setting me up again." I stare at my mother, who looks on the verge of bursting if she doesn't get to speak.

"If you think I'm happier, it's because you haven't been watching every move I make."

Miles coughs out a word that sounds suspiciously like *Holiday*, which has Alex smirking.

My head falls back against the wall, and I scrub a hand through my hair. Glancing at James, I remember the reason I came to see him in the first place.

"As you're all here, I should tell you that a couple of months ago, I asked Arthur to draw up papers to begin the process of changing primogeniture. My current plan is to leave everything to Max."

I'm not sure who's louder in their outburst—my mother or Hendricks.

"What the fuck, Lando?"

My mother doesn't swear, but her explosion is no less angry. "Absolutely not."

"This is Max's future. Were you going to talk to me about it?"

I turn to Hendricks. "Yes, of course. Once it had all been settled."

"Did you sign these papers?"

"I did," I reply and look at James, "but it appears Arthur never received them."

To his credit, James doesn't even bother to deny it. He just reaches into his desk drawer and pulls out a brown envelope.

"I didn't want you to do something you regretted."

"Why would I regret leaving all this to Max? Everything we've built, everything Dad built. Max is the next generation. Besides, it's a backup measure in case I never meet anyone."

"Don't be so ridiculous, Lando."

My head snaps around. "Mother, I don't know if I'm going to get married and have children, but I'm not going to fucking do it with you breathing down my neck only to land with someone else like Caroline."

Her lips purse again. "What about Holiday?"

"What *about* Holiday?"

"You've been spending time together—"

"I gave her a ride home from London. That's all."

I dare not look at any of my brothers. I haven't said one word to them about Holiday since Miles announced my crush at family supper. But it's widely agreed among our family that, of everyone, I'm the worst at lying.

They'll take one look at my face and know the ride home from London is not, in fact, all.

"Serious question here. Are you going to be my second brother to fall in love with an American?"

When Alex and I splutter at the same time, it's almost like we rehearsed it. Leave it to Miles to break the tension by adding more tension.

"I'm not in love," Alex snaps.

This time, all eyes land on him. Miles's, Hendricks's, and mine anyway. My mother rolls hers, though I'm not sure if that's at Miles or Alex or me. Likely all of us.

"What? I'm not. I hooked up with a girl last Christmas, and that's all it was. Nothing more. A hookup. A *fling*."

On second thought, maybe Alex is worse at lying than me.

"C'mon, Al. I'm sure Haven will call you back at some point. Maybe she's busy. Or did you check that you definitely had the correct number for her store?" Miles asks, wrapping his arms around Alex's shoulders and pulling him into a hug.

"Get off me," he snaps in return.

Thankfully, it's enough of a distraction for the conversation to move away from Holiday and back to the reason I'm here in the first place.

"Orlando," my mother snaps. "What do you intend to do with that?"

She's pointing at the envelope on James's desk.

Crossing my arms over my chest, I suck in a cheek. Alex and Miles stop dicking about, and the room falls silent.

"If you promise not to mention my dating life until the end of the year, then it can go back in the drawer."

I don't know why I give the end of the year as a deadline, except by the end of the year, Holiday will no longer be in Valentine Nook.

My mother pushes out of her chair and smooths down her shirt and trousers. "I can live with that."

No one moves until Miles slaps his thigh. "Right. On that note, I'm going over to Foxleigh. Any of you losers want a ride up to the house?"

* * *

I TAKE Miles up on his offer, and he drops me off at the front door.

On the way, we pass the side of the house where the Burlington staff live when they're on duty. It's also where everyone parks their cars, and it's the nearest spot to the kitchen entrance.

"Isn't that the car you gave to Holiday?" Miles points toward the cleanest car in the lot.

The cleanest of all the Burlington Estate cars, anyway.

The rush of adrenaline is instant, even when I try to bat it away, given Miles's presence.

"I don't know."

"It is. I'm certain it is. I recognize the number plate as it's parked outside my cottage every day."

"So?"

"So are you sure you want me to drop you at the front door?" He snorts. "You can just get out here."

I don't bother to deign a response, but when he pulls up at the hall and I hop out, he calls me back.

"Lan, I meant what I said the other day. It's good to see you more like you again. Fuck Caroline and fuck Jeremy. You deserve to be happy, and if Holiday Simpson makes you happy, then I say you should go for it. If you don't believe me, you should take a look at that photo, if you haven't seen it already."

For a moment, I'm too choked up to speak. Miles, for all his annoying habits—of which there are too many to mention—is also incredibly intuitive, kind, and loyal to a fault. Jeremy was his friend too, and I know that neither he nor any of my siblings have spoken to Jeremy since.

"Thanks, Milo."

I don't even bother turning left to my study. I march straight across the hallway and down a short passage to a set of stone stairs, following it until I arrive at my destination.

The scent of sugar and cinnamon fills the air, and I hear Pierre's thick French accent through the door.

Peering around quietly so I can watch without disturbing them, Holiday's leaning over an impressive ball of pastry. She's all red cheeks, puffing away a strand of hair while dangerously wielding a rolling pin like it's a baseball bat.

I rarely come down here, so I wasn't expecting there to be so many people, but I suspect that Holiday's presence has the exact effect on the Burlington house staff as Miles does in the estate yard.

I don't manage to stay secret for as long as I'd hoped.

"Oh, Your Grace. Can I help you with something?"

I turn to find Cynthia, Pierre's sous chef, staring at me as Holiday's eyes snap up.

Busted.

"Oh no, thank you. I just came to find your newest recruit." I smile over at Pierre, who for once isn't wearing his signature frown. "Can I borrow her for a moment?"

He puffs out a response and throws his hands in the air, which could mean both yes and no.

I'll take it as yes and gesture for Holiday to follow me away from the prying eyes of twenty house staff. Her face is impossibly fresh, totally devoid of makeup. But she's smiling, a reaction that is rare in Pierre's kitchen.

My craving to see her has been replaced by a desperation to kiss her, which I fight by swiping my thumb over a smudge of flour on her cheek.

"Hey."

"Hey."

"How's your morning been?"

"Good, how's yours?"

"Better now I've laid eyes on you. What've you been making?"

"*Pies*. Pierre said my pastry 'needs work.'" She air quotes with a roll of her eyes.

I bark out a laugh. "Well, I won't keep you." For what surprisingly isn't the first time, I decide to take Miles's advice and go for it. "But I came to ask if you would like to meet me at The One True Love later?"

Holiday grins wide, rises on her tiptoes, and brushes her lips to mine. "I would love to meet you later."

HOLIDAY

"I *knew* it."

"You're not mad?"

"No. Of course not. *Absolutely* not." Clemmie grins wide. "I knew something was going on when you came over for family supper."

I'm staring at her, trying to find any tell that she's pissed I've been making out with her brother, but I can't. I try one more time. "Seriously?"

"Yes." She reaches across the table and takes my hand in hers. "I think it's great, truly. Not to put any pressure on you, but Lando's been so much happier since you arrived here. The brother I used to know is coming back."

"What d'you mean?"

Clemmie pulls the champagne from the ice bucket and tops off our glasses. I've become one of those women who seem to find any excuse to pop a bottle. What's more, I like it.

I could get used to this new life I'm living.

"Well . . ." Her tongue clicks against the roof of her mouth. "It's a lot of work running Burlington, keeping everyone happy, and managing the complaints, and that's nothing to say of the estates worldwide. Alex manages it mostly, but the buck stops with Lando."

She reaches out, picks up a chip, and scoops it deep into the hummus I picked up from the store. We also have slices of peach pie, which I made with Pierre this morning, and he begrudgingly admitted was *"magnifique."*

Not to brag, but he's right. It might have been the eighth attempt at getting the pastry to the exact thickness Pierre instructed me to—at which point, I was ready to smack him with the rolling pin—but it was nevertheless worth it.

"Keeps him busy."

"You could say that. He's an excellent leader. The problem was Caroline."

Stuffing a handful of chips in my mouth so as not to give away how desperately I want to know everything about this woman Lando planned to spend his life with, I ask, "His ex?"

Clemmie nods. "Yup."

I crunch as quickly but as quietly as possible, hoping Clemmie will continue if I don't interrupt.

"They were very badly suited."

My shoulders slump. I was hoping for something juicier. "Why did he stay with her?"

Clemmie shrugs. "Good on paper, I guess."

It's morbid curiosity, but I can't help myself. "So what was the problem?"

"Everyone hated her. And I mean *everyone*."

She's so blunt in her delivery that I have to cough up the chip dust that was inhaled too quickly. I think about all the people I've met, including Clemmie, who's so friendly toward everyone she meets that it takes her forever to get anywhere.

"Even you?"

"I didn't hate her *hate her*. I mostly felt sorry for her. Being the future Duchess of Oxfordshire is not for the weak, but she expected to be waited on hand and foot, which is not how we do things around here. Lando *works*."

I know. I've seen that firsthand. I think about the ride we took with Thunder and Sunday, and how Lando's eyes never stilled. They lasered in on broken fence posts or cows in fields where they shouldn't have been or trees that needed trimming.

The only time he focused on me a hundred percent was when we made it to the waterfall.

I shift in my chair and recross my legs. Now is not the time to think about *that*.

"What happened?"

"I'm not sure." She shakes her head. "Truthfully, I thought they were heading for splitsville, but he took Caroline on holiday, and they came back engaged. I was away at uni, and Miles called me to break the news."

"Did Miles like her?"

"Miles *hated* her. So you can imagine how that went down."

I chuckle. Of all the brothers, Miles is the one who has no fucks to give. He does what he wants when he wants. His behavior is equally outrageous and amusing, and now that he's stopped hitting on me, I quite like him.

He's gotten into the habit of waving and shouting, "Howdy, neighbor," very loudly every time he sees me.

"I think Miles just hated that she treated Lando like a cash machine, and Lando gave her anything she wanted because it made his life easier. That's what really fucked off Miles. Lando became someone we didn't recognize."

"And then she screwed his best friend—" My scoff drips in disdain.

Clemmie's brows shoot up. "He told you about Jeremy?"

My cheeks burn as I nod. I'm still mortified by my reaction to him telling me when it should have been compassion, but the more I've thought about it—and I've thought about it *a lot*—the more I believe it was the reaction he needed.

"Wow. He doesn't talk about it with anyone."

"He didn't go into detail," I spit out.

I don't want Clemmie to think her brother shares more with me than with his family, but from the smile on her face, I'm guessing she's okay with it.

"So, not to be nosy or anything . . ." She reaches for a fork and casually chips away at the pastry on the pie, though her eyes keep flicking up to mine. "Are you seeing Lando again? Have you . . . you know . . . made any plans?"

Was I that obvious when I was asking about Caroline? If so, I should quit acting for good.

I laugh. "Actually, yes. He asked me to meet him for a drink later."

"Cool. Cool," she replies just as casually and cuts off a giant piece of pie, which she scoops into her mouth. "Omigodthisisgood."

I beam with pride. Academy, take back my Oscar because that pie is my greatest achievement this year.

"Really? You like it?"

"Yes. Wow," she mumbles, taking another huge bite. "Are you enjoying it?"

"Sure am." I nod and pick up my own fork before Clemmie eats it all. "But boy, Pierre takes his job seriously."

Clemmie's eyes brighten as she snorts in amusement. "Yeah, he does. It's why I stopped with roasting a chicken. I couldn't take the disappointment in his tone every time I got something wrong." She finishes the champagne and chases it with a full glass of water. "I nailed that chicken, though."

"Can Lando cook?"

She shakes her head. "Better than I can, though that's not a stretch. One of the pitfalls of having every meal prepared for you. There are other things I'm good at. Hendricks is the only one of us who can legitimately cook."

I hold my hands up. "Hey, I'm not judging. Us kitchen novices have to stick together."

She's just about to reply when her phone lights up on the table, and she catches sight of the time. "Shit. Hendricks is going to kill me. I promised I'd go and help him with the late shift at the vets. I should have been there five minutes ago."

She shoots out of her chair and gathers up her bag. I stand to walk her to the door and am wrapped in a hug.

"I'm so glad you're here, Holiday. I know it's only temporary, but I hope we'll be friends for life."

For a moment, I'm too stunned to speak.

I have my girlfriends back in New York, but Clemmie is the first person I've *truly* made friends with in a long time. My life is so transient, and I exist in circles of colleagues and air kisses, where we cross paths at industry parties or events or on the next film set before we drift off on our separate ways.

But when I hug her back and reply, "You bet your ass we are," I mean every word.

I wait by the front door as she rushes out and down the path. As I'm closing it behind her, two huge magpies land on the fence and stare at me.

Two for joy.

One for Lando, one for me.

If my time in Valentine Nook is destined to become the memory of one more fleeting episode in my life, then I'm making the most of it.

We might have had our dinner together, followed by time in the fountain. But after Lando came to find me this morning and asked if I'd meet him for a drink, tonight has all the ingredients of a proper date.

One I hope will continue where we left off the last time.

The champagne emboldens me to spend the next three hours prepping for my date like I'm about to hit the red carpet.

I soak in a bubble bath, scrubbing myself from top to

bottom. I apply a deep conditioning treatment to my hair. I shave my legs. I wax.

I spread a clay face mask, followed by a sheet mask that promises to remove all wrinkles while plumping my skin to its fullest potential. I follow with toner, serums, and moisturizers that assure me they do the same.

I slather my body in a fragrance that smells so good I almost turn myself on.

But deciding what to wear takes the longest.

I try on four dresses, a cute skirt and top combo I've yet to wear, and jeans and a cute off-the-shoulder tee before returning to the first dress I tried on. A long dress printed with multicolored florals that swirls around my feet. I bought it from one of the village boutiques because it reminded me of the beautiful flowers blooming in the front yards I kept passing.

Pairing it with flats, I add a slick of lip gloss and finish with mascara and run out the door with ten minutes to spare.

I don't spot Lando when I walk into The One True Love, and it's busy enough that there are no spare tables, so I pull out a stool at the bar and sit down. It's the first time I've been in here by myself, and aside from a few double takes as I peer around, no one's staring.

The novelty of being seen around Valentine Nook has worn off, and it brings a huge smile to my face.

I'm still smiling when Eddie appears carrying a large tray of clean glasses. "'Ello, 'Oliday. You look pleased with yourself."

"I think I am."

"Well, good, what are you drinkin'?"

I turn back to the door, in case Lando's arrived, but there's no one by the door except a small dog. "I'll wait for Lando."

"Suit yourself," Eddie replies, turning to put the glasses on the shelves.

I use the time to go through my phone and read all the

messages that have flooded through on the Simpson Family Chat Group today after one of my nephews caught a ball in Little League with his face, knocking out the brand-new *adult* tooth that had just grown through.

I'm debating what to reply when the stool next to me moves, and my head snaps up only for the smile to falter when I see it's not Lando, just a random guy, so I resume with the messages.

"You must be Holiday."

My eyes flick toward the voice. I've been in Valentine Nook long enough now that I'm recognizing people. Whether it's at The Beanery or Valentine Cook or passing down the main street where I'll offer up a smile.

I've *never* seen this guy, and the way he says my name has my hackles rising.

"Have we met?"

The guy pulls a packet of tissues from his pocket and places them on the bar next to a brown cardboard box. I lean back. If this guy's sick, I don't want to be anywhere near him.

"We haven't," he replies, at which point Eddie stops putting glasses away and turns around. "Hello, Eddie."

Eddie, who I've only ever known to be the curmudgeonly grandpa type, looks so menacing that I'm momentarily speechless.

"Get the fuck out," he hisses. "You know better than to show your face around here."

The guy nods and rolls his mouth into a hard line. "If it's all the same to you, I'll wait for the duke to tell me that."

"Your funeral."

Ice cubes clatter as Eddie scoops them up from the cold bin, drops them in a bowl, and slings it across the bar, where the guy thumps down a fist and stops it from going any further.

He neatly lines up the packet of tissues next to it.

Okay, this is fucking weird.

"Are you sick?" I can't stop myself from asking.

Mystery dude huffs out a small chuckle. "Nope. But I say I have about five minutes before I'll need them."

I go back to my messages and try to focus on my siblings arguing over what to do about my nephew's missing tooth, but my eyes are too busy flicking between this guy in front of me and the door where I'm hoping Lando will walk through any moment.

When he does, he marches across the stone floor, barely offers me a glance, and punches the mystery man square in the nose.

LANDO

"A'right, everybody out," Eddie yells. "C'mon. Let's go. OUT. Take yer drinks with you."

There's a scramble of chairs behind me, along with loud grumbles of protest, a yapping Jack Russell, and the sound of glasses being placed on tables. I hadn't realized it was quite so busy when I stormed in, but I guess I wasn't paying attention.

"OUT."

Feet shuffle toward the doors as Eddie's customers slowly make their exit, only to stand outside and peer through the windows. I understand their reluctance and curiosity at what's going on because they need as many facts as possible to accurately spread what will undoubtedly be the most exciting piece of village gossip since the wedding was canceled.

But hey, that's me. Doing what I can to keep Valentine Nook entertained.

I'm shaking out the throbbing in my hand when I spot a bowl of ice on the bar and plunge my fist into that instead. The stinging is superseded by cold, and the pain momentarily vanishes. It's a better solution than the bottle of whiskey I drank the last time I punched Jeremy.

My eyes drift to the floor where he's easing himself to sit using an upturned stool. I regard him for a second, half groaning, half laughing as he leans back against the bar. Blood pours from his nose and his split lip, and his left eye is already puffy. I'm debating if I should help him up but then decide he can stay there.

Dick.

It's the shocked gasp that has me turning, however. Holiday stands to the side, hand covering her mouth, her wide blue eyes glued on Jeremy and brimming with disgust. I just can't tell if the disgust is aimed at me.

For the first time since I walked in, I get a look at her. A really *good* look.

Her rosy cheeks. Shimmery lips. Blond hair tumbling over her shoulder.

Her skin looks so clean and smooth that if it weren't for the wisdom behind her eyes, she'd look far younger than her twenty-five years. Makes me feel like an utter pervert for lusting after her so blatantly.

Especially when my dick kicks behind my zipper.

She's so fucking beautiful with her pretty flowery dress, wearing it for our date, that a profound ache appears in my chest.

Because I've now fucked everything up before it even began.

I was on my way when Eddie called to warn me Jeremy was sitting at the bar next to Holiday, and a murderous rage kicked in. I don't know what he's doing here or what he wants, but it only took one glance through the window to spot him leering at her for me to charge.

It's still there, ire roiling through my blood like a viper ready to strike, even while my entire focus is trained on Holiday and the shock on her face.

"Holiday," I begin softly, stepping toward her slowly, doing my best not to frighten her.

A musky, floral scent floats between us, and the ache in my chest deepens. It's the scent I've been dreaming of since the summer fair. The one I'll forever associate with her.

Holiday's eyes flick to mine briefly, then back to my former best friend. He's grinning like a lunatic, trying to stem the flow of blood seeping from his mouth and nose.

I hate him.

I hate that my first reaction to seeing him with Holiday was violence.

I hate that she's looking at him.

I hate that I'm flooded with shame at what she witnessed, but that I'd do it all over again if I had to.

"Who is that?" Her voice is barely louder than a whisper.

I'm interrupted before I can answer when Jeremy thrusts a hand out to her. "Jeremy Glenroths, delighted to meet you."

Two tiny lines appear between her brows, and she blinks, trying to connect the dots as to why I would storm in here and punch a stranger in the face. But then she looks at me, and I see her perceive the situation. There's a good deal of hurt in there too, and perhaps some understanding.

Air sticks in my throat as Holiday steps forward. Blood whooshes in my ears, and the viper gets ready to strike.

Jeremy's hand is still aimed straight toward her. He's expecting her to take it, though I can promise if he so much as touches her, he'll be on his back again after I rip his fucking arm off.

Except she doesn't take it. Instead, she crosses her arms over her chest and leans forward ever so slightly.

"Hey, asshole, if I'd have known who you were, I'd have punched you long before Lando did."

Well, that was unexpected. I smother a grin.

"Touché." Jeremy reaches for the packet of tissues and stuffs one up his nose. "I see the big man's already told you all about me. Must say, huge fan of your work."

"Go to hell," she snarls in a tone I didn't even realize she was capable of, flipping him off as she spins around. Rising on her tiptoes, she brushes her lips against my cheek. "Take as long as you need."

The pleasure I gain from that small interaction is insurmountable.

The shame morphs into a sizable lump.

My eyes stay on her as she walks away, hair bouncing around. Eddie's standing by the door, ready to let her out. She pulls him into a hug, followed by a kiss on his cheek. Even from where I'm standing, I can see the blush creeping over him.

Hollywood's sweetheart and my defender rolled into one.

And just like that, I become her biggest fan.

She pauses on the threshold and turns, a soft smile lighting her face, and the power of it hits me right in the chest. It's exactly what I need to get through the next hour of my life.

Throwing Jeremy a final deeply withering look I hope I'm never on the receiving end of, she leaves the pub. The bolts clatter as Eddie locks the doors behind her.

I find Jeremy's gaze following her as she passes by the window, and my fists ball. I'm going to kill him.

"Right, you two, the place is empty. I'll be in the back. Try not to break too much," Eddie gripes and trundles off, leaving us alone for the first time since the evening before my wedding.

Ironic that he's also ruined the first proper date night I've had in forever too. And if I have to have a conversation with the dickhead, I'm not going to do it sober.

Spotting a bottle of Glenmorangie on the shelf, I pour myself a large glass and knock it back, followed by another.

"I'll take one of those."

I pause, drumming my fingers against the bar, deciding whether I want to share this bottle with the guy I used to share everything with.

Then decide I don't.

My petty pants fit great today.

"No, you won't."

He huffs a dry chuckle, pulls himself to standing, and rounds the bar. Over the years, we've served ourselves here more times than I can count. He knows where the glasses are, and he knows where the good bottles are. With Alex, Hendricks, and Miles, we would frequently have lock-ins after hours with groups of friends, and in the morning, Eddie would count up the damage and add it to our running tabs.

I don't bother looking at him while I slowly sip. "If you take one more step, I'll black your other eye."

"Jeez. Calm down," he replies but shifts back. After picking up one of the barstools that fell over in the scuffle, he sits on it. "How 'bout that ice? Can I have that?"

I glance down at the bowl. It's now more water than ice, and I've had my fist in it, but I push it toward him anyway. Picking out one of the cubes, he runs it across his swollen lip.

He's silent as he does so, and while I'm not in the business of making things easier for him, I absolutely do not want to spend a second longer in here than I have to. Holiday is my priority, and I have a ruined evening to make up for.

"What are you doing here, Jez?"

He drops the cube into the bowl. "Came to invite you to a wedding. Caroline and I are getting married, if you haven't heard."

I eye him carefully. He was always one who liked to shock, just for kicks. I also know him well enough that their wedding is not why he came to Valentine Nook.

"Don't you want to offer your congratulations?" he asks when I remain silent.

"Not really."

"Do you want to know why we're getting married?"

I swill the amber liquid in the bottom of my glass. "Nope."

"Caroline's pregnant."

My heart stops. My stomach bottoms out. A high-pitched ringing sounds in my ears.

"You should see your face." Jeremy slaps his hand on the bar and barks out a loud laugh. "It's mine, but *wow,* that would have really thrown a spanner in the works. I can imagine Victoria wouldn't take too happily to the news either. How is she, by the way? Do send my regards to the duchess—"

I'm too busy catching my breath with relief to really pay much attention to what he's saying. For a split second, my life flashed before my eyes. The acrimony Hendricks went through with Max's mother nearly killed him, and the prospect of working through it myself isn't something I ever wish to experience.

But once the relief has passed, it's followed by an unexpected pang of sadness. I'd always assumed Jeremy would have been godfather and vice versa when we had children. Now the future of Burlington lies with Max.

"Why are you telling me this?"

"Wanted you to hear it from me before anyone else."

I laugh at that. A big, heartfelt laugh because the thought of him sparing my feelings after everything that's happened is so ridiculous it's absurd.

I'm still chuckling when Jeremy reaches around the bar for a cloth, drops a handful of ice into it, and holds it against his eye.

"So you and the American—"

The laughter dies on my lips. "Don't you fucking mention her name. Don't you even *think* about her."

"Whoa, Your *Grace*. That's quite the temper you've developed," he taunts and moves the ice cloth down to his nose. "You want to know what I find interesting?"

"No, I really don't, but I guess I'm going to find out."

"Cor-*rect*." This time, he gets up, walks behind the bar, and pours himself a glass of whiskey. And I don't stop him. I'm too scared that I'll take another swing at him, and this time, I'll keep going. "You almost murder me because I'm sitting next to a woman you've known less than two months, yet your fiancée falls in love with another man right under your nose, and you don't even notice."

"Your point?"

"My point. *Hmm.* I saw a photo of you and . . . um . . . that *foreign person* who was just in here."

I roll my eyes. "So?"

He glugs the whiskey and places his glass on the bar. I'd almost forgotten how much Jeremy loves a dramatic pause and how much they used to irritate the fuck out of me.

"In four years with Caroline, I never saw you look at her like that. But you know what? *I* look at her like that. I always did, something else you never noticed."

I know what he means.

After Miles told me to check out the photo, I pulled it from the pile of media notices I never usually bother to read. Even *I* was surprised. But not from the way I'm looking at her—like she's the first sunny day after a month of rain—or the way she's laughing at me.

It's the absence of stress and worry.

There's a lightness to my expression. A rarity after two days of meetings and years of living up to my obligations.

Perhaps Holiday *is* my sunny day.

"This is why you came all this way? Because you saw a fucking photo? Or because my powers of observation aren't up to your standard?"

He shakes his head with a scoff and gets up off the stool.

Walking to the other side of the bar, he picks up a brown box, which I'd assumed was Eddie's, and places it in front of me.

"I love Caroline, but I have to admit that for the last six months, I've also been wracked with guilt. I should have handled things differently, and I regret losing you as a friend, but it's a cost I have to bear."

I blink hard at words I never expected to hear. "Are you asking for my forgiveness?"

He shakes his head. "No."

"Then I'll ask again, what the fuck are you doing here?"

His chin jerks to the box. "Everything you ever gave Caroline."

I peer at the box but don't open it. I don't want to look in it.

"It's time to draw a line and start fresh. We're having a baby now, our life is real, and I don't want it to be funded in any way by you. Caroline would have brought it herself, but I don't think she would have been quite as welcomed as I have." He laughs dryly.

"Then give it to fucking charity. I don't want it."

Ignoring me, he tips back the remainder of his whiskey and turns for the door. I expect him to walk out without saying a word, but after he's unlocked all the bolts, he stops with his hand gripped around the handle.

"Take care of yourself, my friend. I hope you find what you're looking for."

I stay where I am, staring at the cardboard box. I marvel at the mundanity of it. That something so nondescript contains so much power.

Taking another slug of whiskey, I rip the seal and open it up.

Inside, I find cases of jewelry, dozens and dozens of leather and velvet boxes. Some black, some navy, a couple of red, but more than that, I find memories I'd forgotten. Blocked.

The ruby drop pendants I brought back from China when

I'd had to travel last minute, the diamond tennis bracelets for the months I'd spent at the yard helping Hendricks during the first winter we were dating, earrings for every complaint Caroline made that I spent more time with Thunder than her.

The last case I pick up is a small black leather one. I don't need to open it to know what's in it. I should have known then that we were doomed before we'd even begun.

Caroline's engagement ring, her second one.

It's nothing but four million pounds' worth of evidence. A sum total of bad decisions I've made in my personal life. A clear-cut sign of everything I should have done differently.

Four million pounds' worth of jewels. Because in my heart of hearts, I was marrying someone I didn't really like, and it was the easiest way to assuage my guilt.

A payoff.

For six months, I've stewed in bitterness and wallowed in my own self-pity. Everyone around me has moved on with their lives.

My mother's words from the last few weeks sound loudly in my head. Hell, even Miles's are ringing in my ears, followed by Clementine's, Hendricks's, Alex's, and somewhere in the background, Eddie's.

They're all right.

I've been happier in the past six weeks than I've been in a long, *long* time.

And it's not because of Holiday, but it's taken her arrival for me to see what was missing.

I think back to what Miles said this morning.

It's time for me to start doing what makes me happy.

Shoving the box under the bar, I call out to Eddie that I'm leaving and sprint out the door.

I have until the end of the year to enjoy my life without anyone breathing down my neck.

And a date to salvage.

LANDO

Holiday's eyes are puffy when she answers the door. *She's been crying.*

"Did you fall down the stairs again?" I ask, immediately regretting it when her tears start up again.

Now is not the time for stupid jokes, but I've never been great with women crying, and there's a box of precious gems in the pub that's testament to that.

But for the first time, I'm determined to see it through and fix it—with more than money.

She shakes her head, and I want to kiss her better. Kiss everything better.

Kiss her until we need to come up for air, and everything's forgotten.

I start by brushing a strand of hair away from her face. "Hey."

"Sorry." She sniffs, swiping her hand under her nose.

I'm pretty sure I know the answer, but I ask anyway. "Why are you crying?"

A fresh set of tears starts up, but through them, she laughs. "I don't know."

"Is it because of me? Have I made you cry? Because if I have—"

"No." She shakes her head. "No . . . you haven't. No. Of course not."

She's so adamant with her response that I know I'm onto something. The tears definitely have to do with me, and I'm wracked with guilt.

"Holiday, you can tell me. Please tell me."

She lets loose a big, long sigh. "It's so dumb."

"If it upset you, it's not dumb."

"Okay, but bear in mind I drank a bottle of champagne with Clemmie earlier," she mumbles, teeth worrying at her bottom lip.

"Got it."

Holiday's face screws up tight before she drops it into her hands. "I thought you punched him because you're still mad at him because you're still in love with your ex."

She says it so quickly, and her mouth is partially covered with her hands so it comes out a little garbled, but once I realize what she said—or rather the *implications* of what she's said—my anxiety vanishes.

She's not looking at me, so she can't see my struggle to hold on to the grin tugging at my mouth. I'm tempted to wait a little longer before putting her out of her misery because honestly, this *feeling*—that this *incredible* girl standing in front of me might be jealous—is intoxicating.

"That's not why I punched him," I say eventually.

"No?"

"No." I shake my head, easing apart her hands until her beautiful, tear-stained face comes into view, and I tuck a finger under her chin. "I punched him because he was talking to you."

"What?" The tears have turned her eyes even bluer than normal, and a whole story of questions and emotions plays out in them before she settles on, "Really?"

"Yes. Really. I don't care about him, and I'm definitely not still in love with Caroline. I'm beginning to wonder if I ever was. But seeing him next to you, looking at you, breathing the same air as *you*, made me insane with rage. So I punched him." I add a casual shrug, like it's no big deal, because the way she's looking at me makes my heart race enough that I need to take the edge off.

I catch the faint remains of pink shimmer on her lips as her mouth drops into a perfect oval.

"I've spent my entire life doing what's expected of me. For once, I'm going to do what I want."

She blinks. I see her breath catch, and the shift between us is seismic. I hold her gaze, blue on blue. The intensity between us builds as quickly and thickly as the air before a thunderstorm.

The delicate curve of her throat works as she swallows. "What do you want to do?"

"This."

My mouth falls onto hers, sealing us together. Flinging her arms around my neck, she holds on tight as I scoop her up and kick the door shut behind us.

I carry her down the hallway, past the ghosts of old memories, and deposit her on the big round hall table. I'm already hard when I step back.

For the millionth time, I marvel at how fucking beautiful she is. That *I'm* the one who gets to see her this way—sitting on the polished mahogany table, dress bunched around her thighs, chest heaving, cheeks flushed with desire.

When her tongue darts out, wetting her lips, my gaze finds a new target. The pink shimmer has disappeared, kissed off by me, leaving behind a mouth I plan to do wicked things with.

Her eyes, no longer puffy or red from crying, drop down slowly and back up, stopping at my mouth.

The ache in my chest returns. My dick throbs with wanting her.

Her dress strap has slipped off onto her shoulder, and I gently replace it. One last act of propriety before I drop to my knees.

Her skin squeaks along the wood as I tug her into me, yank down her underwear, and throw her creamy thighs over my shoulders.

Doing exactly what I wanted to do the last time she was spread out in front of me, I drag my tongue through her soaked slit and suction onto her clit.

"Oh god, Lando. *Fuuck*."

It comes out as a hiss, followed by a thud as her elbows fall onto the table. It's a poor attempt to hold herself up. Peering out from under her dress, I catch her arm flung over her face, teeth sinking into her lip, back arched.

"Say my name again," I demand.

My lips run along her thighs, nipping at them while I use my thumbs to spread her open and lap up her wetness dripping on the wood.

She groans so loudly I feel the vibrations across her body. Her hips push into my face, and fingers spear through my hair, gripping the ends to tug herself closer. If I have a bald spot by the end of it, it'll be worth it.

"*Say* my name." I take another long swipe, my tongue cleaning up every drop of her.

"*Lando*."

"Good girl. By the time I finish with you, Hollywood, your throat will be raw from screaming it."

I want to watch her come. I want to taste her as she does. I want to *devour* her.

Because while this is for Holiday, it's also for me. To make her feel as good as I do and build on this connection we have as proof that there's something between us.

It's not a figment of my imagination.

She's so slick that sliding two fingers inside her and twisting them up rewards me with another garbled moan and a round of unsuccessful thrashing. My arm clamps down across her pelvis, holding her tight as she slips on the table.

She's dripping wet, melting under my touch. The sight of it makes my dick weep. She's entirely at my mercy, whimpering my name.

I've never seen anything like it.

"Easy, Hol, you're making quite the mess." Taking my tongue to her again, she squirms and arches deeper. Swathes of silk cluster around her navel. "You don't want to ruin your pretty dress."

She lets out another loud groan and balls her fists.

There's no traction on the table, nothing to grip onto as her thighs begin to shake, and when I add a third finger, her pussy clamps down hard.

Every inch of visible skin tints pink. Full-body convulsions take hold, her eyes flicker closed, and she explodes in front of me. My dick's straining so tightly in my jeans that I almost follow.

Unbuckling enough to release myself, I roll on a condom, gently pull her off the table, and straddle her across me while she's still drunk on the glow of her orgasm. She teeters on top of me, her knees hitting the hard floor while I wait for her to catch her breath.

The strap has slipped again, and instead of replacing it, I ease it lower, exposing a peaked pink nipple and a rounded golden breast that fits perfectly into my palm. Her eyes lock onto my thumb as I slowly trace along the hint of a tan line.

"Where did I find you?" I ask. It comes out as a whisper, but I couldn't honestly say whether I meant to keep it in my head.

Her response is light and amused, a symphony to my ears. "I believe it was under a waterfall."

She's not laughing a second later after I line myself up and drive into her. I'm not laughing either. All I can think about is how incredible she feels stretched around my cock, the warmth of her pussy as comforting and welcome as brandy on a cold winter's evening.

How perfectly we fit together.

Steadying herself, she pushes her hands under my shirt too quickly and rips. Buttons fly in every direction.

The feel of her fingers running across my chest has me thrusting again, and the sensation of her clenching steals the air from my lungs. I can't even manage a groan.

My hands disappear under her dress, digging into supple flesh while I let her adjust. My thumb finds her clit, slowly circling, and I watch her glazed eyes darken until they're no longer focused.

Her wetness seeps onto my thighs.

"Tell me the truth, Hollywood. That first day you saw me, did you think my cock would feel as good as this?" My words rasp like I've been dragged over hot coals.

She shakes her head.

"Because I never dreamed your pussy to be like this."

Lashes bat at me. "Good?"

"No. Not good. Fucking *incredible*."

Challenge flashes in her eyes. "Yeah? How 'bout when I do this?"

A roll of her hips sends bolts of pressure shooting up my spine. "Ah, *fuuck*. Yes."

Blunt nails rake over my skin as she starts up a slow, steady rocking that almost strangles my cock.

"So tight," I grit out.

"And this?" She leans down, hands splayed across my chest, and her mouth finds mine.

Our tongues tangle. Her kiss is hungry and needy.

I spin us around, and my forearms act as a bracket to

protect her from the hardwood floor. Her legs wrap around me, and that's all it takes for me to fuck her hard, driving inside her while my name drops from her lips over and over.

It's what I need. What she needs.

And when her eyes lock on mine and her body spasms, I'm done for. I spill into her, my cock jerking with every clench of her pussy until I collapse.

We stay silent, staring up at the ceiling. I lived in this house for years, and I don't think I've ever looked up before. I grin into the twilight evening. I've never had sex on the hall floor either.

A profound sense of peace washes over me. Perhaps my ghosts have been "laid" to rest in more ways than one.

Next to me, Holiday lets out a deep, relaxing sigh. When I pull her into me, she fits so perfectly against my side that I'm immediately hit with the realization that this is all temporary. And I'm not sure how I feel about it.

There's saltiness to her skin when my lips press against her damp temple. "What are we going to do when you leave?"

She stays silent, and all I hear is the soft rise and fall of our breathing as we watch the wall where shadows of our fingers entwine.

"I'm not leaving today. Or tomorrow. And when the time comes, we'll figure it out."

"How long have we got?"

"Four months."

"Better make the most of it then," I reply, tugging her under me again.

My mouth finds hers.

I'm not prepared to lose a second.

HOLIDAY

Lando is true to his word.

We are making the most of it.

For two weeks, we've been inseparable.

When it's rained, we've stayed in. When it's been sunny, we've ridden out. I am now fully confident back in the saddle, as long as it's Sunday underneath me and Thunder keeping him focused.

I learned that we're not morning people even though Lando has to be up early most days. So on the weekends, we sleep late.

When Lando's worked, I've hung with Clemmie, practiced yoga, or jogged alone because she refuses to jog with me.

Pierre finally decided I'd mastered the art of good pastry (my words, *not* his), and I've graduated to working with chocolate, a subject I'd only previously known how to eat. Somewhere along the way, during the weeks he's been teaching me, he's decided I need to learn everything about becoming a pâtissier, whether I want to or not.

I'm on the fence, but I guess, at the very least, I'll finally have something to contribute to the Fourth of July and Thanksgiving.

Obviously, Lando appointed himself chief taster, a role he's taken very seriously.

I've spent more and more time in Valentine Nook, enough that I'm now on a first-name basis with Claudia from The Beanery, where I begin my days with a coffee because once Lando leaves, I can't get back to sleep.

Sometimes I sit and eat breakfast on the chairs set on the cobbled street outside, or I'll perch on the fountain wall and watch the morning pass by. I check my daily report from Ashley, which is getting shorter and shorter, and I try not to think about the day I have to start taking calls again, because it'll mean I'm no longer in Valentine Nook.

My shoot in Paris looms, and for the first time ever, I'm not looking forward to seeing Marcy.

In the evenings, we have dinner at the different restaurants in Valentine Nook, where it's become clear how much everyone in the village adores Lando, but none more so than Eddie, who we always stop in and see on the way home.

And while we've been seen around the village, and there's an awareness of Lando and me spending time together, I hadn't realized how fiercely he was protected until no news sightings were reported of us.

My media update from Ashley started and stopped with the photo outside Claridge's.

But I have a feeling that's all about to change today.

"FOR FUCK'S SAKE, MILO, BACK. WATCH YOUR FUCKING BACK," Hendricks screams at Miles, thundering down the far side of the polo field.

There's a lot of yelling. Mostly Hendricks, but also Alex, who both seem to be under the impression Miles can hear them across a space the equivalent size of eight football fields.

"Hen, watch your language," Clemmie snaps, her hands shooting up to cover Max's ears.

It doesn't appear that Max is paying the slightest bit of

attention to his father. He's far too busy watching his uncle, tiny fists gripped around a pair of binoculars, as he gallops toward the goal with four angry-looking riders chasing him.

I've seen Miles in a new light.

Gone is the guy with the permanent smirk and roving eye. He's been replaced by a serious athlete with focus and dedication, tearing down the field. His face is a mask of determination and control with instincts so sharp he's nothing short of dangerous.

It happens so quickly I don't fully understand how, but in a blink, Miles spins his pony around, blocks the ball with his mallet, and slams it between the posts, bringing the score to even.

It feels like I've witnessed a Tom Brady touchdown.

Foxleigh Park crowds go wild.

The stand we're in—the Burlington family stand, which must hold one hundred people—goes even wilder. None more so than Max, who drops the binoculars, jumps up in his chair, and squeals, "WELL FUCKING DONE, UNCLE MILO."

Hendricks is too busy cheering in excitement to notice his son chanting expletives. Lando turns away so Max doesn't see him laughing. Alex ruffles his hair, Clemmie rolls her eyes, and I pick up my drink, feeling happier than I have any right to.

The smile on my face has been a permanent fixture for the past two weeks.

Play resumes, and the ponies get back into position. Hendricks sits and scoops Max onto his lap, leans down to where the binoculars landed on the floor, and loops them around his son's neck.

"Daddy, when can I play like Uncle Miles?"

"When you've eaten all your vegetables."

Max, satisfied with Hendricks's response, settles into his father's chest and resumes his watching. Every time Hendricks shifts forward to yell his support, so does Max, moving as one.

I once went to a polo tournament in the Hamptons, where I was the guest of the title sponsors—a locally made gin brand. I invited some girlfriends, and we spent the afternoon in the VIP tent, sipping cocktails and paying little attention to the day's events.

This is not like that. Lando and his siblings only take their eyes off the field during the changeover breaks. Even Clemmie.

"LEFT," Hendricks yells again. "LEFT."

I can only imagine what he's like as a father on the side of the field, assuming he's not been banned for arguing with the ref and coaches because, based on today, that's just as likely.

"GO CHESTER. GO CHESTER," Max screams.

I lean into Lando and whisper, "Is Chester another player?"

He answers from the corner of his mouth. "Chester is Miles's pony for this chukka. He's very fast with a quick spin. He usually brings him in during the middle chukka."

"How many ponies does he have?"

"Actually, I'm not sure." He turns to Hendricks. "How many ponies does Milo have at the moment?"

It's Max who answers, "Uncle Milo has fifteen ponies at Foxleigh. But some are still too gween." He proceeds to list them all out. "My favorite is Clover."

"Mine too, Maxy," Lando agrees.

I wait until the end of the chukka to ask any more questions because I *get* it.

I come from a sporting family. We grew up loving baseball in the summer and football in the winter.

I learned a long time ago that sport takes priority, and it seems polo is no different.

As the teams make their way off for the changeover, everyone relaxes. Drinks are ordered, and snacks are consumed. Max leaps off Hendricks's lap, picks up a mini polo mallet, and proceeds to charge around the stand, pretending to be his uncle on a pony.

Lando stands behind me, close enough for me to lean into him and breathe in the rich, musky scent I crave when he's not around. His thick bicep wraps around my chest, tucking into my shoulder. When he drops a kiss on my head, I have to physically stop myself from preening because, of all the things I'm learning about Lando, his affection is my favorite.

"Having fun?"

"Lots." I nod truthfully.

Any time I spend with Lando and his family is enjoyable. They're not dissimilar to mine if mine came with giant houses and waitstaff, but the dynamic between Lando and his siblings is the same, along with the warmth and the constant banter.

"So I was thinking . . ." His chin rests on my head. "Next week, when you're in Paris, how about I come with you?"

I spin around. "You want to come to Paris?"

He nods. "I'd like to see you at work. In your environment. I've shown you mine. How about you show me yours?"

My teeth sink into my lip, and I peer up at him. "I'd *love* to show you mine."

In a second, Lando's eyes darken. That delicious, familiar tugging in my pelvis kicks in. I'm pressed so close to him that I feel the swell behind his zipper, and I briefly wonder how far I can push this.

He leans closer, his mouth brushing over the shell of my ear. "Behave yourself, Hollywood. Only good girls get my cock, and I know how desperate you are for it."

Scratch affection. *This* is my favorite.

My brain is firing, trying to find any excuse for us both to leave *right now* when I sense Clemmie jiggling a bottle of champagne at me. "Hol, want a top-up?"

"Sure," I croak, doing my best to steady my shaky hands as I pass her my glass. "Thanks."

As she's pouring, another roar lets out from the crowd. "Oops, we need to watch this. Miles will quiz us later."

"What?"

"Yes, sadly. He'll want to know what you feel were his highlights of the match. I'd go with that last goal, personally."

A laugh rumbles from Lando's chest.

"Why do you think we're all watching so closely?" He winks, his lip quivering as his eyes crease, and I think about how good he looks when he's smiling.

"Where's Miles's yard?"

He turns me back around and points at the far left of the field, past the stands where thousands of spectators are sitting. "See that line of trees? It's beyond there. It's where all the ponies are kept for the Oxfordshire team. And where the England team trains. There's an arena, practice fields, and an exercise pool. It's impressive."

"And Miles *runs* it?"

Lando nods. His stubble tickles my cheek when his head dips over my shoulder. "I know, it's hard to imagine Miles doing anything other than partying and causing havoc. Polo is the only thing he takes seriously."

"Do you play?"

"I can play, but I'm not very good. We all compete in a family tournament at the beginning of every season, but Miles carries us."

While he's speaking, the players gallop back onto the field on fresh ponies. Miles has switched out Chester for a pony as black and shiny as Thunder, who's currently prancing about like a prima ballerina while Miles sits steady.

Even to my extremely untrained eye, I can see he's in a league of his own.

"What about Hendricks?"

"He's better than I am, but no one's like Miles," Lando replies, "except Max."

I peer over to where Max has given up riding the mallet,

and he's now swinging it around. "My brother used to do that with his baseball bat, and now he plays in the majors."

"He has the same talent Miles did at his age, same as our father did." Lando's voice drops and softens. "He'd have loved to watch Miles play for England."

Lacing my fingers into his free hand, I squeeze. "I'm sorry he never got to."

"CLOVER, CLOVER, CLOVER," Max screams as the next chukka gets underway.

"Miles's pony," Lando whispers unnecessarily. "The lucky one."

* * *

THE LUCK WORKS.

By the end of the first half, Miles's team leads their opposition by three goals, and Clemmie grabs my hand before the ponies leave the field.

"C'mon, let's go and stomp divots. But first, I must pee."

"Sure, why not? I could do with a bathroom break too."

She takes my hand and leads us out of the stand, through the crowds, and into the VIP tent. She's keeping her head down, trying to squeeze past unnoticed, and I follow her lead. Sunglasses on. If she doesn't want to be seen, then neither do I.

I assume we're following the signs for the bathrooms, only we turn left before we get there.

"Clem, the bathrooms are over there."

"We're going to different ones. Too many people," she replies as we head back out into the sunshine on the other side of the tent and along a narrow pathway lined with bushes.

Clemmie's eyes are down, and I see him before she does. It's possible she didn't see him at all, from the way she collided with his chest. If I hadn't pulled her back, she'd have fallen over.

I'm about to apologize when I catch sight of Clemmie's face. Her mouth's open, and for the first time since I've known her, she seems anxious. Her shoulders are stiff with tension.

Then I take a look at the guy.

He's the definition of tall, dark, and handsome. Thick brows, chiseled cheekbones, shaded by the ball cap he's wearing, and eyes so brown they're almost black as he stares right at her.

It has all the makings of a meet-cute, an accidental run-in, except I get the impression there's much more to it.

He looks like he should be annoyed, but the way his lips purse makes it seem as if he's holding down a smile. Especially when his head dips with a curt nod that feels more taunting than sincere.

"Lady Burlington," he says, an American drawl that sounds both foreign and immensely comforting after two months in England.

My eyes bounce between them. I wait for Clemmie to say something, but I'm not expecting, "We have to go."

My glasses are dark enough that he can't see me look at him as she drags me off. Not an iota of surprise on his face, and the smile I knew he was hiding tips up.

She's still not said anything by the time we reach the bathrooms—which happen to be near the players' quarters. We pee in silence, then make our way out to where the hordes are.

I thought I'd done well in avoiding the small number of press in attendance, but the moment Clemmie and I step foot on the field, they swarm. We're new blood among all the other celebrities present, cheering on the teams.

Our photos are taken, and I avoid all questions about who I'm here with. Several people come over to speak to Clemmie, then linger as we replace the turf kicked up from the ponies' hooves and press it back into the ground. Twice I'm asked for a selfie, along with a request for my number and several offers if

I ever need a tour guide in England, all of which I politely decline.

The whole time, my eyes jump back to the stand where Lando's laughing with Max and Alex.

It's distracting enough that I almost forget about the encounter on the way to the bathrooms until I look up to find the same guy leaning against the stands, watching us. And the moment Clemmie turns her back, I know she's spotted him too.

"Who's that guy? The one we bumped into."

Her cheeks flush an uncharacteristic shade of pink, eyes darting to either side. She's concentrating very hard on replacing the divot I already trod in. "Santiago Torres."

"He's hot."

Her shoulders slump with a deep sigh. "Yes, *very*."

"Who is he? He sounded American."

"His mother is American. His father is Argentinian. He played polo for Argentina before he got a two-year ban for an illegal bump, which nearly killed Miles. Miles *hates* him. I'm surprised he's here." Her tone becomes tinny, hollow almost, enough for me to want to give her a hug.

"Wow."

She nods, and I wait for her to continue, but she doesn't. Instead, she sucks in a quick, deep breath and changes the subject.

"I've just realized you'll be here for the Fall Ball."

"What's the Fall Ball?"

"It's so fun." Her eyes light up, relieved I'm not pressing her on the scowling mystery guy. "We hold it every year around Halloween in London. It's dinner and dancing, all done in masquerade. We raise money for Lando's charity, which supports helping children grieve when a parent dies. He started it about fifteen years ago."

Now I'm the one pressing in a divot I'd already pressed in because I don't know what to say.

I help with charities. I try to do my bit every year by donating or whatever's required, but truthfully, they tend to all blend into one. But this charity, *Lando's* charity, is a stark reminder of how exactly he came to be the person he is today. Suddenly, I'm fighting the urge to cry.

"Count me in."

"Excellent, and that means we'll have to go shopping."

"How do you raise the money?"

"Donations, ticket price, auction. One year, Miles decided to auction himself. Raised nearly a quarter of a million just for him, but it also ended up in a fight between the three highest bidders outside the venue, which was splashed all over the front pages the next day. We didn't do it again. Safer to stick to one-of-a-kind experiences." She grins, and a giggle bursts out, which sets me off too.

"Why does that seem so Miles?" I snort. "But I'd love to help. I can definitely find something worth donating."

When the bell goes off, announcing the end of halftime, Clemmie loops her arm into mine. I notice that her eyes keep darting over to where that guy was standing, only he's gone. When I turn back to the direction we're heading, Lando's walking toward us.

His eyes are glued to mine. I don't think he's even noticed anyone else. But he has an air about him that compels people to move out of the way when he passes, and for a second, I marvel at him.

By the time he reaches us, a smile stretches across his face. "What are you two gossiping about?"

"I was telling Holiday about the Fall Ball."

I nod, peering up at him. "I'll find something cool to donate for the auction. Maybe a trip to a movie set?"

Lando wears a curious expression, both thoughtful and amused.

I'm wondering what it means when he drapes his arm around my shoulders and twists me into him enough that he can press a full kiss to my mouth with little effort.

It's brief but not too short and gives absolutely no doubt to anyone watching us that we're in a "relationship" at the bare minimum.

"Thank you, Hollywood. That's very kind."

I sense the snap of a camera. There's no way he doesn't either. But we walk off the field and back to the stands like we haven't noticed and don't care.

LANDO

"So tell me what to expect." I put my coffee down and watch Holiday.

We've been flying for thirty minutes. Her fidgeting has grown progressively more fidgety, and I'm not sure why.

I'm certain she's not a nervous flier because she wasn't gripping the armrests on takeoff. She seemed perfectly comfortable settling into her seat, requesting a mint tea, and flicking through a bundle of loose notes she pulled from her bag. She nodded to the pilot when he asked if we were ready to leave, and the moment the wheels became airborne, she turned to me with a blinding smile, following up with a kiss that made me wish this flight lasted longer than an hour.

But if she clicks the top of her pen any more aggressively, it's going to break.

"Hol?"

Her face does that thing where I know she hasn't heard a word I've said.

"What?"

"Are you okay?"

She nods, though it seems more like she's going through the motions of nodding. Head loose from her neck.

"Yeah?" It comes out as a question.

"Let's try again. What's wrong?"

She lets out a long sigh and slumps back in her seat. "Nothing."

"Holiday?"

Her eyes roll closed. "Do you remember when I told you I sometimes think I can leave acting for good?"

I almost laugh. It was the night I kissed her, the afternoon I drove her back to Valentine Nook. One of the best two hours of my life. It's not a day I'll forget in a hurry.

But I just say, "Yes."

"My agent, Marcy, will be in Paris. She's very good, one of the best. I'm lucky to have her, really. She built my career, and she works phenomenally hard for her clients, negotiating top-dollar deals. I'm where I am today because of her—"

Babbling is something I've learned Holiday does when she's nervous, in particular whenever her agent is mentioned. It reminds me of being in investor meetings when bad news is being delivered.

Start with the good stuff, and no one will notice how you've lost one hundred million in land value after a season of terrible weather.

I wait for the but.

"She's bringing me two offers for films next year."

I study the drop in her face. Film offers seem like a good thing, but based on the way her mouth turns down, I'd wager it isn't.

"You don't want them?"

"I don't."

"What are they?"

She shakes her head and adds a sad shrug that pulls at my heartstrings. "I don't know."

"You haven't seen them yet?"

"No."

I'm confused. I've never pretended to understand women, but right now, I really don't understand, which thankfully, Holiday senses and takes pity on.

"If I see them, and I like them, it'll make it harder to turn down. Marcy's so persuasive. If I like them, she'll sense my weakness. But I'm not ready to go back to movies. I have my Oscar, and it nearly killed me." Her head drops onto the table.

I might not understand women, but I know when they're on the verge of crying. And before she does, I leap out of my seat and pull her into my lap on the sofa.

"Do you know what else I remember from the day you told me you could give up acting?"

She shifts on my knee and peers up. Two frown lines appear between her brows. "What?"

"That you'd like to try the theater."

"Oh." She sighs and settles back into my chest. "Yeah."

"Well?"

"I was just being flip. I didn't mean it."

I get the impression she's brushing me off, which, unfortunately for her, doesn't work. Because I become like a dog with a bone.

"Why can't you mean it? What's wrong with the theater?"

She sits up, her eyes flashing, "It's *hard.* Night after night, in front of a live audience."

It's such a ridiculous argument that I scoff in her face. "You don't strike me as the sort of person who'd shy away from something being hard."

"I'm not, but—"

"Have you spoken to Marcy about it?"

"I mentioned it to her once, a couple of years ago, but nothing ever came of it. She said movies are better. More money. Theater's too limited because of audience numbers."

Her hand mindlessly pushes against my palm, twisting them together, staring. "I should look at the offers. They're probably fine for me."

Her tone is so unenthused that I almost laugh. I don't think I've ever heard anything more halfhearted.

"Holiday, I might not know the movie industry, but I do know business. And unless you're prepared to go into something with your whole heart, you have to walk away. Yes, theater is hard, but I bet you a million pounds that being up there and hearing the audience cheering for you every night would be more exhilarating than anything you've ever done on a set."

Her lips mash together, and she stares at me. I can see thoughts flickering as she wonders if I'm onto something. I know this much: if she ever stepped foot on a stage, I'd buy out the front row every fucking night.

"You have a forty-million-dollar contract to sign, and you said it yourself that it'll give you the financial freedom to choose parts you want, not parts you have to take."

She nods silently.

"But nothing will happen if you don't tell Marcy what you want—"

Both of us turn as the privacy curtain parts, and the purser appears.

"Your Grace, we'll be landing in ten minutes. The car is waiting for you."

"Thanks, Mike."

Holiday jumps off my lap and marches down to the bathroom, grabbing a small bag on her way. "Time for me to get my game face on."

The driver transports us through the Paris traffic, pulling up to the George V—where I upgraded the suite she'd been booked to the penthouse with its panoramic city views—by which point Holiday looks tense enough that she might explode.

"Monsieur le duc, bienvenue. Quel plaisir de vous accueillir à nouveau parmi nous. And a warm welcome to you Madame, welcome, *welcome back,"* greets Charles, the head concierge, who's waiting for us when we step out of the car. "We're so delighted to have you stay with us again."

"Charles, toujours à votre poste," I reply, shaking his hand.

"Et comment se porte Madame votre mère?" he asks, always respectful when he's talking about my mother.

"C'est très aimable à vous. Ma mère se porte bien, elle garde un excellent souvenir de son dernier séjour ici."

It's been a while since I've stayed here, but my mother comes so regularly that the proverbial red carpet is always rolled out.

Holiday's head whips around from where she's watching our bags get loaded onto the trolley. "You speak French?"

"Bien sûr." I wink, and behind her dark glasses, I know I receive an eye roll in return. Taking her hand, I plant a kiss on her knuckles. "Come on, *mon petite fromage.* Let's go and see our suite."

Holiday doesn't say a word. Not as we walk across the ornate lobby's marble floor or the plush carpets of the hallways until we reach our home for the next three days. Nothing.

Our bags are placed in the bedroom, and I hand the bellman a couple of neatly folded twenty-euro bills while Holiday drifts over to the balcony doors overlooking the city.

Flipping the Do Not Disturb sign onto the door, I roll up my cuffs, kick off my shoes, and quietly pad toward her.

My arms snake around her belly. "You know, I think it's

against French law to be in a bad mood while you're staring at the Eiffel Tower."

A small puff of amusement pushes up from her chest.

Running my nose along her jaw, I inhale her citrusy scent, and my dick jumps to attention. "You might end up in a French jail."

Her tense shoulders drop a little, and she leans against me. The bulge in my jeans gets tighter. I know she can feel it.

"We wouldn't want that," she replies, turning to look up at me. There's fatigue in her eyes that I haven't seen since the week she arrived in Valentine Nook, but there's also heat behind them.

"What time is your meeting?"

Her watch slips around her wrist when she spins to look. "At three o'clock."

"Which gives us exactly one hundred and forty-three minutes to relieve some of that tension you're carrying. You'll have to get your game face on again, Hollywood, because I'm about to mess it all up."

A perfectly shaped brow shoots up. "How are you going to do that?"

"I'm going to fuck it out of you." If she's shocked, she doesn't show it. Blue eyes fall to my mouth. Her tongue swipes against her lips. "Do you think the French use *fuck*? Or is everything about *making love*?"

She shrugs like she doesn't care, which would work if her eyes weren't already glassy.

"Is that what you want? Gentle lovemaking?" A slow roll of my hips forces her back into the glass doors, pressing into her so she can feel exactly what *I* want. "Or a good, hard fucking?"

My hands push under her T-shirt. Palms smoothing over her soft, warm skin and into her bra, where I tweak a nipple so hard it could cut glass.

Her breath sucks in sharply, and her head flops against the

door, inviting me into her neck. It's a silent demand for my touch, but I'm not falling for it.

She's been quiet enough this morning, and now I want to hear her voice.

I want her to use it.

"C'mon, Hollywood, tell me what you want. Get the practice in now because later, you're going to tell Marcy you want out of movies." My lips breeze along her clenched jaw. "So what's it going to be? Lovemaking or a good, hard fucking?"

I still my hands on her hips. She gets nothing except my hot breath across her skin.

"Fuck me."

I shake my head. "Not good enough. Do you want my cock or not?"

She's so wound up that it's almost too easy to push her buttons. "Lando, this isn't relaxing me. Stop fucking talking and fuck me already."

I lean in, my lips curving as I gently press them to hers. It reminds me of the day at the pool when she stood in front of me, arms clasped to her chest as she snarled, eyes blazing.

It was anger that matched mine.

I wanted to fuck it out of both of us then. I'm going to now.

"I knew you were in there somewhere." Twisting her around so fast she nearly topples, I bend her over the large round marble coffee table by the window. "Palms flat. Don't move."

I strip quickly, my cock springing out toward her while her breath shoots across the reflective black surface.

Making light work of unbuttoning her jeans and tugging them down to her knees, I spread her open as far as she'll go. The sight of her glistening pink pussy lips dripping for me as she's bent over a table is so hot and sexy that I nearly blow on the spot.

I lick my lips and lean down, taking care not to touch her as I push my hands through her hair and fist it.

"You should see yourself, Hollywood. Pretty face, perfect hair, about to get all mussed up because you need my dick so badly."

Her breath comes in jagged bursts.

Gripping my cock, I slide the tip through her wetness to her swollen clit, and back to her arsehole. Her body tenses more with each swipe until she grits out a frustrated, *"Lando."*

Smirking at her back, I position myself at her entrance.

The visual of my cock sliding inside her soaking pussy combined with her hot, forceful clenches as I bottom out short-circuits my brain. My mind goes blank. The sensation is *unreal.*

I will never think of Paris again without remembering this moment.

An extended "fuucck" comes out as more of a hiss, while all I get from Holiday is a punctured groan.

It's not for me to question how she feels this good, but how the *fuck* does she feel this good? Like her pussy is custom-fit for my dick.

My hips roll and flex as I pull out and ease back in, her body tensing each time like she's holding back. Her fingers claw at the cool marble as she curses under her breath.

"Say it louder, Hol. I want to hear you being loud. You want something, fucking tell me."

She groans again before I hear the words. "Faster. I want it faster. *Harder.*"

"Yeah, I can do that. And my cock is so fucking hard for you."

One hand splayed between her shoulder blades and the other gripping her hip, I slam into her hard, making her cry out. I do it again. And again, until I'm thrusting into her with wild abandon and zero finesse.

She uses her voice until she's hoarse, screaming at me to fuck her.

Expletives penetrate the air. Our skin slaps together. And I *fuck* her like it's my job.

Harder, faster until I can't tell who's shaking more. Her or me.

My balls tighten, and at the first strangling grip of my cock, I pull out, finishing her off with my fingers while I fist myself.

Hot ropes of cum shoot across her back, between her shoulders and on her hair until I'm totally spent and collapse onto her.

"Oh my . . . *fuck* . . . Holiday . . . what the *fuck* was that?"

From somewhere underneath me, a giggle escapes. "Well, I'm definitely relaxed. But I don't know if I can walk."

HOLIDAY

Lando's method of relaxation works until I arrive at the address to meet Marcy.

Marcy rushes to greet me, powering out to the car in heels I always long to take off the moment I step into them.

Ironically, they make her appear more French than American.

"Hi, doll, you look *fabulous*." She ropes me into a hug, kissing both cheeks, something she never does, and I have to pull in my smile. "The room's all set up, and everyone's super excited to meet you. We've done preliminaries, and now that you're here, we'll go through the finer points. There's a presentation."

I nod, doing my best to hold my shit together and not let my nerves get the better of me. I don't even know where they're from. I've been in dozens and dozens of meetings like this one, and I never feel like I'm on the verge of a breakdown.

But this, this feels momentous. I *want* this.

This is the next five years of my life.

This gives me the freedom to choose the future I want,

which is probably why I've convinced myself there are a dozen ways I could fuck it all up before the ink is dry.

Three women, the epitome of what I appreciate as truly French elegance, are waiting inside the front doors. They're immaculate and chic—perfect hair, perfect nails, perfect faces—and each wears a lipstick in varying shades of red.

There's no subtlety when their eyes drop to the floor, slowly traveling back up. It's a move I'm used to, one I always prepare myself for. Am I the same Holiday Simpson they were expecting?

I stand straighter, shoulders back, until eventually, dark red lips flicker in approval.

I high-five myself for the online shopping spree I began at eleven p.m. four nights ago, fueled by panic and a bottle of wine. Otherwise, I wouldn't now be dressed head to toe in Chanel, holding a Dior clutch.

I figured I might not be able to speak French, but I can *spend* French.

There's no rushing because they're far too *laissez-faire* for that, but there is still warmth in how they hold their hands out to greet me now that I've met their IRL standards.

"*Bonjour,* Mademoiselle Simpson." Bright red lips smiles. "Welcome. I'm Marie-Thérèse, head of marketing."

"*Bonjour,*" I reply, reaching my limit on the language. "Please call me Holiday."

She dips her head, sweeping her hand out in front of her, and guides me through reception until we reach a meeting room, where I find another six people waiting around a table laid out with designated seating.

An image of my face is blown up on the wall.

It's one I don't even recall having taken. I'm staring straight at the camera, fresh-faced, makeup-free, but there's determination and steeliness in my expression that instantly bolsters me.

That girl up there is ready to take on anything. Therefore, so am I.

"Welcome, Holiday. We're so happy to have you here," Marie-Thérèse begins with her thick French accent before introducing everyone in the room, whose names I find myself repeating in my head so I don't forget them. "Can we offer you refreshments? You flew this morning, yes? You need *café*."

I nod as everyone else titters with light laughter. The typical icebreaker for these meetings. I excel at small talk, even though inside I cringe at how contrived it comes across.

"Yes, but only from England. I won't say no to coffee, however," I add with a laugh of my own.

"*Bon*."

Coffee appears in front of me, placed purposely between a fresh copy of the contract and a tray of pastel macarons displayed so beautifully I want to take a photo to send to Pierre.

We sip and commence with the preamble of more polite chatter, I'm given instruction on the best places to visit during my trip here, and they tell me how much they like New York, but *only* New York. Not America, obviously.

I get the impression that in the period before I arrived, Marcy has played hardball to the point where they no longer want to acknowledge her. Or they're only acknowledging her because I'm present because when we finally get around to starting the meeting, they're studiously ignoring her.

"*Allors*, let's talk scheduling," Marie-Thérèse says with a flip through a thick notebook. "We have a camera test booked for tomorrow, where we'll assess your skin tone, hair type, what works best, what doesn't. And these initial shots will be used to announce our partnership in January—"

I nod.

"Your agent tells us you have press junkets in November,

and you have some films scheduled for next year we must work around, which is no problem—"

I pause. My jaw grits tight as I stare at Marcy, willing her to look at me so she can see I'm absolutely fuming.

"That's not necessary. And nothing's confirmed next year, so we can schedule what you need."

Several pairs of eyebrows shoot up, and I try not to grit my teeth.

"D'accord." Marie-Thérèse leans across the table, fingers steepled. "Holiday, we see this as a partnership between Hollywood's sweetheart and the world's biggest beauty company. We want to collaborate, we want you to be part of our family, and we believe we will have a great future together."

"Thank you." I smile around the room, and for the first time since I arrived in Paris, I completely relax (don't tell Lando). "I'm so grateful to you for the invitation and the warmest of welcomes. I'm excited to join you all on our journey together."

The final page of notes flicks closed.

All that's left to do is sign the thing, and then I remember . . .

"I'm working with a new charity. It belongs to my . . . er . . . friend." *Friend.* That doesn't sound right. It sounds cold and distant even though none of my friends are either of those things. But referring to Lando as one of them doesn't sit well with me, not after what he just did to me. Not after the past few weeks. "I'd like to offer them a prize that money can't buy, and I'm hoping you can help. A trip to a shoot or the opportunity to spend a day with the makeup artists perhaps? Anything along those lines?"

"Holiday—" Marcy starts, only to be interrupted by Marie-Thérèse.

"*Oui,* we can do that."

"Thank you." I smile and suck in a deep breath. "Then I guess that's everything."

I glance at Marcy to see if she has anything to add, but her pursed lips stay clamped shut.

Everyone else in the room watches me, waiting for me to pick up the pen and sign at the bottom of each page of the freshly drawn-up contract. Which I do.

There's a collective sigh of relief, none more so than mine.

I've done it. I've fucking done it.

I've signed the biggest contract of my career, and after we shake hands and get through another ten minutes of chatter and exit the boardroom, not one part of me is surprised—and relieved—to see Lando waiting.

I fight the urge to run into his arms, but before I get the chance to even say a word, Marcy guides me into another meeting room. Her bag drops on the table with a thud.

"Well done, honey. Great work. This will be a phenomenal stepping stone for you. Play your cards right, and they could keep you in moisturizer for life." Catching sight of herself in the mirror, she taps the skin under her chin.

"Thank you," I reply, and I mean it.

She might be overbearing and exhausting, but she's always fought for the best deals.

"You're welcome. My pleasure." She turns back to me, confident in the six million she's just earned herself. Her diamond stud earrings glint in the light as she opens her bag. "Now let's talk about the next eighteen months, and what happened in there."

"Marcy—"

"I'm not happy about it. After the junkets, we have award season. This first movie deal—"

I step in front of her, place both hands on her shoulders, and look her dead in the eye. "Marcy, I'm not ready to go back to movies. I don't want those offers."

"Holiday—"

"No, I don't want them," I bark. I also don't want to go

around and around in circles while she tries to persuade me to take on more roles. "But—"

Marcy's entire body loosens under my grip. "Of course, there's a *but* . . . We can postpone. They'll push for you. You're an Oscar winner now, for Christ's sake. We can change the start date, whatever you want."

"No," I repeat, firmer this time. "I want to do something different."

"Different?" She must be due a fresh round of Botox because the tiniest hint of a crease appears on her brow. "You mean television? That could work. I can see if there's something in development you can lead. *Apple* would be a good fit for you. Or an anthology season. I'm hearing rumors about *True Detective* coming back—"

I swallow hard. "Theater."

"Theater?"

"Yes. I want to try theater."

She steps away from me, blinking hard. "I thought we talked about this."

"Now we're talking again."

"Broadway?"

"Yes." When I think about Lando in the hallway, I blurt, "Or the West End."

"London? You wanna live in London?"

"I want to try theater," I repeat.

She stares at me. I put on my best resigned expression while her lips purse and relax, purse and relax until eventually she decides not to push the subject further.

"Okay, leave it with me. I'll put some feelers out," she says, slinging her giant bag onto her shoulder. "I'll call you when I have something."

Wrapping me in a final hug, she flings open the door and hurries away at her typical million miles an hour off to her next meeting.

I slowly walk toward Lando as he pushes off the wall. "Did you sign it?"

I nod. "Yes, I did."

His chin tips to the meeting room behind me. "And that? You told her?"

"Also, yes."

He darts forward, and his mouth smacks against mine. "Proud of you, Hollywood."

My eyes fall on where the three lipstick girls are standing halfway down the corridor. "What were they saying? I saw you listening."

"They think you're the most beautiful American they've ever seen, and they're excited to work with you. And they're also wondering how you put up with her." His eyes follow to where Marcy is pushing through the front doors. "Two points I happen to agree with."

My lips twitch. "Hmm."

"Are you ready to go?"

"I am."

I revel in the way Lando's palm fits possessively on the small of my back as he walks me out to a waiting car, where the driver jumps out to open the door. Lando hurries around to the opposite side and slips in before I do.

Two large orange bags are waiting in the center console.

"What are those?"

He taps the biggest one. "This is a package my mother asked me to collect for her. I believe it's a Birkin." He holds up the other. "And this is for you."

"You bought me a present?"

"I did."

I'm too greedy to wait until we get back to the hotel, so I tug the ribbon. Carefully easing out the box inside, I remove the lid and wade through reams of tissue to find a small leather folder with a silver buckle and a heart dangling from a strap.

"You didn't seem to have anything to keep your notes together when you were reading them on the plane."

It's so thoughtful, so typically Lando, that my eyes well up immediately. I can feel him staring at me, his expression filled with confusion.

"Is this a good cry or a sad cry?"

I dab at the tears before they fall. "A good cry. A very good cry. Thank you, it's really so kind of you."

"You're welcome," he replies, reaching behind him, "but perhaps these might cheer you up too."

He's holding a beautiful black box covered in swirls and intricate edging. It's the type of box that typically contains a piece of jewelry. My breath catches somewhere between my lungs.

It's better than jewelry, and immediately, a laugh barrels out of me. Only in Paris would a box of donuts be packaged as beautifully as jewelry.

"Donuts?"

"Of course. We have something to celebrate, don't we?"

I giggle and peer at him from under my lashes. "Yes, Gracie. We do."

* * *

WE SPEND the next two days being as French as we can.

We eat croissants. We drink wine. We *make love.*

When I do my camera test, Lando works from a couch in the corner, watching. Too many times, my focus drifts over to him.

We try pastries that would have Pierre weeping. I buy a little box of the chocolates he says I have to beat before I can move on to making other things. We cycle along the Seine. We visit the Mona Lisa and Versailles.

We laugh and laugh and laugh.

And all the while, there's a niggling in the pit of my stomach that feels a lot like a turning point.

My life is about to go in different directions. I just hope I take the right path.

LANDO

"Have you seen this?"

Grabbing my coffee mug before it topples over, I peer at Alex, then at the piece of paper he's slammed onto my desk, easing it out from under his hand.

It looks to be a land purchase order, forestry for sale. Fifteen hundred acres. One hundred million dollars.

My brow knits together.

He doesn't need my authorization to spend anything under half a billion. I trust him, and he has a sixth sense that seems to have protected him from making any lamentable investments so far.

One hundred million wouldn't usually have him so riled up that he looks like he might burst into flames at any moment.

"Can you fucking believe it?"

My eyes scan the words again. Have I missed something? According to this report, the land is sound, borders the national forest in Colorado, and works on a fifteen-year cycle of forestation. I mean, fifteen hundred acres seems a little small to me, but Alex is much closer to the international sustainability programs than I am, so maybe he has a more ambitious plan . . . but I'm still going to need some help.

"Al, mate, use your words."

His finger jabs at the paper. "That's Haven's place. Wylder Ranch."

I read the words for a third time and a fourth. After the fifth, I look up at him and his expectant—albeit *angry*—expression. I'm guessing he wants me to be as outraged as he is, but I'm slow on the uptake this morning.

I should have stayed in bed. With Holiday. And had coffee. But I've been neglecting my duties of late, working the bare minimum the past few weeks, and the work's piled up. I also want to take Thunder out before it rains this afternoon, so I reluctantly got out of bed before the alarm went off and started work.

"I don't see where it says Wylder Ranch."

He almost stabs a hole in the paper, trying to show me the address. "There. 4539 Talisker Summit Road."

"That's Haven's place?"

He nods, mouth mashed together, glaring at it hard enough I wouldn't be surprised if it turned to dust.

"How d'you know?"

"I went there, remember? Miles came to collect me in the morning. It's a stunning place, incredible views of the valley—"

He peters out into a beleaguered sigh and slumps down into the chair by my desk.

Of the five of us, I'm closest to Alex. Hendricks and Miles have each other, and the age gap with Clementine was too big for me to hang out with her all the time. Alex is the one I grieved with when our father died.

He's the one I trusted to lead the international side of Burlington Estates when I decided I wanted to stay closer to home.

Like me, Alex works hard, takes his role seriously, and

doesn't concern himself with trivialities. Over the years, he's had a couple of semi-serious relationships, but because he's not restrained by the same expectations I am, they always ended without the eagerness to make it down the aisle.

Alex dragged me away from the mess of Caroline and Jeremy. He protected me during those early days when I wanted to drink through the humiliation. He's always been there for me.

But looking at him now, it's abundantly clear that my head's been too stuck up my own arse to see how much Alex has been hurting too. And the *hookup,* as he keeps referring to it, was considerably more than that.

"I don't understand. Did she send you this? Did she finally call you back? She wants you to buy it?"

"No, no, and no. It was in my weekly report of potential investments. It was top of the pile."

"Oh." I'm not entirely sure what to say.

"She worked so hard to keep it."

"After her father died?"

He nods. "Yeah. I don't know why she's selling it now."

Running a hand through my hair, I think about the many reasons I invented for how *not* to take on Burlington when our father died, and I had a mountain of advisers. Something I know Haven doesn't.

"Maybe it was too much for her. You said she does most of it by herself. Maybe that's why you haven't been able to get ahold of her. Perhaps she sold the Christmas tree shop too."

He chews on his lip, running his fingers through his thick stubble. "Do you think?"

"Yes." I nod. And for the first time in a long time, I see a glimmer of hope in his eyes. I briefly wonder if that's what I look like when I'm thinking about Holiday.

Alex picks up my mug, sips, screws his face up at what has to be tepid coffee at best, and puts it back down.

"What were you doing anyway?"

I shake my head. "Nothing important."

There's a pile of newspapers on the desk, the top one of which I was flicking through when Alex stormed in. He picks it up, letting out a low whistle, his eyebrows rising the more he reads.

"Someone's been busy."

I reach for the coffee Alex dismissed. "I've been living my life. It's the paps who've been busy."

"I see that."

Splashed across several pages of the worst British tabloids are photos of Holiday and me—Claridge's, the polo match, Paris, and walking into a restaurant in Berkeley Square when she joined me for my monthly trip to London last week. None from Valentine Nook, for which I'm grateful.

I don't normally read tabloids, but the reason James put it on my desk in the first place is that this particular paper, with this particular article, decided to run a comparison between Caroline and Holiday. It covers everything from their net worths to achievements to jobs to education and background.

But the majority of the article focuses on the canceled wedding and the alarmingly accurate reasons why, alongside a picture of Jeremy and Caroline.

In truth, I'm surprised it hasn't been reported on until now, but as hard as I'm trying to find one, it appears I'm all out of fucks to give.

They made their proverbial bed. They have to lie in it. And according to Jeremy, Caroline's bed is exactly where he wants to be.

And I'm no longer bound by shame and guilt. I'm not going to lie and say that I wasn't wearing a small smile when I was declared the victor of this fucked-up comparison.

"This is a good picture of you." Alex bends the page and shoves it toward me.

It's a photo where Holiday and I are walking along the Seine, taken the evening after her first meeting.

I smile at the memory. "Yes, I like it too."

"Uh-oh, they've made it official. 'Lando Burlington, the eleventh Duke of Oxfordshire and England's Most Eligible Bachelor, is off the market,'" he reads aloud, and I hear him chuckling behind the paper.

He can laugh all he wants. I wait for him to reach the bottom of the page, and when he does, he snorts loudly.

"*Ah* . . . the crown has been passed to me again."

"Congratulations."

"Thank you." He tosses the paper contemptuously onto the chair beside him and bows his head. He's silent for a moment, crossing his legs, picking off a piece of thread from his jeans and dropping it on the floor. "What's happening with you two?"

I knew the question was coming, I just wasn't sure *who* it would come from. Since Holiday and I returned from Paris, every family member has acted with uncharacteristic indifference, even Miles. Which means all of them are chomping at the bit for information.

"What do you mean?"

"C'mon, Lando, you know what I mean. It's great and all that you're happy again. I love it. God knows something needed to pull you out of the funk. But *that*"—he points at the paper he tossed—"is more than something. Miles said he's seen you leave Bluebell every morning this week."

I *knew* it. I knew they've all been gossiping about me like they have nothing better to do. I just wish I knew what the answer to Alex's question was.

"I didn't realize Miles ever woke up early enough to spy on his neighbors."

It's a pointless deflection because now that he's begun, Alex is obviously going to take his role as family informant seriously. He can't go back empty-handed, and he continues like I haven't said a word.

"Lando, you're together all the time. What are you going to do when she leaves? Is this just a prolonged friends-with-benefits arrangement? Or more?"

It's a question I've been asking myself.

I know Holiday's time in Valentine Nook is finite. I might not want to admit it, and I certainly don't like it. But I *know.*

Her life and career are back in America, while mine is here. I've been trying to figure out a plan for us when the time came for her to leave, but there isn't one that doesn't involve either of us spending half our life on a plane.

I don't want to be stealing moments between all the publicity and photo shoots, and months on a set wherever she happens to be in the world at that moment. And I doubt she does either.

Some mornings, I wake up next to her, blond hair fanned around the pillow watching her eyelashes flutter as she dreams, her lips parting with each breath, and think I'll give it a few days until I see her again. No big deal.

Only to find myself back on the doorstep of Bluebell Cottage by lunchtime.

One thing's for sure, I no longer have an aversion to going inside. In the space of a few weeks, we've fucked more in that house than I ever had before.

I can't get enough of her.

In the end, I say, "I don't know."

"This isn't just a crush anymore. You're falling for her."

Suddenly, I'm not so amused. I don't need my brother projecting his shit onto me and snap out a reply, "It's not the same as you and Haven."

His brows sink low, and I see a concern I wish wasn't there, especially when he says, "I know. It's going to hurt so much worse."

"I'm *fine*."

My tone is enough of a warning to him not to push any further. He nods and gets up from his chair. "I'm buying it, by the way."

Because his eyes are staring at the pile of papers on my desk, for a moment I think he's joking about the crown for his newly minted England's Most Eligible Bachelor title.

Then I realize he isn't.

"I'm not sure that's a good idea."

"It is."

"Al—"

"Look, even without Haven, that land is incredible, and if we have it, then it stops anyone else from taking it and slapping on another ten hotels that Aspen doesn't need. We can keep it as it's supposed to be. You said yourself you thought a ski lodge there would be good."

"A *ski lodge*, not a tree farm."

"I'll find something to do with it, but I'm telling you now, there's no way Haven wants her parents' place sold for hotels. I *know* her."

I shake my head. "Al, c'mon, be reasonable. You knew her for a week, and you haven't heard from her since."

His stare hardens, along with his jaw, reminding me why he's known as the most stubborn of all of us.

"I *know* her. She didn't just lose one parent, she lost both. She's not selling because she wants to. She was working all the hours to fund keeping it." He throws his hands up, sweeping them around my study. "Take this place. We don't have to worry about money, but that doesn't stop us from working all hours to keep Dad's legacy intact."

My eyes drop to the paper on the chair, open on the picture of Holiday and me.

We both know Alex buying the land has nothing to do with

investment and everything to do with getting Haven's attention. And I realize if the situation was reversed, and Holiday had ghosted me, I'd do anything to try to get her to speak to me again.

"Okay, buy it. If that will help you, if that's what you think is best."

"Thank you." He stops with his hand on the door and leaves me with a parting shot. "You know, you deserve to be happy too, Lan. Try to let yourself."

* * *

I'M STILL THINKING about Alex's words when I make my way over to the yard later in the afternoon to ride Thunder. I haven't called ahead. It's been a while since I've tacked him up myself, and I like seeing him in the stable when I arrive, popping his head over the door to greet me.

I also haven't checked in with Holiday. I want to prove to myself that I can go for a couple of hours and not behave like some pining teenager. I reason that I don't need to know if she's enjoying her day because I already know she will be, as she'd packed up a basket of apples and pears to take over to Pierre.

But the universe has other plans for me.

For a second, I stare at the curve of her legs, imagining them wrapped around me later, just like they were this morning. Her jumper rides up as she raises on her tiptoes and brushes a piece of straw from Thunder's forelock, exposing a sliver of tanned skin I've run my tongue along in recent days.

When he lowers his head to help her, she kisses the white blaze down the front and I'm suddenly consumed with jealousy.

Jealous of my horse.

She spins around from the sound of me laughing at what a

fucking idiot I am, and her smile hits me so squarely in the chest my mind goes blank.

"Hey."

I walk toward her, slowly like I'm savoring the time. "What are you doing here?"

"I had extra apples for Thunder and Sunday. When I'm done with Pierre, I always stop by on my way home."

Of course she does.

"No wonder Thunder's getting fat," I tease.

She slaps me playfully in the chest. I grab her before she can step back, wrapping my arms around her and breathing in her scent of sugar and cinnamon.

"Don't body-shame Thunder."

I reply by taking her face in my hands.

My chat with Alex this morning has me in my head about her leaving, and I kiss her like it's the last time I'll see her.

I want to know how it feels, how I'll feel to have her in my arms one last time.

I sense the moment Holiday realizes it's not a quick kiss, her fists gripping my shirt while I hold her. My tongue sweeps around her mouth, tangling us together, melting into one another. My teeth graze her lips, and I swallow her moans, wanting more.

I will always want more.

We kiss long enough for Thunder to snort with impatience at being ignored. When I let go, her eyes take a second to focus while she catches her breath.

"What was that for?"

"No reason. Just because." I glance at Thunder and clear my throat so she can't see how bad I am at lying. "I'm going to take him out. Do you want to come on Sunday?"

"Sure, can you wait for me to change? I'll be twenty minutes."

I nod. "I'll get them ready."

"Okay." She leans up, plants one more kiss on me, then sprints to her car without another word.

The moment she's out of sight, Thunder nudges me, rests his head on my neck, and whickers a deep sigh.

"Yes, buddy. I know."

Alex is wrong. I'm not falling for her.

I've already fallen.

HOLIDAY

When it rains in England, it *rains*.

Miraculously, the roof is holding up. I've been staring at the crack in the ceiling, daring it to leak, but so far, it's been drip-free. I'm not so sure about the windows because they're taking a beating this morning.

It's so loud I'm amazed Lando's sleeping through it. Sometimes he sleeps so deeply that I have to stop myself from checking his pulse. Today, the quiet snoring tells me all I need to know, and when I slip out of bed, he doesn't stir.

In lieu of a robe, I snatch up the cashmere blanket resting on the chair in the corner, wrap it around myself, and tiptoe quietly downstairs in search of coffee. The last of summer's petals litter the backyard, rain bounces off the patio as it pelts down, and puddles form underneath the fruit trees.

As I'm staring out of the back doors while the coffee machine whirs and chugs, I'm overcome with a feeling of deep sadness.

Summer is over. Fall is coming. The change of seasons is a stark realization that it's getting closer to the day I'll be leaving this little cottage behind.

I know what leaving is like. I'm good at leaving. I'm used to being in one place, working my ass off all hours of the day and night, then saying goodbye.

But it's never felt like this.

This is different.

Emptiness builds in my chest because I don't want Valentine Nook to become one more memory. Somewhere along the way, it stopped being a place I escaped to and started to feel more like a home. A beginning.

I've found a community I've never really had before, where people stop and talk to me—not because I'm famous—because they want to tell me about a new litter of puppies their dog had, give me a jar of honey they just harvested or fresh eggs from their chickens. Or the one I love most—an invite for afternoon tea.

I'm not ready to go. I want to keep it, and I need to figure out how.

I want to see the village in every season. I want to shoot the shit with Eddie at the end of my day. I want to go to London with Lando every month.

When I head back upstairs, it's with one trudge at a time, and I slip under the comforter without Lando ever knowing I was gone.

For the next hour, I watch raindrops smash against the windows. The white noise-esque ambiance both hypnotizes and feels strangely comforting as I lie there trying to map out a plan for the next few months before I have to return to work.

How do I stay? Would Lando want me to stay? Is what we have purely because there's an end date to it? We've built a bubble that could easily burst with the slightest bit of extra pressure, and I'm not sure what that pressure looks like.

My brain aches with questions that have no answers, and in the end, the pull of watching Lando becomes too strong.

I'm obsessed with the way his entire face smooths out when

he sleeps. The weight of responsibilities he carries during the day is gone. His brow relaxes, his jaw softens, and even his beautiful mouth appears too sweet to whisper the filth he knows I love to hear.

If I could draw, I'd sketch him every day, but sadly, I wasn't blessed with that talent.

"I know you're staring at me." His gruff voice breaks through my thoughts, and I have to bite down my grin.

"You don't know shit."

"Oh, you think?" he replies, his eyes still shut.

"Yeah."

Quick as a flash, his fingers shoot out and dig into my ribs, tickling them against my sides until I'm laughing so hard I wheeze.

"Stop. *Stahhp.*"

"Admit you were staring."

I'm laughing so hard I can't speak, and when his fingers move again, I gasp out the words, "Fine, I was staring at you."

"I knew it."

The torture immediately stops, and I'm tugged into his side. His eyes open, and over my shoulder, he spies the coffee mug.

"How long have you been awake?"

"A little while. The rain woke me."

He peers to the window, only now noticing the apocalypse outside. "Hmmm. Guess summer's officially over."

My chest tightens at that statement, and the urge to cry becomes overwhelming to the point I need to turn away.

Lando shuffles the pillow underneath his head, punches it a few times for extra fluffiness, and slides his arm underneath. I'm instantly distracted by the flex of his bicep, and the tears dry up.

"What's that brain of yours thinking about?"

My mouth mashes together. He's so close I can see my

reflection in his big blue eyes, and the way they always soften when he looks at me.

I debate whether to tell him I've been awake for hours, mentally juggling destinations, time zones, and travel time. How long I'll be away from Valentine Nook for my junkets—from him—and how long I can stay when I return. That I'm fantasizing a world in which we can be together, where I don't leave permanently, and Valentine Nook is my base instead of Los Angeles.

A world where I get to wake up next to Lando every day.

But I'm not ready to admit it yet. I also don't know if that's what Lando would want.

"I'm thinking about lunch," I say instead.

"*Lunch?*"

"Yeah, I want to try to make one of your Sunday lunches."

Lando's slash of dark brows rises into his hairline, and his lips twitch because this is a *bold* undertaking.

Sunday lunch, I've discovered, is a ritual in England. One they take very seriously.

I hadn't noticed it so much during the summer, but I walked into The One True Love a couple of weeks ago to find it the busiest I've ever seen. Customers were being turned away due to the lack of available tables. At the other end of the high street, Cupid's Arrow was experiencing the same.

The following Sunday was no different.

"Ooh, Hollywood." Air hisses between his teeth as he sucks it in. "Do you know what you're saying?"

"Yes. It's Sunday lunch. Meat and vegetables." I push out of his arms and sit up. "I think I can handle it. And you know what? I'm feeling confident. Your mom is away, so why not invite everyone over here?"

The crease on his forehead deepens. "By everyone, do you mean my siblings? Are you sure?"

My mouth purses at the skepticism on his face, which only

makes me more determined. It's time I used the kitchen for more than making coffee and baking pies.

"*Everyone.* Isn't this what you Brits do on a Sunday when it's raining? And I don't want to go outside in this . . ." I wave a hand toward the window where visibility is dim. "So why not bring it here? I thought Sunday lunch was about family?"

An amused grin tugs at the corners of his mouth. "Well"—he leans over, smacking his lips to mine—"all right then. We might make an English woman of you yet."

His words are as warming as the cashmere blanket I tossed back on the chair. "That might be the best compliment you've ever given me."

Lando sits up against the headboard and snatches his phone from the nightstand.

"What are you doing?"

"Calling in the troops," he replies, his fingers typing rapidly on the screen. "It's ten now. Shall we say lunch at three? And what're we cooking?"

"What?"

He glances back at me, his fingers paused. "Hollywood, correct me if I'm wrong, but I believe your fridge is empty. If we're making Sunday lunch, we'll need the meat and vegetables. All you have in your cupboards are the ingredients for pastry."

"And that won't work?"

His headshake is so solemn, I can't tell if he's doing it ironically or I got my sarcasm wrong. "I'm afraid not."

"Well then, I'll go to the grocery store and buy it all. You're smart, you know that?"

"I do." He finishes typing his message, tosses the phone to the side, and turns back to me. "But you know *how* I know that?"

"How?"

"Because I'm here with you."

I stifle a giggle. "Wow. Smart *and* cheesy. Isn't it a bit early to be using lines like that?"

"Hmm. I don't know. Let's see, shall we?" His fingers scratch through his beard as he thinks. After a brief pause, he says, "Am I in heaven, or is there an angel in my bed?"

I don't know how he keeps a straight face. It's literally my job to control my reactions, and I'm struggling to do so.

"Actually, this is my bed."

"Ah, true. Okay, well . . ." He taps a finger against his lip. "Nope, that won't work . . ." Leaning over, he peers at my dress on the floor. "Nope, already there." His cheeks puff out with a long breath. "This is tougher than I thought."

"Oh, buddy, it's a good thing you're pretty."

"Yeah, how pretty?"

"Pretty enough for me to do this." My hand slips under the comforter until I reach bare skin.

I softly graze along his shaft, and he lets out a quiet groan as I cup his balls and squeeze gently. The feel of his cock thickening in my palm sets off a throbbing deep in my pelvis. An intense tugging that instantly floods between my thighs.

I love the way Lando reacts to my touch and the way my body revels in the power I hold over him. It's nothing I've ever experienced before—the insatiable need to make him feel good because it makes *me* feel good.

"Fuck," he hisses. "I must be really fucking pretty."

"You are."

His cock is velvet and steel, smooth and straight. If it were possible for dicks to be called beautiful, Lando's would be. Gripping the length, I slowly pump.

"Ahhh . . . *fuck*, Hollywood . . . that's so *good*."

His words spur me on, and I want to bring this guy to his knees. Literally. I want to watch his face as he comes with my name on his lips.

His balls tighten as he gets closer. My fist moves quicker,

and Lando groans louder. I'm so caught up with making Lando come that it takes me a second to realize he's groaning from frustration, because someone's banging on the door.

"Ignore it. They'll go away," I whisper, twisting my palm over the flat end of his dick, covering myself in precum.

But when the banging becomes loud enough to compete with the sound of the rain, the mood is officially killed.

"Hol. *Hol.* You there? Lemme in."

"I'm going to kill her," Lando snarls, and his eyes screw tight.

Bang. Bang. Bang. "I need to pee."

My grip eases, causing another round of protests from Lando. "No, baby, *please*. Don't stop. I'm so close."

"Babe, your sister is outside." I jump out of bed and grab the blanket again. "We'll pick it up later."

"Tell her she's disinvited to lunch."

Rushing down the stairs, I open the door to find Clemmie standing outside, bedraggled and soaked to the skin. There's not a dry inch of her, and when she drops four large shopping bags on the floor and pushes past me to the bathroom, she leaves a trail of tiny puddles behind.

I lug her bags into the kitchen and deposit them on the counter. How did she even manage to carry so many when they're *this* heavy? Tossing a tea towel on the floor to mop up the water, I run upstairs to get her some dry clothes.

She's switched on the coffee machine when I get back down.

"God, I'm so sorry. Something about the rain makes me really need to pee."

"Here." I hand over a pair of my brother's sweatpants, which I packed by accident, and a couple of cozy sweaters I bought online last week. "Your legs are longer than mine, but these should be okay."

"Wow, thank you. That's really kind," she says, pushing the shopping bags across the kitchen counter. "I brought lunch."

Clemmie strips off and switches her wet clothes for dry ones while I examine the contents of the bags—an array of vegetables, a chicken, a side of beef, a leg of lamb, lemons, fresh herbs, several bottles of wine, and three tubs of different-flavored ice cream.

There's no way I'd have thought to buy all this.

"Is this all for today?"

Clemmie nods with a smile. "So there's a choice."

"How did you get here so quickly?"

"I was in the store when Lando messaged. I know you're cooking, but I thought I could help. And remember when I said I make a mean roast chicken . . ." She shrugs her shoulders. "Surprise. Sorry, is that okay?"

Glancing down at all the ingredients spread across the counter, maybe Lando was onto something when he asked if I knew what I was getting myself into. I don't think I did.

One look at Clemmie's eager face, and I yank her into a tight hug. "Thank you. Oh my god, thank you. Yes, help. Please. Roast chicken sounds perfect, and you know . . . the rest."

"Really?"

"Yes. I must have woken up thinking I was Martha Stewart or something. Lando asked me if I knew what I was doing, and I said yes. But I wonder if maybe I don't."

"Well." Clemmie chuckles, easing from my grip. "I can't think of a better reason to do it together than to prove my brother wrong."

"Oh, thank god." I sigh with relief and stick a cup under the coffee machine. "D'you want one?"

Clemmie nods as she puts the ice cream in the freezer. "Yes, please. I suppose it's a bit early to start drinking."

I'm tempted. But I also know that I can't drunk cook my first English Sunday lunch. It gives me a weird buzz that I'm about to do something I've never done before. On the rare occasions I've hosted dinner parties at my place, I've always used caterers or dished out preprepared food. Never *cook* cooked. And I've been so busy baking with Pierre that I haven't yet gotten around to learning the rest.

"Maybe later," I reply, staring at the mountain of food. "How long does this take? We have just over four hours."

"That's plenty of time. We can enjoy our coffees first and decide what we're having." She turns as Lando walks in, looking less than happy. Not that Clemmie seems to notice, or perhaps she's used to him, so she chooses to ignore it and flashes him a big smile instead. "Morning, Lanny. Are you sick?"

"No."

"Why are your lips blue?"

"Cold shower," he grunts, then drops a kiss on my head and takes a large sip from my coffee cup while I hold in a smile. "What are you doing here?"

"I was in the Valentine Cook when you messaged, so I offered my services. Holiday and I are making lunch together."

His eyes flick to mine, twinkling with amusement, and I know exactly what he's thinking.

"In that case, there are definitely too many cooks in here. If you don't mind, I'll nip home and check on Thunder."

I shake my head. "I don't mind."

"Excellent, and that means we can discuss the Fall Ball," Clemmie says through a slurp of her coffee.

"Then I won't hurry back. Don't burn the place down. Remember, the roof is thatched."

I glance out the window, where the rain still hasn't let up.

"I don't think we need to worry about anything catching fire."

* * *

I HAVE a newfound respect for Martha Stewart.

How the hell does she make it look so easy?

It's taken me an hour just to clean the kitchen up. Even with Clemmie's help, we barely had enough time. There's a chicken *and* a side of beef in the oven, the vegetables went in right before Clemmie left to change into clean clothes, and after convincing me I didn't need to stare at the stove while she was gone, I did the same.

I've learned you don't need to be good at cooking. You just need to be good at math because you have to get your timings in precise order for lunch to be ready exactly the way it's supposed to be ready.

I can't remember when I was last so stressed or worked so hard, and I'm not talking about movies. They're demanding but for a different reason. I've busted my ass today.

But I feel like I've accomplished something I don't have a natural talent for, especially the apple pie I spent an hour painstakingly putting together with latticework, just as Pierre taught me.

I'm proud of myself.

I peer around the table I've laid out—simple, classy, totally Martha—I even finished it off with a couple of rose heads from the front yard, knocked from their stems by the rain, which I drop into a few Mason jars. Thanks, *Pinterest*.

Everything happens at once—the timer for the oven goes off as the front door opens, and in sprints Max with a bunch of flowers as big as he is.

"Here!" he shouts, thrusting them at me. I catch them just in time before he rushes back to the front door, where everyone else is entering at a normal pace, including Hamish.

"Sorry. Sorry," Clemmie pants, rushing to shut off the beeping before I can, "I was leaving, then everyone jumped in the car with me, and it obviously took another ten minutes."

I'm still standing in the hallway when Lando walks in,

looking better than anything I could serve up on a platter. "Something smells good," he says, pulling me into him and running his nose along my jaw. "Mmm."

The goose bumps are immediate, and I will never tire of being in his arms. Of him.

"Uncle Lando's kissing Holiday," shouts Max, pointing directly at us in case no one realized we're here.

"Yes, I fucking am," Lando mutters, doing exactly that *again*.

Max's finger stays where it is. "Uncle Lando said a bad word."

"What are you? MI5?"

Max stares at Lando, pondering the question, but runs off to join Clemmie in the kitchen before he decides on an answer.

"Well, isn't this lovely? Don't think I've been invited around for Sunday lunch before," Miles announces, who's last through the door after Hendricks even though he lives the closest.

"There's a reason for that."

"Because you can't handle the fun I bring?"

"Yes," Lando deadpans with a hefty eye roll. "That's why."

Before Miles retorts, I ease out from under Lando's arm, telling them to go pour themselves a drink. I hurry into the kitchen, where I find Clemmie has stopped the beeping and is pulling the chicken out of the oven.

"I'll help," I say, putting the flowers down and grabbing oven mitts to remove the rest. I almost trip over Hamish positioned in front of the kitchen island because he knows that's where the food is going. "Jeez."

By the time we've transferred everything into the cute dishes I found in the cabinet and taken it all through to the dining table, where everyone's patiently waiting, I'm no longer hungry. Hendricks has already started carving, Max is piling roast potatoes onto his plate to the point there won't be any left for anyone else, and Clemmie looks as beat as me.

Plopping into the seat next to Lando, I'm curious why Miles

and Alex are staring at the bottle of wine I opened. It's a red that Lando and I shared at The One True Love. I went back to see if Eddie had more, because I remembered the look in Lando's eyes as he took hold of the bottle. For whatever reason, it seemed special to him, and I wanted to share it again.

"Is everything okay?"

"This wine, Holiday, where did you get it?"

I thumb to Lando. "We had it a while back, and I really liked it. I asked Eddie if he had more and bought some."

"It was our father's favorite," Miles replies so quietly it feels like a punch in the gut.

"Oh, I . . . I'm sorry." My head snaps to Lando, who's looking at his brother. "I didn't realize. I just knew Lando liked it. I hope that's okay," I stutter a reply, feeling a little lost for words. I'm such an idiot. Why did I not ask him why he liked it so much?

Miles silently puts the bottle down. He takes three long strides and pulls me into a hug. My arms swing at my side, too shocked to do anything else.

"Thank you," he whispers in my ear. "And thank you for bringing Lando back."

"Wow, did I just see Milo hug a girl without trying to feel her up?" Alex drawls when Miles steps away.

"Hey, I would never do that," Miles grumbles, only for the corner of his lip to twitch, "but if she can resist my charms, then at least we know she's serious about the duke."

Lando drops his head with a shake. "You're such a dick."

I don't need to look down to know he's laced our fingers together. When our eyes meet, and he mouths, "*Thank you*," my chest feels like it's cracking open.

For two minutes, no one speaks. The only sounds are the knocking of silverware against china as vegetables are scooped onto plates, people deciding between chicken or beef, and Max hungrily chomping away. I have yet to put anything on my plate, but I'm getting a perverse pleasure in watching everyone eat.

Finally, Clemmie swallows her mouthful and sits back. "I think this is the best roast I've ever had."

"Are you allowed to say that if you've cooked it?" I ask.

"Yes, I think so." She picks up her wine and turns to her nephew. "Maxy, what do you think?"

"I love it." He's taking another scoopful of potatoes, which has Hendricks shaking his head in dismay and moving the rest from his reach.

"Hey, Maxy, yours is the only vote I'm looking for." I laugh.

"It's the only one that ever counts," Lando adds, turning to me with a wink.

Miles pats his stomach. "How have I only just discovered I have a neighbor who cooks like this, and she's leaving?"

I pick up my wine, ignoring the lead weight I feel inside me. "It was Clemmie really, but I made the pie for later."

"Where are you going?" Max asks.

I smile at him, taking comfort in Lando's hand resting on my thigh. "Back to America, where my home is."

Although now I'm not quite sure that's true.

His little face scrunches up, and he leans forward. "But how will you kiss Uncle Lando in America?"

Lando splutters next to me, and I pray my cheeks are already rosy enough from cooking for anyone to see me blushing. Everyone else is openly laughing.

"A question we all want to know the answer to, Maxy." Alex snickers.

"Al . . ."

"It's valid. How will we all cope without our resident thespian now that we know she can cook too?" Miles adds, ignoring Lando's warning tone. "I vote she stays."

"Milo, you're dramatic enough for everyone," Lando snaps. "If it were between you and Holiday for an award, you'd win."

I snort out a giggle because it's true. I might be the professional actress, but Miles is the drama queen.

"You think?" Miles clasps his hands to his chest and gives me an idea.

"Wait," I order, rushing out of my seat and up the stairs two at a time to my bedroom. "One sec."

At the back of the closet is the box Ashley sent, which I never unpacked. Ripping off the tape, I ease out the biggest of the leather presentation cases and run back downstairs.

I hold it out to Miles while everyone else looks on curiously.

"Here. For tonight only, this can be yours."

He cautiously removes it from my hands, placing it on the table in front of him. Pushing the clasp, Miles lifts the lid and peers inside. His eyes flick to mine, one thick dark brow raised.

Gripping his fist around the statue, he eases it out. "I'd like to thank the Academy—"

Clemmie gasps, her hands shooting forward. "Holy shit, your Oscar. Miles, gimme."

He snatches it out of her reach. "Nope. It's mine. Holiday gave it to me. You all heard her."

"Milo, come on. Let me have a turn."

"I have a BAFTA and a Golden Globe upstairs too, if either of those work."

Clemmie's eyes widen. "Ooh, Golden Globe."

Laughing, I run back upstairs and retrieve the rest, then place them on the table. I watch everyone fight over who gets what first, and it's so much fun. A familiarity about it reminds me of my own family—the bickering, the warmth, the love.

Not that Lando could move to America anyway because he has Burlington to run, but I can't imagine him ever leaving his family. Even the idea of us meeting somewhere in the middle for a month at a time seems far-fetched as I sit here and zone out. I'm once again thinking about the list of options I mentally pulled together before Lando woke up this morning and strike half of them off.

"You're so talented, Holiday. You really deserved these," Clemmie says, holding the BAFTA mask up to her face.

"Thank you." I smile at her, but it's fake. I want to cry.

"I agree. New York was a masterpiece." Lando takes my hand and brings it to his lips. "And you were pivotal."

My head spins around. "You watched it?"

He grins from ear to ear. He's as proud of himself as I was when we finished cooking lunch. "I've watched everything you've done. Took me a month, but I watched them all."

My mouth drops. I'm speechless. I have no words. They're all gone. He's never once mentioned it. Not even a hint.

"My favorite is the one where you're dating that guy from Boston, but you love rival baseball teams." Clemmie giggles. "Best romcom ever."

"Nope." Lando shakes his head. "Hated that one. I like New York."

"Only because there's no kissing in it," Miles shoots out, before adding, "It wasn't my favorite."

"What's your next project?" Alex asks, filling everyone's glasses.

No one notices how much he's pouring because all eyes are on me for my answer. Even Clemmie's, and she already knows everything.

"Um . . . well, I recently signed a beauty campaign that begins in the new year. I don't know where the first shoot is yet, though. But acting-wise, there are no movies right now. I want to try my hand at theater, so my agent is looking for something suitable."

I *hope* she is. She messaged me to say something potential had come to her and she'd let me know once she had more information, but that was over a week ago.

Under the table, Lando squeezes my hand.

"Well, count us in for the first night." Alex smiles, though he's looking at Lando.

"And in other news," Miles says with a grin so wide his dimples disappear into crevices, "did you hear Al's been on a shopping spree? He's bought Haven's place."

From Clemmie's gasp, I can tell this is new news to her. It's new news to me too, but I'm not quite as invested in the story. Everyone's heads turn to Alex, whose smile has turned to a glare directed at Lando.

"I didn't say a word," he protests with his hands held high. "I swear."

Alex runs his fingers along the edge of his wineglass and lets out a resigned sigh. "Whatever, I don't care."

"I support it. That place will make a great yard. Get some winter polo in over there."

"We're not turning it into a yard. And I didn't buy it for the company. I bought it privately, for me. Or will have once the paperwork goes through."

Hendricks lets out a low whistle down at the other end of the table. "Have you heard from Haven? Does she know you're buying it?"

Alex shakes his head. "Nope. And can we please change the subject?"

"Sure thing." Miles turns his attention to his nephew. "Maxy, what do you want to talk about?"

Max taps his little chubby finger against his chin while he thinks. "Um, Hamish chewed Granny's shoe, but I'm not supposed to tell anyone."

For a second, it's silent enough that you can only hear the raindrops. Then Alex bursts out laughing, followed by Max, and like dominoes, everyone goes until we're all laughing. And that's how the rest of the afternoon continues, through more bottles of wine, apple pie, and all three tubs of ice cream until the sun goes to bed and the rain stops.

I have a feeling we could have gone for longer if it hadn't been Max's bedtime. Because they all came together in one car, they have to leave together too. By the time we say goodbye, I know it's not just Lando I'm going to miss dearly when I leave this place.

Lando closes the front door and wraps his arms around my waist. "Bravo, Hollywood. I can't believe you survived that and came out unscathed. In fact, I think my siblings would happily trade me for you."

"I don't know about that." I chuckle. "I think they like you a lot."

"I think I like *you* a lot. Even more than I did this morning."

"Oh yeah?"

"Yeah." He nods, and I'm immediately taken back to what we started but never finished.

The moment I peer up at him, I'm done thinking about how sad I feel or what I'm leaving behind. For now, I need to live in the present and keep my promise of picking up where we left off.

"Hey, I love your sweater," I say, tracing a pattern on the front of his chest.

He glances down at the black ribbed cashmere. "*This*? Um, thanks."

Sinking my teeth into my lip, I hit him with my best fluttering lashes and drop my tone. "Yeah, and I'll love it even more on my floor later."

A flash of Lando's baby blues is followed by a panty-melting smirk. "It's a good thing you're pretty."

"How pre—"

My question turns to a squeal as Lando throws me over his shoulder and makes for the stairs.

"I'm about to show you, and this time, no one's interrupting us."

LANDO

It's alarming how quickly I've gotten used to leaving Holiday in bed while I get ready for the day. Or how many mornings I've stayed in bed working because I wasn't ready to leave.

Getting up and getting out has always been my ethos. I have a business to run, and it won't happen if I'm not in the yard or at my desk by eight o'clock. Except, *miraculously*, the world doesn't stop if I arrive at the yard by ten instead.

Over the past few weeks, it's become harder and harder to slip away while she stays sleeping, which has everything to do with the day Holiday is scheduled to leave. It's no longer months away, but weeks. Seven, to be precise.

On the flip side, the length of time she's been in Valentine Nook has turned from weeks to months. So many months it's hard to remember what it was like here without her. It's hard to remember the person I was before she burst into my life with her celebration donuts, Hollywood smile, and huge heart.

In the hallway, the floor creaks, and my head pivots to see Holiday walking through the open door. She's all legs under the white T-shirt which barely covers her arse, blond hair mussed up from a night of sleep, and the smile that rivals the sun breaking the horizon.

"Coffee, Your Grace."

She steps carefully onto the bed, managing not to spill a drop from the two mugs she always fills to the brim.

"Thank you."

She drops down, cross-legged. One of her knees rests against me, and I reach out to stroke up her thigh where her Californian tan has disappeared as quickly as the summer. She says nothing as she picks up a book from her bedside table and opens it. It's one of four books she has on the go, and there's something about how we can sit in silence—her reading, me working—when we can quite as easily spend a day nonstop talking.

And we can *talk*. We talk, and laugh, and have sex. It's all incredible. But *this*, this quietness, there's an intimacy to it I've never had before. It fills my chest with a kaleidoscope of colors, warming me to the depths of my soul and reaffirming what I've known for a long time. Maybe since the day I met her.

I love Holiday Simpson.

But typically, our peace is interrupted by a ringing. Holiday drops her book, picks up her phone, and looks at me with a quiet kind of excitement.

"It's Marcy. She might have theater news. I should get it."

I glance at the clock. "What time is it where she is?"

"She gets up super early. Or goes to bed late."

Why doesn't that surprise me? From the little I've seen and what Holiday's told me about her, it doesn't seem like the woman sleeps.

"You take it. I'm going to jump in the shower," I tell her, dropping a kiss on her head.

I pad into the bathroom and stand in front of the mirror. Out of habit, I open the drawer for my toothbrush and razor, but when I look down, they're not there because this isn't my house anymore. I don't live here, and I stopped shaving.

"Idiot." I chuckle with a shake of my head and pick up my toothbrush from the counter *where I left it last night.*

I'm reaching for the tap when I hear an excited squeal, and my ears prick. Peeking around the door, I see Holiday where I left her, but with a smile lighting up her face. Hell, it lights up the entire room as she nods along with whatever Marcy's telling her.

"Hmm, seriously? With no audition? Holy shit, that's amazing . . . yes . . . yup. Marcy, you're incredible—"

I turn back to the sink, and the smile on my face is as big as Holiday's.

I'm guessing she's got something lined up with the theater, and I'm so fucking proud of her.

And not just from this. I've never met anyone who's so sure of themselves. So driven to go after what they want and stand up for what's good for them in all aspects of their life. She needed a break, she took it. Had a fall, got back up. Wanted to learn something new, and now she's on her way to being Pierre's pastry chef.

It's more than I've ever done, that's for sure.

My path was laid before I was born, and I've never deviated from it.

I expect her to join me in the shower, but after ten minutes, I get out, and she's still talking. Only this time, her tone is vastly different. Harder. For a second, I don't recognize it as hers.

"No. *No,*" she repeats, but louder. "Marcy, I was very clear . . . I have an engagement . . . I can't leave before then—"

I stop running the towel over my hair and stand still.

"Fuck, Marcy, that's not fair. They can't do this—"

The pitch of Holiday's voice changes. Becomes higher.

"No. I'm not doing the shows. Someone else can . . . I was

told the end of November, not the beginning . . . I can't leave yet . . . *No* . . . Do something . . . You're my agent, for fuck's sake."

My stomach drops. The beginning of November is three weeks away. I wait for more confirmation of what I don't want to hear, but instead, there's a loud thud, followed by a muffled sob.

When I come around the door, I see her phone on the floor across the other side of the bedroom. Quietly, I retrieve it and place it back on the bedside table.

"Hollywood? What's going on?"

Her neck crooks toward me as I sit on the bed. Her face is screwed with frustration, and she swipes away a tear.

I wait while she gathers her thoughts, teeth worrying her lip. I want to tell her it can't be that bad, but I don't. The beginning of November is still ringing in my ears.

Throwing back the covers, she pulls her knees to her chest and wraps her arms around them. "I . . . uh . . ." She takes a deep breath and flashes a smile that doesn't reach her eyes. "Do you want the good news or the bad news?"

"Let's go with the good news."

She nods. "There's a new production starting of *Cat On A Hot Tin Roof*. They want me for the role of Stella. Rehearsals begin in April. Opens in July. I have to meet with the director, but apparently, I don't have to audition."

My mouth drops. I forget about the phone launched across the room or the fact there's still bad news to come. She got what she wanted.

"That's incredible. I'm so proud of you."

She nods. "Yes. It really is. On Broadway. My name will be in lights."

"Where it belongs," I tell her, though my excitement deflates slightly. "New York isn't far—"

"No, it's not."

"Is that the bad news? New York?" I grin. "It's not that bad." My words peter off when another tear falls down her cheek.

"My schedule for the press junkets has been brought forward a month."

"Okay . . ."

"I have to leave the night of the Fall Ball."

I don't know what to say, and I feel like I'm missing something, which probably comes from me knowing absolutely nothing about the movie industry. I don't want her to leave early, but then I guess all it means is she'll return sooner.

"Okay, how long is a junket? A week? Can you come back after?"

"They'll take me up to mid-December. Because I won last year, the studio wants to push me out more." Her lips mash and twist.

"Six weeks isn't so bad."

"After that, award season begins again, and it's going to be busy. *Intense.* I'll be traveling . . ."

From the way she's chewing her lip again, I almost don't want to ask. "How long is award season?"

"Finishes mid-March."

"March?" That's five months away.

Half an hour ago, I had seven weeks to figure out what to do when Holiday left. Now I have three weeks before she's gone for five months. A month ago, I was of the decision that when she left, we'd have to say our goodbyes, but I've long changed my mind. I don't care about living life on a plane.

I have a plane. I'll make it my office. I'll put a better bed in it.

"I have to be back in London for BAFTA. That's in February." She shrugs, plastering on another one of those fake smiles I hate. "Wanna be my date?"

Taking a deep breath, I slide closer to her and wipe my thumb across her cheek to remove another tear. "I would love to be your date. I'll be your date to anything you ask me."

Watery blue eyes flick up to mine. "Really? All of them? Even the American ones?"

"I'd be honored, and the rest we'll figure out. It won't be that bad," I say, hoping I sound more convincing out loud than I do in my head.

"You think?"

I nod. "Do you still get Christmas or New Year?"

"I'll be with my family for Christmas," she says quietly.

"New Year, then." I smile at her, trying to make it as reassuring and genuine as possible. "We'll figure it out. Remind me how long the show will be on Broadway?"

"Six months total, three for rehearsals, three for the show. Ends in September."

I do a quick mental calculation. It's October now. Over the next eleven months, Holiday will be free for a total of one month, plus a few snatched days here and there. There's no way to sugarcoat it—the situation is shit.

"Well," I begin, "we'll have to get really good at phone sex then, won't we?"

The corners of her mouth lift with a weak smile.

"And don't forget, I have my own plane, ready to go at a moment's notice."

"Yeah?"

"Yes." I shake her knees, still tucked firmly into her chest. "C'mon. It'll be an adventure."

I can see she's not buying it, but I don't want to tell her I know how she feels. That I'm not ready to give her back. That I've fallen in love with her. Because I saw her face when Marcy told her about the role she'd been offered and how happy she was. I'm not taking that from her. I'm going to show her I'm as excited as I could possibly be.

For once, I'm not going to be the worst liar in my family,

because telling her how I feel amounts to nothing but selfishness on my part when the world is waiting for her to return.

I lean in and kiss her. "Okay, I'm going to get dressed and head to the yard before someone sends out a search party."

I'm almost at the closet when she calls me back, her voice barely audible. "Lando, what if this is all it was supposed to be? A summer fling. Temporary."

"It wasn't," I tell her firmly.

This time, I'm not lying.

I refuse to believe that something temporary could make me feel like my heart is breaking.

HOLIDAY

"What d'you think of this?"

Spinning around, I find Clemmie standing in front of the mirror, wearing a full-length, strapless black-and-white gown. She has one hand holding her hair up and away from her neck, and the other is deep in a pocket—a detail I'm a huge fan of.

She looks stunning.

I walk slowly around her—examining the structure, the weight of the material, the cut—with the meticulous eye I've refined over years of being dressed by professionals.

"I love it."

"Really?"

I nod. "Yes. Absolutely. It's beautiful. So are you."

She glances at me through the reflection in the mirror. "Would you wear it?"

"Definitely."

She twirls. The heavy asymmetrical hem billows around her, and she looks every inch an English lady, tall and regal with perfect cheekbones and a nose I know plenty of women would beg their surgeon for. She's made for the red carpet.

"I'm going to take it. I'll have a masquerade mask made to match." She splutters with a giggle. "Can't say that five times in a hurry."

"You should. It really suits you." I smile my best smile at her, teeth and everything, trying to make it reach my eyes because she really does look incredible. "And who doesn't love a dress with pockets?"

"I know. It's what swings it for me," she replies, stepping back into the dressing room.

I turn back to the rack of sweaters I was flicking through.

It won't be long before the calls begin, requests to dress me ahead of awards season, and that's without knowing whether I've been nominated again. If I have, the calls triple. My stylist will manage everything. She'll whittle it down to five designers and five designs per ceremony for me to choose from. We've worked together long enough now that she knows what I like and what suits me, and I trust her.

But looking at the gown Clemmie's wearing, I'm picturing myself in it, and Lando next to me in his tux, looking handsome as all get-out. He wouldn't look anything else, my English duke. He'd turn heads, and he'd cause whispers on the carpet. Everyone would want to know who the hot guy holding my hand is.

Part of me doesn't want to stay for the Fall Ball because I don't want to see how good he looks. Then I'll know exactly what I'm missing out on when I walk the carpets alone.

Because as much as Lando professed he wanted to be my date, I saw in his eyes that they were only words meant to make me feel better. I did the math. I'll barely have time to come up for air during the next year. And we both know it.

So Lando won't be next to me on the carpets. I won't get to take his arm, walk side by side as reporters clamor for my attention, and I won't feel his hand on my thigh when we take our seats.

The Fall Ball is in a week. I'll smile, and twirl and do what needs to be done, then fly out to New York before midnight. Lando will become a fond memory, and I'll be the same to him. *Just a fond memory.*

It makes sense. We should cut our losses before someone gets seriously hurt. It will be painful enough as it is. Better to rip off the Band-Aid now.

"I need help," Clemmie squeaks from the confines of the dressing room as she walks out backward. "I'm stuck."

I rush over to her, tugging on the zipper until it comes loose and Clemmie can slip out of it.

"Have you decided what you're wearing?" she puffs out from the other side of the dressing room door.

I shrug. "Ashley shipped over a couple of dresses for me."

"Cool, so we can have a trying-on session for those too?"

"Sure. If you'd like," I say, happy that she can't see my face because I'm sure it's clear I'd rather do anything but.

I couldn't bear the thought of going shopping for the Fall Ball. It felt like I was buying a dress for a funeral. I knew I had enough at my place in Los Angeles that could work instead, so I asked Ashley to ship over a couple that would be suitable.

It makes me feel better about what I'm planning to do.

I don't deserve a new dress when it's only going to be worn for breaking a heart. Two hearts, if you include mine, though I'm beginning to wonder if I don't have one.

The door of the changing room swings open. Clemmie's back in her jeans and sweater and has the ballgown draped over her arm. She takes it to the register and holds it high on its hanger so it can be rung up. I go back to flicking aimlessly through the piles of sweaters and cozy fall clothes. Normally, I'd be stockpiling them and burning a hole in my AMEX, but I can't even find it in myself to look at them properly or with any enthusiasm.

And when my phone pings with a message, I welcome the distraction and open it.

MARCY: First L'Oreal shoot scheduled for New York, January fifteenth after the Golden Globes. You good with this?

I'M TEMPTED to reply that I'm not. They should make the shoot in London, or Paris, or Valentine Nook, but what's the point?

HOLIDAY: Yes, fine.

MARCY: Good. Also, I have the final proofs back from the test shoot. You look good. Perhaps my favorite shots of you, ever. Image 4 is *heart eyes* emoji.

I OPEN the file she sent in her message, and a dozen images of my face stare back at me. Each is different. Close-up and full body, smiling and not smiling. Or in the case of Marcy's favorite, caught unaware and laughing my ass off.

She's correct. I do look good. I look happy.

Lando was sitting out of shot, and I know I'm laughing because he'd fallen asleep on the couch, exhausted from a night of French-style lovemaking. The makeup artist had whispered to me in her thick accent that he was a sexy older guy, but I'd called him a lightweight.

He hadn't been asleep at all, just faking it. He'd overheard the entire conversation and promised to show me the meaning of the word later. The rosy cheeks I'm sporting in the picture aren't from blush, that's for sure.

The memory is a stark contrast to the way we've drifted through the past two weeks, painfully aware our ending date is near. There's been an unspoken intensity between us—clinging to each other every night, making love, lingering goodbye kisses every morning.

But I know we're only prolonging the inevitable.

The heartbreak has already begun.

"What's that?" Clemmie asks from over my shoulder when she's done paying.

I turn the screen to her. "My test shots from Paris."

She snatches my phone away and peers hard at each image. "Holy moly, you look incredible. So natural. You're glowing. Wow. Send me the list of those products they used on you. I want to look that good."

I'm not going to tell her the reason I was glowing had nothing to do with L'Oreal products and everything to do with her brother.

Instead, I force a laugh and change the subject. "Where are your bags?"

"They're sending them to Burlington," she replies, then notices my empty hands. "You're not buying anything?"

"No, not in the mood."

Clemmie sucks in her cheek and I feel her studying me. She hasn't asked me why I'm not as chirpy as usual, but she knows. She sees Lando almost more than I do, and I know he's gone back to being as short-tempered as he was when I arrived. I heard him shouting at Miles after he left my place yesterday morning.

"Are you in the mood for a drink?"

I bark a laugh. I'm so grateful for our friendship. I have to work on not letting my throat constrict too much, or the tears will flow. I can't have that because if I start, I'm not sure I'll be able to stop.

"I'm always in the mood for a drink."

She loops her arm through mine. "Then let's go."

The air is crisp as we walk down Valentine High Street.

Halloween decorations are being strung up from the lamp-posts, and pumpkins large and small are scattered around each store entrance. The wisteria has died off into gnarled ropes climbing up the walls, fitting well with the spooky vibe, and some stores have entwined it with witches and ghost silhouettes.

I'm so busy trying to commit all the details to memory that I don't notice Mrs. Winston walking toward us until I almost bump into her. She's holding an enormous bunch of carrots.

"Oh, Holiday dear, excuse me."

I take hold of her arm before she falls. "Sorry, Mrs. Winston, my fault, I wasn't looking where I was going."

"Not to worry. I'm glad I bumped into you girls," she says, her head bobbing between Clemmie and me. "I've just made a lovely batch of blackcurrant jam. I'll drop some over to your cottage. Or better yet, you must come over for tea to try it. I'll make scones."

"We'd love to," Clemmie replies for both of us.

"Good, good. I'll be in touch. Next week perhaps." She smiles, offering a little wave of the carrots as she does. "Anyway, must dash, need to get these to Churchill. Enjoy the rest of your day."

"You don't want to take that goat with you, do you?" mumbles Clemmie, before Mrs. Winston is out of earshot. "I think this might be the year he meets his demise if he's caught in the apple orchard again."

My laugh dissolves into a sob, and I'm wiping my face.

"Don't worry, you don't have to cry," she continues, wrapping her arms around me. "I'm sure it won't come to that. Churchill will live forever."

I see what she's doing, and I'm grateful. I know she'll listen if I want to talk about Lando, but I truthfully don't know what to say.

When we start walking again, I notice a crowd waiting

outside Agatha Chase's Love Emporium. Way more than usual, and there's always a lot because it's easily the most popular store in Valentine Nook.

I guess broken hearts are big business.

"Wow, Agatha's busy today."

"It's some special full moon, and Halloween's coming up. It's her second busiest time after Valentine's Day." Clemmie shrugs, slowing her stride, but with no intention of stopping.

After Clemmie pulled us away from her on my first trip around the village, and Lando practically sprinted in the opposite direction, I decided maybe it was best if I didn't investigate. But now I'm tempted, so I stop.

It's the big pink neon signs for love potions, spells, and rituals that pull me in. Giant amethysts have been placed in the window next to times and openings for tarot readings, and crystal baths promising to heal your female energy.

"I want to go in."

"Okay, but take it with a pinch of salt. She's kind of intense." Clemmie sighs and walks toward the door.

I thumb to the back of the crowd, consisting of mostly teenage girls. "Don't we need to get in line?"

"No." She shakes her head. "They're here for readings."

I follow her into the store, and I'm immediately hit with the scent in the air—sweet and thick from the burning incense—and it makes me feel lightheaded.

It's surprisingly spacious inside, set out like an apothecary, with shelves of drawers filled with herbs you can scoop out yourself, and bottles of colored liquid labeled with names such as "Love No. 1," "Full Moon Protection Spray," and a dozen different "potions." It's gimmicky, but it's cute, and I kind of wish I hadn't waited so long to come in.

A couple of women are being kept busy behind the counter, while another restocks shelves. I'm wondering where Agatha is when I hear a jangle of bracelets behind me. When I turn around, she's standing in front of me. Up close, she's much younger than I thought, maybe in her fifties, with flawless skin and piercing green eyes. It's her long, pale gray hair that gives the impression she's closer to one hundred.

"Hey, Agatha," Clemmie says.

"Hello, Clementine, my dear, your heart's still brooding, I see. It won't for much longer."

"Thanks, but I didn't ask."

"You didn't need to," Agatha replies haughtily.

My head snaps to Clemmie because I haven't known her to brood over anything. She's never mentioned a guy to me, and I'm so distracted that I don't notice Agatha reaching for my hand before it's too late.

"You must be Holiday."

I nod eventually. "Yes."

As she stares at me, her eyes lose focus. "I've been waiting for you to come and see me—"

I snatch my hand away and turn to Clemmie, whose mouth is pursed tight. She wasn't kidding when she said Agatha was intense. I've been in here a minute, and I already know I can't bear the idea of her telling me that things happen for a reason, or I'm doing the right thing, or love will find me again.

It feels like that's exactly what she's going to do.

In the end, she says, "Perhaps Orlando will see sense soon." I have no fucking clue what that means.

Clemmie tugs on my arm. "Good to see you, Agatha. We're going to look around."

"As you wish. I just took delivery of some new crystals you might like. They're in the corner."

"Thanks."

As much as Agatha might be a little kooky, the store is beautiful. We spend far longer than I expected to in here, but there's so much stuff. In the end, I buy a pink tourmaline and rose gold pendant, which promises to connect to my heart and help me receive love and joy. God knows I need it.

I also buy one for Clemmie because I'm going to miss her just as much.

As I'm paying, Agatha drops in a bottle of Full Moon Protection Spray along with a twisted posy of sage and palo santo, and tells me she'll see me soon. I don't have the energy to correct her.

We leave as a group of girls enters the store, and it only takes one to ask, "Are you Holiday Simpson?" before they're all requesting selfies.

I agree on one condition—that Clemmie is also in the photos.

I don't know why I did it, but I do know these pictures are going up on social media because this is my *real* life. Where I'm famous enough that people want any tiny piece of me they can get, so they can then brag about it.

And somewhere deep in the recesses of my brain, I think that if Clemmie's in them with me, it means there's evidence that for a little while, my life here was real, too.

LANDO

I normally don't like wearing a masquerade mask, but hiding behind it for a few hours tonight has made it easier to pretend I'm happy.

We've drunk, we've danced, and we've raised a lot of money. Holiday's contribution—the opportunity to join her on a photo shoot—went for thirty thousand pounds to a hedge fund guy I work with as a present for his daughter's eighteenth birthday.

I've shaken hands, I've hosted the auction, and I've worked the room.

And all the while I've kept one eye on the clock, ticking down until the very last second before Holiday has to leave, hoping it might slow time. It hasn't.

Witching hour is fast approaching, and I feel like I've barely seen her all evening.

Even now, when I have a moment unbothered by people wanting to come and talk to me, Clemmie's dragged her away to the dance floor to introduce her to some friends before she says goodbye to everyone she's met.

Watching her smile and laugh at everyone who's not me is

infuriating. It's what has me wrapping my fingers tightly around my whiskey glass when all I want to do is hold her hand and cling on for dear life.

Yet I can't take my eyes off her.

She's never looked more beautiful. She's never looked more *Hollywood* in a black gown that hugs the perfect curves of her body I know so well. Gone are the tousled strands constantly falling loose around her face, replaced by a slicked-back twisty thing without a hair out of place.

Red lips, thick black lashes, shimmery cheeks. It's no wonder every single guy in here can't take their eyes off her. I've seen them follow her around the room all evening, admiring, leering, and wanting to get close to her.

She's taken more selfies tonight than I have in my entire life.

She's the starlet they all know and love.

But she's never looked less like the Holiday I know. *My* Holiday. The one who wears jeans and a T-shirt, feeds donuts and apples to my horse, cooks lunch for my family, and falls asleep crooked in the bend of my elbow.

I hate it. I hate sharing her. I hate that I have to give a piece of her back to her fans after tonight.

"Another Fall Ball done . . ." Miles yawns, leans back in his chair, and peers around at the remnants of our evening—a table littered with discarded champagne bottles and empty glasses. Cups of coffee are untouched. "Which means we're on the way to Christmas. How are we feeling about it this year, Al? Good, bad, indifferent?"

We all look at Alex, though I don't expect him to reply, and he doesn't. He just picks up his whiskey glass and downs the contents.

Alex isn't a fan of Christmas, given our father died in December. Alex had always blamed himself for it even though he's the only one. The rest of us use December to celebrate Dad's life.

Ironically, while I was escaping the fallout of my almost wedding, Alex came out of his shell last Christmas. In hindsight, that was all after meeting Haven, and as she's made it clear she wants nothing to do with him, it's likely Alex will once more retreat, and relieve me from the title of grumpy brother starting December first.

My gaze flicks back to Holiday and Clementine, who are now talking to my mother and a group of her cronies. I need a distraction, and this conversation is as good as any.

"What's happened with the property?" I ask, mindlessly checking my watch for the hundredth time. The countdown hasn't slowed.

Alex traces his finger around the rim of his glass and shrugs. "Nothing. Not a peep from the real estate team. I offered the hundred million, and then it stalled. The lawyers can't get a hold of anyone."

"What are you going to do?"

"Nothing. What can I do?"

"You can start by coming to the after-party." Miles leans over and refills Alex's glass. "C'mon, Al. It's Henners's big night out."

My lips twitch in amusement while Alex rolls his eyes.

Since Max came along, putting the brakes on Miles's and Hendricks's wild partying, the Fall Ball has become the only night of the year Hendricks really lets off steam. Max stays back at Burlington with Birgitta, while we stay at the family base in London—our house in Eaton Square—because Hendricks has decided he needs the hundred miles or so between Valentine Nook and the city before he can totally relax.

He also takes advantage of a lie-in the next day, but any

more than one night away from Max, and he begins to get twitchy.

"Al*ex* . . ." Miles whines. "Please come. *Pleaaase.*"

Ignoring the uncanny impression of Max, Alex peers over his whiskey glass at me. "Lan, you in?"

I shake my head. "No, I'm taking Holiday to the airport."

My watch says twenty minutes to go. It's like time is speeding up. We're going down a hill, and momentum has gathered until we're hurtling to the bottom.

"Oh shit." Hendricks winces. "I didn't realize that was today. Sorry, Lan. How are you feeling?"

"Not great," I reply. No point lying.

"But you're going to see her again. She's coming back, right?"

I nod heavily. "Yes."

"When?"

I'm doing my best to answer the questions while ignoring the sinking feeling in the pit of my stomach, the one that's a lot like a lead weight dropped into a lake.

"For New Year's," I say, as cheerily as I'm able. "She has all the promo for this movie before then, and then she has the premiere."

Miles leans forward, his hands steepled together. "Are you going to be walking the red carpet with her?"

"She hasn't asked."

I look at the three of them. A couple of minutes ago, they were all joking, laughing, and taking the piss out of Alex. Now they look sad. They're all wearing an expression that reinforces my suspicions—that when Holiday says goodbye to me, it won't be in a "see you in a month" way.

It's going to be forever.

Her mood has changed in the past week. I want to attribute it to the stress of packing her things more quickly than she expected and instructing her assistant on what needs to be collected and what she's taking on the plane with her, but I know it's not. So many times, I stopped myself from saying she could get it when she returns, and that it'll be waiting for her.

Call me chickenshit, but I haven't wanted to hear her say she wouldn't be returning.

"But the awards start in January, and she asked me to accompany her for those."

Their collective sigh of relief does nothing for my anxiety.

"Something to look forward to then." Hendricks smiles, always the optimist.

My time checking has become obsessive, but when I glance up, Holiday's walking toward me, and this time, when people try to stop and talk, she ignores them.

"Hey, you're not the Duke of Oxfordshire, are you?"

I turn in my chair, pull her onto my lap, and bury my nose in her neck. I don't even care who's watching. I need this.

"That depends," I mumble. "Who's asking?"

"Just a lil' ole actress," she replies, wrapping her arms around my shoulders and squeezing me until my soul aches and a barrel of tears pushes up my throat.

"Don't go."

When she stiffens, I know I didn't keep the words in my head like I meant to, and just like that, she eases herself off my lap and moves closer to my sister, who swings an arm around her shoulders. It reminds me that I'm not the only one who doesn't want Holiday to leave.

"Clem, you coming to the party? Holiday, what about you? Can't you delay the plane for a couple of hours?"

Her mouth rolls together, and she smiles sadly at Miles. "Ah, I wish I could. But I have a meeting in the morning. The studio sent a plane to make sure I got back in time."

"Boo," he grumbles, standing to give her a hug. It's the type of hug he gives Clementine, and that in itself is enough to break me. "You'll always be the best neighbor I've ever had. Don't be a stranger, okay?"

"Okay," she replies quietly, easing out of his arms and into Hendricks's.

My throat tightens further with each of my siblings she hugs.

There's no "see you soon" or "you must visit us again" because everyone's too wary of me and our situation.

I stand, waiting, and when she's ready, she turns to me with her hand held out. We walk out of the ballroom in silence. No one stops us. No one asks for a selfie. People take one look at our faces and know it's not a good time.

The car is waiting to drive us to the private airport just outside of London. Except when we step outside, it's not the car I expect—the one with *my* driver.

And it's then I know.

Holiday turns and looks at me, big blue eyes glistening with tears.

"Holiday, what's going on?"

"Just listen." She holds her hand up. Her expression takes on a steeliness, and I find myself bracing. "It would never have worked. Long distance sucks."

The lead weight hits the bottom of the lake. This can't be happening.

"Holiday—"

"Lando, we both knew this had an end date. Why don't we just call it what it was—an incredible summer? Let's not ruin it."

"We're not going to ruin it. Why would that happen?"

Her features harden along with her tone, and I briefly wonder if she's practiced this. "Because I'm telling you that's what *always* happens. The time difference alone is enough to kill it. You're getting up as I go to bed."

I'm still holding her hand, and I pull her into me. "Holiday, we'll figure it out. I promise. We can get through a little time difference."

"Don't make promises you can't keep. When I'm working, I'm completely immersed in what I do. I don't have time to worry about when we're going to be together next. We'll end up resenting the hell out of each other in a matter of months."

I shake my head. "We're stronger than that, and you know it. I'll be by your side for the awards."

She doesn't look at me when she replies. "I think it's better if I do them alone."

"Holiday, come on . . ." My tone is pleading, whiny almost, but I can't help it.

With a sigh, she places her hand on my chest, palm above my heart where I know she can feel it beating wildly. I wonder if she realizes that these days it only beats for her.

Rising on her tiptoes, she presses her lips to mine. Letting go of her hand, I hold her face and kiss her like I want to strip the red off until her mouth is the one I'm familiar with.

It's hard, needy, and fraught with everything we need to say to each other but can't. But mostly, it's sad. Desperately sad.

And when I taste the saltiness of her tears, my heart totally breaks.

"I love you," I tell her for the first time, one last attempt at getting her to change her mind and come back to me. "Holiday, please, we said we'd figure it out, and we will. The time difference can't be the reason we don't stay together."

She doesn't reply but leans into the car and pulls out a box. A fucking box. That her things are in this car, and she planned it all without me realizing it, is a final twist of the knife.

"Wait until I'm gone. Okay?"

I'm numb, barely noticing her placing it in my hands. I'm too focused on her face, committing it all to memory—the color of her eyes, the perfect heart shape of her lips, the determination in the jut of her chin.

It's what brings all my anger to the surface. Holiday has made her mind up, and I don't get a say. *Again.*

"You're not even going to give us a chance? This is bullshit. Please, Holiday, don't do this to us."

She slides into the car, gathering her gown around her, and when she's done, she pulls the door closed. Her palm presses against the window, and it's the last thing I'm left with as the car sets off.

I stand and watch until they pull into traffic.

I don't bother going back in. I can't face the looks of pity on my brothers' faces—or the tears I know Clementine is crying—because they'll set off my own.

Instead, I get in my waiting car and request my driver to take me back to Valentine Nook. As a final *fuck you,* we pass four buses with her advert on the way out of London, taunting me with the perfect body I know every inch of.

I'm still holding the box she handed me, and I notice an envelope tucked neatly under the ribbon for the first time.

The laugh I let out is dry and full of scorn. Of course it's addressed to Thunder.

Dear Thunder,

I so enjoyed getting to know you and Sunday. I'm sorry that I won't be around to visit again.

Look after your dad, tell him he's the best thing that ever happened to me, and I love him.

Your friend,

Holiday x

P.S. Pierre has promised to always bring you donuts.

. . .

INSTEAD OF TAKING me to Burlington's front door, I instruct my driver to drop me at the stable yard where Thunder is sound asleep.

"Look what Holiday made you," I whisper as I creep in quietly and wake him enough to receive a grunt in reply.

Kneeling, I break it in half and hand over his midnight snack. It's only when he smells the sugar does he open his eyes fully.

Thunder's velvety lips quiver around the jam oozing out, and with a snort, he nudges me for the rest. When he's done eating, he lays his head down and goes back to sleep.

Only when I settle next to him in the hay and lean on his soft belly do I allow my tears to finally fall.

HOLIDAY

For the first time in five months, I step onto United States soil and fall straight into my brother's arms.

"It's gonna be okay, Hol . . . I promise."

"You . . ." *Sob.* "Don't know . . ." *Sob.* "That . . ." *Sob.*

"I do. And you know how I know?" he replies, squeezing me tight and rubbing my

back in that soothing way he's always done when I'm having a crisis.

I take a big sniff. "How?"

"Because that's what you always tell me."

If it's possible, Tanner's words make me cry even more. I'm also sure I've never said that, and if I have, then I'm clearly a bigger idiot than I already thought I was. Because right now, I can't imagine it ever being okay.

"And I'm all for you crying it out right here in the middle of the tarmac, but as it's four in the morning and I'm freezing my nuts off, it would probably be a better idea to get in the car."

Easing out of his grip, I take the edge of his sweater and use it to wipe my nose, just like we did when we were kids. Yes, it's gross, but it always raises the tiniest smile.

"Feel better now?"

I shake my head. "No."

"That's the spirit." He winks, tapping his fist to my chin. "Now, let's . . ." He becomes distracted by something over my shoulder. "Holiday, what the fuck is that?"

I spin around, and the tears start up again. Not that they stopped at any point over the past nine hours since I left Lando standing on the steps of the Dorchester Hotel. I'm severely dehydrated. But along with the tears, I do manage a slight smile at the sight of the air steward wrestling Willard the bear—as I named him—down the narrow steps of the plane.

I could have left him to be packed up and sent back with the rest of my things, but as Lando gave him to me, I didn't want to risk him being damaged.

"That's Willard," I wail, topping it off with a loud sniff. "The bear Lando gave me after I won the coconut shy."

"I still don't know what's shy about a coconut," Tanner mumbles with a shake of his head. "Okay, get in the car. That thing will have to go in the back seat because he won't fit in the trunk with your bags."

I do as I'm told because truthfully, I'm also freezing cold. Once I make sure everything's been packed into the car, I settle into my seat while Tanner wrestles Willard into his until finally we're ready to leave.

I turn to him as he starts the engine. "Thank you for coming to get me, Tanny."

The smile I offer him is weak, but it's also so grateful. I honestly couldn't have faced landing on my own and having a car service take me to Tanner's apartment, where I'm staying until I fly back to Los Angeles in a couple of days.

"Of course I was coming to get you. I'm not going to let my sister cry her eyes out by herself." He tuts. "We'll be home soon, and Brady will be awake. He'll make his auntie Holiday feel better. Then you can get some shut-eye."

"What about Millie?"

"She has class this morning, so she'll go back to sleep for a bit too I think."

Millie, Tanner's wife, is a student at Columbia and took a year off when she got pregnant. She started back at school at the beginning of this semester, and now that Tanner's in his off-season, he's doing the bulk of the childcare, along with the help of both ours and Millie's parents, who don't seem to be able to stay away.

He's also paying for a nanny, though I'm not sure what there's left to do once the grandmothers are done for the day.

At this time of the morning, and with Tanner's driving, we reach Manhattan in less than twenty minutes. I spent so much of the past two years in this city, yet now it feels alien to me. The air, the chaos, the fact that everything is on the wrong side. Although it's so different from Valentine Nook, it may help me move on quicker and forget faster.

I'd be a big fat liar if I said I wanted to do either. I don't deserve to forget. The moment I begin to feel normal, my punishment should be picturing Lando's face as I rode away. Telling myself I've done it for his own good is no comfort whatsoever.

Millie waits by the elevator doors the moment they open into their apartment, and of course I start crying again. I'm too tired and too fragile to cope with her kindness at waking up to greet me, or at Brady looking impossibly cute in a little orange onesie covered in pumpkins and a hood with a brown stalk sticking from the top.

She reaches out to hug me, careful not to squash her son between us. "Oh Hol, don't worry, we'll talk it through, but it'll be okay . . . *whoa* . . . that's . . . *big*."

"She's cried the whole way home," Tanner grunts from behind me as he drops Willard on the floor next to my bags, lets out a long sigh, and rests his hands on his knees. "That thing is fucking heavy."

"I didn't cry the whole way," I grumble. "I stopped when we drove through the Lincoln Tunnel."

"Sorry, I stand corrected."

I watch as my brother kisses his wife and takes his son from her arms. My heart aches acutely from that one simple gesture. Up to this point in my life, marriage and children have never been an aspiration. I have enough nieces and nephews to suffice for the moment, but witnessing it now, it's hard to imagine I'll ever find that type of love with someone when I've blown it with the one person I could see myself growing old with.

My face crumples all over again.

"Oh, Hol—"

"I'm fine." I wave Millie off and hold my hands out for Brady.

He's got my brother's blue eyes, which I guess are mine too. His chubby little cheeks bulge as he smiles at me.

"Hey, buddy, you got big, huh? Do you remember Auntie Holiday?"

"Mmm, sure did," Millie replies. "It's like walking around with a kettlebell all day."

I laugh. "If kettlebells looked like you, I'd be in the gym more often."

Brady raises his palm and rests it on my face. His sweet baby scent fills the air, and it's calming enough that waves of tiredness begin crashing over me.

"Hey, I think I'm going to catch some sleep before my meetings this morning."

Millie takes Brady back. "The guest room is all set up for you. Sleep as long as you want. I'm going to do the same. Tanner will be here all day if you want to hang out with him, and I finish class after lunch."

"Thank you."

I pick up my bags, and before I head down the hallway to my room, Tanner hugs me tightly, whispering, "I promise it'll be okay. We'll figure it out when you wake up."

I can't quite bring myself to believe him, so instead of answering, I just smile. The moment I close the bedroom door behind me, I drop everything on the floor and power up my phone.

I hadn't wanted to check it at all during the flight—some fucked-up form of delayed gratification—because it was easier to hold on to a tiny sliver of hope that I might have a message from Lando when I land, than listen to the louder voice saying I'm too stupid for even thinking he'd ever speak to me again after I left.

CLEMMIE: Miss you already.

CLEMMIE: How was your flight?

MARCY: My call's been canceled, so we can meet earlier. Eleven a.m.? My office?

MOM: Welcome home, sweetie. See you at Tanner's tomorrow. Have you got tickets to Late Night for your dad and me?

CLEMMIE: Miles's after-party sucks. I'm going to bed. Still miss you.

AFTER TRIPLE-CHECKING that there's nothing from the one person I want to hear from, I collapse into bed with a fresh onslaught of tears.

* * *

I GIVE up on trying to sleep, and when I see myself in the bathroom mirror, I decide the time would be better spent praying for a miracle to make me look human. Because that's what it's going to take.

Last night's makeup is streaked down my cheeks, and my eyes are completely bloodshot and the puffiest I've ever seen them. Two attempts at washing my face don't improve much, so I text Ashley and ask her to have a spa service come around this afternoon to give me the full works before I appear on national television.

Because there's no way I can step outside looking the way I do, now I'm back in the US, where my face is displayed on every other billboard.

I'm reluctant to even leave the bedroom, but the sound of Brady's gurgling while Tanner talks to him is too tempting to stay. But it's the second voice I hear that has me stopping short, because it's not Millie.

Sure enough, my agent is sitting at the breakfast counter drinking coffee while Brady stares at her from his bouncer as she spins the balls on the mobile in front of him. If it wasn't so weird, it would be comical, because Marcy—as she's told me many times—is not a baby person.

"Hey." It comes out as a croak, and I'm sure I see Marcy wince the moment she spots me, but it could just be from my eyes being fuzzy.

"Welcome back." She smiles.

She definitely winced. Her smile is far too big and cheery to be genuine.

"What are you doing here? I thought we were meeting later? Did I get the time wrong?"

Marcy shakes her head. "No, doll. I just thought I'd pop by, haven't seen little Tanner since he became a daddy. We can do our meeting here instead."

That suits me. The longer I have to fix my face, the better. But I frown.

Along with not being a baby person, Marcy is also not the

type of person to "pop by." Everything about this situation I've walked into immediately makes me suspicious. I'm guessing it's because the past few weeks I've been too pissed to talk to her.

"What's going on?"

"Nothing. I wanted to see you before the craziness begins. It's going to be a busy end of the year," she adds, like she thinks I'm not aware of how busy my life will become.

I'm about to jump back onto the Hollywood juggernaut.

Taking a deep breath through my nose, I blow it out in one long puff.

"D'you want another coffee?"

"Sure."

I flick on the machine, wondering if it would be easier for me to have it administered intravenously. Marcy and Tanner are talking about the World Series, which Tanner's team crashed out of in the third round of the playoffs, and I zone out while they discuss trades for next year and who's likely to win the title this season.

When I'm done, I place a coffee on the counter in front of her. "Here you go."

Her eyes roll down to the cup and back to me. "Well, this is worse than I thought."

I frown because she hasn't even tried it. "What does that mean?"

"Holly, sweetheart, you look like you haven't slept in a month, and that you've done ten rounds with Mike Tyson"—she waves her hand around dismissively—"or whoever's boxing these days."

I guess we're not talking about the coffee.

"I know I look like shit, but why d'you think that is?" I snap. "I told you I didn't want to come back early."

She calmly picks it up and sips. "You're under contract, Holiday. There's nothing I could have done."

Her voice is softer than I've ever known it to be, empathetic almost, and it nearly pushes me over the edge.

I can't cope with Marcy being sweet to me right now. I need her to be the bullish badass agent she always has been.

I need someone to shout at who'll take it without getting offended, and I need someone to blame for getting me into this situation, for having to take a break in the first place because I'd worked too fucking hard for too fucking long and was about to fucking collapse.

If that hadn't been the case, then I wouldn't have been in England.

And we all know what happened in England.

Most of all, I need someone to blame for falling in love with Lando when I had no business doing anything of the sort.

My eyes burn, and the heaviness in my chest presses down until I almost can't breathe.

"But," Marcy begins, "I do have some news you might be interested in."

I swipe away the moisture and assess her through narrowed eyes. "Go on."

"The paperwork hasn't been signed yet on *Hot Tin Roof*, so it's my duty to tell you another request has come in. The budget isn't as big, and it's for two months instead of three—"

Using the heel of my palms, I rub against my temples. I thought she was going to tell me something good. But two months is still two months, add in rehearsal time on top of that, and it may as well be a lifetime. It doesn't solve anything.

"The director is Hamish McTaggart. He won the Tony last year for that play on Broadway about R.B.G. He's super hot right now."

I nod. I saw that play, and it was good. But I still don't see what the point of her telling me is.

"And it's playing at the Donmar Warehouse."

My ears prick, though I'm still too focused on my own self-pity and broken heart to immediately realize what she's saying or its implications.

"Holiday, are you listening to what I'm saying? The Donmar Warehouse is in London."

Oh my god. She's right. "Are you saying there's a play in London that wants me?"

"Yes."

"When is it starting?"

"Rehearsals in April, again. Same timeframe."

"I'll take it."

Marcy's lips purse. "I haven't even told you what it is."

I don't tell her that I don't care. It could be a revival of Barney with me dressed as a purple dinosaur dancing on stage every night, and I'd take it. Because *London.*

"What is it?"

"Shakespeare, *Twelfth Night.*"

It feels like forever since I laughed, but I can't help myself. I'm transported back to The One True Love and the little table in the corner where Shakespeare may or may not have written one of his plays—maybe it was this one. The other thing that flashes in my brain is Agatha Chase telling me she'll see me soon.

Perhaps she was onto something.

"Shakespeare is perfect."

"I had a feeling it might be, and after that, there's a potential movie to begin filming next November. A legal drama, location Europe but predominantly London, which I trust will also be suitable."

That's nearly a year of being in England. Yes, more than suitable.

Rounding the counter, I wrap my arms around Marcy and hug her tight. The pressure in my chest has vanished, and my tears have finally dried up, replaced by the biggest smile.

"Give me a pen and I'll sign right now."

The next few weeks of press suddenly seem like a breeze to get through, and I'm already coming up with a plan to beg Lando for two things—his forgiveness at leaving and to be my date again.

I can't even find any nerves swirling at the possibility he might say no. I don't care.

All that matters is that I'm going to see Lando again.

LANDO

I don't think I've ever been so unhappy in my entire life.

It's been five agonizing days since Holiday left, and for four and a half of them, I've been trying to figure out a way we can be together. The only plan I've come up with is for Alex to take over Burlington and for me to oversee operations from a New York HQ that doesn't exist yet. But if Alex agrees, then I'll be flying over to find an office as soon as the plane is fueled.

If he doesn't, then . . . well, I haven't gotten that far.

I've only made it to The One True Love, where I'm shivering next to the blazing fire with Hamish at my feet while I try finding my solution at the bottom of a pint.

One look at me and Eddie cleared the back room so I have it to myself, just like I did on my first date with Holiday.

My head falls into my hands. Christ. What a mess.

"Well, hello, fancy seeing you here."

My head snaps back up at the sound of Miles's voice. "How'd you find me?"

"Eddie called."

Traitor. I scowl over at the bar, not that he cares. He misses

Holiday as much as everyone else, but when my mother walks around the corner, my scowl narrows and aims at Miles instead. My mother, whom I've been avoiding.

"I've been looking for you everywhere."

"Congratulations," I grunt. "You found me."

"Yes, and I see you've decided to stop shaving again, darling."

My head snaps up. I'm not in the mood for this shit. If they thought I was hard to be around after Caroline, they haven't seen anything yet.

"Mother—" My voice carries a warning tone for whatever she came here to say, which she obviously decides to ignore.

"*Orlando*. I am your mother—"

"Don't even think about trying to set me up on another date. I'm done."

Her mouth purses, and she stares at me for a second until her face softens. She scooches in next to me, and just like she did when I was younger and having a bad day, she pushes her fingers through my hair. It's oddly comforting and lulls me into a false sense of security.

"I know I promised not to interfere, but I lied. Do not let that girl get away."

The all-too-familiar tightening of my throat happens again, and it's really starting to piss me off. I shift back along the leather booth.

"She broke up with *me*, Mum. What am I supposed to do? I can't force her to change her mind. It was her decision, not mine," I snap, but I can't help it. I'm angry. I'm sad and angry with Holiday for giving up so easily. "We're going to be on different continents for a year. There's literally no time to see each other."

Not sure why I'm trying to convince my mum when I can't even convince myself.

"Find time," she responds before standing. Helpful as

always. "Anyway, must go. I said I'd pop over to Mrs. Winston's to discuss the Christmas fair."

On the way out, she passes Miles, walking back to the table carrying two pints of beer, one of which he places in front of me. He pulls out the opposite chair and sits down.

"Did Mum tell you to go after Holiday?"

"Something like that."

"I think you should."

"Don't you start." I swipe the foam from my top lip. "She's got an amazing role on Broadway. Short of moving the theater to London, there's nothing I can do."

Hmm. There's an idea.

Miles shrugs and gets out his phone. "I have something that will cheer you up."

"Nothing's going to cheer me up."

"How much d'you want to bet?"

I groan, "Miles, if you're going to be deliberately annoying, then I'd rather be left alone if it's all the same to you."

Unfortunately, it doesn't deter him. Quite the opposite. "Okay, no bet, but how about you shut up and listen? This morning, I was watching one of those American chat shows they have, you know the ones on late every night, and Holiday was on it."

"I'm not interested," I lie. I'm very interested. I can't help it. I want to know everything she's doing. I just don't want anyone else to know that's what I want.

I need time to lick my wounds in private. If that includes watching her on some goddamn American TV program where she's smiling and laughing and moving on with her life while I'm here being my most miserable self, then so be it.

It's bad enough that twice this week I've seen Holiday's face staring at me. Once from the back page of the *Financial Times*, where a full-sized ad had been taken out for the same Gucci campaign that's on the side of the buses. The other was a movie poster for her upcoming film.

I'm never going to escape it. Her beautiful face will follow me for the rest of my life.

I've already told the board that my monthly meetings in London will need to be conducted remotely until next year.

Miles slaps a set of headphones in my palm. "Stop being a dick and watch this."

I don't have the energy to argue.

Sitting back, I stare at the screen paused on Holiday's face. Immediately, my chest seizes. Even a little pixilated, she looks beautiful, and she looks happy. She's in her natural habitat.

This is where she belongs, not here in Valentine Nook surrounded by cows. I was stupid to ever think it could be a possibility.

I press play, but I'm so focused on her face that I barely hear what the host is laughing about as he shuffles his question cards.

"That's good. Now tell me what you've been doing since you won your Oscar. Has it been crazy?"

Holiday turns and smiles at the audience. As she does, there's a split second when she looks directly into the camera, and it feels like she's looking straight at me.

"Actually, no. It's been very peaceful and relaxing."

"And is it true you met an English duke?" He pronounces it dooke. Just like Holiday does.

I barely breathe as Holiday laughs. A sound I'd almost forgotten. "It is."

"I can't blame you because this guy . . . *wow*, I didn't know they made English guys who looked like this—"

My eyes almost get stuck from rolling so hard. What an idiot.

But then one of the shots of Holiday and me in Paris fills the screen, followed by the polo match, and one from the Fall

Ball I haven't seen before. The studio audience claps and squeals, and when the camera pans back to Holiday on the sofa, her cheeks are pinker.

"Are you going to be inviting us around for afternoon tea, *guvnor?*"

"You know, Jimmy, maybe I will."

"Can we have those little cucumber sandwiches?"

"Sure." She laughs again. "I'll see what I can do."

"Now what's next after the movie? What's lined up for next year?"

"I'm trying something new. I'm heading to a stage in—"

I'm losing the will to live. I have no idea why Miles wanted me to watch these unless it was to cause me more pain for whatever slight I've done to him. Then I hear two words that have me rewinding.

"I'm heading to a stage in the West End, but that's all I can say right now."

Rewind.

"In the West End."

I glance up at Miles. "This has to be a mistake."

He shakes his head. "I don't think it is. There's another one."

Miles takes his phone back and brings up another video. Again, Holiday's talking to the host about her time in England and how she's not done yet. That she'll be returning at the soonest possible moment, and she's going to be starring in the West End next year.

"She knows the West End is London, right?"

Miles frowns. "I'm going to take a wild guess and say yes."

"I don't understand." Why would I understand? It makes no sense whatsoever.

"I think she's found a way to come back to you, buddy." He leans over and punches my arm. "Congratulations."

"So what? I haven't heard from her? Does Clementine know? Am I supposed to wait until I have confirmation?"

"Fuck no. You go and get her," he says like he has experience chasing girls who reject him.

Miles has zero experience with this.

I'm reeling from the onslaught of information, so my wits aren't as quick as they usually are. Therefore, when Agatha Chase marches straight up to our table, I have no way of escaping.

"Hello, Orlando."

I groan because she's the last person I want to see right now. I'm also mildly irked that not only does she never address me properly, she calls me *Orlando*. A name no one calls me except my mother, and that's when she's annoyed.

"Oh Agatha, please do fuck off. I'm not in the mood. You were right, okay? Yes, I'm alone. Yes, I will be alone forever. Happy?"

Agatha scoffs hard. "And I thought Miles was the most dramatic Burlington."

"Hey," Miles protests. "I'm right here."

Agatha's eyes slice down to Miles as though she's only just noticed him.

"Hmm. Yes, so you are." She tuts and focuses back on me. "Orlando, if you bothered to let me speak, even for a minute instead of rushing away from me every chance you get, then I'd be able to finish what I was telling you."

"I don't want to hear it."

"Well, you're going to." Her words snap out so forcefully that I'm momentarily stunned. "If you marry out of duty, you will be alone forever. If you marry out of love, it will survive the test of time and distance."

"What?"

"You never let me finish, and all you took from what I said was being alone forever. But that's not what's written out for you. You have several paths ahead."

Next to me, Miles sneers loudly. "Where's it written?"

"In the stars."

Miles tips his head back to look at the ceiling, which I'll admit raises a small smile. "You don't honestly believe in all that, do you, Agatha? C'mon, isn't it all a little far-fetched?"

"Only to the unenlightened, Miles," she replies, haughtily. "If you opened up your heart a bit more, then you'd be able to accept the love you crave so deeply."

"I get plenty of love, thank you very much."

It's clear exactly the version of "love" Miles is talking about, to which Agatha raises a withering eyebrow in response.

Thankfully, Clementine arrives before the pair of them get into an argument, and squeezes into the booth next to me. She almost looks as sad as I feel. I'm tempted to ask her if she's heard from Holiday about this West End business. But I don't want to know the answer because if she has when I haven't, I know it'll make me feel doubly shitty.

"Oh hey, Agatha, how's it going?" she asks, almost absent-mindedly, before thumbing behind her. "D'you two know who that woman is at the bar? I'm sure I just heard her asking for directions to Burlington. I think she had an American accent."

Miles and I turn around to see a woman with dark blond hair and a tiny baby strapped to her chest talking to one of Eddie's bar staff. She's not very tall, and she's pretty, if a little tired looking, which would be understandable if she's just become a mother.

The longer I stare, I'm certain there's something oddly familiar about her, but I meet so many people it's hard to remember them all.

"Maybe. I'm not sure. I'd need to get closer to know."

"Same. I swear I've seen her before. She's definitely hot, so it's possible . . ." Miles begins, before his face drops in panic. "Shit, I hope that's not my child."

Agatha's also staring hard at the woman now talking to Eddie. "It's not. That child is Alex's."

"Oh, thank god," Miles replies, before his head jerks back in Agatha's direction. "Wait, what did you just say?"

"That child is Alex's," she repeats calmly, not like she's just dropped an atomic bomb of information. Then because she's Agatha, and a law unto herself, she walks off as quickly as she arrived without another word.

Clementine's intake of air is so sharp she splutters. Miles spins around again to stare harder, and then I realize where I've seen that girl. The last time was standing in the middle of a bakery in Aspen waiting for Alex to say his goodbyes.

The answer hits Miles at the same time. "It's Haven."

"Alex's Haven?" whispers Clementine.

"Shit, what do we do?" I down the remains of my glass only for Miles to keep me from standing.

"*We're* doing nothing." He points hard at my chest. "You're going to LA. Clementine and I will deal with Haven."

I glance at my sister, who seems as shocked as I am by the turn of events.

"Milo, I can't just fly to LA."

"You can. The plane is fueled and waiting. James is outside in the car ready to take you, and I packed you an overnight bag, which is also in the car."

What the hell is happening right now? An hour ago, I was nursing my sorrows and minding my own business. Now the girl Alex loves is standing in The One True Love, holding a baby, and I'm heading to get Holiday back.

The most shocking of all, however, is that Miles has volunteered to deal with whatever the situation is, without making a joke of the whole thing. He seems totally serious.

Clementine claps her hands far too enthusiastically. "It's like a real-life movie ending."

I frown at my sister. "I don't know where she lives."

Miles pulls out his phone and taps the screen, only for mine to buzz with a message. I look down to find a photo of a package with an address label for Los Angeles. "Now you do."

"How did you get it?"

"Holiday's assistant was at Bluebell yesterday packing up boxes. I happened to pop by and say hello. While I was there, I saw the address label."

"You really think I should go?"

"*Yes,*" Clementine and Miles insist in unison.

"You heard Holiday. She's coming to the West End. So go and bring her back." Miles adds, "And I can't believe I'm saying this, but what if Agatha's right too?"

"If she's right about me, then she's right about that." I nod in Haven's direction.

"One shitshow at a time," Miles shoots back. "Now will you please fuck off? James is outside waiting."

I don't even know why I'm thinking about it.

Of course I'm flying to Los Angeles.

* * *

EVEN IN NOVEMBER, Los Angeles is mild enough to wear a jumper without feeling too cold, but I'm shivering nonetheless. Shivering, shaking. Same difference. Because it's from the same bunch of nerves playing go-karts in the pit of my stomach.

The Hollywood sign is bright white, lit up against the darkening sky. I haven't spent a lot of time in Los Angeles before. It's not a city Burlington Estates has any interest in, but as the evening draws in, I'm taken aback by how vast it is. The lights of the city stretch into the distance and disappear over the horizon.

I'm in the back of an SUV heading to the address Miles gave me. Up front, a little blue dot moves quickly toward the red arrow on the GPS map, and the closer it gets, the quicker my adrenaline spikes. I've been traveling for twelve hours, it's approximately two a.m. back home, and I've slept for a total of four hours.

It's a lethal combination that poses a set of questions I don't want to think about, but I will absolutely blame Miles for if everything goes tits up.

It's evening in Los Angeles. What if Holiday isn't home? What if I've got this all wrong? What if she's getting ready for a date?

My fists clench, and my nonexistent fingernails dig into my skin so hard they almost draw blood.

The driver slows down and turns to me. "Sir, we're here."

I peer out the window and see what amounts to a tall gate in a very high hedge. But that's it. There's no driveway or entrance—just this gate in the hedge.

"This?"

The driver nods.

"Are you sure this is the right place?"

He turns and looks at me, like I dare question his map reading.

"That's the address you gave me."

I get out. I left my overnight bag on the plane, which in hindsight was kind of stupid, but I guess if this isn't the right place, then I'm heading straight home.

"Where's the garage?" I ask, trying again, because I know Holiday has a car here, so if this is her place, where does she keep it?

The driver points at a dark green garage door flush to the hedge I hadn't noticed before. It's kind of ingenious having a camouflaged house.

"So I guess I just ring the buzzer?"

When he rolls his eyes and mumbles under his breath, I decide to cut his tip in half. Where's the brotherly solidarity? Surely, he can see I'm on the verge of a nervous breakdown.

I stand in front of the gate and count down from ten. When I reach one, I decide to count down from twenty.

"You want me to wait here?" the driver calls out, cutting his tip again.

"Yes," I snap.

"Is the buzzer not working?"

This time, I ignore him and press down on the button. "Okay, here goes nothing."

"Yeah," barks a voice I recognize immediately.

"Holiday?" Silence stretches out, so I buzz again, only this time it goes unanswered.

I spin around to the driver, now back in the car. "You heard someone answer too, right?"

He shrugs in response.

I'm about to try a third time when the lock spins and the door opens wide.

Standing in front of me is the woman I love with my whole heart, the one I know I want to spend the rest of my life with, wherever that will be. I'll follow her anywhere.

Except she's looking at me like she's seen a ghost.

"Lando? What are you doing here?"

I'm too busy staring to be able to form words. All the words I rehearsed on the flight over have vanished.

"Lando?"

"I'm miserable," I blurt. "I can't even last a week without you."

Her hands fly to her mouth, and she lets out a loud sob, which I take as a good sign, so I continue.

"I've been trying to figure out a way for us to be together, and I came up with a pretty good solution, but then I heard a rumor that perhaps you might be coming to the West End. So before we go any further, I want to double-check you know the West End is in London, and there's not another West End somewhere in America."

"You flew here to check I knew where the West End is?" she asks quietly from behind her palm.

I nod. "Yes."

"How did you know?"

"Miles saw one of your chat shows and showed me," I reply. "Is it true, you're not going to New York? I don't have to set up headquarters there because you're coming to London?"

"I changed my mind." She shrugs, and her hands fall to her side. When she smiles at me, it's like I can take a full breath again and she's the one administering oxygen to me. "I heard London is the place to be, and you know, there's someone over there I kind of like."

"Oh yeah?"

"Yeah." She smiles. "Super tall, long legs, black hair. Answers to the name of Thunder."

A smirk curves my lips. "He will be pleased to hear that. I think he's missed you nearly as much as I have. Everyone's missed you nearly as much as I have. I've missed you the most."

This time, her shoulder drops low. "Not as much as I've missed you," she replies. "I'm so sorry, Gracie. I'm so sorry for what I put you through the last week, and for leaving and not believing in us. It just made me realize how much I love you and how miserable I am without you." She trails off into a sob.

"I'm here because I believed enough for both of us." I swipe away a tear. "Does this mean we can go home? Because I can't leave empty-handed. I'll be strung up and hung from the Valentine Arch for returning without you."

"Well, as it happens, another interview was added to my schedule. One of your London chat shows, so if you've got a spot on the plane, I could do with a ride."

"Even if I didn't, I'd kick people off for you."

When she giggles, I smile. I've so missed that incredible sound.

"I was hoping, if you'll still have me, I could come back to Bluebell once the award season is over."

I shake my head. "Bluebell won't be available, I'm afraid. It's no longer up for rental."

I pause, and Holiday's smile freezes. I can see her brain working overtime already.

"You'll have to come to Burlington, if that's suitable for an A-lister of your caliber."

Her mouth drops. "Burlington? Really? You're asking me to move in with you?"

I nod. "I am. If you're going to be working all hours, I want to make sure the ones you have for me aren't hampered by traveling."

"Even when the traveling is over a field?"

"Yes. Even then." I wrap my arms around her. "I love you, Holiday Simpson, and I'm done with being apart from you. So what do you say? Will you move into Burlington?"

She lifts onto her tiptoes and flings her arms around my neck. "I'd love to."

EPILOGUE

Holiday

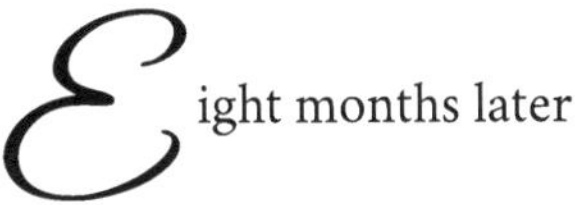

ight months later

"ENCORE. ENCORE."

My heart hammers against my ribs as I rush back onto the stage, greeted by a standing audience cheering, whistling, and hollering, and take a deep bow. A second later, my co-stars join me, followed by Hamish McTaggart, our esteemed director, carrying a giant bouquet of roses.

"My star," he says, taking my hand and kissing it before handing me the flowers.

From the size of Hamish's wide grin, you'd never know he'd thrown a tantrum only hours before. Or that nearly every main cast member threatened to quit at some point during the rehearsals because they couldn't take any more of Hamish and his histrionics. You'd think he was the first person to ever direct Shakespeare.

But tonight all is forgiven, and Hamish can bask in the glory of applause for as long as he needs, and I'll be doing the same because *man,* do I deserve it. We all do.

I thought I'd known hard work before, but theater is a whole different beast—exhausting, exhilarating, and utterly terrifying—and I'll be back here again tomorrow night to do it all again, and twice on Saturdays.

Theater comes with a thrill I can see myself getting addicted to. The adrenaline rush of stepping out in front of a live audience and praying you don't fuck up your lines. I've never been a fan of roller coasters, but I bet it feels the same. In comparison, a movie is slow and steady, filtered, and you rehearse your lines over and over until you nail them.

Then it's all tied up in a pretty little money-making bow.

Early reviews are in, and they're all saying this production of *Twelfth Night* will sweep the Olivier Awards next year, including best actress for me in my role as Viola—"my best work to date." And for the first time ever, I think the critics might be onto something.

But I couldn't have done any of it without my number one fan and biggest supporter, currently beaming up at me from the middle of the front row—Lando—along with his siblings, his mom, and my parents. Marcy was here for the first week of pre-shows and once more declared the phone would be ringing off the hook with requests for me, which I'm happy with.

We've agreed to one project a year, wherever that may be, because Lando has said he'll join me.

Since the beginning of the year, he's been a permanent fixture next to me on the red carpet, which, to the amusement of his brothers, set off a slew of fan accounts featuring #hotenglishduke. I might have had Ashley "like" a couple of the posts for me.

Lando would be happy for it to die a painful death and never discuss it again, but Miles, being Miles, won't allow that to happen. Since the first social post, any new ones are shared in the Burlington family chat group and rated.

I don't hate it.

The cast and I take one final bow before the curtain falls, and for a minute, we all stand there, breathless. We did it. We got through the pre-shows and opening night without any fuckups, no lines forgotten, and no entering from the wrong side. Nothing.

We're still on the stage, so our squeals of excitement are silent as we jump around congratulating and hugging each other, and the collective relief that we're one show down is palpable. We don't even stop when Hamish tries to calm us for post-show notes. In the end, he gives up because he's eager to get to the opening night party for a stiff drink just like everyone else.

I'm floating on a cloud of happiness when I bump into Isobel, one of the production assistants.

"Holiday, would you like me to pop those in water for you? I'll put them with the rest."

"Yes, please."

"And you have a visitor," she adds with a smile.

I shove the bouquet at her and sprint down the stairs, then along the corridor to where the principal dressing rooms are. The scent of roses hits me before I reach mine, and when I enter, it's like I'm walking up the path to Bluebell Cottage because flowers cover every available surface and the floor.

But I don't notice any of it because Lando is leaning against my makeup table looking more handsome than I've ever seen him, backlit by two dozen bulb lights.

The socials would have a field day if they could see him now.

"There she is." He grins, holding his arms wide open for me to fall into. "You were incredible. I'm so fucking proud of you."

I breathe him in, like I always do. He smells like mine, and if I can end every day in his arms exactly like I'm doing now, I'll die happy.

Leaning back, I hold his clear blue stare. "You really liked it?"

"I *loved* it. Broadway next."

My eyebrow shoots up, and I muffle a laugh. "I think we have enough to plan for the moment, don't you?"

Twelfth Night runs for two months, and at the end of November, I begin filming a new legal drama set in the echelons of European security. Somewhere between that, I'll take on the role of a lifetime as Lando's wife.

He proposed to me a couple of weeks ago.

After two months of intense rehearsals, Hamish had graciously given the cast a weekend off before the preview performance, which was to take place ahead of opening night. The second we were allowed out, I jumped into Lando's Aston Martin and hit the gas until we reached Burlington to spend a glorious uninterrupted forty-eight hours.

We arrived just in time for family supper, which so happened to be almost exactly a year after my first Burlington family gathering.

And just like last year, fireworks were included.

The following morning, we woke early to take Sunday and Thunder for a long ride across the fields, checking on this year's calves, and then visited our favorite spot on the estate. The one where we met for the first time.

While Lando tied up the horses, I walked in ahead through the canopy of trailing vines and wisteria to find the crop of rocks next to the waterfall had been laid with a picnic. A bottle of champagne sat in a cooler next to a bowl of bright red strawberries, along with a giant donut with multicolored frosting that I knew Pierre had made.

And while all that was incredible, the little black box sitting in the middle of the donut was what caught my eye.

I could sense Lando's footsteps behind me, along with his anticipation. I don't remember breathing when I bent down to pick it up, but when I turned around, Lando was on one knee, looking nervous.

My nerves got the better of me, and I squealed yes before he'd even asked the question.

"Hollywood, can you let me have my moment?" He sighed, with the mother of all eye rolls.

Biting down a smile, I placed the box in his hand. "Sure, go ahead."

"Thank you."

Opening it up, he tipped out a smaller velvet case hidden inside and took a deep breath.

"Holiday Simpson, I've loved you since the first time I saw you right here in the glen. You came into my life at a time when I couldn't have needed you more. I was completely lost, but you found me and showed me the way home. Home to you. I know marrying me means you take on all of this too, but if you say yes, I promise I will never stop trying to make you the happiest woman on the planet. And I'll always be your biggest cheerleader."

By the time he cracked the lid, silent tears were running down my cheeks. Inside was the most beautiful ring I'd ever seen—a huge diamond, set in the thinnest gold halo and a band of pavé stones.

"It's stunning," I whispered.

"A family heirloom," he added. "You really like it?"

"I absolutely love it, just as much as I love you."

With shaking hands, Lando placed it on my finger, and we didn't leave the waterfall for the rest of the morning.

Since Lando came to Los Angeles, we've tried to keep our life together as private as possible, something that's not always been easy. Which is why we decided to keep our engagement a secret for as long as we could.

Only two people know, my dad and Tanner. Everyone else will find out at dinner tonight, which sadly Tanner couldn't attend because he's in the middle of his season.

"Maybe we do. But wishful thinking for next year." Lando smiles, taking the opportunity to smack his lips to mine. "I have something for you."

Reaching into his pocket, he pulls out a small black box and holds it out in his palm. It's exactly like the one he gave me at the waterfall.

"What's this?"

"Open it."

When I see what's inside, I don't know whether to laugh or cry (happy tears). I'm looking at a gold band, on top of which is a thick circle of amber pavé stones, topped with a rainbow of tiny precious gems. It looks exactly like a donut.

Carefully removing it from the velvet casing, he slides it onto my finger, which happens to be empty because my engagement ring is safely locked up while I'm performing every night.

"Something's been bothering me about your engagement ring, and I couldn't figure out what. Then it occurred to me that your engagement ring is a Burlington family ring passed down through generations, and while you're the rightful owner of it, you aren't the first owner. Or the first person I gave it to," he adds sheepishly. "So I had this made. Something for *us*. A donut just for you, and you can wear it whenever you need to celebrate."

I'm trying my best to mop up my tears without damaging my makeup, but it's impossible, so I give up.

"You made me a donut."

"I did. I think it's quite fitting for the future Duchess of Oxfordshire."

I bite down on my lip. It's going to take me a long time to get used to that. My mom is already freaking out that Lando's a duke.

"I love you so much, Orlando Burlington. I can't wait to spend the rest of our lives together."

His hands cup my cheeks. "Then let's start with getting the hell out of here. Everyone's waiting at dinner, and then we can go on to the after-party, which you know is all Miles and Hendricks are excited about."

"Best idea you've ever had." I laugh, and it takes me all of five minutes to change and retouch my makeup.

Thanks to L'Oreal, I have that down to a T. The first campaign was such a hit, they've asked to extend the contract, but I haven't decided yet.

"Ready, Hollywood?" Lando asks, holding his hand out.

"Sure am, Gracie," I reply.

"Then let's get this show on the road."

THE END

ALSO BY LULU MOORE

The New York Players

Jasper

Cooper

Drew: The Vegas Edition (extended prologue)

Drew

Felix

Huck

The Tuesday Club

The Secret

The Suit

The Show

The New York Lions

The Third Baseman

The Shake Off

The Baller

The Strike Zone

Home Run

The Oxbridge Series

Oar With Friends

You Float My Boat

The Valentine Nook Chronicles - coming September 2025

Once Upon A Christmas Tree - OUT NOW

Valentine Nook

Wylder Ranch - November 18th

Honeysuckle Lane - Feb 2026

Foxleigh Park

Burlington Hall

Made in the USA
Middletown, DE
09 September 2025